Dev smiled. "What's the harm in a kiss?"

"I don't want to start this. I'm not very good at drawing lines. It's kind of a genetic thing."

"You?" he said. "I've never seen a woman draw a straighter line, or walk one, either." With his thumb, he traced the full lower lip he had every intention of taking between his teeth. "One kiss. Now. Here. This night only."

Jenna backed away until she was leaning into the gate, but he followed. She braced one hand against his chest.

"Please," Dev said, disbelieving that he was reduced to begging, but hungry enough to beg just the same. The dim light wasn't enough to see the change in her expression, but he could feel it as the pressure of her hand against his heart relaxed.

"Just one kiss," she said.

Consent given, he could afford to linger. He savored Jenna's scent, her sigh, the silken feel of tender skin at the base of her throat. He indulged each of his pleasures and more, but didn't yet kiss her.

She wriggled away from his touch and then framed his face with her hands. "If you're going to kiss me, just do it."

"Americans," he said, "always in a rush."

Also by Dorien Kelly

The Last Bride in Ballymuir

Available from Pocket Books

Hot Nights in Ballymuir

DORIEN KELLY

POCKET BOOKS
New York   London   Toronto   Sydney

This book is a work of fiction. Names, characters, places and incidents are products of the author's imagination or are used fictitiously. Any resemblance to actual events or locales or persons, living or dead, is entirely coincidental.

An *Original* Publication of POCKET BOOKS

POCKET BOOKS, a division of Simon & Schuster, Inc.
1230 Avenue of the Americas, New York, NY 10020

Copyright © 2004 by Dorien Kelly

ISBN: 0-7434-6459-1

First Pocket Books printing March 2004

10 9 8 7 6 5 4 3 2 1

POCKET and colophon are registered trademarks of Simon & Schuster, Inc.

Cover design by Jae Song

Manufactured in the United States of America

For information regarding special discounts for bulk purchases, please contact Simon & Schuster Special Sales at 1-800-456-6798 or business@simonandschuster.com

Acknowledgments

Researching this book was a pleasure. I am grateful for the wonderful people—and incredible cuisine— at Tapawingo, in Ellsworth, Michigan.

My heartfelt appreciation goes to Chef-Owner Har- lan "Pete" Peterson, Executive Chef Stuart Brioza, Chef Todd Draper, and Pastry Chef Nicole Krasinski. And Todd, my special thanks for your patience and humor while enduring my odd questions!

To Chris Fletcher,
for hauling me out of the fire countless times!

Chapter One

It takes a woman to outwit the devil.
—Irish Proverb

On a spring-perfumed Tuesday morning, the devil arrived in Ballymuir, wearing a hand-tailored Saville Row suit and driving a black Porsche 911. Other than Jenna Fahey, none in town seemed to recognize him for who he was. Of course, she was the only one he nearly mowed down in the narrow street outside Spillane's Market.

Though shaken, Jenna survived. The delicate heads of organic lettuce she had charmed Mr. Spillane into holding aside for her were, unfortunately, victims.

"Two years in Ireland and you still don't know which way to look before stepping off the curb," Jenna's best friend, Vi Kilbride, teased as she helped her gather the remains of what was to have been salad at Muir House, Jenna's restaurant. "I'm thinking we'll hire a keeper for you. Male, preferably."

Jenna ignored her friend's comment. She had men enough—a kitchen filled with them, actually—talented, hard-edged, beloved lunatics.

The Porsche, whose driver she had seen with a near-death sort of clarity, had pulled into a spot uphill. Her lip curled as she checked out the high-performance, lettuce-killing machine. The car was every bit as out-of-place in this quiet corner of Ireland as she'd been when she'd arrived here two years ago, determined to make Ballymuir a bastion of haute cuisine.

A lone head of lettuce rested atop a car across the street. First looking right, then left, instead of the near-fatal reverse order, Jenna crossed. She lobbed the lettuce to Vi, who stood with a handful of people who'd come out of the market to see what the growling car and screaming woman had been about.

Before rejoining them, Jenna wiped her damp and gritty hands on her jeans. The sky was clear now, but it had rained soft and steady just before first light. Promise of even more rain clung to the jagged, purple-hued mountains that held Ballymuir hard to the sea.

Jenna pinned on a smile and resorted to humor, her favorite crutch in stressful moments. "What's the last thing that goes through a chef's mind when she hits a car's windshield?" she called from mid-street.

"This is one of those American jokes, isn't it?" asked Mr. Spillane, rubbing a hand over his thinning gray hair. "Never do understand 'em."

"Her . . ." As she reached the sidewalk, Jenna scowled, her thoughts interrupted. The Porsche's driver was jogging downhill, straight toward her. She knew his type—rich, self-important, always in a hurry. "Ass."

Black hair, dark eyes, charcoal suit, he was six feet of breathtaking arrogance come to town. Her body's reaction to his undeniable perfection was chemical. And irrelevant.

"I'm so sorry. Are you all right?" he asked as he closed in on her.

Interesting. German car, British plates, and Irish accent. Quite healthy-looking, too, though an Irishman with a tan was highly suspect—practically a crime against genetics. Irishmen burned and peeled, or weathered to a ruddy finish. They did not look as though they'd just dropped in from Cap d'Antibes for a visit. For the first time she found her "always in the kitchen" pallor problematic.

"If by all right, you mean not dead, I'm fine." She could do nothing about the pasty tone of her skin— no doubt made even paler by her brush with death— so instead she straightened her red sweater.

Not that he would have noticed. After a cursory glance that she imagined was to be sure she had no severed limbs, he had turned his attention elsewhere. This was no great surprise; she wasn't the sort of woman that men tended to linger over. Look . . . yawn . . . move on.

"I didn't even see you step out onto the road," he said, pushing back the cuff of his white shirt and checking a chunky gold watch that Jenna knew cost more than most people in Ballymuir could hope to save in a lifetime.

"How could you see anything, traveling at the speed of light?"

"Let me replace the . . ." He frowned at the crushed green stuff interred in its crate.

"It was organic butter lettuce."

His gaze again flicked over her. "Let me replace it for you."

"That's a fine offer, to be sure," elderly Breege Flaherty opined from her spot next to Vi. Trust Ballymuir's citizens to insist on being part of the action. No neutrality here, even on matters as mundane as trampled produce.

Americans had a few quirks of their own. Being born and raised in Chicago meant that Jenna's southern belle act was shaky, but how was this false Irishman to know?

"You'd do that for me?" she asked, hand neatly settled over her heart.

The eyelash flutter might have been overkill. Vi was making a sound perilously close to gagging. Jenna shot her a quick glare.

The man simply smiled. One slightly crooked eyetooth rescued him from Hollywood perfection. That, and the fact that Jenna found something very calculating about his expression.

"After running you down in the street, it's the least I can do." He reached into his breast pocket and pulled out a billfold.

Ah, cash, the great placater. She should have expected this, but something about the almond tilt of his eyes had briefly disarmed her.

"It's not that simple," Jenna said as crisp new euros appeared. "You see, Mr. Spillane, here, has to order the lettuce a week in advance, then if we're lucky, it actually makes it from Holland."

"We've not much call for the organic stuff, outside of Jenna and one or two other blow-ins with odd ideas about food," the grocer apologized.

Maybe it was because this stranger was a highly unsettling echo of everything she'd been trying to leave behind, or maybe it was because she remained ticked off over her lettuce, but whatever the reason, Jenna upped the ante . . . just to see what he'd do.

"The wholesaler in Tralee might still have a case," she said. "Or if that doesn't work, there's always Killarney. Two hours—maybe four—and we'll be even."

There, she'd called his bluff—another man of flash but no substance.

His smile didn't waver. With a graceful economy of movement, he stowed the money and flipped open a cell phone. One push of a speed-dial button and he was all business. "Margaret, I'll be needing a case of butter lettuce—"

When Jenna cleared her throat, he amended, "Make that *organic* butter lettuce delivered to—"

"Muir House," Breege's friend, Edna McCafferty, supplied.

"Muir House," the man echoed. "In Ballymuir, and no later than ten thirty, if you could." He smiled. "What would I do without you, Margaret, my love?"

"Pick up your own damn lettuce," Jenna said just under her breath.

"Sorry? I didn't catch that," he said as he returned the phone to his pocket.

She repeated the thought with sterling diction. "I

said, without Margaret, you'd have to pick up your own damn lettuce."

Their eyes met. A startling sort of awareness coursed through Jenna. She looked away first, then realized the error of her choice. One never looked away from the devil.

His smile was slow, easy, a thing of damned beauty. "Without Margaret, that, I would. Now if you'll excuse me, I'm late for a meeting. Have a grand day, everyone."

His long stride covered the incline to his car, and Jenna watched his every step.

"So that's Dev Gilvane," Mrs. McCafferty practically crooned as the Porsche disappeared over the crest of the hill.

Dev. At least his parents had recognized what they would be raising.

"I knew his mam, back when. The boy has her eyes."

Only a woman on the passing side of eighty would see Dev Gilvane as anything less than a full-grown man.

"Right, now. You can scarcely remember yesterday's supper, let alone what Kate Connelly's eyes looked like," Breege Flaherty was saying. "She's been off to Dublin thirty years and more."

Edna ignored her friend. "He's staying with Muriel O'Keefe, I hear. Paying for all three rooms so he can have some privacy, too. His name's always appearing in those London gossip columns—you know, the one filled with premieres and benefits. A prominent financier, they call him. He's nearly a star like that Bono."

"Who?" Mr. Spillane asked.

"You know, that young jackeen with his music."

"You've not seen him out your way, Jenna?"

Trapped between the warp and weft of the conversation, the best Jenna could do was blink.

"They're meaning Dev Gilvane, not Bono," Vi prompted.

Jenna was sure that even after she'd spent a full decade in Ballymuir, she still wouldn't be able to keep up with the free-for-all talk. She became too enamored by the music of the words to catch their meanings. And more and more, she found herself slipping into the cadence of their speech.

"Um . . . no. Any reason I should?"

"I've read that our boy's quite the grand man with the ladies, too," Mrs. McCafferty said. "I thought maybe he'd have brought a girl to dine—a model or actress, perhaps?"

"Sorry, but it's just the usual suspects this time of year," Jenna replied with as much sincerity as she could muster. She had no appetite for models, actresses, or playboys. She'd worked hard to escape from her high-maintenance and high-drama family.

Mrs. McCafferty remained undaunted. "We've hope yet. He's told Muriel he's just here on holiday, but she's seen him paging through the real-estate listings over breakfast. Just think of the glamorous types we'd have coming our way if he were to move home."

Breege's silver brows rose into an arch. "Ballymuir's never been his home."

"Ah, but it could be a yearning for his roots. He might be looking to settle in." Edna rubbed her hands together, as though warming to the prospect of glory and glamour strolling the streets of the village.

Breege laughed. "Have you been nipping at the *fuisce*? Just where would someone grand like Mr. Gilvane be settling in? Our manors are no more than piles of ruin."

"Well, it takes someone mad as an Englishman to bring back one of those old hulks," Mr. Spillane pointed out.

All gazes settled on Jenna.

"Not-not that I'm meaning an insult," the grocer stammered. "It's a fine thing you've been doing with Muir House. Why, I was saying to my Kathleen just the other day that—"

"It's okay, Mr. Spillane. Really."

And it would be far better for all of them if she could stop Seamus Spillane's torrent of words before he got going. He was a nice enough man, but had no Off switch that she could find.

In any case, Jenna realized that settling at Muir House had been an act of insanity. All the same, now it was home and hearth. What these people didn't know—not even Vi—was that the place wasn't exactly hers, as they all assumed. To hear that this Dev Gilvane was sniffing around knotted her stomach.

"I suppose we'd all best get on with our days, too," Vi prompted. Jenna caught her friend's worried glance and reminded herself that she'd do well to hide any hint of emotion around Vi, whose perceptiveness bordered on the unnatural.

Mr. Spillane picked up the case of lettuce. "To the rubbish with this."

"It seems such a waste," said Edna McCafferty as she began to wrestle the box away from the grocer. "Surely with a bit of soaking, there will be some left to save."

Not more than a handful of bruised and ragged leaves, according to Jenna's practiced eye. Still, it was this sort of "something from nothing" attitude that had made Ballymuir thrive while other equally isolated villages diminished to roadside ghosts.

Breege weighed in on Edna's side of the battle. "You'd best let go, Seamus," she said to the grocer. "You know Edna can take you if she's got a mind to. Besides, it seems to me that Jenna should decide the fate of the lettuce. It's bought and paid for, is it not?"

Mr. Spillane released his grip. "Aye."

Edna held her prize tighter.

Jenna issued her verdict. "It's yours, Mrs. McCafferty. Would you like my recipe for chilled lettuce soup? It's a hit during summer teatime."

"Soup? I was thinking just to give the greens a good dollop of mayonnaise and all would be right."

Organic lettuce reduced to a mayonnaise delivery device. If that wasn't the work of the devil, what was?

"I'm sure it will be wonderful," she lied.

"What with mayonnaise isn't?" replied Mrs. McCafferty before she and Breege made their way up the street to the small house they shared next to the surf shop/bookstore.

Jenna and Vi said their goodbyes to Mr. Spillane. Instead of heading toward the harbor, where her studio was located, Vi followed Jenna to her car. Once there, Jenna's friend strategically placed herself between Jenna and the driver's door.

Jenna looked up at Vi, who had several inches on her in height. What she saw didn't improve her morning. Vi's green eyes held a determined glint, that of a warrior readying for battle.

"Don't get started," Jenna warned.

Vi crossed her arms and leaned against the car. "Ah, so it's to be the standard ritual of you denying you're troubled and me prodding until you can take it no more?"

"Nothing's bothering me. I couldn't be better."

Vi flicked a lock of her long red hair over her shoulder. Nothing was permitted to stray out of line when she was in one of these moods. "Right, you are. And it's not just that Dev Gilvane crossed you, either. Though speaking of the man, I don't suppose you noticed that he was incredibly—"

"Full of himself?"

"Gorgeous, perfect, fine enough to eat."

"Says the vegetarian. Though if you think he's that hot, have at him. He's all yours."

Vi laughed, the sound rich and musical in the cool air. "In any other circumstance, I might, but he's not meant for me, you see?"

"Then who is he meant for, Edna McCafferty?"

Her friend's smile grew broader. "Are you telling me you didn't feel it? The sun shone brighter when you two spoke."

Jenna shifted uncomfortably. Vi's brand of Celtic mysticism was far more entertaining when focused on someone else. Especially because Jenna had felt something—what, exactly, her cautious heart refused to consider.

"I *feel* that I'm now twenty minutes behind schedule. I *feel* that I need to come up with a replacement for my spring salad because we both know that man's never going to get me any lettuce. And I *feel* that you're just a bit too smug for your own good."

All of which only sharpened Vi's resemblance to a sleek, contented feline, albeit one wearing a bright blue woolen cape. "Smug and optimistic, actually. I'd be tidying my bedroom for a bit of company, if I were you." She stepped aside and motioned at the car with a flourish of her hand. "Now, be off."

Jenna opened her Nissan's slightly rusted silver door. "If I didn't love you like a sister—"

"You'd hate me like one," Vi finished. "And don't be thinking I've forgotten to ask what's bothering you. I'm just waiting until I have you as a captive audience. I'll visit for a meal and a chat tonight around eight."

Vi waited for no answer before strolling away, and Jenna had none to give. She took solace in knowing that eight o'clock tonight meant closer to nine, since Vi operated on the relaxed concept of Irish Time. Still, whether Vi's interrogation was to be twelve hours off or twelve days made no difference. One bit of dissembling and Vi Kilbride would squash her flatter than the devil had her lettuce.

Dev Gilvane pulled into his parking spot at Cois na Mara. Lovely name for a house that—like many things from the 1970s—was best viewed blindfolded. Still, with the nearest hotel over twenty miles away and most bed-and-breakfasts not game for a long-term guest, the odd little place was a godsend. He supposed in time he might grow accustomed to its pseudo-gothic architecture, though he didn't plan to stay long enough to test the theory.

Dev grinned in spite of himself as he neared the strangest aspect in this landscape of the bizarre. The front garden was crowned by a replica statue of Dublin's well-endowed fishmonger and folk-song legend, Molly Malone. He hadn't quite worked up a polite way to ask Muriel O'Keefe, the bed-and-breakfast's owner, what Molly was doing in the yard. It had been bad enough when he'd asked what Cois na Mara meant.

"Why, near the sea, of course," she'd replied in tones thready with shock that an Irishman wouldn't know this.

Perhaps the fact that the sea was a faint sliver of Dingle Bay blue on the horizon had thrown Dev. Or perhaps it was because since leaving Ireland at age eleven, he'd spent no more than the occasional holiday here. His Irish was limited to the stock vulgarities that were the first words a boy learned in any foreign tongue.

All these years later he had to admit to a passing curiosity over what the Irish for "near nothing at all" might be. A more honest name for Muriel's house, if less alluring.

In a gesture rich with unintended irony, his employers at Harwood, a behemoth of a British real-estate concern, had sent him here on assignment as a reward. When settling on Emerald, they'd chosen the wrong Isle. Now, Capri or the Greek Isles came to mind as appealing spots.

Dev reveled in his career as the king of all site finders. Some souls had a nose for wine; his particu-

lar gift was a nose for sheer hedonism. He could pin-
point a travel trend and then create a resort to cater
to desires a guest didn't even yet know he or she possessed.

When Trevor, his boss and mentor at Harwood,
had presented him with this "marvelous opportunity
to see home," for the first time ever Dev had given
his superiors short shrift. Rather than fully explore a
land he'd prefer to avoid, he'd traveled directly to his
mother's county of birth.

True, he'd done slightly better than toss a dart
over his shoulder at a map of Ireland. Mum was always waxing bloody poetic about the beauty of
Kerry. And though he could remember virtually
nothing of a childhood trip to Ballymuir, he'd
thought that surely something here would suit his
needs. And it appeared that something might. All the
better for him to be quickly back to his London
friends and diversions.

As Dev passed Molly, he gave her a friendly pat
on her bronze bum. He bounded up the steps and entered Bric-a-Brac Central. Muriel instantly appeared,
wiping her hands on a frilly blue apron she wore
over nondescript trousers and top.

"And so how was your morning drive?" she
asked.

Before pulling the door shut, he took a speculative
glance outside, wondering if the Molly statue
weren't rigged to be some sort of advance warning
system. He'd never made it past the entry without
Muriel materializing and her farmer husband
bounding out the back door for the hills beyond.

"Rain-free, at least." As he imagined it wouldn't

do much to endear him to Mrs. O'Keefe, he kept to himself the fact that he'd nearly killed one of the locals. And for quite the same reason, he was visiting Ballymuir in the guise of a tourist. The more picturesque a location, the more hostile its residents to the idea of development.

"Can I bring you some tea, or some of my scones?" Mrs. O'Keefe asked. "They're fresh-baked, you know."

Dev pocketed his car keys and edged toward the stairway. "Thanks, but no. You filled me up with your wonderful breakfast."

Muriel cooked meals large enough to feed a legion. He'd had buttery fried eggs, rashers, toast, and juice, and enjoyed it all to excess. Both his tailor and personal trainer were going to go around the bend when he finally made it home.

"Well, if you're needing a bite later, just come to the kitchen and I'll fix you a plate," his hostess called after him.

Dev took the steps two at a time.

"Home," he muttered as he came to the door with the numeral 2 painted on its plain wooden surface.

Once inside, he slipped out of his suit coat and hung it in the wardrobe that sucked up most of the room's space and light. His accommodations were essentially a purple floral closet with delusions of grandeur. Sort of the Royal Suite for Dwarfs . . .

After debating whether to change into more casual garb, then rejecting the idea because work was work, even when conducted in a backwater, Dev grabbed his briefcase and cell phone, then made his way downstairs.

If he were staying at the Clarence in Dublin, he'd have a suite with an enormous postmodern desk and a minimum of two phone lines. Here, he had a corner of a dining table in the breakfast room. Claiming an addiction to current events, he'd persuaded Mrs. O'Keefe to let him run a line for his computer from the jack in the entryway. In exchange for the access, he'd agreed to cover her telephone bill for the time he was a guest. Muriel's appeared to be a far-flung family. Yesterday, when he'd come back from his soggy and fruitless drive, she'd been chatting it up with a third cousin in Brisbane.

Dev opened his laptop, plugged in the phone line, and got down to work. His favorite Internet search engine took less time to spew a list of results than it had taken him to type in a single name: Jenna Fahey.

Based on what he'd heard about her at the pub the prior night, he hadn't expected Muir House's chef to be so . . . feminine. Soft brown curls, a full mouth meant for kissing, and hazel eyes bright with wit weren't chief among the attributes he appreciated discovering in a potential adversary.

After noting her face, he'd permitted himself to look no lower. He was a lover of women—their scents, their laughter, their mystery. This was business, though, and he refused to regard Jenna Fahey as a woman.

He wished for an Amazonian ball-buster, bloody cleaver raised in clenched hand and invective spewing. That sort was all the easier to take in battle. Ah, but he could still defeat the pretty chef, and if circumstances compelled, he would.

Dev leaned against the straight wooden back of

his dining chair and closed his eyes. None of these were thoughts conducive to efficient business, and being in Ireland was damn distracting enough. Resolved to be done with this, he began opening links to Web sites and became acquainted with the seamless public persona of Jenna Fahey, a rare two-star chef, restaurateur, and daughter of a rich and privileged American family. It was what went unsaid that intrigued Dev.

He flipped open his cell phone and called his personal assistant. "Margaret, I've just forwarded you a list of Web sites to review. When you've finished, contact our security department regarding the background on Jenna Fahey. And I'd like a reservation for one at Muir House at eight o'clock tonight." He paused, then added, "Not under my own name. Use Malone, Molly Malone."

Dev wasn't sure what motivated this sudden yen for anonymity—not to mention egregious absurdity—but he had learned to trust his instincts. They had saved him from the fire more than once.

"Eight o'clock, it is," Margaret replied, unruffled that her employer had morphed into a woman.

He began to launch his usual "What would I do without you?" but the words died in his throat. From the depths of his imagination came a smooth American voice saying, "Why, make your own damn reservation, of course."

Instinct told Dev Gilvane that Muir House and Jenna Fahey were to be anything other than business as usual. And how he dreaded the thought.

Chapter Two

Though there is no bone in the tongue,
it has frequently broken a man's head.
                                        —IRISH PROVERB

Himself's replacement lettuce arrived at noon, accompanied by a massive—almost funereal—arrangement of red roses and a prettily worded note of apology. After reading it, Jenna dumped the note in the middle of a bin of fish guts stripped from the evening's plaice entrée. The flowers she had Niamh, her dining-room manager and hostess, break into small, tasteful bouquets, then remove from her sight. When the time came, Jenna planned to deal with their sender just as efficiently.

If, as Edna McCafferty had speculated, Gilvane really was in the market for a piece of Irish paradise, he could do no better than Muir House. Even Jenna had to give a nod to the irony of making herself vulnerable through success. After almost two years of careful budgeting, and detailed, grueling work, the house verged on acceptability.

Courtesy of her mother, who remained far too engaged in her social schedule to ever visit her elder daughter, Jenna had received a shipping container packed with fine—and now repatriated—Irish antiques. Only four of the nine bedroom suites remained to be refurbished. As for the restaurant, its reputation was substantial, if not exactly the stuff that stoked a chef's fantasies.

At the moment the kitchen was its usual frenzy of elbow-to-elbow activity. The scents of roasting garlic and simmering fish stock competed for airspace, while Hector and Saul, Jenna's Portuguese and Israeli line cooks, traded friendly obscenities and jockeyed to grab the best of the day's supplies for their respective spots on the line.

Aidan, Jenna's second-in-command, watched the pair with his face in its usual stony set, as though he couldn't understand what sin he'd committed to be consigned to this Babel of language, accent, and attitude. Of course, as kitchen veterans, both he and Jenna knew that nomads like the line chefs would soon grow restless and move on, and others would arrive to take their place.

Once she was sure preparations were running smoothly, Jenna closeted herself in her office, which had once been one of the house's smaller salons. There, she settled in behind her desk and perfected the night's menu, complete with birthday and anniversary greetings for honored guests. In Jenna's culinary gospel, presentation was everything, both on the plate and beforehand.

Odd thing was, she'd never been especially interested in expanding that philosophy to her own appearance. She was trim and tidy, but lacked the fillips and filigrees of style shown in her food. Admittedly, as the changeling child of the tall and golden Fahey clan, her raw ingredients were none too spectacular. Still, she could live with the lack of looks since she'd also missed out on the Fahey brand of arrogant insanity.

The last of fifty menu copies was humming off the printer when the clatter of the kitchen was silenced by shattering glass. Jenna bolted from her chair. In the narrow hall between the kitchen and the dining room she found Evie Nolan, world's laziest waitress, scurrying away from a rack of broken water glasses. The fact that Evie was moving more quickly than a stroll was damning evidence.

"Evie?"

"Yeah?"

"Care to tell me what happened?"

"Dropped 'em," she said in a bored voice, while sticking out her ample chest a little farther, as though to note Jenna's minimal allotment of the same.

"So clean them up."

"Me?"

Hiring Evie had been a case of horse-trading— apathetic Ms. Nolan in exchange for her father's "on call" expertise as a heating-and-cooling man—so Jenna overlooked a lot. All at the expense of what she suspected would before long be a full-blown ulcer, courtesy of more than Evie.

"Of course, *you*," she said before walking to the alcove that held the bus station and emerging with a broom. She handed it to Evie, who looked at it as though she'd never seen one before. "Start cleaning."

Jenna picked up the glass rack; six or so had survived. She brought them to the dishwashing area, then returned to supervise Evie before she managed to disappear.

The waitress executed a few apathetic passes of the broom at the remaining shards, then paused in her non-effort. "Forgot to tell you. I took a call earlier. Molly Malone's comin' to dinner tonight."

"Sure, just like the entire Kerry hurling team was coming last week." Prank calls weren't limited to American kids. In Ireland, the rule seemed to be a cell phone for every child and to each an unlimited calling plan, even on this relatively remote finger of land.

"So I was wrong about the team," Evie said with a "you can't blame a tart for hoping" shrug. "This one was real enough, though. The woman sounded like a Brit, all proper and snotty like she had a stick up—"

Jenna cut in with the precision of a surgeon. "How many in the party?"

"One."

"What time?"

"Forgot."

"I don't suppose you got Miss Malone's phone number?"

"Had nothing to write with."

All in all, it was a good thing that Evie frequently missed her shifts.

"Oh, and you had another call. . . . Some girl asking for you. This one was American-sounding, you know, like—"

No point in finding where Evie thought Americans kept a stick. "Did she leave a message?"

"I told her to ring back. Nothin' to write with, remember?"

"Great phone skills you have there."

Either Evie hadn't often been on the receiving end of sarcasm, or she simply didn't care, for all she eked out was another half-attentive, "Yeah."

Stomach doing its burn-and-clench act, Jenna took the broom and sent the waitress to fold napkins. As for the mystery of the second call, she'd deal with that when she found the time. Even an American who hadn't been home in ten years knew a Yank or two, though in her case, virtually none she cared to speak to.

Jenna glanced down at her hands gripping the broom. Her knuckles shone white and bloodless. She would be useless until she calmed. After quickly finishing the cleanup, she stepped out of the house. Walking the hard silver-green turf that passed for a lawn, she circled the place that had become her life.

By anyone's standards, Muir House wasn't perfect. Successive generations of builders, each with a separate vision, had cobbled together a massive structure. The gray stone and mortar house, with its two not-quite-matching wings, sat with its back to the sea. Still, it suffered from the salt wind and winter storms. Paint flaked from the tall blue shutters flanking the ground-floor windows, and it seemed to Jenna, who could envision all that her home *should* be, that a half-finished air clung to the place. But it was nearly hers, and she'd fought to make it so.

Acceptance had been gradual. At first she'd been considered sort of an amusing sidebar to village life: the odd American girl scraping years of grime and neglect off a house that most of the older locals would have preferred to see crumble. Then, slowly, life changed, and Jenna became convinced that her restaurant was meant to be.

Germans biking the country roads would happen upon her, have a meal, then go tell their wealthy friends about the undiscovered gem they'd found. More would come the next month, then more, then came a brief mention in a regional travel magazine.

Next the foodies had arrived in search of something new. Veteran diners and critics all, some had been referred by chefs Jenna had once worked under, and some had just arrived on their own. They'd venture to the wilds of Muir House and feel that they had one-upped their friends on Mediterranean cruises.

The last to come were the locals. It was Jenna's guess they'd been waiting to see if she killed off any of the tourists with her cooking, as those were more easily replaced than people willing to live here year-round. Even now, in Ballymuir they gossiped at O'Connor's Pub about perceived oddities such as mango chutney and pasta any color but white. Jenna didn't mind, just so long as they came back and experimented anew another night. And they did.

All in all, she was lucky. Ireland's voracious economy was slowing, a sign of danger for businesses such as hers. One more reason that Dev Gilvane with his greens and roses and empty words loomed as such a threat. She had seen his type before—in fact, had nearly married a man much like him. She could guarantee that he was well-damned. Now, the trick would be to make sure he quickly departed for warmer climes.

"You're mine," she reminded her home as she finished her loop and rounded the corner to the kitchen's back door.

Aidan stood on the stoop, wearing one of his rare smiles.

"You've a call from *Irish Gourmet* about the shoot they've scheduled," he said, referring to a glossy magazine that had recently entered the marketplace. Not so very long ago, the magazine's title would have been deemed an oxymoron, right up there with jumbo shrimp. "But if you're too busy talking to your house, I can always tell them to ring you later."

Jenna's laugh was weary. "No, I'll be right there."

There was no rest for the obsessive.

At exactly eight Dev walked the broad flagstone path to Muir House's front door. Low shrubbery of some sort or another disguised floods that gave a wash of light to the walkway. He knew that the sea was just on the other side of the house. The tang of salt perfumed the air, and the water's subtle rush and whisper beckoned to him. This morning's brief drive-by of the property and snoop down the private lane had been just enough to tease, as was this visit.

Tomorrow, he promised himself. Tomorrow he would walk the land and see if this sense of promise bore itself out, or if it was just the wishful thinking of a man who'd sell his firstborn—if he had one—to be quickly home.

Muir House was lovely, sure enough, and well-tended, a fact that surprised and regrettably added to the property's value. The deep lacquered red of the front door shone evenly, and the bronze hardware felt smooth beneath his touch.

Dev stepped inside, and for an instant the oddest sensation gripped him. It was as though he'd seen this place, or dreamt it. Even the sweet scent of beeswax was an echo of sorts. But no, this was impossible. He'd never stepped over this threshold, not once.

He took a brief glance at his face in the large, gilded mirror that stood above a semicircular table facing the door. The look of shock he wore was enough to make him turn away. He shook his head, freeing it of the momentary muzziness. Low music— a harp, perhaps—played from inside. He drew a steadying breath and moved toward the sound.

Just the other side of the entry, a slender woman waited. Not Jenna Fahey, fortunately. He'd like a look about without her watching him. From what he'd already seen, she was no fool to give him run of the house. And about now, his second-born would be on the block to change that sorry fact.

"Welcome to Muir House," the hostess said. "Do you have a reservation with us this evening?"

"I do. It's under the name of—"

Jenna Fahey appeared from what Dev surmised was the dining room. "Molly Malone, unless I miss my guess."

"Dead on," he replied, schooling himself to be patient, not to anticipate her.

"You need a shave, Molly, if you don't mind my saying so."

He said what he thought she might want to hear. "You, on the other hand, look lovely."

She glanced down at her chef's clothing of a white jacket and checked pants, then back at him. Though she said nothing, the skeptical arch of her brows beneath curly brown hair let him know that she found his words hollow.

Dev smiled anyway. "I was afraid if I made the reservation under my own name, you'd have barred the door."

"It takes more than an attempted hit-and-run to make me turn down a customer this time of year, Mr. Gilvane."

"Call me Dev."

Instead, she called him nothing at all. "Would you like to have a seat in the library while you look at the menu?"

He suspected that even if he didn't, she would have led him that way. After she had him settled in a wing chair in front of the fire and was bringing a glass of single-malt Scotch his way, Dev had to concede a measure of respect.

"Has your restaurant been open long?" he asked as she set the glass on a small table to his right.

She looked about and her expression softened. That is, until her gaze returned to him. "Almost two years, and if I'm going to make it three, I need to get back to the kitchen. Evie will be your waitress this evening. I hope you enjoy your meal."

She nodded a goodbye and turned away, but hesitated, then swung back around. "Oh, and I'd recommend the plaice. It's fresh from the harbor this morning."

Her broad smile made her appear momentarily different. Nearly beautiful, he'd say, were she not an adversary.

"I'm afraid I'm not much for fish," he replied.

For his honesty, he received a tart "Too bad. I thought it suited you very well." Then she walked away.

Before long the hostess reappeared with a menu. "Evie will be by to take your order," she said. "Until then, enjoy the warmth."

Dev toyed with his Scotch and watched the orange-red glow of the fire in the grate. He wondered why at the scent of burning peat, so many of his expatriate friends would develop a sudden and bizarre longing for the auld sod. It was dirt, he thought with an unsentimental sniff, nothing more.

Evie appeared and led him to his table, a small, private spot for two in a windowed alcove of the dining room, perfect for a pair of lovers or a sole diner who'd rather not spend his meal front-and-center. The waitress hovered with a degree of interest he'd have found amusing, if it weren't so blatant. He half-wondered whether she planned to personally place his linen napkin, then check it for fit.

For matters of personal safety, Dev expressed interest in the lobster ravioli appetizer, forcing her to depart. One could certainly credit Muir House with a friendly staff.

Dev looked about. The dining room wasn't especially full, though as the restaurant's owner had pointed out, this was the off-season. As far as he was concerned, gray and wet Ireland held no on-season. But his was not to judge, merely to do.

He nipped through his appetizer—a surprisingly tasty morsel, though he wondered what machinations one had to go through to obtain fresh lemongrass out here. The chef was indeed a determined woman.

As Dev ate, he took note of architectural detail around him. The house, though big, wasn't especially ornate. He knew from his brief Internet looksee that the property had been in an English family for centuries—a lodge of sorts, built and expanded through the years on the enormous scale that conquerors generally preferred. Not that he blamed his English friends for taking this land. Then, as now, it was likely ripe enough to have fallen into their hands.

Dev's cell phone chirped, and his hand went automatically to its holster to retrieve it. Based on the surly glances from the neighboring diners, a ring tone other than "Hail Britannia" might have been better received.

"Hello," he murmured, trying to be as inconspicuous as a man could while waving the Union Jack.

"Gilvane? Barrett here. Did you—"

Static consumed whatever Sid from the New York office might have been saying, then there was nothing at all. Dev blew out a frustrated breath, flipped shut the phone, and sampled his Scotch.

The phone rang again.

He mouthed a "sorry" to the scowling couple to his immediate right. "Sid?" he tried again.

"I've got some questions on the Costa Rican deal. Was the assumed vacancy rate—"

Again he was cut off.

Balls.

This time Dev held the cell phone at the ready. Two notes, no more, played before he answered. "Sid?"

"Where the hell are you . . . Siberia?"

"Close enough," Dev replied, rotating his Scotch glass so the liquid sheeted against the sides.

Someone had arrived tableside. Dev's gaze traveled up checkered pants, white jacket, tense jaw, and teeth bared in a patently false smile.

"Mr. Gilvane, I'm afraid we have a rule—"

He was certain this woman had more rules than a fish had scales. He raised his right index finger in the universal sign for "hang on a sec."

Her mouth wasn't bearing up well under the strain of that smile. She looked as though she'd like to give him another sort of one-fingered salute that he saw most often in the United States.

In Dev's ear Barrett was barking in true Manhattan style, "Hey, let's talk about that vacancy rate before you disappear, huh?"

"Mr. Gilvane." She stretched his last name as thin as her obviously waning patience.

Balls again.

"Give me two minutes," he said to Sid, then flipped the phone shut.

"Maybe you missed the note on the menu," she said in an undertone, "but we ask our patrons not to use cell phones inside the house. It detracts from the dining experience."

"Fine, then. Where might a patron enhance his business experience?"

"The terrace?" she suggested, eyeing the dark

business suit he hadn't bothered to change out of. "It's warm enough outside. I'll show you the way."

He'd scarcely stood when Sid rang again. At the same time Muir House's owner gestured for him to follow.

"Minutes must be shorter in your part of the world," he said to Sid as he followed the chef. For a small woman, she walked with a long stride, affording him little opportunity to do more than take in a few general impressions of the artwork-lined hallway that she ushered him down.

One small painting to his left looked to be an original Jack Yeats, better suited for full-time guard in a museum than life in a drafty corridor. Next to that was a large, modern work, a brilliant slash of hillside green meeting lavender and gray. It held a sort of vitality that made Dev slow, just to feel the current pass through him. The signature in the lower right corner was a bold, purple *V Kilbride*. No one he'd heard of, though his knowledge of art encompassed only what various girlfriends had tried to persuade him to like, such as the prohibitively expensive Mr. Yeats.

They reached the end of the hall, and his hostess opened a large door set between long and narrow glass windows.

"One second more," he said to Sid, who likely didn't hear since he hadn't yet shut his gob.

Jenna Fahey was far more liberal than he in her concept of "warm." Dev was tempted to turn up his jacket collar against the chill of the wind that met them as they stepped outside. But if Her Highness could take it, so could he.

And it seemed that someone else wasn't particularly bothered, either. A woman stood at the far reaches of the terrace, her back to them. As with the front of the house, the rear was lit low with landscape lighting. It didn't illuminate the other guest very well.

"I've reformulated the spreadsheet six ways and it's still not working, Gilvane," the New Yorker groused in his right ear.

Next to him, his escort called to the other woman, "What are you doing out here?"

She turned and walked toward them. Dev recognized her as one of this morning's near-miss bystanders. She was tall, not in the way of his thin-unto-death model girlfriends, but in a more substantial fashion. Her hair was a rich, startling shade of red. It suited her, though perhaps not another woman on the planet.

"I've been counting the stars," she replied, then shot an amused glance Dev's way. "There appears to be a new one tonight."

"More like a black hole," he thought he heard Jenna Fahey say. Believing he had to have been mistaken, Dev quelled his smile. It was difficult to placate Sid about the cost of Costa Rican resort property and eavesdrop at the same time.

"Sid, give me tonight to look at the numbers. I'll e-mail you straight away." So it was to be another miserable night spent in Muriel O'Keefe's breakfast room surrounded by bad oil portraits—so to speak—of the Holy Family. This was his penance for avoiding religion, no doubt.

"How long?"

"Four hours at most," he promised his coworker,

then hung up, his sole comfort that he'd be a managing partner with Harwood long before Sid could grasp the thought. Dev slid his phone back into the clip at his belt.

"So you'd be Dev Gilvane," the redhead said, earning an annoyed sigh from the woman next to her. "I'm Vi Kilbride," she continued, extending her hand.

"Violet, technically," the chef added.

Vi—or Violet—gave her friend a steely glare. "Vi will do."

Jenna Fahey laughed, and Dev found the sound unacceptably pleasing.

"Vi," he repeated, hoping to distract himself from positive thoughts of Ms. Fahey. "By chance, the 'V Kilbride' of the canvas in there?"

She smiled as they shook hands. "Observant man."

"When it suits him."

She had a sharp wit about her, the chef, and he'd prefer she turned it on someone else. Perhaps herself.

"I need to get back inside," she said with an impatient glance in the direction of the door. "Are you having dinner, Vi?"

"I am."

"Would you care to join me?" Dev offered. One could learn much over a shared bottle of wine.

"That would be gra—"

Vi stopped, then frowned downward. Dev's gaze followed. One white chef's-variety sneaker was planted atop her utilitarian brown shoe. This time there was no fighting his smile.

"Another time," Vi amended, then nudged her friend away.

They returned to the house and traveled down the broad hallway together. Jenna Fahey finally launched the line of questioning he'd anticipated since arriving. "And you're in Ballymuir, why, Mr. Gilvane?"

"Do you often interrogate your customers?"

"Not on a regular basis, but with you I'm willing to make an exception," she replied. "If it helps, call it a payback for my brush with death."

"And here I was thinking the payback was the flowers, but since you must know, I'm on holiday."

She actually slowed her hurried, American-girl pace. "Here? In April? Interesting choice. You seem more the five-star, coddled type."

"Ah, but there's no shortage of coddling at Muriel O'Keefe's."

Vi laughed. "He's got you there, Jen. And if you're concerned about Dev's welfare, perhaps you should let him room at Muir House."

She gave a quick shake of her head and moved along once again. "I'm selective about my guests."

"What she's saying is that after fixing four suites to open guest rooms, she's allowed no one to stay, yet," Vi said. "She's even shown me the door on a night fit for none but fools."

"Not true!"

"But close enough. She guards her privacy, our Jenna. Fine practice for a woman destined to be in the public's eye, wouldn't you say?"

Jenna, who was most definitely *not* his, answered instead. "I doubt I'll ever be quite as popular as Mr. Gilvane." She gave him a last, narrow-eyed stare. "You do have the cell phone switched off, don't you?"

"Of course," he lied.

"I'll leave you here, then," she said as they approached the corner they'd first rounded from the dining room. "Do you need help in finding your table?"

He gave her the smile that had conquered corporations. "I found Muir House readily enough, didn't I?"

It was wrong to toy with her this way, but it was also a grand diversion. She marched off without another word, but none was needed. Her last, low hiss had delivered her opinion of him with sibilant accuracy.

Past eleven at night the restaurant would have been quiet but for a surfeit of Kilbride siblings. Still, Dev Gilvane was gone, and that gave Jenna peace enough. He had shown great skill in baiting her, and she'd shown even more talent in setting herself up. The sane solution would be to bar him from her property. And she'd do it, if she thought it would stick.

Seeking comfort in routine, Jenna began her nighttime ritual. First stop, the kitchen. There, Patrick Kilbride, who shared the job of night porter with his twin brother, Danny, was scrubbing the floor. Since moving to Ballymuir this past winter, both the Kilbride twins had shown themselves to be hard workers, putting in time at their older brother Michael's woodworking shop, then each here two nights a week. Whatever it took to get Patrick through the grueling job of making the well-used floor immaculate once again—even vintage Pearl Jam at full throttle—was fine by Jenna.

In the dining room labored Danny, earning extra money to spend on the girls by waxing and polishing the room's oak wainscoting.

"Great job," she called over his music of choice—techno-pop, God help the Irish. He waved his free hand, but never stopped working.

Jenna joined the female Kilbride in front of the library fire. At the tangy smell of the burning peat—so distinctively Irish—comfort seeped into her bones.

"It seemed a good night," Vi said from deep within one of the pair of cream brocade wing chairs, angled to form a quiet place for talk.

"It was, and busier than I expected, too," Jenna replied as she eased into her seat.

"This is just the beginning."

"Then I hope I survive the rest," she half joked.

"You will, but not without a battle or two." Vi paused long enough to lift a glass of water from the side table and take a sip. "And it seems I'll be joining you on that front. I need to go to back to Kilkenny for a few days."

"It's not your mother or father, is it?"

"No, I need to visit the Design Centre to check on my inventory, though I don't suppose I'll be able to escape the city without at least dropping in on Mam and Da. I'm nearly three months overdue for my semiannual 'when are you going to marry, or at least stop making that awful art' speech from Mam." She gave a mock shudder. "You'd think I'd moved quite far enough away when I came to Ballymuir."

Since family wasn't Jenna's favorite topic, she said nothing.

Vi smiled. "I've got you speechless, do I? Then

now would be the time to ask if perhaps you'd keep an eye on Roger while I'm gone?"

Roger was Vi's dog. He was a stumpy-legged, happy terrier of some indistinct sort, and the perfect calming influence on his volatile owner. He was not, however, an acceptable influence on a restaurant kitchen. And even with her lack of experience, Jenna was pretty sure she wasn't what one would term a "dog person." They were too messy, too tough to control. The closest she owned to a pet was Harold, an ancient lobster she'd inherited along with his tank when a friend's seafood restaurant in Dingle had closed down.

"Why not have Roger stay with Michael and Kylie?" she asked, referring to Vi's elder brother and his wife, married not yet a year and so blissfully in love that sometimes Jenna found it difficult to witness.

"No, they won't do at all. Every time I leave the dog with them, he comes home horribly spoiled and looking as though he's contracted the bloat. They feed him as though he's a wolfhound. What better place to leave him than with a chef? He'd thrive under your special brand of neglect. You're too busy cooking for the rest of the world to overstuff him—or even decently feed yourself."

Jenna shrugged. "The shoemaker's kids go barefoot, and all that."

"You'd do well to consider yourself now and again, you know."

"I think of myself every day."

Vi snorted. "You're confusing self and what you do for a living. You busy Americans have a knack for that, I'm thinking. I suppose it makes one rich enough. But to have no time to watch a fire, let alone dance in front of one?"

Jenna smiled. "And that would be something you have a knack for."

"True," she said complacently. "Tonight while you were off restoring perfection to your world, I was having a chat with my friend, here." She gestured at the bricks of peat, burning down to their last. "Interesting what a woman can see that way." She studied Jenna. "You'd best paint one of those unfinished bedrooms black."

Jenna was accustomed to these odd starts of Vi's. Her friend gave no particular name to the skill she had, this way of sensing things to come. To Vi, it was as natural as drawing breath—nothing suspect about it.

At first Jenna had been far from a believer. Even now she didn't want to really, truly believe that such a thing could be possible. Yet she'd been startled by the truth of Vi's pronouncements enough times that she now tended to hedge her bets.

"Black." The color brought only one person to mind. "You *were* joking about bringing Gilvane under my roof, weren't you?"

"Mostly, though there's much to be said for holding one's enemy close . . . especially that one." Her smile shimmered with sexual speculation. "Some sizable benefits there, I'd be guessing, though I'll take mercy on you and not ask you just why he makes you so nervous."

"Thanks for holding back."

Unlike Evie, Vi enjoyed a nip of sarcasm and

could hand back the same. "Just one of my many services."

Silence settled on them. Vi stretched out her long legs and sighed at the fire. Jenna found herself oddly transfixed, too.

"It's Gilvane and more I'm seeing," her best friend eventually said. "Lightning and shadows . . . You'd best be prepared."

Falling in too deep, Jenna made herself look away from the random licks of flame.

Preparation.

Ah, now there was something at which she'd attained virtuoso rank. Plans and backups, strategies and counterstrategies, when it came to this, she was in her element. She'd been raised in a household where the ability to hold her own was the difference between survival and utter humiliation. But even then, the enemy was known, tangible. It had been her father, who was brilliant, sarcastic, and incapable of love.

"Can you get any more specific than approaching darkness?" she asked Vi.

Her friend stood and stretched. "Afraid not," she said, leaving, as any good poet would, interpretation to the listener. "I don't suppose you've some fresh mint leaves in that magical kitchen of yours? I'm feeling a bit of a headache coming, and mint tea's just the thing." She was halfway to the door—no doubt off in search of mint—when she added, "Oh, and you're a love for watching Rog."

Had there been a choice?

Chapter Three

Don't make a bid until you've walked the land.
—IRISH PROVERB

The room was warm and the bed heavenly soft. Jenna dreamed she was seventeen again, sailing on Lake Michigan with her little sister, Reenie. They were happy—which was how Jenna knew it was a dream—laughing as a spray of water came across the Sunfish's small cockpit. She could feel the damp chill against her fingers.

Dream and reality merged. Jenna bolted upright.

"Eew!" She wiped her wet hand on her feather-down comforter and glared at the creature bedside. "You've got one cold nose, dog."

In answer, Roger trotted off. Vi, who was stretched across the foot of the bed, laughed.

Jenna greeted her with a grumpy "Have you ever thought of knocking?"

"I did, but since your bedroom and the front door are miles apart, little good it did me. You're a sound sleeper," she observed. "That's a sign of a soul at ease."

"Or one who's exhausted." Truth was, she'd spent far too much time staring at the ceiling last night. Striving to control the uncontrollable was one hell of a hobby, but it was all Jenna had. Much as she tried not to worry about Dev Gilvane or obsess over the number of stars bestowed upon her by food critics, when the kitchen was silent and there was nothing left to distract, her brain proceeded with gusto.

Vi sat upright, then flicked her long red hair over her shoulders. "You should have a drink of whiskey before bedtime. My nan swore by it."

"From what you've told me, your nan also swore by a mutton-fat poultice for burns."

Vi winced. "Some of her cures are more appealing than others. So are you ready for your visitor? Rog promises me he'll be no trouble at all."

The topic of conversation had wandered across the room. Currently he was by the wardrobe, snuffling at Jenna's work shoes, a canine gourmet delight.

Jenna stretched and yawned. "Is the sun even up yet?"

"As up as it's likely to be," Vi said. "Something nasty is clinging to the mountains, which is why I'm here so early. I'd like to be on my way before it visits the shore."

"All right," she said, pushing aside the covers and swinging her feet to the ground. "I'm up."

Vi crawled off the bed and smoothed her crimson silk trousers and black top. The outfit had to be one of her creations; she seldom wore store-bought. Vi retrieved her square, velvet patchwork sack that Jenna privately thought of as her friend's witch's bag—filled with items to frighten and amaze. Reaching to the bottom, Vi pulled out a pair of black chopsticks.

"I shouldn't be gone longer than two days," she said, knotting her hair atop her head and securing it with the sticks. "I'll ring you if anything pops up."

"Like?"

"An old lover, if I've any luck at all."

Jenna padded over to the wardrobe. She opened the left door and scowled at her muted image in its tarnished glass. If she had less pride and more sense, she'd take up her mother on the standing offer to meet in Paris and shop. But since her frequent-flyer mother couldn't seem to make that extra hop to Ballymuir for a visit, Jenna preferred to hold fast to her pride.

"Take your time. I'm sure Roger and I will come to an understanding." She glanced at the dog. He was licking the sole of one shoe. Definitely gross.

"What, no promises to give him a spot on your pillow and snackies every morning?"

Jenna smiled in spite of herself. "I'm holding out for someone taller . . . and human."

Vi came to stand behind her. She settled her hands on Jenna's shoulders and smiled at their reflection in the wardrobe door. "Good enough. Speaking of which, do your best not to kill Dev Gilvane while I'm gone. I'd hate to miss the show."

It was a pleasure to know that at least she hadn't lost her entertainment value.

Half an hour later Vi was on the road, Jenna was mostly conscious, and Roger was doing a happy-dance by the kitchen's back door. Jenna frowned. Maybe it was more of a jiggy, gotta-go dance. All told, it wasn't worth the risk to discover the difference.

"So everything's under control?" she asked Aidan, who was displaying some prodigious knife work on an eggplant, or aubergine, as it was called in this part of the world.

"It will be as soon as you get that feckin' dog out of the kitchen," he said in a mild tone that fooled her not at all.

"Point taken," Jenna replied, impressed that he'd gone for the subtler *feck* rather than his usual word of choice when in a high-stress situation. Jenna suspected that Aidan would remain placid in a hostage-taking, nod to sleep if at sea in a gale, but mess with his kitchen, and he'd have your guts for garters. Ready to escape, she reached for her waxed jacket and cap, where they waited on a hook by the door. Outside, the sky was silver with a light mist that made for the classic Irish "soft day."

As soon as Jenna had the door open, Roger shot out like a greyhound off to the races. Or at least as close as a dog with legs the size of a chicken's could come.

"So we're taking a walk?" she called, fussing with the toggle at the top of her buff-colored jacket.

Roger didn't seem inclined to answer. Luckily, he had chosen to follow Jenna's usual path for a walk—across the drive, through the field, and up the hillside she shared with her next-door neighbor, Mr. Horrigan, and his countless sheep. While Roger sniffed and marked, then scampered across the matted wet turf, Jenna took the straight route to her favorite thinking spot.

Though the view down to Dingle Bay was incredible, it was not this alone that drew Jenna. On the hillside's peak, amid sheep, random boulders, and tufts of hardy grass, stood an ogham stone, a marker carved in a simple alphabet of lines and slashes by people long gone.

Since oghams dotted the Kingdom of Kerry, this particular stone drew only a passing mention in the guide books. Every now and then Jenna would spot a couple of the more determined breed of tourists—those free of tour buses and leprechaun T-shirts—hiking to the ogham. She trusted that they would treat it with the same respect she did. Worn as it was, it was meant to outlive her.

When she made the peak of the hill, she called for Rog, who seemed to think that he was destined to herd Mr. Horrigan's sheep.

"They're not listening, pal," she called.

Roger yipped his reply, getting an annoyed bleat from one of the ladies in the pack. Jenna paused to trace her fingers up the rough marks that ran on the side of the stone, which was almost as tall as she.

"Hello, Tennac." Technically, she'd been told by Mr. Horrigan that what part of the stone could still be deciphered read *Tennac, son of* . . . , but that was an unwieldy greeting.

In the brief time she looked away, Roger had wandered. For a short thing, he could move quickly.

"Dog!" she howled as the canine bolted across the broad sweep of rocky field, toward Mr. Horrigan's house. "I swear I'm going to make you into a stew!"

He paused just long enough to look back, and Jenna could have sworn the little beast laughed.

Excitement coursed through Dev's veins. It was almost sexual in nature, the thrill of knowing he'd found the right spot, the *perfect* spot, for Harwood. He was sure a therapist would have a tidy retirement, unknotting his business drive from his sex drive.

He walked the path from the shore to the house, imagining the wonders an enormous budget could create, and thanking whatever divine powers that had interceded long enough to keep Jenna Fahey off his tail.

Dev wished for a better day for photos, but guessing none was in the offing this century, he pulled a digital camera out of his jacket pocket and started taking photographs for his initial report to his employers.

Today Muir House had a dour look about it, with its hewn-stone walls echoing the heavy sky above. Still, unlike any other historic property in the vicinity, it possessed a roof—a fine selling point, indeed. Dev framed and shot, checked the results, and moved on to another angle.

All the while, he kept an eye out for the resident phone-hater, who he was sure would be equally unenamored of cameras. Especially when pointed at what she deemed hers. After he'd circled the house, he opened the rusty and protesting gate to a walled garden and captured that, as well.

"Bloody brilliant luck," he assured himself as he left the garden and trekked back up the drive. "Couldn't do better."

Ahead lay the stone fence marking the front of Muir House's property. He'd left his car roadside, or at least as much on the side of the road as one could manage with the encroaching hedgerows. Still, traffic was minimal, and he was feeling blessed today. Which, of course, could have been the after-effects of a night spent with Mrs. O'Keefe's benign portraits of Madonnas, babes, and such smiling down upon him.

Dev hesitated before leaving. His initial memorandum would be a masterpiece with an aerial shot. Unfortunately, he had neither a helicopter nor a clear sky. He cast a critical eye on the hills leading to the mountains beyond. Distances could be deceiving in this mostly treeless landscape, but it didn't look too far a climb to give him what he needed. And it wasn't as if it were actually raining. This was more a mist permanently suspended midair.

He'd gamble his car's unblemished state a while longer. Dev pocketed his camera, wished for other than custom Italian leather shoes, and began walking.

What should have been an invigorating stroll soon became something more treacherous. The spongy green turf had a way of making the ground look deceptively smooth, and Dev's footwear was no match for the foot-swallowing holes or the amazing quantities of sheep dung. The hill's peak seemed to draw farther away with every step he took. Head down, he forged on. *Quitter* wasn't in his vocabulary.

"Going hiking?"

At the sound of that dreaded American voice, Dev drew to a stop. Behind him stood Jenna Fahey and a ridiculous-looking dog tied to a fat rope lead. He felt his mouth begin to pull into a smile at the sight of the creature.

And at Ms. Fahey, too, if he were to be honest. She wore a deep green canvas hat with its brim curled up. On one side was a clump of what he supposed were flowers made of the same fabric. Between the hat and a jacket that looked to be made for someone twice her size, the chef resembled an elf gone cute but very wrong.

"You almost passed me by," she said.

Rather than confess that his favorite shoes were conspiring to kill him, and that it was all he could do not to tumble arse-over-heels back downhill, he said, "You blended in with the landscape."

Her hazel eyes, which he had to admit were really quite beautiful, had narrowed. It took so very little to set her off that he could find almost no sport in it, but on a sodden Irish Wednesday, it would have to do.

Jenna didn't mistake blending in with the landscape for a compliment. But there remained worse fates. She could look as overdressed as the false, snooping Irishman in front of her. And she knew he'd been snooping because that was all he was dressed to do.

She didn't want to think about his absurdly inappropriate shoes, so instead she eyed his jacket. Black, of course. It looked as though some pricey British designer had been taken to the countryside to shoot pheasant, then translated the experience into an ersatz "outdoorsman" line. Gilvane was one water-logged slave to fashion, since the weather had passed soft and settled on downright wet.

At least the rain had slowed his reconnaissance activities. One of his jacket's diagonally slit pockets bulged, and she was certain it wasn't with a dead bird. Jenna modified the classic Mae West line.

"Is that a camera in your pocket, or are you just happy to see me?"

He smiled. For once it appeared to be wholly uncalculated. "Interesting question, but I'm wondering what the dog might have done to deserve a noose so large," he asked, pointing to the rope she'd borrowed from Mr. Horrigan.

"He broke canine rule number one—stay."

"And you are a woman for rules, aren't you?"

"There's nothing wrong with structure. Structure is good." Had she actually said that aloud? Annoyed with herself, Jenna pushed her jacket's cuff, which had slipped too low. She drew a slow breath and tried to wrest back control.

"So did you come up the hill to see Tennac's ogham?" she asked. His blank expression was exactly as she'd expected. "No? Then what would bring you here?"

"The view?" he suggested.

"In town they say you might be looking for a new home. Is that true, Mr. Gilvane?"

"Dev," he prompted, but she ignored him.

"So is it true?"

"Do you always believe rumors?"

"This one, I do. And before you ask, Muir House isn't for sale."

Her hat began to droop in the front, and a rivulet

of chilly water hit the tip of her nose. Gilvane, with
no hat at all and his dark hair slicked back, was far
too handsome for a cold, wet man. He watched her
discomfort as she tried to readjust the hat's brim
with her dog-less hand.

"Virtually anything is for sale when what's offered is tempting enough," he said, then reached out
to adjust her hat. "What would it take to tempt you,
Jenna Fahey?"

God, he was good, lowering his voice to an intimate inflection as he asked the question. Nearly a
master of his craft, he'd missed with only his eyes.
Instead of promising abandoned passion, there was a
flash of something odd that Jenna couldn't identify.
Surprise, maybe. But the bottom line was that she'd
dealt with better manipulators. She'd been sired by
one, in fact.

She stepped away. "I'm the planning sort. The
structured sort. Nothing tempts me."

"Nothing? Even saints are tempted."

She was no fool, but when this man smiled, she
might as well have been, because an insidious sort of
warmth started simmering inside. "You'd know,
wouldn't you, Gilvane?"

He slicked back his dark hair with one long-
fingered hand. She closed her mind against an image
of that same hand spanned against her hot skin.

"Not '*Mister* Gilvane'? I'm thinking we might
have made some progress."

"Progress toward what?" Her voice wavered, and
she hated the weakness it disclosed.

"Why, temptation, of course."

Fine, she was a fool, and a total one at that. She

had just managed to challenge the devil in the game
he played best. Jenna tugged on Roger's tether. "I'm
leaving. Snoop outside all you want, but stay away
from my house, or—"

"Oh, I know the penalty for breaking the 'stay'
rule," he said with a wry nod at Rog. "I'm just waiting
to see the prize for teaching you about temptation."

Jenna did the only thing she could. She fled Dev
Gilvane as quickly as one stumpy little dog would let
her.

Late that night Dev sat in front of his computer in
Mrs. O'Keefe's breakfast room. The lingering scent of
the plump raisin scones Muriel had baked to go with
tomorrow's breakfast kept him silent company. Determined to overstuff him, she'd left three "just to
tide you over till morning."

Food and temptation, the two seemed to be walking hand-in-hand for Dev today. He was having a far
easier go at facing down the scones than he was at
forgetting about that moment on the hillside this afternoon. In the rain and the muck and the seething ill
will, he had known a startling moment of clarity.

Something in Jenna Fahey had spoken to him of a
raw newness—of possibilities he'd never considered—
and it had shocked him. Everything in his life was
polished to a hard sheen; generally, he liked the lus-
ter. But looking at Jenna today, her full lips un-
painted and her face wet in spite of that hideous hat,
he had wanted her. It was a momentary madness,
he'd told himself then. Yet here he was, hours later,
still wondering about her taste. Oranges, perhaps . . .
tart, sweet, and ripe.

Dev grinned at the thought. She'd have him skewered and over a spit should he even try to kiss her. Ah, but it was grand to have a bit of a distraction while trapped in Ballymuir, and he'd never met a woman more in need of distraction herself.

He focused on his computer and scrolled through the last batch of information he'd requested from Margaret. His heart seemed to halt, then drum faster when he read the final memorandum.

"Jesus," he muttered, then gave an apologetic glance toward Himself's portrait on the wall. "Incredible."

Jenna Fahey, queen of the manse, didn't own Muir House. He was certain that the chef had intentionally omitted this fact. Frowning, Dev rubbed his hand over his forehead as he tried to decide what this news meant to him. And that quickly, he caught the error in his thoughts. He was treating this far too personally.

This is business, he reminded himself. Business had never turned from him or left him wanting; he owed it his first allegiance.

It was to his benefit that the American didn't own Muir House, for she had made her position clear. He'd wager that the property's true owner would be more easily bought.

And as for Jenna Fahey's fate?

Gaze fixed on his computer screen, he considered the merits of the situation. Someone as driven and talented as Jenna deserved a brighter setting than this back corner of nowhere. After a measure of time to adapt to the idea, she was certain to see its logic.

So all is grand in the business realm. But what of those

weeks before a deal can be struck? asked an insidious voice from deep inside. *What of pleasure?*

Dev smiled. Surely someone as intelligent as Jenna would be able to separate business matters from a budding mutual attraction. And surely they could explore this attraction to their common satisfaction.

Or so a man could hope.

Either way, he would do his job as he always did—to bloody perfection, for that's what made him Dev Gilvane.

Chapter Four

The one who is idle is generally making mischief.
— IRISH PROVERB

Friday was one of those off days in the kitchen: bad timing, bad temper, bad choices. Jenna placed the blame at the expensively shod feet of Dev Gilvane. She'd spent all of Thursday waiting to find him skulking about outside, or worse yet, ensconced like royalty in her dining room. He had never appeared, and that had served only to heighten her aggravation. The only thing worse than dealing with a problem was the anticipation of having to do so.

By noontime Friday she and Aidan had twice come to words over the lamb entrée. By one even Roger had done the sensible thing and taken refuge. He was hunkered down under the scrubbed-oak table in what had once been Muir House's minuscule original kitchen, but had more recently been transformed to sort of a war room, where Jenna tested recipes and fed the troops.

Jenna herself had retreated there by four, only to have the dishwasher storm in, announce that the busboy had grabbed her bum and she wasn't that sort of girl, and then flee Muir House. Given the several witnesses to the bum-grabbing, Jenna had sent him packing. In Muir House's hierarchy, the dishwasher was afforded a measure of preferential treatment. It was the job toughest to fill and the one which Jenna most hated doing.

With luck, she'd persuade Emer, the dishwasher, to return tomorrow. The dust had scarcely settled from Emer's and the busboy's hasty departures when it was time for family dinner—the meal the staff shared just prior to the restaurant's opening hour.

While the staff ate, Jenna reviewed the night's menu with them, making sure everyone could recite the ingredients, down to the smallest whisper of cumin in the medallions of lamb tenderloin. She would, of course, corner Evie and privately quiz her again before the guests arrived—Remedial Table-Waiting 101.

Aidan, who had stepped out of the room to take a phone call, came back in just as Jenna was launching her descriptions of the farmhouse cheeses new to the night's menu.

"Ah, Jenna," came Aidan's hesitant voice from behind her. "You've someone here to speak to you."

"Tell them I'm not here," she said, impatient to get through the detail work.

"I can't do that." He gestured to the doorway behind Jenna. "She can see you."

Jenna turned and looked at the tall and slender young woman standing in the kitchen doorway. She had the nervous look of a job-seeker.

The baseball cap pulled low over her face made Jenna think "American," but the rest, including unwashed, almost-dreadlocked dark hair, worn jeans, and too-tight shirt could have been any college student sitting on a sidewalk anywhere from Bourbon Street to Dublin's O'Connell Street, offering to braid hair for beer money. Much as she needed a dishwasher, Jenna had a rule about not hiring people who wouldn't meet her eyes, and this one was fixated on her shoes.

"I'm sorry, we've filled all of our open positions," she said.

The girl ran shaking hands down her jeans. "Jen, it's *me*."

Jenna stilled. *"Reenie?"*

The girl nodded and finally raised her gaze.

It was like a hammer to the heart, seeing her again. Jenna moved closer. It had been six peaceful years since she'd seen her sister in person, but only a matter of weeks since she'd glimpsed a candid photo of her in the "Celeb" section of a weekly magazine—not at all a Fahey place to be found. Still, the last Jenna knew, Maureen had golden hair, designer clothing, and an aura that exuded glamour.

Jenna ushered her a few steps outside the war room's doorway. "Has your father seen you lately?"

"He's your father, too," Maureen Elizabeth Fahey said, in what was quite possibly the worst choice of words.

They stared each other down. Jenna wasn't sure whether she was supposed to hug her or even if she wanted to, so she settled for giving her sister a tentative pat on the arm.

"It's good to see you. Are you visiting in the area?"

"Sort of."

"Reenie, how do you *sort of* visit?"

Hazel eyes so like hers showed a flash of irritation. "No one's called me Reenie in years," she said, drawing out the last word as if it had been decades since she'd abandoned her childhood name. "My name is Maureen."

"Fine, Maureen then. But you still haven't answered my question."

Maureen toyed with her silver thumb ring. "I'm looking for a place to stay."

"Why here?"

"Is it such a big deal to want to visit my sister?"

It was an enormous thing, and they both knew it. Too much had stood between them for too many years to pretend otherwise.

A sheen of tears glimmered in Maureen's eyes. "I thought it would be nice. . . ."

Reenie was her father's child, a solid ten on a scale of ten in manufactured drama. Jenna had been the quiet one, always on the outside of her father's circle of interests, unable to please and ultimately not caring whether she did.

If she let Reenie in, Jenna was giving up privacy with little offered in exchange, except storms of emotion, euphoric highs, and tumbling lows, messy and unwanted. But if she turned her away . . .

"You're welcome to stay," she said, knowing she'd

never be able to stomach the guilt of booting her sister—no matter how estranged—to the street.

"Okay," Maureen said, vulnerability disappearing as quickly as free food in a pub.

Suckered again.

"Is there someone who can carry my backpack up to my room?"

"You mean, other than you?" Jenna clarified.

Her sister nodded.

"No," she said, then gave her a Fahey smile. "This isn't life with Mom and Dad. There's no maid to clean up after you, no one to do your laundry. If you stay, you'll have to take care of yourself, and then some."

Her sister looked around as if seeking the fastest route of escape. "I could pay you room and board."

Apparently the grunge version of Maureen remained allergic to work. No surprise there, Jenna thought, remembering the joy that child Maureen had taken in creating chaos, then watching others clean up after her.

"We both know where your money comes from," she said.

"Since when do you care if it's Daddy's money?"

"I've always cared—I just haven't always had the choice. You pitch in or stay someplace else. My home, my rules."

Maureen laughed. "God, you sound just like Daddy."

The words stung. "Next rule. Don't talk to me about him."

"Have it your way," Maureen said with a shrug. "Where should I put my stuff?"

"Just a second," she said, then stepped into the war room, where everyone was doing their best to act as though they hadn't been avidly eavesdropping. "Aidan, would you mind picking up with the cheeses and finishing with dessert?"

And then she rejoined her sister. "I'll show you to your room."

Maureen allowed herself to relax as she stepped in line behind Jenna. Visiting her sister wasn't much of a plan. Then again, she wasn't much of a planner, but she was catching on. Now that she had a place to hide, she could lose the disguise she'd bought straight off a girl's back in Paris. With luck, the temporary hair coloring she'd used would live up to its billing, too. And tomorrow she could contact a friend who wouldn't rat on her. She could send her real clothes to . . . what *was* the name of this town, Bally-something?

Not that she'd actually seen a town—more like a few blocks of buildings. Of course, she'd been in shock at the time over actually having taken public transportation, a desperate move to lose pissed-off people. When, grimy and exhausted, she'd climbed off the bus from Dublin by way of every miserable village the driver could find, she'd had enough of the common life. Finding someone to drive her the rest of the way to Jenna's had cost her close to the last of her cash. No big deal—she still had her very best friend, credit.

"Where's your bag?" Jenna asked as they walked down a posh hallway.

"Outside—by the front door."

"You might as well get it."

They went back to the front of the house. Maureen grabbed the backpack before Jenna changed her mind and sent her curbside, then followed her up a curved, sweeping staircase. This place definitely wasn't the dive that her father's passing, amused comments had led her to expect.

As for her sister, Maureen expected nothing—literally. It had been years since she'd seen her, and that had been just a quick hello. Jenna had been working in Paris, and Maureen and her mother were staying in the family apartment for Easter vacation. Back then, Maureen had been a geeky teenager, thrilled to have a glamorous big sister who was a Parisian chef. Except Jenna really hadn't been much more than a glorified slave, with no time at all for Maureen.

And that hadn't changed. It wasn't as though she wanted rose petals strewn at her feet, but a hug or something might have been cool. She lacked the energy to be angry, though. If she didn't focus on the basics, like food and rest, she was afraid she was going to lose it.

Soon, though, she'd have that bed to fall into. From what she could see, the second floor of her sister's house wasn't as done-up as the first. There was no fancy art on the walls and the carpets weren't the expensive Persians she'd seen below. Jenna passed a number of closed rooms, then stopped.

"I haven't had this suite open in a while," her sister said while opening a door. "It could probably use an airing-out. The shower works well, though. I had the plumbing upgraded a few months ago."

They stepped inside. The room was stark in its simplicity, just a large bed with a lofty black comforter, and an armoire and a pair of armchairs of dark wood. The plaster walls and moldings were painted white, and the drapes hanging over a long bank of windows were white, too. The only notes of contrast were a ceiling painted a rich crimson and an antique, gilded mirror above the bed. Not exactly the Ritz, but not so shabby, either.

"The bathroom is through the door to your left," Jenna said.

Okay, so she was a little ripe. Sam, the king of scummy ex-boyfriends, was a believer in Method acting, and she was beginning to see his point. At least as it pertained to getting in character, not as it pertained to screwing actresses.

Shoving the miserable creep out of her thoughts, Maureen walked to the bed and ran her hands over the comforter.

"Black—my favorite color."

Her sister looked half-amused and half-annoyed at what she'd considered the most nonconfrontational words she could come up with.

"Figures," Jenna said.

"What figures?"

"What if I told you that someone you don't even know said you'd be coming?"

"I'd say that you're in need of serious drugs. *I* didn't even know I was coming here until . . ."

Maureen trailed off, looking around the room.

"Until what?"

She didn't want to say it, didn't want to sound as totally off-the-deep-end as her sister. So she walked over to the armoire, opened its doors, and stared into the emptiness. The words escaped on their own. "Until I had this really vivid dream the other night, okay?"

"Welcome to Ireland" was her sister's reply. Then she left.

Well past eight, Dev sat in on a conference call with the London and New York offices. It was a blessing he'd gone the full distance and picked up a new phone for Muriel. If he'd been lacking a speakerphone, his left hand would have been locked into a claw and his ear fallen off by now.

Did these people never stop talking? He didn't know who to blame it on: the Americans, the Japanese, or the international business community as a whole, but he was damn tired of sixteen-hour workdays. At least back home the knowledge that he had a night with some excitement awaiting him assuaged the pain. Here, he had one American chef who was growing more intriguing by the minute.

As Sid in New York again worried about the Costa Rican numbers and how resort occupancy rates were tanking, Dev glanced at his watch. His dinner reservation at Muir House was for eight-thirty. Last night he'd been late in returning from traveling all the possible routes to Muir House from Shannon Airport in County Clare and had been forced to eat pub grub. He deserved a decent meal and perhaps a bit of diversion with Jenna Fahey.

"Trevor," he said to his boss in London, "I've another meeting I need to attend. Could you reach me by cell if there's something requiring my input?"

The answer was "yes," the first one he'd gotten tonight.

Minutes later, as Dev drove the coast road to Muir House, he stewed over the negative responses that Trevor had given him. No, he couldn't return to London and finish his site report from there. No, he wasn't needed on the wrap-up of the Costa Rican deal. No, there was no reason to pop back to the city to attend the monthly divisional meeting. He was to relax in Ireland.

Relax? The idea was absurd.

He'd spent his first eleven years "relaxing" in a drab suburban outpost of Dublin, and it wasn't a memory he cherished. Then his parents had come into some money and his mother had packed him off to boarding school in England. For about three months he'd hated her for making him leave home, and he'd hated everyone at school, too. He'd been a miserable little bastard until he'd learned to fit in. After that, he'd never looked back.

What most disturbed Dev about the strange undercurrents in tonight's call was the thought that this Ireland assignment might be a prelude to a permanent post. He had no intention of refitting himself to Irish life, not even if it was to be in a city as cosmopolitan as today's Dublin. He was a Londoner by choice, and that would never change. He'd made a full life for himself, including the boon of female companionship who shared his goal of ultimate pleasure with minimum impact on work schedules. And when it seemed that they risked becoming too intimate, he would neatly move on. No pain. No messiness.

Dev pulled into one of the two available spots left in the gravel car park adjacent to the restaurant. A full house tonight, it seemed, and a glorious night for it, too.

Though he was late and not in the best of moods, Dev found himself in no particular hurry to dash up the walk. Instead, he strolled. The breeze carried a mysterious hint of tropical warmth, and the skies were remarkably clear. Tonight, banishment to the terrace would be little punishment.

Once in the house he glanced at his watch. He was nearly ten minutes past due, but it seemed he needn't worry. Niamh the hostess was graciously apologizing to a group of six that they'd have to wait a wee bit for their table, now that they were an hour-and-a-half beyond their scheduled arrival. Apparently ten minutes late was nearly early in Ballymuir.

"I'll be right with you, Mr. Gilvane," Niamh said before ushering the other party to the library.

When she didn't return straightaway, Dev waited as patiently as he knew how—which was saying little. "Curiosity killed the cat" his mum would always chide after rescuing him from one childhood scrape or another. Pity about that cat's fate, but curiosity was what kept him moving. It was a ravenous hunger, and just now he wanted not only a meal but a better sense of Muir House's interior layout.

The difficulty with buildings this old—and not of especially notable origins—was that it was nearly impossible to find a set of architectural plans. He'd done his best to guess what might be behind the windows in the photos he'd taken, but it was just that—a guess.

The hostess was still missing. He could ask for no better invitation to go wandering. Instead of following the main hallway toward the bar and dining room, Dev branched off to the right. Kitchen sounds grew louder. He glanced down a short hall where the floor was covered in terra-cotta tile rather than the thick runner under his feet, and wisely passed it by.

Farther down on his right was a door with a brass plaque that read Private. He assumed it was part of the house's living quarters. He could have honored the sign, but then he wouldn't have been Dev Gilvane. Slowly he turned the knob, frowning as it squeaked. He'd have thought that everything in the chef's world would be well-oiled and running to perfection. Dev pushed the door open just enough to peek inside. He winced at what—or more accurately, who—awaited him.

Jenna Fahey stood in profile, her head bowed and her arms wrapped about her midsection, pulling her white jacket closer to her curves. His first inescapably male thought was that he hadn't before noticed what fine breasts she had. Yes, she possessed a perfectly perky American shape. And he was a drooling dog to be noticing such things, especially when he was no better than a trespasser.

She lifted her head and looked to the doorway. He considered retreating, but it was too late. He was well seen. Her arms had dropped to her sides and she'd tucked back her shoulders.

"Mr. Gilvane." She sounded less than thrilled. He, on the other hand, was looking forward to another of their friendly chats. He wondered if he might have been a prizefighter in a prior incarnation.

"Call me Dev."

"No, thank you," she said, as though she were passing up dessert. "What are you doing in here?"

"Looking for the loo?"

"Behind a door marked Private?"

"It seemed a possibility."

"Unlike you, I try to be straightforward. This is my office. You'll find the men's room marked—amazingly enough—Men, in the opposite wing."

Her hair shone under the light of the small crystal chandelier hanging in the center of the room. There seemed to be so many shades of brown in her curls, everything from chestnut to a glint of deep auburn. He wondered if it could be as impossibly soft to the touch as it looked.

"Am I losing you, Mr. Gilvane?" Her foot tapped an impatient rhythm on the hardwood floor.

It was then that Dev took note of another drooling dog, this of the canine variety, sitting at Jenna's feet.

"So you've freed him from his noose?"

She glanced down, almost as though she'd forgotten she owned a dog. "Oh, you mean Roger. He's come to see things my way."

From the direction of the kitchen, the clanging sound of metal hitting an object equally hard drew their attention. Jenna muttered something under her breath that could have either been a curse or someone's name.

"Are you all right?" he asked.

"I'm fine."

Fine was one of those terrifying, catch-all female words, applied to a rainbow of truths ranging from "I'm truly doing well" to "In less than a nanosecond

I shall implode." She looked to be verging toward the darker end of the spectrum. Odd as it was, he felt an impulse to comfort her.

"Really, is there anything I can do to help?" he asked.

"Unless you're willing to take over for the world's worst dishwasher, no."

He glanced down at tonight's iteration of a black suit. "Sorry, I didn't come dressed for it."

He wasn't accustomed to women looking him over and finding him lacking, but this one clearly did.

"How about this, then?" she said. "You could try playing me straight and tell me why you're snooping around Muir House. You're not the horse-and-hound, country-lord type."

For the first time in as long as he could recall, Dev dipped into the well of banter and came up dry.

"I guess you meant to ask if there was *almost* anything you could do." She shook her head. "One thing about you, Dev Gilvane, is that you never fail to disappoint."

Dev worked up a mock hiss of pain to cover true sting of her dart. "Hit dead on."

Niamh appeared in the doorway. "So we haven't lost you altogether," she said, then gave Dev a pleasant smile.

"Not for lack of trying," muttered her employer before saying in clearer tones, "Mr. Gilvane is ready to go to his table."

Niamh was hardly an armed guard, but the effect was the same. Dev was escorted back to the public domain. And in what he could only view as a punishment, Evie of the endless chatter appeared to be his waitress again tonight.

After he'd settled in with his obligatory single-malt Scotch, Evie leaned closer, thrusting her bosom at him.

"I traded off with Brien, over there, to get you again tonight." Dev wasn't quite sure, but he thought the waitress might have winked at him. Then again, it could have been a facial tic, which he found a far preferable explanation. There was something sly, almost feral, about her that set his teeth on edge.

Just then the sound of breaking glassware cut into conversations, bringing a momentary, startled silence to the room. Dev's curiosity must have shown on his face.

"Oh, that's the owner's sister," Evie said in confidential tones. "She's washing up the dishes and doing a right poor job of it, too."

"I didn't realize Ms. Fahey's sister worked here," he replied while mentally riffling through the family information that Margaret had sent him. Beautiful and quite spoiled, Maureen Fahey was supposed to be a full-time party girl.

"You're ahead of us if you even knew she had a sister. Jimmy—he's the busboy who was let go today, all because of that cow, Emer—anyway, Jimmy and I were guessing that she'd been hatched from a pod. She's not even human. Everything has to be perfect. She had a bloody fit when I couldn't remember that tonight's farmhouse cheese was a Gubeen. Like milk from a Ballycotton cow would taste any different."

Dev watched to see if she'd even draw a breath, but her lung capacity seemed to be up to the task.

Evie yattered on. "So then herself's sister shows up at the door, and she's no sooner unpacked than she's put to work behind the—"

In a case of classic timing, Dev's cell phone chirped the opening notes to "A Soldier's Song." Thank God he'd remembered to change the tones to Ireland's anthem. Bad enough that Evie's oversolicitous hovering was earning him jaundiced looks from his neighbors.

After giving the closest diners an apologetic grin and shrug, he waved off Evie and flipped open the phone. When he glanced back up, the waitress and her round tail were already swinging toward the kitchen.

"Gilvane here."

"Dev, it's Trevor. A few questions have popped up on the Ballymuir site. Do you have a second?"

"Yes," he said, while thinking, *and possibly not much more, given Muir House's chef.*

"So you say this house is outside town?"

He kept his voice low and eyes down, better to go undetected. "By a few miles along the coastline."

"And the roads? Will there be access problems for coaches?"

"The road is tight, but no more so than on the Ring of Kerry," Dev said, referring to the county's more heavily visited Iveragh Peninsula.

"Grand. Get to work, then. Though we all agree with you that thirty acres is too small a site. Start talking to adjacent property owners. We need to be certain we can get our hands on enough to build a golf course. Is there sufficient open land?"

Dev briefly mourned his ruined shoes. "To the extent one can call rocks with the occasional clump of topsoil land, yes, there's plenty open. I'll go visit the neighbors tomorrow."

"Start with Mr. Horrigan," Jenna Fahey advised from the spot she'd taken just behind him. He wondered how long she'd been there. The way his luck had been running since landing in Ireland, his guess was too long.

"I'll ring you back later." Dev closed the phone without waiting for an answer.

Jenna greeted neighboring tables, with a special smile for a silver-haired man, then pulled out a chair opposite Dev. He was quite impressed by the genial expression she'd pinned on, as though they were old friends about to chat.

She opened his menu and pointed to the pretty little script at the bottom about cell phones, cigarettes, and cigars.

"How'd you know I took a call?" he asked.

"You annoyed Evie, which is never a good move."

The tongue-flapper scorned, Dev thought.

"Hand it to me," she said, her gazed fixed on the phone currently sitting above his dessert fork.

"I've switched it off." It was a lie of which he'd grown fond.

"And you'll switch it back on as soon as I leave the room."

He smiled his most charming smile and got a deadpan stare in response.

"I can excuse the occasional phone call," she said in a soft voice intended to stay between the two of them. "What I can't excuse is the sheer amount of guts it takes for you to sit in my house and talk about buying it out from under me."

He opened his mouth to deny the charge, but she stopped him.

"I know you were talking about Muir House. I'd ask you to leave, Mr. Gilvane, but it would cost me too much in gossip. Now give me the phone."

Dev handed it to her. As she rose and looked down at him, he felt an uncomfortable emotion, one so old and unfamiliar that it took him a moment to name it: guilt.

It was enough to put a man off his food.

Jenna left. A chastened man, Dev ordered and ate in silence, then retrieved his cell phone and returned to Cois Na Mara. There, he lay awake long into the night contemplating the female capacity for mucking up a male's mind. Business was business, damn it all.

Muir House on a Sunday was meant to be a peaceful place; it was the first of the two days each week that the restaurant was closed. Jenna usually began her time off by attending morning mass at St. Brendan's in the village. Even without looking at a clock, the light in her bedroom this particular Sunday was enough to tell her that she'd overslept. She felt groggy, almost drugged, and her head pounded as though she'd drunk her way through the Bordeaux section in the restaurant wine cellar.

She stretched and nudged Roger with her foot. He was still out cold, curled in a nearly perfect dough-nut O. Amazing. She'd had no idea that dogs could snore so loudly. Of course, she'd also had no idea that she'd ever permit a dog to sleep on her bed. Roger hadn't deemed the topic open for negotiation.

Jenna folded back the covers without smothering

Rog, then sat up. That simple move pushed her far enough to consciousness that last night's unsettling events returned to her—Maureen, Dev Gilvane . . . and the bottle of red she'd polished off by herself at two in the morning. She flopped back against her pillows, gave it a heartfelt "feck," and slept an hour more.

When Vi came to retrieve Roger just past noon, Jenna was awake, if not pleased with the state. Princess Maureen was still in her chamber, no doubt waiting for a handmaiden to come tend to her.

Jenna and Vi settled in the blue salon, another of the rooms Jenna kept off limits to guests. Here she kept her personal mementos—family pictures, a candid shot of her with Paul Bocuse, one of her idol chefs. It was a warm, cheerful place that she'd taken care to make her own, and not just an amalgam of her mother's decorators' tastes.

On a day when her skull wasn't threatening to split open, Jenna would have enjoyed the daylight shining through the room's mullioned windows. Today it hurt. Keeping to the shadows, she edged her way to a chair. Once settled, she took a sip of her coffee, which she'd spiked with a shot of Jameson's.

"So, how was Kilkenny?" she asked as the hair of an Irish dog worked its way through her system.

Feline that she was, Vi had draped herself across a pale blue velvet settee and reveled in the sun. Roger stretched out on the Aubusson rug, nose on paws, ready to nap.

"Kilkenny was grand," said Roger's mistress. "I saw quite a bit of an old friend—all the interesting parts."

Jenna, who hadn't seen the interesting parts of a male in quite some time, decided to forego that line of chat, and just maybe punish Vi a bit in the bargain. "And your mom, how is she?"

"Mam was on her best behavior. We bypassed the career speech and covered only marriage." Vi's red brows drew into a slight frown. "Though she did threaten a visit to see how Pat and Danny are getting along—as good an incentive to get them to call her as I can imagine."

"I'll bet."

Vi's mother had been in Ballymuir last summer for Michael and Kylie's wedding, which Jenna had catered. Mrs. Kilbride had been talented at letting everyone know how put out she was to be there, without actually saying so.

Jenna downed the last of her coffee and considered having some more. With whisky, of course.

"So has that Dev Gilvane been about?" Vi asked.

Jenna's heart kicked up a notch. She was trying to string together an answer that had nothing to do with what she really felt—not that she'd even pinned that down—when Her Royal Highness strode into the room. Today's wardrobe choice was a ripped T-shirt with faded lettering about "Sorority Rush Week" and what looked to be a pair of army surplus pants—definitely not the Fashion Week material Jenna had seen in those Paris candids of her sister.

Reenie's hair was strange, too. The white girl's attempt at dreadlocks was gone, and it was no longer yesterday's muddy brown. Unfortunately, neither loss was grounds for improvement. Now her hair flirted with a scary, streaky almost-gray. Jenna tried not to stare.

"Vi, this is my sister, Maureen," she said.

Vi's gaze rove between the array of family photographs on the mantel and the girl in front of her. Jenna thought her friend did an admirable job of not sounding a variation on the "whatever the hell happened to you?" theme, as she had yesterday.

Vi stood and extended her hand. "It's grand to meet you."

Maureen ignored the offered hospitality and squinted at Vi. "Right. You, too."

This was the product of serial expulsions from expensive boarding schools and private colleges? Their father should have offered to build a wing on a charm school.

Reenie turned the same hostile look on Jenna. "Food?"

"Kitchen."

"I looked there. Nothing's cooked."

"So cook it." Paybacks were indeed a bitch; she'd spent two hours after closing taking care of the carnage in the dishwashing area.

"Can't cook."

"Eat fruit," Vi suggested in a tone that made it clear she was thinking of less palatable offerings. Jenna held back a laugh.

Maureen was less amused.

"Phone?" she snapped.

"My office."

"Which is?"

"By the kitchen."

Maureen stalked out of the room, Vi laughed, and Jenna decided on one more medicinal coffee.

"And, yes, before you ask, black's her favorite color," she said to Vi.

Vi smirked. "I wasn't feeling the need to ask." She bent down and scratched Roger behind his ears. "Despite the rain cloud following her, it's grand she's here. Did she tell you why she's come?"

"Not really. Talking to her is like talking to Dev Gilvane. You get answers, but none of it's real."

"Well, I won't be opining on Gilvane since I've not been around him when his guard is down, but with your sister, everything you need to know is right there."

"Such as?"

"She's angry, for one."

Jenna shrugged. "Who isn't? Emer walked out last night, so I persuaded Reenie to run the dishwasher."

Vi laughed. "Persuaded? You mastered subtlety while I was gone?"

"Fine, I coerced. But it's not like a little work would kill her."

"Ah, so now we come to the thick of it."

"There is no thick, okay? She's my sister, but when you come right down to it, I know half of Ballymuir better than I know her, and I'm perfectly all right with that."

"Of course you are."

"And if she thinks I'm going to change a single damn thing I'm doing just because she decides to waltz in, she's dead wrong. No one messes with my system. No one. Besides, I've been here two years and not one family member has come to visit."

"And it's not bothered you at all."

Jenna got up from her chair and grabbed her mug. "I need more coffee."

Maureen stood in the doorway, her face pale and

mouth pulled tight. Time looped its way around Jenna, then pulled tight. She saw a pouting Reenie at age four when Jenna didn't want to play dress-up, an angry Reenie at age eight when Jenna was fifteen and had no use for her, and a crying Reenie at age ten as Jenna packed her bags and left.

"Maureen . . ."

Reenie at twenty gave it a blunt "Bite me."

After she was gone, Jenna walked to the window and looked down to the shore. The tide was in, and the water lapped at its upper boundary of round, storm-washed boulders. Too many people, too many problems. She was better at being alone.

"Spring is on us," Vi said from behind her. "I was thinking this morning that we need a bonfire."

"Any reason in particular?"

Her friend's answer was simple. "It's Beltane Eve and there's much to burn."

Chapter Five

The big house has a slippery threshold.
—IRISH PROVERB

Jenna had long known that the true definition of "futility" was engaging in a battle of wills with Vi Kilbride. If she decreed a Beltane Eve bonfire, a bonfire there would be. According to Vi, in the old time this night marked the beginning of the year's fruitfulness. New couples would love, fields would grow fertile, and fresh fire would be brought into the home. In these fast and modern days, the day was more an excuse for a gathering, not that Ballymuir ever required a reason.

By late Sunday afternoon Jenna had pulled together an enormous pot of thick and spicy vegetable soup and baked a basketful of baguettes. Before long the house would fill with Kilbride men and women, and the restaurant's staff and friends from the village. Outgoing Vi would be her buffer from all of them.

Jenna stood on the terrace, the soft sea breeze eddying around her. Vi and Maureen were closer to the water, at the stone ring. Last fall Jenna had given in to Vi's firebug ways. Choosing to contain what she couldn't control, Jenna had selected a flat spot just above the slope to the bay and built a broad, low circle of stones to hold the flames. She sometimes wondered where Vi had lit her fires before having run of Muir House. With luck, not in her tiny yard on the edge of town, in sparking distance of her weekends-only, next-door neighbors' costly thatched roof.

Vi was showing Maureen how one properly stacked wood. It looked as though even Reenie had the good sense not to argue. Vi created her blazes with the same artistry that Jenna used when selecting seasonings for her recipes—bit of birch, kiss of oak, and twig of alder. The fact that Vi's brother Michael had started building custom furniture always added to the exotic mix. Jenna imagined there weren't many Irish fires fueled by mahogany scraps.

Deciding that she'd left Vi to suffer Reenie alone long enough, Jenna descended the wide terrace steps to the rougher land beyond. She was three-quarters the way down when a male voice called her name. Jenna stopped and looked back. Damn. Gilvane. She had enough to distract her without letting last night's anger rise again.

"Go away," she answered, again picking up her pace. "We're closed."

He pulled even with her in no time. This afternoon he was dressed casually, in jeans and a nubby charcoal-colored wool sweater—a relaxed sort of black. Jenna wondered if he ever had an off day, one on which his smile wasn't up to full wattage or his grace abandoned him. She doubted it.

"What do you want?"

"I've come to apologize," he said almost unwillingly.

She didn't want this from him. She had him neatly compartmentalized and couldn't bear the thought of him straying.

"I get the feeling that you don't apologize often. You might as well save it for someone who cares."

He moved in front of her and stayed her escape with a hand on each shoulder. Her heart sped to his touch, and Jenna resented its betrayal.

"Ah, but you see, this is an apology *I* care about," he said. "I'm sorry for last night, and if you'll stand still long enough, I'll make you some promises."

"Fine," she said, mostly in hopes that he'd take his hands off her. She angled a bit to her right and saw that Vi and Maureen had both stopped working and were watching avidly.

He held fast. "First, I'll admit to an interest in Muir House. It's a beautiful place."

She shrugged from his grip. "I know."

"And," he said, moving to keep in front of her, "whatever my interest, I promise that from today, I won't use my visits here to advance it."

"Then why visit?"

"For the pleasure of your company?"

She laughed, but could feel flattered color rising on her face. Or maybe it was shame that she'd even think of wanting him to be attracted to her. She'd fallen for some bad types, but never an outright thief of all she loved.

"Pleasure? Good one, Gilvane."

"It's the truth, and I'm amazed that you can't see it. If I were to disappear tomorrow, would you not miss me a little, miss at least the thought of being tempted?"

Would she? Her answer frightened her. "I'd miss you as much as I miss—"

He'd reached out and was touching her hair. She swatted his hand away. "Stop that."

He smiled as though he held a secret. "If I didn't visit, I'd miss you, Jenna Fahey. I'd miss knowing all those things I want to know. . . ."

She stilled, curious what it was the devil didn't already know.

"Hey, are you going to come help, or just stand there?" her sister shouted.

There was a certain irony to being saved by the brat.

Dev turned and looked. "What are they doing?"

At Vi's broad smile and wave, Jenna gave in to the inevitable. "Making trouble," she said. "We might as well go down, or they'll come up."

They joined Reenie and Vi at the circle's edge. Vi's firewood had been laid in a woven pattern that was nothing short of art. For an instant Jenna was held by a flash of a vision of druids, wicker cages, and sacrifice. Nonsense, she knew, but she shivered just the same. Dev glanced over at her. She did her best to present a surface calm. He was already too adept at pinpointing her weaknesses.

She introduced Dev to Reenie, who inspected him with much the same critical interest Jenna would a quarter of beef on restaurant delivery day. Vi, on the other hand, slathered on the charm.

"So, Dev Gilvane, I've been hearing that you're from Ballymuir."

"Dublin, originally," he said. "And London now. My mother was born in these parts, but I've visited just once."

"Look at all you've been missing," she said, casting an arch smile in Jenna's direction.

She'd never seen Vi appear discomfited, but with one quelling look, Dev Gilvane accomplished the impossible. Since Jenna wanted no matchmaking hand shoving the middle of her back, she didn't feel especially sorry for her friend.

Dev walked the perimeter of the circle. "Among other things, I'm surprised I missed this the other day."

"When you came snooping?" Jenna asked.

He paused and smiled. "Yes, when I came snooping. Is this a ruin of some sort?"

She felt as though she'd just been presented with a wonderful gift. "It's the remains of a beehive hut," she improvised, ignoring Vi's surprised expression.

"A what?" He was apparently the rare Irishman who lived free of Irish history.

"Little circular dry-stone buildings," she said. "You'll find a lot of them on the hillside out Slea Head Road. Monks built them centuries ago . . . nobody's sure why. Some think they were rooms for meditation or a stopping-over point on a trek."

He glanced up at the house, then back to the fire ring. "So this is an archeological site?"

"Yes. Unfortunately, it's limited what I can do with the property."

The dubious angle of his brows and his casual "interesting" made her suspect she'd pushed it too far.

Vi seemed to be recovering her capacity for speech. "Speaking of local treasures, we'll be having a Beltane bonfire tonight. Would you join us, Dev?"

Jenna possessed none of her friend's psychic powers, but the man would have to have been both numb to brain waves and ignorant of body language to miss her unspoken *no!*

He hesitated just long enough to let her hope she could relax for the night, but then said, "A fire? Yes, I think I would."

Of course. What more natural an attraction?

Her best friend appeared content with the results of her meddling. "Brilliant! Come at sunset."

"Can I bring anything?"

"Just yourself," Vi replied.

Which, in Jenna's obviously extraneous opinion, was one item too many.

Gilvane soon departed. On his heels, Maureen escaped, claiming a disabling but invisible splinter in her palm. Jenna lingered to try to pin down Vi.

"Did you have to invite Dev Gilvane?"

"On Beltane Eve, I most surely did." She walked a circle around her wood, nudging a piece here, loosening one there. "Otherwise the night would have been like having a sweets table with no sweets."

"He's not sweet, trust me on this."

"But he's something to you, isn't he? And you've been away from the banquet quite long enough. In the time I've known you, I've not seen you look twice at a man, except Dev Gilvane."

"What woman wouldn't look twice?"

"Many," Vi said, turning from her half-finished creation. "He'd be a bit much for most—but not you."

"Smart women."

Her friend frowned. "If his being here bothers you, I'm concerned. And while I'm worrying for your sanity, just what was that line you spun about beehive huts?"

"A disincentive. He wants Muir House."

Vi shrugged. "And I'd like to fly."

Jenna looked to the sky dotted with plump white clouds, then to her home. "You might not get your feathers, but at least in theory, Muir House is something Gilvane could have. I don't own it."

"*What?*"

The alarm in her friend's voice fed Jenna's anxiety, which had been dining well enough already. "I said I don't own Muir House."

"And you never told me this?"

"Yeah, well, what kind of clairvoyant are you? You should have already known."

"You act as though I'm some sort of all-seeing goddess. I don't know what you ate for breakfast, how much your utility bills are, or if you own this land. Though I'd be thinking that among the three, you might have mentioned the last."

"It's not the kind of thing to just pop into conversation, okay?"

Vi snorted.

"Look, when I found Muir House, I tried to buy it,

but the best I could do was work out a lease. The owner is a little odd." Which was like saying that Vi was a little bossy. "And I haven't stopped trying, either, but it's tough to get her attention. This property isn't up on her list of interesting topics."

"I'd say you'd best interest your absentee landlord before Dev Gilvane finds the truth."

Jenna crossed her arms over themselves and held on tight. "He hasn't said anything, but I'm pretty sure he already knows."

"Ah."

"Yes, *ah*."

"And now?"

She'd been hoping someone would answer that for her. But since even Vi, wise beyond her years, could see no quick solution, Jenna launched her plan, hoping it didn't sound as hollow as it seemed to her. "I'm going to get my solicitor to step up pressure on Miss Weston-Jones—"

"British, I take it?"

"Hyphenated, elderly blue blood. Think butlers, musty clothing, and fox hunts."

Vi shuddered. "I'd rather not."

"Anyway, all I can do is hope for the best. Maybe Miss Weston-Jones will rejoin Earth. Or maybe I can outbid Gilvane even if he does make an offer."

The sole bright spot of being a Fahey was trust-fund money at age twenty-one from her paternal grandparents, but the restaurant start-up costs had nearly tapped Jenna's share dry. There was always her father, though. She could ask, and given his mood, he might agree. Of course, he might also change his mind the very next day. Life with Martin

X. Fahey was like riding out the swings of a pendulum.

"One thing's for sure," Jenna added. "No matter what happens, I don't want word of this loose in town. If possession is nine-tenths of the law, maybe the illusion of ownership will push me the rest of the way."

Vi gave a negative shake of her head. "I can't see it happening. You know what they're like, how gossip spreads."

"We've had a lot of new gossip fodder move in over the past few months. I figure everybody's busy enough dissecting your new French neighbors."

Vi laughed. "True enough. I heard the other day at the market that some believe they're smugglers. It will be weeks yet till consensus is reached on exactly what they're smuggling." The set of her face grew more serious. "But as for Dev Gilvane? Tales of beehive huts aside, do you think he can't be swayed from wanting Muir House? I've seen you be persuasive enough."

"I don't know. Maybe. I'm not . . ." She trailed off, trying to think of some way to describe the effect he had on her, but could come up with nothing that explained the nerves jittering just beneath her skin, the mix of fear and anticipation. "I'm not myself around him."

Vi smiled. "Or perhaps you are," she said. "Perhaps you're exactly who you're meant to be."

Now, there was a thought to inspire true terror.

Afternoon slipped into evening. Soup simmered and Clannad's traditional music played over the house's sound system. Vi walked the shore, Reenie hid, and Jenna lolled in an armchair, leafing through the pages of a picture book on Irish gardens. One day she'd turn her attention to Muir House's walled garden and make it give more than the herbs it grudgingly sheltered. Perhaps some apple seedlings so that someday she could make sweet apple tarts straight from the garden. Or cut flowers for the restaurant tables . . .

Then it struck her that she was making plans for a future that might never come. Jenna shut the book and closed her eyes. She'd always been so confident, assuming that hard work would bring success, that the risk of improving Muir House would be met with reward. And it would, though perhaps not hers.

One thing was certain—keeping Dev Gilvane from Muir House would only increase its cachet for him. She knew his type, living for the challenge and the short-term thrill. She feared that she and her house were nothing more than that, and they both deserved far better.

"Your friend the witch says to tell you that the guests are arriving."

Jenna opened her eyes and took in her sister's hostile expression—one constant in a changing wind. She rose.

"Vi's not a witch." Exactly.

Maureen smirked. "She also says you should wear green."

Jenna looked down. She'd already changed into the soft, green woolen sweater Vi had given her for her last birthday, and was half tempted to go change again just to keep her friend's ego in check.

"Witch, for sure," Maureen decreed, then left.

Jenna opened her front door to see a line of people walking from the parking lot. The sight reminded her of her favorite childhood cartoons with their depictions of ants raiding a picnic, except these foot-soldiers were bringing the food to her.

"Honey cakes," said silver-haired Breege Flaherty, pressing a parcel in Jenna's hands. She winked. "They'll keep you fit for May Day and chasing the men."

Her companions laughed.

"Breege, you'll have Jenna thinking we're all pagans," said Kylie O'Shea Kilbride, her arm looped through her husband's.

"There's nothing wrong with a spot of fun, and at my age she'd best be having it for me."

Michael brushed a brotherly kiss against Jenna's cheek and said, "It's grand to see you and grander yet the way you've opened your house to us."

"Any time," Jenna replied. The words were heart-felt. Ballymuir had given her a home. A welcome was the least she could offer in return.

Michael, Kylie, and Breege were no sooner on their way out to the terrace than Evie Nolan came through the door, pushing a bottle of wine her way. After the waitress scurried by, Jenna checked the label and realized that she'd just been gifted with the Pouilly-Fuisse that had turned up missing in last Monday's cellar inventory.

Sweets and milk candies, kisses on the cheek, her heart and arms were full. Even Father Cready, the sole priest in town, arrived. "Observing only, if you get my meaning," he'd said with a wink as cheerful as Breege's.

One man remained unaccounted for. As much as she'd objected to his coming, she felt strangely let down that he wasn't there. It was a strong lure, the hum of excitement that came with seeing Dev Gilvane. Yet Beltane Eve, even for a skeptic like her, was no night to be toying with temptation.

Putting aside thoughts of dangerous pleasure, she carried her bounty to the dining room and set it up on the round eight-top table in the center. She'd just finished admiring her handiwork when a voice came from behind her.

"Waterford, is it?"

Jenna turned to see bed-and-breakfast owner Muriel O'Keefe pointing at the chandelier.

"Must be the devil to dust."

Jenna laughed. "It is."

Dev stood beside Muriel, looking as though he believed he'd taken a giant step toward martyrdom. Jenna pressed her hands together, ignoring the school-girl rush of adrenaline.

"I'm here to keep an eye on the boy, what with May Day coming and unwed women about." She nudged Dev forward and then thrust a package at Jenna. "Stout cake for you. Couldn't get the husband to move from the sofa, though," Muriel said, her head turning this way and that. "I've never been inside, you know. Food's too fancy for our sort. I've heard it's quite grand, though, velvet upholstery and tassels from the lampshades in the library. Mind if I have a look-see?"

"Of course not," Jenna replied, hoping Muriel wouldn't feel let-down at the lack of tassels. She set Mrs. O'Keefe's heavy cake on the table, then slid it from its paper sack. "The library's back by the front door and on the opposite side of the hall."

Muriel strolled off, leaving Jenna alone with Dev. She fussed for a minute, tucking Muriel's bag into the brass wastebasket to the right of the fireplace. She'd felt many things in his company, anger—or a cousin to it that she chose not to name—being the most frequent. But now she was awkward, absent of words, and uncertain what to do. He wasn't helping, looking at her with an intensity that made her blood rush.

"Green suits you," he finally said. "It brings out the color of your eyes. They're really quite fine, you know?"

He sounded almost surprised when he said the last. She couldn't decide whether to be amused or flattered. Either way, she knew his words were genuine, not one of the empty compliments he handled so facilely.

"Thank you. I should, ah . . ." The word *run* ringing loudly in her mind, she gestured at the doorway.

"Have you ever seen a Beltane fire?" he asked, settling a hand on her waist and ushering her down the hall.

"Not Beltane," she said, quickening her stride to avoid his touch, "but Vi's burned plenty of others. The last one was because it was a Thursday, and I think the one before that was in honor of Mr. Spillane down at the market getting in a new shipment of Nutella."

He laughed. "According to Mrs. O'Keefe, this one's different. She said something about lust and hayfields that I preferred to miss."

"The good news, Gilvane, is that the closest hay-field is at least a mile off."

"If that's the good news, I'd hate to be hearing the bad."

They were on the terrace by then, even better news to Jenna since the tensile strength of Dev Gilvane's tall, fit body and a cushion of hay were concepts she didn't dare connect.

Diversion surrounded her. Clusters of people chatted and laughed, far more than had come by way of the front door. Jenna and Dev were separated by the crowd, but she could still feel him watching her. Now and again their eyes would meet, and he would smile. It was the same look he'd worn in that unsettlingly intimate moment when he'd touched her hair. And again, it shook her.

As true darkness neared, everyone drifted toward the stone circle. Seeking camouflage from Dev, Jenna hid among the tall Kilbrides. Pat and Danny were busy competing for Maureen's attention, who was equally occupied by looking bored.

Vi, who stood next to Jenna, asked, "Ready, then?"

"As ready as I'm going to be."

In a voice strong enough to carry around the circle, Vi said, "First, my thanks to Jenna Fahey for giving me my fire while making sure I don't burn your houses to the ground. She's a kind woman, indeed."

The crowd laughed and applauded. Jenna tried for a true smile, but as always it was the nervous stretching of her mouth that embarrassing public praise produced.

When everyone quieted, Vi continued. "Michael, Pat, Danny, and myself had a grandmother who was nothing short of magical. She could calm a heart ill-at-ease and grow a lush garden in the poorest soil. Nan would always say that with every drink came a story, and if one were a Kilbride, with every story came a song. I've had the drink, so you can be guessing what will follow."

"And before we're too old to hear you, if you might," prodded Michael, to the laughter of those gathered.

"No one loves you like family," Vi teased.

At that, Jenna's and Maureen's gazes clashed and then withdrew. No one could punish quite like a family, either. Jenna looked back to Vi.

"For the benefit of those among us who are not up on our Irish, I'll be singing a song about a maid seeking her lover on Beltane Eve," Vi said. "Now, because these are Irish lovers, needless to say, they don't get matters quite right." She smiled. "After all, we must have our ghosts to keen and rattle their chains in the darkness."

Because she was Vi and this night was to be a dream brought forward from the old days, she sang unaccompanied, in the old style. And because she was Vi, everyone stilled and listened. When she was done, there was no applause, just a respectful silence. Jenna drew it all in, the whisper of the water lapping the shore, the emotion almost palpable on the salt breeze, and the sense that this moment carried so much more than its surface truth.

"Well, then," Vi said after a moment's pause to shake off whatever sprits held her while she sang, "I'd say it's past time for a fire."

She picked up a long branch, knotted and gnarled

as an old man's finger. The very end of it was wrapped tight with cloth and thick with wax—Vi's well-tested fire-starter.

"Father Cready, if you would?" she said.

A man never far from a cigarette, he pulled a pack of matches from his pocket and lit the very end of the branch. It smoked for a few seconds, then gave a bright flame. Vi raised it skyward.

Instead of spearing it into the center of the circle, as Jenna had seen her do so many times before, she said, "You light the fire, Jenna."

Jenna took the torch and dropped it into the middle of the stack. Paper and kindling caught with a rushing sound that pulled the breath from her. She averted her eyes and quickly stepped back.

The collective roar of the fire-revelers drowned the sound of the fire, but echoing even louder than that was the rapid beat of her heart. She turned to work her way from the flames, but Dev stood in her path.

She could feel his gaze upon her, as hot as the fire, but far more focused, more intent. And in herself she felt power and terror and something waking . . . something that was best left dormant.

Jenna fled.

It might have been Vi Kilbride's haunting song affecting Dev. It might even have been the two glasses of wine he'd drunk, though God knew that on countless other nights he'd had more and never felt this reckless. But it was neither of those things; it was Jenna Fahey.

He had made his promise and he would keep it.

While on Muir House's grounds, he would not pursue his interest in the property. Here he stood, walled off from business, left only with hot, hungry desire.

He scowled at the fire. He was a city-dweller, with a city-dweller's sophisticated soul. He should leave and not return until this hunger had passed. Except he couldn't.

Dev left the bonfire and scanned the crowd on the terrace for Jenna. The lights of the house cast enough glow that he could see her in silhouette, standing with a male. Dev walked toward them. Her companion was a tall, gray-haired man he recalled seeing at a neighboring table the first night he'd dined at Muir House.

Dev half-wondered at the tension gripping him. He had never thought himself the jealous type. Then again, he'd had little to be jealous over once he'd found his footing in life. Whatever this feeling was, he'd satisfy it and hope it would fade.

"Walk with me," he said close into Jenna's ear.

"No." She shook her head. The motion brought her scent to him—smoke and woman. "I have guests. . . ."

The man she'd been talking to wore a knowing look. Dev ignored him and settled his hand against the nape of Jenna's neck, letting his fingers toy with those satiny soft curls. She shivered, but accepted his touch.

"Come away," he whispered again and could feel her sway toward him.

Ah, so near was satisfaction. So near that he wanted to seize it and run.

"Brendan, if you don't mind?" Jenna said to the

older man, her voice sounding so calm that Dev's nerves pulled even tighter. *Could she not feel this?*

"Minding has nothing to do with it. I'll see you Tuesday dinner, as always," the man said. "Enjoy the night."

Dev gave a curt nod and allowed Jenna no time for speech before he had her off the terrace and moving away from the house.

"Would you mind slowing down?" she asked.

"I'm walking too quickly for *you?*" That was ripe.

"What do you want?"

What he wanted and what he would say were different creatures. "Your time. Spend the day with me tomorrow."

"I can't."

"Why?" he shot back.

They reached the walled garden. "I need to run my inventory lists and update orders." She sounded breathless, whether from the fast walk or something else, he didn't know, didn't even care. He wanted simply to bend her to his will.

"So you take no day for yourself?"

"Why would I?"

"To do something for the sheer pleasure of it, or is that against your many rules?" he mocked.

"And you've got some reason to think that a day spent with you would be sheer pleasure?"

"In a word, yes."

"Well, my word's *no.*"

Hands on her arms, Dev backed her the few steps to the garden's iron gate. If he would not see her tomorrow when this mood had passed, he had to taste her now.

He took one hand from her arm and settled it against the warm skin of her face. Slowly he drew it downward, his fingertips picking up the pulse hammering in her throat. So she, too, felt the madness.

"Jenna," he said.

She averted her face. "Don't kiss me."

He smiled at the way she'd telegraphed her desire. "What's the harm in a kiss?"

"I don't want to start this. I-I'm not very good at drawing lines. It's kind of a genetic thing."

Excuses.

"You?" he said. "I've never seen a woman draw a straighter line, or walk one, either." With his thumb he traced the full lower lip he had every intention of taking between his teeth. "One kiss. Now. Here. This night only."

She backed away until she was leaning into the gate, but he followed. She braced one hand against his chest. It would be no huge crime to steal this intimacy from her, yet he couldn't bring himself to do it.

"Please," he said, disbelieving that he was reduced to begging, but hungry enough to beg just the same.

The dim light wasn't enough to see the change in her expression, but he could feel it as the pressure of her hand against his heart relaxed.

"Just one kiss," she said.

Consent given, he could afford to linger. He savored Jenna's scent, her sigh, the silken feel of tender skin at the base of her throat. Back at the fire someone began a quick reel on the fiddle, but Dev moved more leisurely. He indulged each of his pleasures and more, but didn't yet kiss her. He smiled as her impatience grew.

She wriggled away from his touch and then framed his face with her hands. "If you're going to kiss me, just do it."

"Americans," he said, "always in a rush."

He let his mouth near and, at the same time, brought a hand to the back of her head so that she couldn't pull away. She'd given no time limits, and he meant to be thorough. So long as his mouth didn't leave hers, it was just one kiss, was it not?

He started with the lightest of pressure—a tease, nothing more. God, her mouth was soft. Angling for a better fit, he tasted her plump lower lip. She'd been at the sweets table, for he was sure she wouldn't taste this sugary on her own. Not with her nip-at-the-world attitude.

Her hands settled at his shoulders and she relaxed into him. Satisfied she didn't intend to cheat him, Dev put himself into the pleasure of the kiss, but Jenna arrived there first. Her tongue dipped into his mouth, then retreated. Startled, pleased, he lured her back. And when she stayed, trouble also came.

He had kissed countless women—more, he was certain, than he could recall. But this, it was different. He tasted her, learned the heat of her mouth, the slick feel of her teeth. His palms skated down her sides, then back up under her sweater to touch breasts he knew were a perfect fit for his palms. She trembled; he shook like a spotty, overanxious teenager.

And with this one kiss he felt himself growing impossibly hard, embarrassingly close to a brink he had no intention of crossing alone. Or clothed.

Dev pulled back and tried to slow his ragged breathing. He jammed his hands into his trouser pockets, pulling the fabric away from a painfully tight fit. Jesus, he was near to owing her another apology, and he was well past his limit already.

"One kiss," he said in a voice he scarcely recognized as his own. "One night." And he left.

Heart hammering, Jenna leaned against the cold, rough metal of the garden gate. She closed her eyes and listened to Dev's footsteps echoing against the stone pathway.

So this was what desire felt like.

If he'd led her back to the house and up the stairs to her room, she would have gone, guests be damned. If he'd stripped her clothes from her right here at the gate, she would have done the same to him. She had stopped thinking, had lived for the rush of sensation coursing though her.

And now that she'd done it, there was no turning back. She had been right to be afraid to touch him.

She would have been safer standing in the fire.

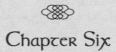

Chapter Six

A cowpat is all the wider for stepping on it.
—IRISH PROVERB

On Beltane morning in Ballymuir, it seemed that God got down to business. Jenna woke with a start, sat up, and took stock of her surroundings. She couldn't lose the feeling that something had shifted. Even the sunlight sneaking between the drapes was finer, clearer. If she were Vi, she'd call this new acuity of her senses magical. But she was a practical woman, so she'd credit the first restful night's sleep she'd had since Gilvane's arrival.

Jenna pushed aside her covers and padded to the bank of windows overlooking the shore. She tucked the central window's drapes into the bronze arms fashioned to hold them, then unlatched the windows and pushed them out, bringing a spring-laden breeze and the music of a songbird into her home. She breathed deep.

Little remained of the Beltane Eve gathering. The remnants of its fire were now reduced to ash resting neatly within the stone circle. No people cluttered the landscape, and she loved the emptiness of it. Not barren, but serene.

Mise en place—everything in its place—a crucial concept in both cooking and life. Last night's fire would be consigned to memory and last night's kiss dealt with. She wasn't insane enough to think that she could forget the feel of Dev's mouth on hers or the thrumming of a long-sleeping pulse that had come fully, instantly to life. But she could work around the inconvenience, deal with it as she had so many other events not occurring according to plan.

After all, it was May, promise was in the wind, and all things were possible. Even a measure of personal peace. Jenna let the sunshine kiss her face and permitted herself to daydream. Between one heartbeat and the next, blaring music shredded her thoughts. A screaming, Jimi-Hendrix-come-back-to-haunt, guitar riff filled the house.

She wheeled away from the window. "Mau-*reen!*"

Shouting had felt good, but accomplished nothing. Jenna sprinted downstairs to the library, where the house sound system's controls were hidden. She pushed the concealed latch to the cupboard built seamlessly into the wainscoting and cranked down the receiver's volume knob.

She turned to her sister, who was reclining on her side like Cleopatra awaiting a perfectly peeled grape.

Her wet hair was twisted into a tight knot at the back of her head. Jenna couldn't quite catch the color—maybe not as scary as yesterday, but still miles off normal.

"So how long did you have to feel out the woodwork to find the sound system?" Jenna asked.

"Good speakers," Maureen replied.

If this was to be a battle of non sequiturs, she might as well land a few of her own. "What's up with the hair?"

"I need to go into town." Her sister ladled enough sarcasm onto the last word to melt acid.

Picking on Ballymuir was never a wise choice. Jenna tugged up the drooping shoulder strap to her camisole, then left. In the sanctuary of the kitchen, she poured herself some coffee from the pot Maureen must have managed to make all on her own. Who said pampered rich girls didn't have marketable skills?

"I said I need to go to town," Maureen repeated from behind her.

So much for sanctuary. Jenna walked to the war room and sat at the oak table. Her sister moved to the opposite side and glared down at her.

Jenna sifted through various diplomatic approaches she might take, but none suited the opposition as well as the truth. "Reenie, I still have no clue what you're doing at Muir House."

"Okay, how's this? I'm here because I didn't know where else to go." The comment was no less sarcastic than her others, except this time Jenna detected a whisper of truth.

"Are you in trouble?"

Her sister laughed but didn't meet Jenna's eyes. "Like there's something Daddy couldn't buy my way out of? I just needed a break, okay?"

She'd learned long ago that her father's dollars came with a high emotional price. "If you're in trouble, you can tell me."

"And I'd know that based on the ten minutes of conversation we've had in the past five years, right? You've made it pretty clear that you have no use for me."

"I'm sorry for what you overheard me saying to Vi the other day, but at least I'm trying. Why don't you do the same?"

"I'm here, aren't I?"

Jenna ran her thumb up the handle of her coffee mug, feeling a rough, worn spot in the thick pottery's glaze. "Do you remember what it was like when I lived at home?"

Maureen shrugged. "Kind of."

"If you think back, you'll agree that just being someplace isn't always the same thing as trying."

She knew by Maureen's shuttered expression that she was getting nowhere. A cowardly sense of relief at not having to discuss those last, ugly days outweighed the regret that she and her sister had never learned to communicate.

"I said I need to go into town. It's after eleven. I was in your room twice this morning and even held a mirror in front of your face to make sure you weren't dead. Since you're not, would you give me a ride?"

Loud music . . . high drama . . . everything amplified. She wondered whether Reenie saw their father's reflection when she looked into her mirror. If she did, the thought apparently didn't weigh as heavily into her choices as it did into Jenna's.

"Are you going to answer me?" Maureen demanded.

Jenna sipped her coffee and winced at its bitter taste. "I hadn't planned to leave the property."

"Hiding from someone?"

The rhythm of Jenna's heart lurched. She looked closer at her sister, trying to decide whether Maureen's comment had been based in knowledge, perception, or guesswork.

"I'm not hiding, just kicking back for the day," she lied. "Why don't you take my car?"

"Can't drive. Never had a reason to."

"Incredible." No driver's license but probably enough frequent-flyer miles to open her own airline, such was the life of the Fahey Princess Royal.

"Now will you take me, *please?*" The obligatory politeness was followed by a baring of the teeth that didn't quite pass as a smile. "Or are you really hiding?"

Jenna wasn't philosophically opposed to a little hiding; that was how she'd happened across Ballymuir in the first place. She refused, however, to let her baby sister get away with this dominant-female, leader-of-the-pack routine.

"Be ready in half an hour," she said.

The road to Ballymuir was a narrow one and often interrupted by stray sheep or oncoming trucks that required both lanes. Over time Jenna had learned that the best way to drive it was with a measure of good-natured fatalism. Since there was no way of knowing what was around the next curve, she might as well own the stretch she was on.

Beside her, Maureen flinched from the tall hedgerow lining the roadside as though green, leafy claws were about to push through the car's window and rip her from her seat. Her face was chalky-white, and Jenna regretted that her sister was wearing sunglasses. She would have loved to have seen a little abject terror in her eyes.

Closer to the village, where the houses grew tighter together and sheep fewer, she almost got her wish.

"Holy sh—" Maureen gasped at the same time Jenna eased out of a curve and braked in order to avoid a bicyclist coming at them in the center of the road.

Jenna smiled at the sight of Brendan Mulqueen, one of her favorite customers, who over the past year had become a friend, too. He was no Irish country gentleman in tweeds and a cap pedaling to town with pipe clenched between yellowing teeth. Somewhere past fifty, Brendan was handsome, vital, and also incredibly fit from his years as a sculptor. With his black racing gear and high-tech bike, he looked ready to join Team Ireland and seize the yellow jersey in the Tour de France.

She moved closer to the roadside, rolled down her window, and waited for him to pull even.

Brendan dismounted from his bike. Holding it with one hand, he leaned down a bit to greet her. "Grand fire last night, Jenna, though I missed you at the end." His broad smile reminded her of another man's, one she was struggling mightily not to think about.

"Mulqueen, you'd live longer if you took the side of the road."

He chuckled. "I've lived damn long enough already. And all it takes is one tour bus sending you into rose briers to start taking the middle. I have more trust in those drivers' instincts than I do in their goodwill."

She smiled. "You've got a point." It seemed sometimes that the locals were viewed as speed bumps impeding the tourist flow.

Maureen gave an impatient sigh and a low, muttered, "Any time now."

Seeing no way around it, Jenna made introductions.

"Brendan, this is my sister, Maureen. Maureen, this is Brendan. You might have seen him at the fire last night."

Maureen slid down her sunglasses to appraise him, then nodded.

"You're welcome to Ballymuir," Brendan said. "What do you think so far?"

"I think I'm looking forward to getting out."

He laughed. "Thirty years ago I said the same thing myself."

"And you're still here. You must be a slow learner."

"A leisurely learner," he corrected. "There's much to sample in Ballymuir if you know where to look."

She nudged her sunglasses back up the bridge of her nose. "Right."

Brendan shrugged. "All the less to take over our corner of paradise," he said to Jenna. "I'll be seeing you tomorrow night. Stop by my table and have a chat if you could. I've a few questions for you about Mr. Gilvane."

"You'll find better authorities in town."

He laughed. "So they'd be thinking. *Slán*," he said, friendly Irish for "see you." He mounted his bike and pedaled off.

Jenna shifted back into gear and took the final two tight turns into the village proper, hiding her smile as Maureen braced her hands against the Nissan's dashboard.

"If you drive like this, what do you do for fun—walk blindfolded off cliffs?"

Jenna's answer was simple and not without certain parallels. "I run a restaurant."

"That's your job, not fun."

"Believe it or not, the two can coincide from time to time."

Her sister scoffed. "I'll stick with unemployment, thanks."

Jenna pulled into a spot in front of O'Connor's Pub. She switched off the car and looked at her sister.

"Across the street from the harbor, you'll see some low, white buildings on a hill. I'll be in the one at the top of the group. That's Vi's studio."

"Stocking up on potions?"

"No. Patience," Jenna said. "Be there by two, okay?"

"Like I can blow that much time in three blocks of civilization. I'll see you at one." Maureen climbed from the car, slammed the door, and stalked off.

Potions were sounding better by the second.

*   *   *

As far as Maureen was concerned, walking in Ballymuir was like stepping into a twisted Irish version of *Brigadoon.* She'd seen a cell phone store as Jenna drove into town, and an ATM, too, but those were about the only pieces of evidence she could find that she hadn't been sucked back in time.

And the word *sucked* hit dead-on. As she trudged up a hill that would freak out a mountain goat, she checked out store windows. There wasn't a piece of clothing that someone under eighty would voluntarily wear, and she couldn't figure out where to buy some decent music. She needed news—current news—and she had a sneaking suspicion that she was screwed.

Some old guy tottered out of a doorway painted bright yellow.

"Hey," Maureen called, "is there an Internet café around here?" She didn't plan to ask her control-freak sister if she could use her computer. All Maureen needed was Jenna peering over her shoulder at evidence of how massively she'd screwed up her life.

"Dingle's the nearest, and that's five miles off," he said. "Though if you go down by the harbor, stop to see Vi Kilbride in the arts village. She'll get you a message home, if that's what you're lookin' for."

Not even close.

"Thanks," she said, keeping the "for nothing" to herself.

He nodded and walked on.

She looked another block up the steep incline to where she'd seen the cell phone store. With luck, it hadn't been a hallucination. She'd left her phone in Sam the scum's suite at the Ritz.

Using Jenna's telephone, Maureen had managed to get hold of Afton, one of a few friends she was pretty sure she could trust. Afton had promised to send Maureen the clothes she'd left behind. In exchange for a favor to be named later, of course. Maureen knew that when Afton came up with a payback, it would be big-time, but Maureen had no choice. She was out of what her father defined as the world's most valuable commodity: leverage.

Maureen paused a moment to catch her breath. God, she was out of shape. Maybe it was time to focus less on being a size two and more on getting some muscle tone. Or not. She stepped into the store, which was about the size of one of her walk-in closets back in her family's Lake Forest home. It held not only cell phones but televisions, stereo equipment, and power tools. No wonder the place was called O'Connor's Everything.

Behind the counter she found one of her favorite kinds of people, a guy anxious to please. He was also young enough to still have a pulse, and decent looking, with black hair and blue eyes. Too bad he was a male and thus, by definition, scum.

"Well, this rules out ritual sacrifice." At his blank look she explained, "You're the first person I've seen in town who isn't old enough for retirement. I figured you'd all been taken to the mountainside last night and sacrificed. Where is everyone?"

"Working," he said with a shrug. "Some here, some in Tralee. I'm Lorcan O'Connor and you'd be Jenna Fahey's sister, Maureen."

She liked the way he pronounced her name, as if it ended with a satisfied sigh, so she decided not to give him too much crap. "How did you know who I am?"

"Same way as everyone else. You had Johnny O'Shea drive you to Muir House."

She guessed that was supposed to be an explanation.

"Here to visit, are you?" he asked.

Might as well give them something to talk about. She'd hate for Ballymuir to be left out when there was a ninety percent chance that the rest of the world was gossiping about her.

"I'm on the run from the Hollywood mafia."

He laughed. "Sure you are."

"So, Lorcan, can you set me up with a phone?"

He could and did in less than twenty minutes, ten of which he used to hit on her. As if she'd be going with him to his da's pub to hear a session—whatever that was. She was seriously done with men.

She pocketed her phone, pleased that she had at least one connection to the real world. "One last question, where can I find a newspaper around here?"

"There'd be Spillane's Market," her new best friend offered. "Down the hill and on the opposite side of the street."

"Thanks."

"Are you sure you won't be comin' to the pub tonight?" Lorcan said as she opened the shop door. "There's a group of us, so you don't need to think of it as a date unless you're wanting to."

She'd give him points for determination. And

really, when it came right down to it, anyplace was
better than sitting at Muir House, waiting for Jenna
to say something nice. She turned back.

"I don't suppose you could give me a ride?" she
asked.

He let loose an involuntary sort of *ha!*—as though
she'd knocked the wind from him. His face turned a
dull red as he struggled to hold in laughter.

She was so goddamn sick of being the butt of
jokes. *"What?"*

He tamed his grin. "You'd best be saying 'lift' instead of 'ride.' If I were to give you a ride, it would
mean, well . . . we'd have to be getting naked first."

Maureen felt scarlet creeping up her face, too.
English as a foreign language was making Paris seem
bizarrely appealing. At least there she knew the
slang, including how to bilingually tell Sam Olivera
to get stuffed.

"Thanks for the tip," she said.

"Eight o'clock, then?"

Both hope and testosterone apparently sprang
eternal in the Irish male. Maureen knew she'd regret
this, but she was becoming so skilled at regret that
she didn't even care. "Sure. See you then."

She gave him her best smile and was gratified in
an impersonal sort of way to see that it still worked.

Screw you, Sam.

Jenna was walking down Patrick Street toward the
harbor when Eamon Nolan, her heating and cooling
man, leaned out of his shop's doorway, looked up
the street and down, then furtively motioned her
over.

"Hi, Mr.—"

She trailed off when he shook his head.

Really curious now, she crossed to his side of the street. She smiled when, like a spy from a B movie, he took a quick drag from the cigarette he held pinched between his fingers and thumb, then disappeared into his shop. She wondered if she was going to be expected to pass some sort of "the black swan flies at midnight" code.

The shop door's hinges squealed as Jenna opened it and stepped inside. She took a moment to let her eyes adjust to the dim light. Boxes of parts lay in a huge heap halfway up the front windows, and everything was coated with both the scent and yellowish haze of cigarette smoke.

Despite the mind-bending mess, Eamon Nolan was a magician with all things mechanical. He'd never had to order a part to fix either her house's ancient furnace or her restaurant's state-of-the-art systems. It was all in here, somewhere. As was Eamon himself.

"Mr. Nolan," she called.

He stepped from behind a black curtain shrouding a doorway at the back of the shop. The tiny hairs on her arms stood as she speculated on the level of chaos deemed necessary to be hidden from customers.

He stubbed out his cigarette in an enormous ashtray filled with its dead kin. "Just checking to be sure Evie hadn't come in the back way. She's supposed to be cleaning today."

Jenna was sure that the odds were better on thirty rain-free days.

"Anyway," he said after another look over his shoulder, "I thought you should be knowing that Dev Gilvane was here first thing this morning. He's after the plans for Muir House."

The news shouldn't have stung. Last night had been a momentary madness. She still knew nothing about him, except that he was semi-Irish, could kiss to start a dead woman's heart, and was a total bastard for wanting what was meant to be hers.

"I see," she said to Mr. Nolan. They were short words, easier to push past the tightness gripping her throat.

"I told him I didn't have any such thing, that I was a 'do it as you go' sort of man even though I've got a full set of plans right in me desk."

"Well, thank you," she said for lack of anything better.

"Word at the pub is that he's looking to build a private hunting retreat," he said in a conspiratorial tone. "Wild game and birds and such. Do you think—"

From somewhere in the mess a telephone rang.

"Don't leave," Mr. Nolan commanded, then disappeared behind the black drape.

Jenna took a moment to push aside the irrational hurt and think her way through the problem. The outcome was apparent; if Dev wanted plans, he'd find a way to obtain them. She was far better off controlling the information.

From the back room came the elevated noise of Mr. Nolan yelling at someone, ending with the sharp smack of a phone being treated with minimal respect. He reappeared, his expression sour.

"Evie," he said.

Jenna responded with a diplomatic "Ah."

"So about this Gilvane," Mr. Nolan said, "what have you heard?"

She was smart enough to work her advantages, whether it might be especially fine spring lamb for the restaurant or knowledge of Ballymuir's hunger for gossip.

Jenna moved a little closer. "Between us, I heard that he's establishing his own religious sect. He needs land for a—how shall I put this delicately?— retreat house." At Mr. Nolan's blank look, she added, "Have you noticed how he's always wearing black?"

"Aye, now that you mention it. . . ."

Jenna waited as the seed she'd planted took root. The older man's horror was both apparent and gratifying. "Jesus, are you talking about a *cult*? Animal sacrifice and devil worship and the like? You'll not be selling to him, will you?"

"Never."

"I was right to send him away with nothing."

Jenna skirted the fact that it would have been an enormous breach of her trust to do otherwise. "He'll be back," she said instead. "And when he does show up, I want you to sell him the plans for the mechanical systems."

Mr. Nolan's dark brows chased after his receding hairline. "What?"

"Do it for a lot of money. Take the most ridiculous sum you can think of and double it." All the better to empty Dev's pockets.

"And you're sure about this?"

"Very," she said. "But you might want to remove

an update or two . . . and tell him about the faulty wiring and how the plumbing has never worked quite right."

"And should I be dropping word of a wee problem with the roof?"

She laughed. "I do believe we've reached an understanding, Mr. Nolan."

He shook her offered hand. "Indeed we have."

Jenna smiled as she returned to the street. Here at least she had Dev Gilvane beat dead cold. She knew how to work the system in Ballymuir.

Maureen knew that it wasn't especially rational to be scared to look in a bunch of newspapers. It wasn't as though events could be erased just because she chose not to acknowledge them. Still, she was taking the chicken's path through Spillane's Market—a random selection of aisles that didn't include her ultimate goal.

An old guy who looked as if he might have once been a professional wrestler stood behind the counter of the single check-out lane and watched her.

"Grand day, isn't it?" he said as she passed by him yet again.

"Yeah, wonderful."

She should have stayed away from Sam Olivera, never should have opened her heart to him. Now that he'd hurt her, she'd still have to see his image on television, in the papers . . . everywhere. And since she couldn't blame Sam for that, she chose to blame the media. Her love/hate relationship with the press had swung to hate. In fact, if she stopped to think about it, pretty much all her life had taken that turn.

But she had to stay mad because the alternative of heartbreak was unacceptable.

Maureen strolled down an aisle filled with canned goods, pretending rapt interest in the oxtail soup. Who the hell would eat that? On to the jams and jellies. She stopped. The chocolate spread didn't look half bad, and she had a sinking feeling that very soon she'd need its comfort. She grabbed a jar and moved on.

Okay, enough of the coward's waltz. Maureen forced herself to walk to the end of the aisle and stop in front of the piddling display of magazines and papers.

The bottom shelf was filled with teen pop garbage and a really scary number of anglers' magazines. Why the obsession with fish? Maureen flinched as she realized how central that question was to her current disaster.

The next shelf up held the tabloids. She wished she had the self-control to just walk away, to know that anything in them was beneath her notice. Except it wasn't. Maureen set the jar of chocolate spread at her feet and pulled the first bottom-feeding rag from the rack.

There was nothing about her on the front page, though that was usually reserved for claims of stars impregnated by aliens. Hand shaking, Maureen prepared to peek inside. She wasn't much of a praying girl, but figured that the shock value of a Maureen-to-God page just might get the Big Guy's ear.

Please, God, let me duck this one, and I'll be better, I swear I will. I'll—I'll—

She racked her brain for some kind thing she could do—something that wouldn't involve being near sick, germy people or take up too much of her time—but came up blank.

I'll do something really good.

Vague but better than nothing.

She thumbed one page in and still found nothing. She was relieved enough to remember to breathe. Maybe this bargaining-with-God thing really worked.

One more page . . .

Shit.

She didn't look at the photo very carefully before closing the paper. She'd lived the moment. Sam with that tramp of an actress. The placement of said tramp's hand where it was most likely to get a rise. The waiter passing by with the tray of fish. Grabbing the tray had been sheer fury, dumping it on Sam and the tramp, incredibly satisfying, and the flash of the photographer's camera, horrifying. No, she really didn't need a picture to remember. She squeezed her eyes shut against angry tears.

The bright side was that now she didn't have to think of anything good to do for God. The dark side was that for the rest of her life, she was going to be haunted by one stupid picture. And Sam Olivera was going to kill her.

She'd spent the past five days telling herself that it was going to be okay. Maybe the paparazzo hadn't gotten a clear shot. Maybe no one would bother to pick up the photo even if the scum-wad did. Yeah, and maybe she'd wash her sister's dishes for the rest of her natural life.

She lifted the stack of papers from the rack and carried them to the counter.

"All of them?" the old guy asked.

"I'm not finished," she said, then returned to check out the competition. There they were: she, Sam, the fish, and the tramp.

She carried the full load to the counter, smacked it down, then went back and retrieved her fix of chocolate.

"Do you take credit cards?" she asked when she returned.

"Aye." He counted the number of copies in each pile of papers, then focused on her with sharp green eyes that seemed to carry something she wasn't used to seeing: pity.

"The news is no different in the fifth copy than the first," he said.

"Unfortunately."

"So you'd be Jenna Fahey's sister?" he asked as he rang up the items.

She supposed it was better than being known as a fish-flinger.

"Let me guess. Johnny O'Shea told you," she said.

"Nah, I saw your photo on page five. You're much prettier in person, you know? And if that boy would rather be with the other girl, he's not only a right bastard but a fool, too."

Holy shit, she was going to cry!

Maureen grabbed the charge slip, scrawled her signature, and hurried from the store with a bagful of humiliation.

Outside, she pulled the chocolate spread from the bag and dumped the papers in the closest trash bin, her contribution toward keeping Ireland clean. She hugged the jar against her chest and glared at the glorious blue sky.

Next time she'd stick with Satan.

Chapter Seven

The seeking of one thing will find another.
—Irish Proverb

Jenna was walking the hill to the arts village when the growl of costly German engineering came up behind her. One to learn from her mistakes, she took to the far edge of the sidewalk and wrinkled her nose at Dev's black convertible Porsche as it passed. Once, just once, she'd like to be prepared to see him. He pulled his car into a spot two buildings downhill from Vi's, then got out and waited for her by his car.

She didn't wave because that would send a welcome. Instead, she nodded a neutral acknowledgment that equally failed to cover her anger and uncomfortable sense of inevitability.

Today he'd dressed less like an executive and more like a regular human. Though she hated to admit it, the change suited him. He was the sort of man who could make a pair of blue jeans look like art. As she neared, she noted the wariness in his dark eyes and the tight set to his mouth. A mouth she now knew was hot and intoxicating. There was no turning back, either from that awareness or from him. She could just slip by, though.

As she passed, he pulled in step beside her. "Inventory done and lists made, I take it?"

Jenna's stride faltered. It was a Monday, and she'd forgotten. For the first time in almost two years she'd fallen out of the routine that was her savior.

"Yes, they're done," she replied, though anxiety at the oversight had begun to simmer.

"What a comfort that must be."

She didn't appreciate the edge to his voice. "Do you want something, Dev?"

"A great many things, actually. Though at the moment what I most want is for you to stop running away from me."

"I'm not running, I'm walking."

"Do you plan to pretend that last night didn't happen?"

"No."

He laughed, but it wasn't an especially charming sound. "Ah, well then, that explains your hurry."

She swung in front of him and jabbed her finger toward the low-slung building before them. "This is my friend Vi's studio. I'm going inside and you're not."

Vi had her crimson half-door propped open, no doubt for more light, which she craved the way Jenna did calm. It seemed that Vi stood a better

chance of attaining her desire. After giving Dev a
threatening look, Jenna stepped inside.

He followed, of course.

Vi was digging through the drawers of an old
apothecary's chest. Based on the jumble of ribbons,
feathers, and seashells that were scattered across the
worktable, Jenna couldn't begin to imagine what she
was seeking. Vi looked up as they entered.

"This is an unexpected sight." She tilted her head
and appraised them. "A fitting one, too," she added.

Dev stepped around Jenna, who'd been doing her
futile best not to let him venture farther.

"And this," he said with a broad sweep of his
hand, "is an amazing sight."

Jenna had been coming to Vi's studio for so long
that while she wasn't blind to its exotic treasures, she
tended not to focus on them as much as she once
had.

Vi had taken what was once a plain, white
cottage-like building identical to the other five in this
government-funded enclave and put her stamp upon
it. She'd had four large skylights installed so that
even on a cloudy day, the space never seemed dim.

Silk banners adorned with her bold Celtic designs
waved in the breeze sneaking in the front door. On
one table were displays of the bead and shell jewelry
and vivid stationery that Vi made when the whim
struck her. Baskets brimming with hand-painted
scarves and panels of fabric were tucked into every
available nook, and large paintings—again, mostly
on silk—decorated the walls. It was not a subtle setting, but then Vi was not a subtle woman.

Jenna watched as Dev walked from place to place,

lifting a scarf from a basket and letting it slip between his fingers. One corner of his mouth briefly curved upward as he fingered the silk. He looked her way, and the spark of heat in his eyes made her pulse jump. She glanced away. She needed no reminding that he was a sensual man. In fact, she'd be better off recalling that he could also be a devious one.

"You're a woman of many talents," he said to Vi.

She laughed. "A lack of focus is what it's called by those who think they're in charge of me. But I like what I do well enough."

"As you should," he said. "Your work is incredible."

Vi positively shone. If she was susceptible to Dev's flattery, what chance did the rest of Ballymuir stand?

Jenna needed to cut this short. "Time is money, Gilvane," she said. "So unless you're planning to spend a whole lot of cash, get out."

"Jenna, that's hardly hospitable," Vi chastised. "Whatever's wrong with you?"

"Nothing."

She looked clearly skeptical. "Perhaps a cup of chamomile tea. Or one of my nan's purges," she added with a nip of asperity.

Some best friend. "Thanks, but no."

Dev settled his hands on Jenna's shoulders, part caress, part controlling measure, and wholly unappreciated.

"I kissed Jenna last night," he said to Vi, "and I'd very much like the chance to kiss her again or at least talk to her, but she seems intent on—"

Jenna escaped from his grip. "Outside. Now."

"My pleasure," he replied, then favored her with a smile that was slow, sexy, and incredibly irking.

"Very fitting, indeed," Jenna heard Vi say as she marched out the door with Dev trailing behind.

She made it exactly three steps past the stoop before losing the rest of her temper. "It's not fair of you, dragging Vi into this."

To the left of the studio door was a graceful wooden bench that Vi's brother Michael had made. Dev sat and stretched out his long legs before saying, "Fair? An interesting concept, that. The real thing's rarer than a unicorn, too."

"What do you want?"

"For you to come for a drive with me."

"Why?"

"For the pleasure of it, of course. There's no rain threatening, it's warm, and you're lovely."

She crossed her arms over her ratty Chicago Bears T-shirt. "You had me going until the 'lovely' thing."

"If you think you're not, then someone's done you a disservice."

She looked away and heard his impatient sigh.

"And if I haven't already given you reason enough," he said, "let's not be forgetting that we have matters to discuss."

Very true. Rules needed to be established. The first was that Dev Gilvane was never to kiss her again. Still, she had other obligations. "I'm meeting my sister here. I need to drive her home."

"I'll give her your keys," offered a meddling friend lurking somewhere just inside her open door.

Dev laughed, apparently content to have Vi interfere when it suited his purposes.

"She can't drive," Jenna called. "And would you mind giving me some space?"

"I'll run her home, Dev can bring you back to your car, and yes, I would very much mind. You don't seem to be able to handle this on your bloody own."

Dev stood. "I'd say that's settled." He pulled his keys from his pocket, tossed them in the air where they jingled brightly, and then caught them. "I'll be back to visit, and with plenty of cash," he said to Vi, who had given up any pretense at affording them privacy and joined them outside.

Vi shooed Jenna along. "Well, go on."

Jenna could have held her ground on sheer principle, except somewhere beneath her mistrust of Dev Gilvane, there grew a desire for his company. She was, in fact, even more susceptible to his charm than Vi.

She fired the Irishman her best scowl. "Fine, then. Move it along, Gilvane."

Once Jenna became certain that Dev didn't feel the need to test the limits of his expensive vehicle on the Dingle Peninsula's challenging roads, she relaxed as much as she was able to in his presence.

The wind pushing through her already curly hair was going to give her rasta-girl dreads that would put Maureen's arrival hairdo to shame. Jenna didn't care. She was thankful, though, that she'd taken the sweater Dev had offered for a little extra warmth. They didn't talk, other than Dev asking if there was anyplace she'd like to go and Jenna directing him inland.

When they crested a rise in the road, it felt to

Jenna as though she could simply lift her arms and fly. She laughed with the exhilaration of the moment. Dev looked over. When their eyes met, she was drawn into something even more intimate than the kiss they had shared, and her heart flew with the rest of her.

She glanced away and realized that their turn was fast approaching.

"This left!" she cried.

Up for the challenge, he wheeled the Porsche onto the narrower lane she'd indicated.

"Would you mind parking just up ahead?" she said, pointing to their right. He did as she asked.

The first time Jenna had seen the ruin of Kilmalkedar church, the wild fuchsia lining the road had been in brilliant, glorious bloom. She'd been wandering, newly broken-up with Claes, her boyfriend, who'd been a glib, wealthy man—not unlike Dev. She and Claes had become engaged after a brief and incredibly intense courtship. Jenna had been sure it was fate. He'd decided otherwise when he discovered that just because she carried the Fahey name didn't mean he'd be welcome in her father's inner circle.

Ireland had been Jenna's refuge from another round of familial humiliation. It had also ultimately been her rescuer.

On this Beltane Day, fuchsia plump unto bursting still draped over the stone walls enclosing Kilmalkedar, breaking only where a gate had been cut for entry to the churchyard. So much else about her life had changed, though. Claes had faded to a memory, not even one with which she associated much pain. She had carried forward a measure of caution, though.

She glanced at Dev, who had turned off the car and was looking around as though searching for some good reason to be there.

"Let's walk," she said.

They left the car, and Dev pocketed his keys. Now that they were no longer moving, the May warmth had caught up with them. Jenna pulled off the sweater he'd loaned her. When she'd just finished wrestling with the oversize garment, she caught him looking at the swathe of skin exposed where her T-shirt had pulled away from her jeans.

"That's me—whitest girl on Earth," she said to cover her awkwardness.

He merely smiled. That alone was enough to make her pulse trip. She tossed the sweater onto the car seat, then led him toward the churchyard.

In the field just across the lane, sheep were bleating. At the gate stood two elderly men dressed in the utilitarian clothes of serious farmers. They chatted in Irish. Jenna loved the exotic sound of the language, though she'd been an abject failure at learning it herself.

She gave them a friendly hello and received one in return. The sharp gravel of the lane gritting beneath their feet, she and Dev walked to the break in the wall surrounding the ruined church.

"Come on in," she said to him as she climbed over the high stone threshold that, at least in theory, was supposed to keep out livestock.

"Cheerful spot," Dev commented, raising a brow at the graveyard surrounding Kilmalkedar.

"You should see it on a foggy day. It's like something out of a horror movie."

He laughed. "And you sound so very pleased."

She shook her head, then absently combed her fingers through her tangled curls. "It's not just the graves and the ruin. You need to look closer . . . *feel* the place."

"Starting with the sheep manure just in front of us?"

Jenna smiled in spite of herself. "Are you sure you're even the smallest bit Irish? Where's that dark, contemplative nature?"

"Pounded out of me in a fine British public school," he replied. "Though I still have the occasional desire to martyr myself for a hopeless cause—which I have mostly ignored."

"Well, indulge me here, Gilvane. Be a tourist in your motherland. Have a look around."

And before he could blow away her hopes for a relaxing afternoon, Jenna ventured off. She walked carefully, for as warm and lovely as the day was, the tall grass was still wet and slick, and the pathways hard to find.

There had been a funeral sometime recently. Wooden folding chairs were stacked and waiting under the eaves of the small, crumbling church for return to a drier place.

Here and there modern gravestones, polished black with gold lettering, sat in well-tended sites. Mostly, though, there were markers so lime-encrusted, rough, and ancient that nothing was left to read in what could be seen through the shaggy grass holding them captive.

But everywhere was a sense of collective power, a subliminal hum just beneath the range of hearing, vibrating in the bones, filling the mind. It was this that brought Jenna back to Kilmalkedar.

She walked to the tall ogham stone that aligned neatly with the church's gaping entry—no coincidence she was sure. Kilmalkedar's founders had been her kind of people: practical, efficient souls building on a site that had likely held meaning before Christianity. Out of habit, she ran her hand up the rough, timeworn lines and slashes chiseled into the stone's side. The rock was cool and damp under her palm.

Dev had joined her. "Can you read it?"

"No," she admitted.

He chuckled. "Then I don't want to know what you're doing."

She patted the admittedly phallic rock. "Feeling somewhat insignificant by comparison?"

He grinned. "Actually, no, except as it pertains to finding the lure of your pet ruin. I'm trying hard enough, but I'm afraid I'm just not seeing it."

"Doesn't it give you a sense of belonging? As though we're all working toward some common purpose?"

"To all be buried here, then? I'd had my heart set on a grand memorial in the center of London, perhaps with myself in full naval regalia."

"Go ahead, tease me. I still think there's something beautiful about this place."

"In a bleak, you'll-be-needing-antidepressants-soon sort of way, yes," Dev conceded.

She laughed. "Thanks."

In addition to the primal hum that she wouldn't raise with Dev the Unbeliever, the evidence of family, even lost ones remembered, appealed to Jenna. Maybe because her family, though powerful for generations, had bizarrely little sense of past. There was no ancestral home handed down, but a series of places where Faheys had formerly lived and a handful of places where they did now. There were no portraits of long-departed relatives, no family anecdotes, no communication among the living. There was only her father, Martin, the last mad kingmaker, and her mother, sure to always remain one family residence ahead of Martin.

She walked a ribbon-thin path around to the back of the church. She could hear Dev following behind. To her right lay an enclosure of several stones protected by a rusted iron rail. A statue of what she supposed had once been the Virgin but now looked more like a ghost, drew her. She stopped when she saw the surname on a marker at the figure's feet.

Jenna looked back to Dev. "Connelly. Isn't that your mother's people?"

He frowned. "How would you know that?"

Yes, he had much to learn about Ballymuir. "The same way I hear about anything else—in town, of course."

"They all know who my mum is? I told only Muriel."

"Well, there you go . . ."

He shook his head. "No one's said a word to me."

"They probably figure you've already met your mother."

The smile he gave her was vague, at best. He left

the path and circled the enclosure, the wet grass slowing his pace. "I suppose it's possible these could be relatives. My mum hasn't spoken much about her past. A mention or two, but nothing more."

Something wasn't playing right.

"And yet you decided to look for a house in Ballymuir. Why?"

In the number of times they'd talked, which were few when viewed in light of last night's kiss, she'd never seen him this uncomfortable. He began to speak, paused, then started again.

"It seemed a good place."

The diplomatic thing would be to let this go, except she was no diplomat. "But why? You had to have had a reason."

"Did I?" he shot back.

She'd provoked him. The thought pleased her. Why should his life be free of turmoil?

"Most people do, Gilvane. It can't be some sort of longing for your roots. You're not exactly a frequent visitor."

"What, more gossip in town?"

"Of course. Other than attending parish hurling matches, it's the local pastime. So why Ballymuir, Dev? Are you planning to grow old and gray there?"

His anger was nearly palpable. Ignoring the tall grass, he walked toward her in long strides. "I had a thought, the time, and the money, so here I am . . . for the pleasure of it."

He moved even closer. With the uneven ground behind her, Jenna couldn't step back.

"Is there nothing you do for pleasure?" he asked.

She wanted to run, a ridiculous impulse. She was

miles from her car and had only this angry man to get her there.

"I, ah . . ."

What *did* she do for pleasure? It seemed to have sifted from her life. That both he and Maureen would have asked her this today frightened her. She was accustomed to no one looking beneath her unremarkable, capable exterior.

"Nothing, Jenna?"

"Don't change the subject."

"Ah, but I haven't. I told you I'm here for the pleasure of it." He reached out his right hand and followed the curve of her jaw, then the line of one cheekbone.

Even as she clenched her fists, steeled herself to resist this diversion he offered, her eyes slipped shut.

"Pleasure," he whispered, his mouth just brushing hers. He kissed her forehead, the very tip of her chin. He teased her mouth and the sensitive skin of her throat. One broad hand settled at her nape and with a slight pressure urged her to him.

Alchemy, she thought. *Passion from anger.*

"God, I love the taste of you," he said, then followed thought with deed.

The low hum that was so much a part of this place vibrated through Jenna, filling her, echoing so loudly in her head that it masked the mad rush of her heart. She twined her arms around Dev's neck and held fast in the storm.

Endless open-mouthed, hungry kisses, life demanding to renew itself, power seeking release, her world shook with it. She had never known a sensation like this. Dev's hands moved down her sides, one sweeping low on her back to hold her closer. The hum grew more distinct.

Jenna wrenched away. "I can't." She was panting.

Dev's chest rose and fell no slower. "Let me take you back to your house. Let me make love to you."

"No." The word escaped as a hoarse whisper.

"Pleasure, Jenna. Just for pleasure. No promises, no entanglements."

She had no skill at this. And no desire to risk her heart and expose her inadequacies all in one precipitous act.

"Nothing is just for pleasure." She looked away and repeated, "Nothing."

"But it can be," he said. "If you'd let it."

"I don't know how. And I don't want to, either," she quickly added when she realized the opening she'd left him.

He shook his head. "Saint Jenna of the Rules. I'm thinking you're more Irish than both sides of my family combined."

He mocked . . . and he hurt. Jenna smoothed her shirt, erasing all evidence of his touch. Rules guided, they protected when no one else cared enough to.

"It's time to go." She walked away, leaving him little option but to follow.

Ballymuir waited just over the next rise, too close to be ignored. Though Dev was relieved to be gone from that dank ruin with Connellys planted deep in its soil, the village sounded no more inviting. She'd told him to take her to her car by O'Connor's Pub, and once there, Jenna would flee. Her intent was clear in the way she braced herself against the car's movement, fighting force and gravity with the same stubbornness—and ultimate futility—that she fought the attraction they shared.

Before he spoke, he needed to reason his way through this knot he'd found himself in—both physically, he thought with a rueful downward glance, and otherwise.

Jenna had asked him the one question he wasn't prepared to answer: Why Ballymuir? And in evading he had found himself faced with another unanswerable query: Why Jenna Fahey?

He wanted to feel the clasp of her body with a primitive intensity that shocked even him. Despite his current state, a few truths remained apparent. He knew enough of Jenna to recognize that she would not separate business from pleasure with any amount of grace.

For her, everything funneled into a single path. He supposed that was a common enough female trait. He'd just never before been mad enough to want a woman whose needs extended past wanting him, too.

He slowed until he could nearly count the buds on the wild roses next to the road. "I'll be leaving for a few days . . . three at the most. But when I come back, I want your time, Jenna. I want your attention. I want *you*."

She gazed out the windshield as though he hadn't spoken.

Dev tried again. "There's no avoiding this. Something is happening between us."

"I don't want you."

Her denial angered him more than even those

prods at his past—dead kin and attachments to the land he chose not to die in. She wanted him; he was sure of it. He had felt it in the beat of her heart, tasted it in the wildness of her kiss, and already he hungered for more.

"It's a rare talent you have for fighting the inevitable," he said, willing himself to grip the steering wheel less tightly.

"There's nothing inevitable about us." The color high on her cheeks and raised pitch of her voice told him that she had begun to suspect otherwise.

"There is, but until you want to deal in truths, I won't be touching you."

She sat mutinously silent. He looked away from the road long enough to catch a glint of something new in her hazel eyes. Fear? Curiosity? He could only hope it was the latter. That, at least, he could work to their mutual advantage.

"Ah, but when you're ready," he said, "I'll have had time to think about all the ways I want to bring us pleasure. And this isn't arrogance speaking, but certainty. Looking at you is a pleasure, tasting you, an even greater one. Feeling your skin against mine . . . learning your secrets . . ." He paused, starved for air, starved for her. He wouldn't give her the power of this knowledge. "No martyring yourself, Jenna. When you come to me, no games. Just sheer pleasure."

He'd said all he could without giving too much of himself away. Blessedly, they were in front of the pub. Dev pulled to the curb. Jenna scarcely waited for him to come to a halt before opening her door.

"Don't come back, Dev. Don't do this," she said, then left.

Dev shook his head as she marched down the sidewalk, and then climbed into her little silver car. She was a fine runner, Jenna Fahey. In time she'd face reality. They were both well caught.

Chapter Eight

There's neither lowly nor noble,
but down a while and up a while.
—IRISH PROVERB

Sheer pleasure.

Dev's phrase lingered in Jenna's thoughts, a whispered promise following her by day and heating her dreams by night. He was taking his toll. Tuesday and Wednesday had been marked by a series of kitchen mishaps. None had been dire, but all had been the result of her frayed nerves, already too close to the skin.

And even one of her usual comforts—visits by Brendan Mulqueen—had been marked by strangeness. On Tuesday he had called her to his table, asked all she knew about Dev, and then the next night, not arrived for his standing dinner reservation. One more unsettling event layered over Dev's whispers of pleasure.

It wasn't as though she didn't deal in matters of pleasure. Her restaurant thrived because she brought pleasure to others. The perfectly prepared meal, the warm welcome, the beauty both on the plate and in the surroundings, all of it the product of rigorous standards created to attain pleasure. But sheer pleasure for herself? That was a luxury she couldn't afford, had she even wanted to.

On Thursday when Jenna awoke, her first thought was of Dev. He'd be back to Muir House; she couldn't wish him away. Pushing aside his all too vivid spectre, Jenna rose, made her bed, and then made her way to the bathroom.

Next to her enormous white porcelain bathtub sat a wicker hamper brimming with bubble baths, salts, scented oils, and loofahs that her mother had sent her the prior Christmas. Instead of ignoring its contents and readying a shower as always, Jenna hesitated. Pleasure and temptation . . .

She looked away, then turned on the tub taps and ran the shower curtain around the chrome oval ring suspended from the ceiling. She stripped and showered like a good soldier. Business as usual. Work as usual. Life as usual.

By seven she sat in front of her computer catching up on news from her e-mail loops—buddies from the business gossiping about critics and ratings and how Jenna had snagged the upcoming *Irish Gourmet* photo shoot. Word was also out that *Guide Eireann* had begun updating their restaurant reviews. For Jenna, it would be another matter conspiring to keep her sleepless. One more star granted by faceless, anonymous critics would gain her the notice she needed throughout Europe.

Of course, everyone had a theory regarding these mysterious souls. Eoin, who ran a bistro up in Sligo town, said it was a portly middle-aged man, balding and dour, who'd skewered him. James in Dublin claimed it was two women doing the circuit to the east this year, both tall brunettes—sisters, perhaps; royal bitches, for certain.

Refusing to fall victim to stress, Jenna exited her e-mail program and grabbed the black notebook that held her schedule and ever-growing to-do list. She headed toward the kitchen, where she found Aidan sitting at the oak table in the war room. He wasn't much for displaying either highs or lows on his craggy features, but he appeared tense as he paged through the kitchen's recipe binder.

"You're here early," she said.

"Just wanted to be on time for the meat delivery, that's all," he replied.

Which wasn't due for another hour and a half.

She made coffee, poured herself her morning mug, and offered one to Aidan, who turned her down.

"Think I'll sharpen me knives," he said, then left for his prep area.

Her man of few words was verging on none. Jenna knew better than to ask why. If he wanted to share with her, Aidan would do it in his own time. Instead she checked her notes for the day.

Thursday was always butchering day. As soon as she'd hired Aidan, Jenna had turned over to him the duties of breaking down cuts of meat to servings, then preparing them for storage in the cold room. It was her least favorite job, and Aidan performed it with the skill of a surgeon—little waste and portions so close in weight that even her digital scale could scarcely discern the variation when she spot-checked.

While he cut and prepped in the back, Jenna finished her coffee, then set up in the front of the kitchen to make the pasta to be used over the weekend. All told, she was much happier up to her elbows in flour. She was well into her task when the telephone rang.

"Damn."

Jenna grabbed a white work towel from the stainless shelf in front of her and cleaned her hands the best she could as she hurried to the war room, where the only phone in the kitchen was located.

She looped the towel over the back tie to her apron, then picked up. "Muir House."

"Ms. Fahey?"

"Yes?"

"Howard Keene here."

Howard was the Tralee solicitor she'd hired when she'd stumbled on Muir House. He had negotiated a lease clause to give her the option to purchase the property at market value, plus one to reimburse her for any improvements she might have made, should she be unable to meet market value.

At the time it had been the best they could do. Honoria Weston-Jones had been hesitant to part with family property, even though she was perfectly willing to let it rot. Jenna had figured that odds were good she'd outlive Honoria, and that Honoria's heirs would be happier with cash than a piece of Irish real estate convenient to nothing. And as for someone bidding against her and driving up value, God knew she couldn't imagine anyone else being interested in the place. It had sat vacant for decades.

Since time was no longer her friend, Jenna had called Mr. Keene late Monday afternoon and asked him to hurry along the sale negotiations with Muir House's absentee owner.

"Do you have some good news for me, Mr. Keene?"

"I'm afraid not. Miss Weston-Jones's solicitor is reporting a certain degree of . . . ah . . . inattention on his client's part. As he's well paid to cater to her eccentricities, I don't expect he'll be moving the process along."

"So what now?" she asked.

"Perhaps it's time for a more direct approach."

"Meaning?"

"When matters bog down in official channels, one might consider another route."

"Are you telling me to call her?"

"Now, I couldn't be doing that in an official capacity, as we both know she's represented by Mr. Faber. But . . . perhaps you might have decided to ring her up—without mentioning it to me, of course."

"Of course," Jenna replied.

"And should we receive more positive news from Mr. Faber, you'll be the first to know. Literally."

After some obligatory small-talk about whether it was a soft day in Ballymuir because it was looking none too promising in Tralee, and how he'd seen a fine mention of Muir House in the newspaper the other day, Jenna and her solicitor said their goodbyes. Forehead and palms resting against the wall as though she were waiting to be frisked, Jenna allowed herself one bleak "feck."

"Jenna?"

She stepped back.

Aidan, looking like the mad butcher of Ballymuir in his well-used apron, stood in the doorway. "You'd best be seeing this."

"Don't tell me there's something broken in the kitchen. I was pretty sure that everything that could break had already."

He shook his head and motioned for her to follow him. "You had a delivery."

"More meat?" she asked, then immediately realized he wasn't heading to the back door, but the front.

"No. It's for your sister, but she's not about."

No shock there. Maureen hadn't been out of bed before noon the past two days.

Jenna stepped into the front entryway.

"Out there," Aidan said.

She swung open the door, and her eyes widened. A legion of tan luggage emblazoned with the designer's initials seemed to have disgorged itself from a red van, which was now disappearing down the drive. Cases of ranging sizes lined the steps.

She turned back to thank Aidan, but he was already gone. As she counted up the bags—eleven of them—fat drops of rain began to fall from the sky. She closed the door and climbed the stairs to Her Royal Highness's room.

Her sister was sprawled facedown on the bed, out cold. Wadded up tissues and rumpled pieces of clothing were scattered across the bed and on the floor. Using her right foot, Jenna swept a path through the mess and nudged her sister on the shoulder.

"Maureen, wake up."

"Don't wanna. Go 'way."

"Your luggage is here."

"So bring it up."

"Like hell." Jenna yanked back the black duvet and the white sheet beneath.

Dressed in an oversized T-shirt and baggy flannel pants, Maureen curled up like a shrimp in the middle of the large bed and dragged a pillow over her head. The muffled comment from beneath the pillow didn't sound promising.

Jenna began pulling open the drapes, bringing gray daylight into the room. "I've made a point of not complaining when you've disappeared each of the past three nights. I've even made a point of not asking you where the hell you've been. But I'm not your servant, got it? Now, go downstairs and get your luggage. You might want to hurry, too. I'm not sure how all that fancy leather is holding up to the rain."

That, at least, got Maureen to move.

Satisfied, Jenna returned to her office and readied to deal with Honoria Weston-Jones.

Miss Weston-Jones wore her spinsterhood with great flair. Her clothes were vintage 1950s, as was her hairstyle. An ill-tempered cairn terrier named Buttons was her boon companion, and Jenna was convinced that Honoria nipped into the sherry with her morning tea and continued from there. In fact, from what Jenna had seen on her one visit, she had her suspicions about Buttons, too.

Calling Honoria directly was a calculated risk, and not one easily quantified. On a good day the woman was incredibly sharp. If, however, she was in her whimsical state of mind, there was no dealing with her. Still, it was time for Jenna to marshal her strengths.

Jenna closed her office door. After double-checking Honoria's number in her computer's address book, she said a brief prayer to the gods of flighty minds, then dialed. When Honoria answered, she worked up her most positive voice.

"Miss Weston-Jones, it's Jenna Fahey. How have you been?"

"Fine, now that Markham has finally exterminated the moles in my garden."

Honoria seemed to believe that the world was well-acquainted with the details of her life and followed them avidly.

"Glad to hear it." Whoever Markham was. "And Buttons, is he well?"

"His rheumatism is acting up, but he forges on, the poor dear. He forges on."

Miss Weston-Jones also spoke in stanzas, as though she'd been a bard in a prior life. Bad poetry tended to give Jenna a headache. Or in this case, amplify the one in residence. She pinched the bridge of her nose between her thumb and index finger. "I hate to disturb you, but my solicitor says there's been some holdup in the purchase negotiations."

"Purchase of what?"

"Muir House."

"Someone wants to purchase Muir House? That old ruin?"

God save her from batty women. "I do, Miss Weston-Jones."

"Are you daft, girl? Whyever would you want to do that?"

"I've been leasing it from you . . . running a restaurant." She racked her brain for some other hint that might help. "I sent you some clippings a few months back."

"Ah, yes, so you did. So you did. The place slips my mind. Savage land, Ireland. Haven't been there since '72, or was it '73?"

"I was wondering if perhaps we could wrap up the deal soon?"

"I never discuss finances over the telephone. It's an uncouth instrument."

"Well, if you could have your solicitor talk with mine . . ."

"Come pay me a visit, dear. You could take me to the Grosvenor Hotel for tea, as did that nice Mr. Gilvane yesterday."

It took a moment for Jenna to get past the blow to her solar plexus and ask the obvious question. "Dev Gilvane?"

"Why, yes. Do you know the boy? Charming, isn't he?" she pushed on, not really caring whether Jenna knew Dev. A blessing, since Jenna was still struggling for a response that didn't include the phrase *duplicitous bastard*.

Devlin Gilvane might have promised sheer pleasure, but he was proving far more adept at delivering sheer hell.

Maureen wasn't so much hung-over as she was willing herself dead. Sure, three pints of stout at O'Connor's Pub last night had been like two pints too many, but a throbbing head was the least of her problems. She was wet, ticked off, and not even interested in getting dressed until sometime the next millennium.

She glared at the luggage she'd just dragged up the stairs, piece by rotten piece—only three of which were really hers. It looked as though Afton had packed every single item of Maureen's clothing in the Fahey Paris apartment, down to the last floss-sized thong.

At least now Maureen knew for sure that her mother wasn't in Paris. Even if she hadn't missed Maureen, she would have definitely noticed that her set of Vuitton had disappeared. Of course, she might have just shrugged and picked up the custom Hermès she'd had her eye on. Maureen sighed and flopped in the middle of her bed.

This was one of those rare times when she longed for a normal family, one in which her parents even noticed that she existed. But no, she wasn't nearly as important as checking out Armani's new line or brokering a deal that got you a German ambassador in your hip pocket. She was just Maureen, good for decoration at cocktail parties and not much else.

She wondered if Sam was still in Paris, and whether he'd had his share of the actress yet.

She wondered why she cared.

And most of all, she wondered how she could be crying again. Out of tissue, she groped around on the mattress for the least-used, but gave up when she remembered that they were knotted in the covers at the foot of the bed.

A knock sounded at the door. Jenna, of course. Ms. Up-At-Dawn-Almighty-Important Jenna.

"Go away," Maureen called.

"Reenie, come on, let me in."

Reenie. Maureen longed for those uncomplicated Reenie days of old.

"I have orange juice," her sister wheedled.

Maureen rolled onto her back. "Is it fresh squeezed?"

"You have to ask?"

"Okay, you can come in." But only because she wanted the juice.

As Jenna entered, Maureen sat up and cleared a spot on the nightstand. Jenna set down the glass she carried. She looked as though she were about to sit on the edge of the bed, but thought better of it. Good thing. That would have been too big of a jump on the sisterly scale for Maureen to believe.

As Jenna walked to the windows and looked outside, Maureen scooted upright and tried her orange juice. It was perfect, annoyingly so.

Without turning to face her, Jenna asked, "Did you have any plans for today?"

"Why? Do you have some toilets that need scrubbing?"

Her sister swung around. For the first time since she'd arrived, Maureen really looked at Jenna instead of just giving a passing glance meant to avoid an order to dust some furniture or kiss customers' butts.

Funny, but she had never thought that she and Jenna looked as though they'd sprung from the same gene pool. Maybe Jenna had been short-changed in the height department and didn't have the Fahey golden hair, but they were definitely related. And at this moment she saw some of her own unhappiness mirrored in her sister's eyes. If she hadn't already hardened her heart, she might have felt sorry for Jenna.

"Okay, here's the deal," her sister said. "I need something to go right today. Aidan's in the foulest mood I've ever seen, I've got business problems making me crazy, and as usual, I'm attracted to a thoroughly rotten guy. So that leaves it up to you."

"This isn't your lucky day, is it?" Maureen drawled.

"Luck isn't the goal. Just survivability."

She could relate.

Jenna flicked one hand in the direction of the windows. "The rain seems to be wrapping up for the morning. Would you like to come out to the garden with me and dig around?"

Maureen was about to produce her best "Dirt? Surely you jest?" sneer when a years-old memory drifted her way. She and Jenna were kneeling in a dirt patch, marking the row-ends of newly planted seeds with sticks. Maureen could even recall the press of soil beneath her bare knees and the sound of the music on Jenna's radio.

"Remember the vegetable garden we planted at the summer house one year?" she heard herself blurting.

Her sister looked startled. "You remember that? You couldn't have been more than five years old."

"Oh, I remember. Mom had a hiss that we'd upset the gardener by digging in his beds, and only the radishes grew."

Jenna smiled. "Yeah, but they were great radishes."

Maureen tried another sip of the juice. "Is your garden here any better?"

"Not by much, and I need to get it fixed up." She frowned, then added, "I've decided that it's time to start renting out rooms—you know, do the county manor thing. For the rates I'd like to charge, this place has to be oozing Irish charm."

Simply because it made her feel a little better, Maureen pointed out the obvious. "You're not exactly the charming-hostess type."

"Not voluntarily, but I'm also out of ideas for other ways to increase my cash flow." She ran a hand through her hair. "None of this is your problem, though. I was just hoping we could spend some time together."

Maureen tried to speak, but there seemed to be a huge lump in her throat. *Jesus, more tears?*

"Or not," Jenna said with a chilly shrug that Maureen was beginning to recognize as part of her sister's armor.

"Give me a few minutes to get dressed," she said. The trick would be finding one outfit in the dozens Afton had sent that wouldn't remind her of being with Sam. Maureen stared at the bed in an effort to hide the moisture rimming her lower lids. "I could use some time outside."

*   *   *

Impulse had led Jenna to Maureen's room, and now impulse had her standing in the middle of a garden. Both acts were proof positive that impulse was a thing to be avoided. She grimaced as she looked around. Except for the corner she'd conquered for her herbs, the nearly two-acre space was distinguished as a garden only by the high stone wall enclosing it.

She wasn't sure that Maureen would show up and was even less certain she wanted her to. All she wanted was out of the house for an hour or two, away from the pressure that had her near to breaking. She couldn't spot a *Guide Eireann* critic, control Dev Gilvane, or make herself happy, but she could tame nature. Temporarily, at least.

The groan of the rusted garden gate caught Jenna's attention.

"You call this a garden?" Maureen said, standing with her hands on her narrow hips, just inside the entry.

Jenna smiled. "Only in the loosest sense."

Just as Maureen was dressed for gardening only in the most general of ways. Her hot-pink high-tops had a newspaper print that complimented her short black skirt and plunging black v-neck top. Jenna ignored a twinge of jealousy over the fact that she'd look like a stump in an outfit like that.

"Did some unpacking, I see," she said.

"Yeah, it's great to be a girl," Maureen replied with her trademark sarcasm. "So what are we going to do out here?"

Determined to keep matters light, Jenna retrieved the photo album she'd set on the bench beneath a scabby-looking, nearly dead pear tree. "I brought this for inspiration. Edna McCafferty, one of the older ladies in the village, gave this to me when I opened the restaurant. Her mother was a maid in the house in the early 1900s."

Maureen hovered next to her as she flipped through the old sepia-toned photographs. The album was a visit to an era long gone. Standing just outside the garden gate, serious-faced women in fussy dresses and enormous hats stared into the camera's eye.

Jenna turned the page, pausing to look at a glasshouse that was once located adjacent to this garden. Not even a hint of it remained. There were photos, too, of the interior of the walled garden, which had once been very formal, with neat stone-lined pathways and a small boxwood maze. Like the glasshouse, the maze was now a ghost.

"Wow," Maureen breathed as she looked at a picture of roses so lush that even seeing them in shades of brown didn't detract.

Jenna smiled. "It was something, wasn't it? It would take a fortune to restore the garden to what it was, but I figured at least I could uncover some of the pathways."

"With what, a bulldozer?"

"No, those." With her free hand, she pointed to two worn flat-bladed shovels she'd unearthed from a shed at the back of the house. During renovations, one contractor or another had left them behind, probably figuring they'd outlived their usefulness. "We'll just scrape back the turf."

"Yeah, right."

"I'm serious. This could be a great way to burn off some stress."

She carried the photo album back to the bench and picked up the shovels. Maureen grudgingly accepted hers.

Jenna used one sneaker-clad shoe to show Maureen the edge of the path. "Let's start here."

"The first sign of a blister and I'm out of here," Maureen said.

Stubborn sod had grown inches thick over the slabs of stone shown in the old photos. The digging took more effort than even Jenna, who was accustomed to huge projects, had imagined. Other than Maureen's muttered curses when her shovel slipped, they worked in silence for a time.

"Have you ever been in love?" Maureen eventually asked.

Jenna worked the shovel beneath the earth as she turned the question over in her mind. "Once, I thought I was."

"Claes?" Maureen asked.

Jenna nodded.

"When Mom met him, she thought he was a jerk."

"It would have been helpful if she'd shared the information. How about you?"

"Yeah, I've been in love. I wouldn't advise it."

Jenna paused long enough to use her forearm to wipe the perspiration beading on her forehead. In the way only Kerry clouds could, they'd drifted off to sea and left a cornflower-blue sky overhead.

"So what happened?" she asked.

"He wanted someone else more."

The tightness in her sister's voice told Jenna that this hadn't been a distant event.

"The curse of the Fahey sisters," she said, thinking of Claes, of Dev Gilvane, and most certainly of their parents. "To always stand in second place."

Maureen sighed, then set aside her shovel. "Do you think maybe if—" Whatever she'd been about to say faded as she cupped her hands above her eyes and looked skyward. "Do you hear that?"

The sound registered simultaneously with Maureen's question. The low thunder of a helicopter was audible long before the beast came into view. Jenna dropped her shovel and shaded her eyes from the sun. The chopper flew along the shoreline, directly toward them. Ballymuir was not a place of casual pilots, let alone sleek black helicopters. And she knew with certainty whom this one held.

"Dev," she said, giving the name the full weight of her anger.

"Dev?" her sister echoed. "He's the guy who had you pinned to the gate the night of the bonfire, right?"

Jenna turned on her sister. "You *watched?*"

Maureen didn't even bother to feign embarrassment. She laughed. "The way my life's going, I'll take my thrills anyplace I can find them."

Its noise ricocheting off the hard surface of Muir House, the helicopter swung low over the structure. Jenna had never felt so damned impotent.

Without thought, she grabbed a chunk of turf and fired it skyward. "Bastard," she growled.

Maureen hooted with laughter, but Jenna was too

furious to care. She didn't have to see what Dev was doing to know that it involved a threat to her home.

The chopper circled, then headed over the water.

"I dunno," Maureen said once she'd calmed enough. "There's something kind of sexy about a guy in a helicopter. Are you sure you want to scare him off like that?"

It wasn't working, anyway. He was coming straight at them.

Once he was nearly overhead, Jenna winged yet another piece of sod. Maureen wrapped her arms across her middle and howled again.

Jenna watched her projectile travel no more then twenty feet and then tumble back to the ground. She should have tried harder back in her high school phys ed classes. The helicopter briefly dipped, as though taunting her, then headed back along the coastline, north and east.

Maureen wiped at the tears gathered under her eyes. "Jeez, and I thought Dad was the only crazy Fahey in the bunch."

"I'm not crazy, just . . ."

Just what?

Seeking out Maureen, coming to the garden, lobbing dirt at Dev . . .

With luck, impulsive acts were like accidents. She'd had her three and could get on with life.

Until the next three arrived.

Chapter Nine

Everyone having a go at the head of a hake.
—IRISH PROVERB

Returning indoors carried its own set of problems, but at least being buzzed by a helicopter wasn't among them. As Dev disappeared over the horizon, Jenna and Maureen grabbed the photo album, stowed the shovels, and retreated.

Once again within Muir House's sturdy walls, Maureen asked if she could use the computer to catch up with the world. Jenna logged Maureen onto the Internet, then left to the kitchen. The news inside Ballymuir was wild enough for her.

Because it was still the restaurant's slow season and the meat order was correspondingly small, Aidan had finished his butchering some time ago. He now stood at his spot on the line, rapidly cutting carrots into julienne sticks for Muir House's herbed, upscale version of Irish stew.

Niamh had arrived. She was reading through the night's menu and simultaneously joking with Emer, the dishwasher who'd kindly returned after the grabby busboy had been "made redundant," as she'd put it. Jenna found that particular Irish turn of phrase gallingly inaccurate, since redundancy had nothing to do with it—the busboy's position remained unfilled.

The sharp sound of clattering metal captured Jenna's attention.

"Mother of God," Aidan said from between clenched teeth. His knife slid from the work surface to the floor. Under the best of circumstances, the man was pale, but now he'd taken on a grayish cast. He had one hand clamped over the other. Blood seeped from between his fingers. Jenna calmly led him over to the old porcelain sink by the back door.

"Let me have a look," she said.

He took the good hand off the bad. Blood welled from a deep cut at the base of his thumb and dripped into the basin. His breath hissed from between his teeth when she gently prodded one side of the sullen wound. It was deep enough that Jenna, who had her share of scars from cuts and burns, felt squeamish.

Niamh, well accustomed to the emergency drill, handed Jenna a clean towel, which she clamped over the cut. Emer, who'd come to peek over Niamh's shoulder, squeaked at the sight of all the blood.

"Go get yourself a drink of water, Emer," Jenna directed. She could hardly afford to have her dishwasher faint.

Jenna looked back to Aidan. "Felled by a carrot, huh?"

He scowled. "It's nothing. A bit of tape and I'll be right enough."

His response was part of the secret code. Short of a severing a finger, chefs never admitted to pain.

"Nice try. Niamh, drive him to Dingle."

"You think I'm needing Dr. McIntyre?" he snapped, referring to the physician who ran the closest clinic. "That I'm some sort of bloody pansy boy?"

"I wouldn't argue the bloody part, okay?"

"I've got no time for this," he said.

"If I don't send you, Deirdre will be after me with an ax." Deirdre was Aidan's wife and as high-strung as he was low-key. "Now, stop wasting my time. Go to Dingle, get sewn up, and come back."

This, Aidan could appreciate. "I'll get me jacket," he said to Niamh. To Jenna he added, "Not a word to Deirdre."

After he walked away, Niamh said in a low voice, "She's expecting again and angry as hell."

That, at least, explained Aidan's bleak mood.

"You'd think by now they'd have figured out what causes pregnancy," Jenna said, earning a laugh from Niamh.

Aidan and his wife had three boys under the age of four. Jenna could see why Deirdre might be feeling a bit testy at the thought of adding another to their pack so soon.

Once Aidan and Niamh had hurried out the back door, Jenna thoroughly cleaned the accident scene, then checked out her remaining kitchen staff. It was not an attractive picture. Saul hadn't shown up, and

Hector looked as though he'd been scraped out of a gutter after a night of partying. Which, knowing Hector, probably wasn't far from the truth.

Lately, instead of taking a spot on the line, Jenna had opted to oversee matters. In addition to supervising her staff, she'd acted as an expediter, orchestrating orders so that each party's food arrived together and with appropriate spacing between courses.

With Aidan now out of action, it looked as though tonight she'd be in front of the fire. The thought cheered her. Now she'd have no time to dwell on Dev Gilvane.

Jenna set up her favorite tools, then adjusted the small bins and dishes of chopped chives, capers, julienned vegetables, and the like that made up Aidan's *mise en place* so that they suited her work habits.

She'd corralled the best of the sauté pans, knew her equipment was calibrated to perfection, but still something wasn't quite right. Jenna rolled her shoulders like an athlete readying for competition, but that "in the zone" ease still eluded her. She needed to break out the big guns.

"I'll be right back," she said to Hector, who briefly turned his bloodshot eyes her way.

Jenna cruised to her office, where she kept her lucky hat, a vintage 1994 Chicago Cubs cap. Maureen had apparently seen enough of the world. The chair in front of the computer was vacant. Jenna pushed it back into its appointed spot. On the desk to the right of the monitor, the printer's little red light was flashing, signaling its hunger for more paper. She wasn't surprised that Maureen lacked the manners to re-stock what she'd used.

Jenna pulled out the printer's paper drawer and refilled it. She was about to turn away when the printer began to hum, readying to spit out another page. Curious, she lingered. An image emerged of a gorgeous guy with an equally beautiful woman. After it dropped into the tray, Jenna picked it up and read its caption: *Newlyweds? Sam Olivera and actress Chloe Weston.*

She shrugged. Her access to American films was limited, to say the least. She set the paper on the desk, in front of the monitor with its screensaver of a chorus line of dancing carrots. Aidan would love that.

The printer began to hum again. Hooked, Jenna waited. This time three people were in the photo: this Sam person, Chloe, and *Maureen!* Make that Maureen and what looked to be some lovely fresh trout she was raining on the seated couple.

"Jeez, Reenie, you don't mess around," Jenna murmured.

She felt a hesitant sort of admiration for her sister's ability to seize the moment. Jenna had never known that kind of anger or passion, except maybe when she'd lobbed dirt at Dev Gilvane, but even that had been a pale shadow of Maureen's act.

She set the picture atop the other and briefly considered hunting down Reenie, but rejected it as unwise. With her track record in matters of the heart, what advice could she possibly offer?

Jenna opened her desk's bottom right drawer, pulled out her lucky hat, and jammed it, bill to the back, on her head. There was one place where she still stood first. It was time to rock and roll.

At precisely eight o'clock in the evening, Dev presented himself to Niamh. After a look at her reservations book and one at her watch, she gave him a smile and a shake of her head.

"You're allowed to be a bit late, you know," she said as she reached for a menu. "It can't be good for you, being on time as often as you are."

Though he'd not raise it with the hostess, he suspected that showing up at Muir House at all would prove to have ill effects. Until Jenna he'd never had a woman try to knock him from the sky. Of course, until Jenna he'd never given a woman reason to want to.

"What would you recommend tonight?" he asked Niamh as they strolled toward his usual cocktail location in front of the fire.

"Anything," she said. "Jenna's cooking this evening, and you can do no better in all of Ireland."

He'd do better by being able to talk to her, but if she was to be anchored in the kitchen, he had little hope.

Frustrated, Dev settled in his armchair. Soon Muir House commenced its magic, and the tension began to leach from him. Odd, but the scent of the peat fire had begun to seem almost soothing. Niamh had a tumbler of single-malt to him before he'd even had a chance to ask. There was a comfort to this place that he'd sorely regret to see lost. He swallowed his Scotch along with a gulletful of guilt—a bitter drink, but what he deserved.

Vi Kilbride slipped into the companion to his chair. "I've been waiting for you and your cash to come back to the studio," she said. "Where've you been?"

"Off earning more." And for the first time ever, taking no pleasure from his efforts.

"So you're one of those men who thinks he can never have enough money?"

"There are limits."

Her smile spoke of a knowledge he didn't especially want to share.

"I saw some of your work in a gallery in London yesterday," he said with hopes of distracting her.

"It travels here and there," she replied, dismissing his effort with a casual wave of her hand. "So have you kissed Jenna again?"

"And this would be your business?"

She smiled. "Since your announcement the other day, I'm thinking it is. But if you're feeling shy, I'll just ask her."

Dev blew out a slow breath as he considered the ascending degrees of hostility in the words Jenna might use to describe him.

"I'm a topic best not addressed."

Vi nodded her thanks to Niamh, who had just brought her a glass of white wine, then said, "But you're also a topic not easily ignored, both here and in London. I've been doing some asking about . . . and hearing things that worry me."

He saluted her with his Scotch. "It's kind, your concern for my welfare."

Vi watched him with a formidable intensity. "You'd do best to tell Jenna the truth, and quickly, too."

He didn't require Vi Kilbride to know that. Tonight was to have been about the truth, had he found the time and place alone with Jenna.

Dev's cell phone chirped and his hand went automatically to the small holster at his belt. He'd meant to leave the phone in his room, had been sure he'd done so, in fact.

It would no doubt be Sid Barrett, who had magically appeared in the London office yesterday. Of course Dev wasn't supposed to have been there. He had parlayed his visit with Honoria Weston-Jones into a stop at headquarters, where he'd found Sid behind *his* desk, looking far too comfortable. Dev was no fool. A power play was being made at Harwood, and he had been dismissed from the battlefield—sent back to Ballymuir with only his lieutenant, Margaret, left to protect his flank.

He bit down on his anger and managed a civil hello.

"Dev?" asked a female voice.

"Mum?" The hell with unexpected, this was shocking. Had Margaret forgotten to send the monthly flowers? Or more dire, transfer the usual funds to his mother's account?

"I've been leaving messages at your flat," Katherine Gilvane said. "Not even that Fifi girl answered."

He smiled. Mum was never subtle in her disapproval. "Her name was Marie-Christine and she's back in Monaco now."

"Permanently, I hope."

Dev leaned forward to glance around the chair and see if Jenna's cell phone radar had homed in on him. So far, he was in the clear, though Vi Kilbride looked all too interested. He pulled back into the shelter of his chair and kept his voice low.

"Look, Mum, I'm in the middle of something at the moment, but I promise I'll ring you up—"

"Well, that's why I'm calling you. I'm in London and thought perhaps we could have a visit tomorrow."

"Normally, that would be grand, but I'm afraid I'm away from home just now."

"Oh."

Her disappointment nibbled at his patience.

"So where are you?" she asked.

"Ireland."

"What?"

"Ireland," he repeated, giving every syllable its due.

"Anyplace in particular or just touring?" Her voice was so dry that Dev wondered if the floor beneath his chair was about to become parched and crack open.

"Mum, I've been nowhere near Dublin. If I were, you know I'd call."

"Where in Ireland?"

Dev massaged his forehead with his free hand. This would lead to nothing but grief, but a man could hardly lie to his own mother. "I'm in Ballymuir."

She laughed. "No, really. Belfast is it? Or Cork?"

"Ballymuir."

"Well now, isn't this an interesting twist?"

Vi waggled her fingers at him. "You'd best finish up." She smiled and waved to an approaching someone.

Dev followed Vi's line of vision. Jenna, was, of course, taking the direct route. Her hair was wild, as though she'd just dragged both hands through it with no thought as to direction, and her face was rosy and warm looking. She was neither polished nor elegant, but he wanted to taste the salt on her skin. Not that she'd be letting him.

"I'll ring you in the morning," he said to his mum, "but just now—"

He offered no resistance when Jenna neatly removed the phone from his hand. Actually, he knew some relief. Explaining *why Ballymuir* and *why now* to his mother lingered low on his list of enjoyable acts. Ah, but Jenna, she ranked high indeed.

"I'm sorry," she said, "but Mr. Gilvane has developed an unhealthy attachment to his phone. As his therapist, I'm afraid I have to terminate this call . . . for his own welfare, you understand?"

She switched off the phone, then looked at Dev. "More business?"

For once, truth was his ally. "My mother, actually."

"Right."

Vi Kilbride watched the exchange as avidly as he might a balls-out brutal rugby scrum.

"Jonquil yellow, I'm thinking," she said.

"What?" he asked at the same time Jenna snapped, "Don't start."

"Jonquil yellow is your mam's favorite color, am I right?"

Mam. He hated the provincial sound of the word. "Yes," he said, "my *mum* likes yellow." At least that's what Margaret had told him.

"You'd best get someone painting," Vi said to Jenna, who gave a narrowed-eyed glare in return.

"And soon," Vi added.

Dev was beginning to find her smile wearying.

"First things, first," replied Jenna while she turned his cell phone over and then over again in her right hand as though the act were some sort of dexterity exercise.

He gestured at the phone. "So what's it to be? Locked away in a safe?"

"That would be too kind."

She turned heel and marched. Dev followed out a morbid sort of curiosity. When she pushed her way through the kitchen doors, he hesitated. A foreign land awaited, one where he would be at a disadvantage. But she did have his phone.

"Brave," Jenna commented after the doors had swung shut behind him. She walked to a holding tank containing one grossly oversize lobster in his— or was it her?—dotage. Once there, she slipped the battery from the back of Dev's phone and tossed it to him.

"This shouldn't hurt a bit, Harold," she assured the creature in the tank, then dropped the guts of the phone into the water. She seemed to relax as it settled to the bottom. Dev came to stand beside her. They both watched Harold languidly wave an antenna in the direction of his new companion.

"So be honest, who were you talking to?" Jenna asked.

"My mum. Really."

"Your mother?"

While it hardly brought them even for the truths he had yet to give her, Dev was pleased at the level of alarm in her voice. Better a confession to a fellow sinner.

"Mum, mother . . . one and the same," he said.

She muttered something just under her breath, then grabbed a cap and an apron from the corner of a nearby countertop.

"Okay, that was a screwup," she said as she tied the apron into place. "And much as I'd like to grovel, I need to get back to work. You're going to have to get out of here."

Such were the spoils of his moral victory.

Dev pocketed the battery to his cell and made his way back to his seat by the fire, only to find that he was now alone. He didn't really regret Vi Kilbride's departure. In her presence he felt as though he were being held to a higher standard, one he wasn't willing to attain. At least, not for her. Jenna, on the other hand, made him wish that he could give her mountains green with meadows, rivers rich with fish, a kingdom to call her own. Instead, he was bargaining a rocky one from beneath her feet.

Dev reached for his Scotch glass on the small, round table where he'd left it before witnessing the murder of his cell phone. The drink was gone, no doubt taken to his dinner table to wait for him.

A quick glance to the bar with thought of a replacement drink turned to a longer look. The bartender had been cornered by a weeping woman. It appeared to be one of those ugly end-of-the-affair encounters. She clutched a purse of some sort with both hands, as though holding on tightly would serve to right the rest of her life. As with any man trapped in a hopeless situation, the bartender wasn't saying much. No words were preferable to the wrong ones.

The woman's weeping rose to a full wail. Dev glanced about the room to see if any other diners were watching. Other than a gathering of amused staff, he saw only the gray-haired man from whom he'd lured Jenna the night of the bonfire. Again tonight, the man bore the expression of one who'd seen it all and had learned to laugh at most of it. His gaze met Dev's and he gave a subtle, rueful shake of his head.

The woman's wail gave way to a torrent of French. Unlike Irish, this language Dev knew. It seemed that Padraig, the bartender, hadn't been honest about his marital status. The woman, half burly Padraig's size, began swinging her handbag with the lethal accuracy of a martial-arts weapon.

Dev stood. He was of two minds, one to flee and one to somehow intercede. One thing was certain, after witnessing this, he'd have a care when crossing a Frenchwoman.

"*Cochon*," she howled, then added a shrill translation of "*p-e-e-e-g*," should the bartender have had any doubts. She swung again, just tagging a hideous blue-and-white porcelain pug that had been decorating the corner of the bar. The dog toppled and shattered on the wood floor. No great loss, to Dev's eye.

The third blow was the Frenchwoman's finest yet, catching the bartender square on the face. He reeled backward, then, like any good Irishman, bled with great flair. One hand clamped over his nose, he left the room.

Just then, Vi Kilbride reappeared. She took the dis-
traught woman by the hand, and in perfectly ac-
cented French even a Parisian couldn't scorn, told
her she'd run her home now, that with sleep, all
wouldn't be so bleak, and that the Frenchwoman had
been right, Padraig was more pig than prize.

After they left, the room was silent except for the
whispers of the gathered staff.

The gray-haired man looked at Dev. "I'll be checking on Padraig," he said.

Dev nodded, assessed the situation, then did what
he did best: issued orders. While Evie fetched Jenna
and another waiter picked up shards of pug-ugly
china, Dev surveyed the remaining staff.

"Any bartenders among you?" he asked.

"No, and we're running short tonight as it is," answered a girl wearing the black-and-white of the
restaurant's serving staff. "We've two out in the kitchen
and no busboy, which means the food's coming slow
and the rest of us are clearing as well as serving."

Opportunity beckoned. Lending a hand would
pacify a certain American chef, who was no doubt
preparing to go for his throat over today's helicopter
flight.

"I'll play publican tonight," Dev announced. He
wasted little time deciding whether this impulse was
grounded in the desire for good community relations
on behalf of Harwood, or in the hope of a more intimate reward from Jenna. It was a grand thing when
one could be both honorable and self-serving in the
same act.

At his offer the few staff members still milling
about gave "whatever suits you" shrugs and left.

Dev stepped behind the bar and made note of its setup. He slipped out of his suit jacket, draped it over a low stool tucked in the corner, then poured a half-shot of Scotch.

"Bloody brilliant," he said, and then raised the glass to himself.

Chapter Ten

He'd wriggle his way between a tree and its bark.
—IRISH SAYING

Despite the knowledge that Dev Gilvane was lying in wait, Jenna had found the zone, and what a sweet place it was. This was why she had become a chef, not to deal with front-of-the-house hassles or half-reliable suppliers. It was about the perfect turn of the wrist and the searing heat of the line.

Without turning from her sauté pan, she called to Hector on the broiler, "How much longer on the beef?"

"Up."

Jenna turned and readied a plate for her entrée. Just then, Evie came into the kitchen.

"Dev Gilvane's says he's needing you," she said from her spot opposite Jenna's station. The comment ended with an innuendo-laden snicker.

Jenna turned away. She had enough matters to juggle without adding Evie. "I don't have time to talk with guests tonight."

"And here I was thinking he's more than a guest."

"Save it," Jenna ordered as she turned back to plate the Dingle Bay scallops on a bed of saffron basmati rice and added tiny dollops of caviar garnish. She slid it across the counter so that it was next to Hector's beef. "Your food's up, Evie. Take it and get out."

"But—"

When the waitress still lingered, Jenna added a blunt "*now.*"

Evie's mouth took a sullen downturn as she gathered her plates. "You needn't get nasty with me. And your Mr. Gilvane's tending bar."

"He's *what?*"

Having gained the upper hand, the waitress left.

Jenna rounded to the other side of the counter, yanked off her lucky cap—which wasn't working worth spit—then wrenched out of her apron.

"Cover for me," she called to Hector, who said something in Portuguese that she suspected translated to "get stuffed."

In the library she found Dev Gilvane behind the bar, just as advertised. Instead of his usual evening attire of a custom-tailored suit, he'd discarded the jacket. His shirt's cuffs were folded midway up his tan forearms. Jenna took in his broad shoulders and the bit of skin at the base of his throat, where he'd unbuttoned his collar. A thought flitted through her mind, one of how it would feel to put her mouth just there. How warm he'd be. . . . If his heart would beat swiftly . . .

She forced her gaze upward and was relieved to be irritated by the intimate twinkle in his dark eyes. He appeared content, at ease, the lord of *her* damn manor.

"Where's Padraig?" she asked.

"Nursing a bloody nose in the men's room. I don't believe it's broken, though."

While she tried to process this information, he cheerfully added, "Padraig's nose, not the facilities."

"Thanks."

She looked around for some hint of what might have happened. Only one item other than her bartender was missing. "Where's my Portmeiron dog?"

"That hideous thing on the bar? A victim, luckily."

She had liked that statue, dammit. "A victim of what?"

"Padraig's girlfriend, who discovered there's already a Mrs. Padraig. Strong arm on the woman—she swung a mean purse."

"Great." Padraig down, Saul missing, Aidan home sleeping off the remnants of a reaction to the painkiller he'd been given. Not to mention the busboy she had yet to hire. Muir House had reached critical mass.

"So, shall I get Rose her cocktails?" Dev asked, then gave the waitress a friendly smile. "I'm glad to help."

Jenna's answer was fast and certain. "No."

She could always put Evie behind the bar and have Niamh take over the waitress's tables. Or not, she amended as she recalled Evie's Beltane gift of the restaurant's wine. To his credit, Dev wasn't prone to the theft of objects as small as bottles. He was more about taking the entire property.

Niamh appeared. "Evie claims she's having a migraine set in and needs to go home. I'll handle her guests."

Evie wasn't sick, and Jenna knew a payback when hit by one. She asked a question born of sheer desperation. "Have you seen my sister?"

Niamh shook her head. "I looked, but she's not about."

It occurred to Jenna that she, too, hadn't seen Maureen since they'd been chased inside by the helicopter this afternoon. Automatically she glared at Dev.

He moved from behind the section of antique mahogany pub counter. "Pride stuck somewhere mid-throat, is it?"

"This has nothing to do with pride." A lie, but it sounded good.

"Ah, then it's having to be grateful to me."

"So, shall I . . ." Niamh prompted.

"Yes," Jenna said. "And thank you."

Niamh departed, Rose waited for her drinks, Hector was no doubt tearing apart the kitchen, and Dev looked at his watch.

"You've got a good bit of the evening to go," he pointed out.

"I know." Jenna fiddled with the cuffs on her jacket. She wanted to owe him nothing, but she was trapped. "Do you think you can handle this?" she asked.

He laughed as he stepped back behind the bar.

"I've handled five-hundred-million-pound acquisitions, so I doubt a whiskey and water will throw me."

She gave a dismissive flick of her hand. "Those are just zeroes after a number. If you don't know how to make a drink, ask Rose or Niamh."

And then it was back to the kitchen to cajole a hungover Portuguese chef into finishing the night.

Jenna sent the last meal out of the kitchen at ten. Another hour past that and she and Hector had finished their cleanup. Hector found himself a belated hair of the dog, Niamh and Rose filled pepper grinders and sugar bowls, and Jenna worked up the energy to deal with Dev.

Gratitude for his help battled with a very healthy mistrust of the man. That was a difficult enough mix without adding in the simmering sexual curiosity that she couldn't quell. Stalling, she stopped in the ladies' room. There, she washed her hands with lavender-scented soap, winced at the pale and tired face looking back at her in the mirror, and then did her best to fix her hair. Giving good looks up for lost, she left.

When she arrived in the library, she saw no sign of Dev, but he must have heard her.

"And they say the Irish drink," he said from deep within a wing chair in front of the dwindling fire. "Try a group of Americans."

Danny Kilbride, who was wheeling in the vacuum cleaner to give the rugs their nightly once-over, nodded in righteous agreement.

"F— uh, damn right," he muttered.

Willing her aching feet to hang on just a bit longer, Jenna walked to the fireplace. Dev smiled a greeting. He was more sprawled than seated, his black hair was nearly untidy, and for the first time he looked tired to her.

"Americans? Ah, the McGuire party," she said. One wealthy set of parents, three grown children with spouses all seeking their roots equaled an enormous dinner bill and apparently, even a bigger bar tab.

"Yes, the McGuires. What the hell is a Manhattan, other than an island?"

Jenna smiled. "A drink I was sure died before we were born."

"As it should have," he commented.

Niamh drifted in. "If there's nothing else you're needing, Jenna, I'll be on my way."

"I'm all set, and thanks for covering tonight. I don't know what I would have done without you."

"Tried to do it all yourself, of course," Dev supplied.

Niamh chuckled, then said, "I'm glad to help. It's part of the business, though if I run off to Majorca for some sun next week, I expect you'll not complain."

"At least not to your face," Jenna joked. "Speaking of running off, have you seen Maureen at all?"

"Not once," Niamh replied.

Danny Kilbride looked up from his work. "I saw her down to O'Connor's earlier. She came in with Lorcan, but—" He stopped short and fussed with the cord to the Hoover.

"But what?" Jenna urged.

"I shouldn't be talking. It's not my business."

"But it's mine, Danny. What happened?"

He turned a shade of red close to that of his hair and stammered out an answer. "She—she was drinking, you see, and not just a little. Lorcan was none too happy. And then she left without him."

"Alone?"

"No, with a group of students. Americans." The last word was spoken with a certain lack of fondness.

"What time was this?" Dev asked.

Jenna was startled by his question. He scarcely knew Maureen.

"No later than nine," Danny replied.

Jenna checked her watch and frowned. She wasn't Reenie's keeper, but still she would have expected her sister to say something before taking off for the night.

"Maybe I should check the village," she said.

"Pat's still there," Danny said, referring to his brother. "I could ring him." He'd pulled his cell phone from his pocket before Jenna could even thank him.

While he dialed, then talked, Jenna sent Niamh on home, assuring her that everything was under control. The burn in Jenna's stomach told her she'd overstated the case.

Danny hung up and said to Jenna, "No sign of her."

"Thanks for checking," she said. Worry moved upward, becoming a physical ache at the back of her neck.

Danny switched on the vacuum.

Frowning, Dev stood. "Your office?" he suggested over the noise. She nodded her assent.

As they neared the service hall to the kitchen, another thought struck. "Did you get to eat tonight?"

He paused a fraction, gave a low laugh, then said, "No, and until you asked, I'd forgotten."

"Well, let me make you something before you take off, okay?"

"I won't be leaving until your sister is home," he said very matter-of-factly.

His concern over Maureen had surprised her, but these words set her back on her heels. "You don't have to stay."

"And you don't have to be alone."

She considered which was more unsettling: waiting for Maureen in solitude, or with Dev Gilvane. Her conclusion was unexpected. "Maybe you could stay for a while."

"As long as you wish."

He was working his way past her defenses, and it frightened her. She reached for familiar ground. "Would you like an omelette?"

"Perfect," he said.

They entered the kitchen, and Jenna tried to relax. "Let me get a few things together," she said, but Dev was already occupied by gazing into Harold's tank.

She'd almost forgotten. Cell phones swimming with lobsters . . . It seemed that impulse had taken up permanent residence.

"Do you think your friend, here, would mind if I retrieved my phone?" Dev asked.

"Probably not, but if you're waiting for me to apologize for putting it there, don't." As low as the act had been, it had also been immensely pleasurable.

"It was nearly deserved," he conceded.

"Nearly?"

"Had it not been my mum, I'd give you full dispensation." Dev pushed one sleeve past his elbow, flexed his fingers, then said, "The creature looks old enough. He doesn't move very quickly, does he?"

"No more than a slow crawl," Jenna said as she pulled a couple of eggs from the reach-in fridge beneath the front of the sauté station. "At least, I don't think so. He's never had much in the way of incentive."

She stood in time to see Dev dipping his hand into the tank.

"Well, let's hope he doesn't find my fingers appetizing. That's a fine lobster . . . *stay*," he directed Harold.

Jenna held back a smile. "I'm a bad pet owner. I haven't trained him yet."

Dev came up with his cell phone. His pleased smile was almost enough to tempt her to drop the phone back into the tank.

"This is your pet? What about the little dog on the big rope?"

"Roger? He's Vi's. I was just watching him."

"That's a relief. I thought he'd been hanged for poor behavior."

"Funny," she said. "I'll be right back." She headed to the walk-in refrigerator and gathered a plum tomato, some fresh herbs and scallions, and a bit of cheese.

When she returned, Dev was using one of the kitchen's white utility towels to dry the remains of his phone.

"This has been one bloody long night," he said.

And destined to grow longer yet, unless Maureen called or returned. Glad for even the simple distraction of an omelette to make, Jenna busied herself seeding and then dicing the tomato.

"Your sister," Dev asked, "has she done this before?"

He seemed to have picked up on her thoughts. This knack of his gave her a sense of having known him for more than the several days that had passed.

"No, but Maureen hasn't been here long." She hesitated. "I really don't know her that well. Like, not at all."

"Ah," was all he said in return.

Heat crept to Jenna's cheeks. Though her words had felt cleansing, this was no confessional, and despite the cult rumors she'd been happy to spread in Ballymuir, Dev was far from clergy of any sort.

For the first time that she could recall, she had overstepped. Usually, she failed to reach far enough.

"I'm sorry," she said without looking up from her work. "You don't need to hear all this. I'll just stick with the cooking."

"No, tell me about your sister," he urged. "I'm an only child. I've had none of the name-calling and whatnot. Or at least, I've had it only with my schoolmates, and I was always on the receiving end."

He was giving her something of himself, easing her past her embarrassment. "Well, with Reenie, it was kind of a brief and glorious battle. I'm eight years older, so we really didn't do much growing-up together. And what little we did just proved my father's theory that I'm a changeling."

"A changeling?" he echoed.

"You know," she said as she whisked the eggs, "the real baby is taken away by the spirits and a cursed replacement left in its place."

"Your father said this?"

"I overheard him talking to my mother one night. The next morning I asked my nanny what the word meant."

"I'm sorry for that."

She shrugged, trying to downplay the lingering hurt. "It's no big deal."

"The unconditional love of a parent is a big deal, indeed." His mouth curved into a brief smile, as though he was amused by the American phrase delivered with an unmistakeable Irish accent.

"With my mum, at least I've known love," he said. "And I'm thinking your father must be mad, in any case. That's nothing to say about one's child."

Jenna fell silent. Matters of family were matters of peril. Omlette finished, she slipped it onto a plate.

"Follow me," she said to Dev, then headed to the war room.

While he ate, she fought back worry.

"Do you think I should call the Gardai?" she eventually asked.

He shook his head. "No, they'd think you were another anxious American. It's been only hours. Give her the chance to come home on her own. She's hardly unsophisticated."

Jenna turned over the image of Reenie dumping the tray of fish. "I don't know. I'm beginning to see that she puts on a good front, but it doesn't run too deep."

Dev stood and gathered his plate and cutlery. "Shall I wash this up?"

"We'll leave it for Emer. If she doesn't have a mess waiting for her, she worries about losing her job."

He laughed. "There's not much difference between my position and your dishwasher's, then."

A passing comment, but one that led to a question that had been bothering her for days. Jenna showed him where to stack his dishes, and added hers from her cooking, too. As they left the kitchen, she said, "You know, you've never said exactly what you do for a living, Dev."

Timing and quick reflexes: with these skills Dev had seized success. But here—*now*—when Jenna had given him the opportunity to bring out the truth, he found himself unwilling to inflict hurt. Except that through delay, he would only make matters worse. Buying time, he asked where she might like to wait for her sister.

"My office," she replied.

They were there all too soon.

"Let's sit," he said, gesturing at a thickly cushioned blue sofa.

Dev settled next to Jenna. She was close enough to touch, should he be so foolhardy. Shadows lingered in her hazel eyes, and she held herself with wariness.

"We should talk about this afternoon," he said. "We need to get it out of the way."

She looked down at her hands. His gaze was drawn there, too. Her nails were blunt, but her fingers long and surprisingly delicate-looking. A mysterious mix, just like the woman herself.

"About the helicopter, you mean?"

"Yes, that, and what I'm doing in Ballymuir, too." He summoned the truth. "Jenna, we both know that I haven't been on holiday, but I also haven't been looking at Muir House for myself."

She watched him, so silent, so still, that it seemed almost torture to sit under her steady gaze.

"You could have been honest with me days ago. Why now?" she finally asked.

He was a man of many words, endless flowing phrases, but now that he needed them, they had fled. "Because now I want no misunderstandings. Now there's more to us than this damn house."

"Is there?" Her words carried a bitterness that seemed deeper than their current mess, unpleasant as it was.

"You know there is." He reached out to touch her hair, but she drew back.

"Don't touch me," she said. "Just talk."

"If that's what you wish. I'm with Harwood International, out of London. It's—"

"I know what Harwood is. Let's move along."

Dev abandoned any hopes for a diplomatic approach. "I'm second-in-command of the resorts division. I was asked to scout a site in Ireland."

Her smile was anything but pleasant. "And you've settled on Ballymuir? Galway's too pedestrian, Kildare overdone?"

"Jenna—"

"I asked you at Kilmalkedar and I still want to know—why Ballymuir?" She fired the question in a quick cadence, yet so controlled, almost dispassionate.

"I came here because—because—" He dragged in a breath and tried again. "I can't tell you why I came here. I don't know myself, except that the name was familiar, and faced with an unacceptable assignment, it was the easy choice. . . ." He trailed off, leaving unspoken the odd feeling that instinct had lured him here, too. He was better damned a bastard than a lunatic. "Don't take this so personally," he said.

"It couldn't be any more personal. Have you suggested Muir House as a site?"

"I've forwarded information." And done more, including securing an option on adjacent land.

"So Ballymuir was the easy choice," she said. "Then what about the easy solution? If there's more to us than my home, prove it."

He knew the impossible path she was taking, yet still he asked, "How?"

"Pull Muir House from consideration."

"I can't."

"I see. Not so easy, then, is it?"

"You don't bloody see at all." He turned to what he knew, what he could account for in pounds sterling. "This is business, Jenna. Cold, impersonal business. What would you have me do—tell them now that I've met you, wanted you, hell, hungered for you, that it would be wrong to proceed? That *I* was wrong?"

One finely arched brow curved upward, but she left him to slog in his guilt, which was quickly turning to something that felt like anger.

"It doesn't work that way, and you know it," he accused. "You grew up a Fahey. Your father has a finger in most everything, right? Have you seen him or his friends turn away from a deal because their hearts soften?"

She stood and put a distance between them. "I try not to be like my father or his friends. You've confessed now, Dev. I don't see what point there is in talking about this. Instead of fighting just you, I've got a multinational corporation going at me."

He left the sofa and closed in on her. It pleased him to see anger in her eyes. Anything was better than chill indifference.

"The point in talking is this." He drew her closer and, despite her unwillingness, kissed her, took her mouth, owned it, and commanded more. But beneath the demand, one word repeated in his thoughts: *please. Please soften, please bend, please want as I do.*

But she was stubborn, Jenna Fahey. She would not accede.

God, how Dev Gilvane could kiss.

It was a low act, a desperate act, trying to sway her with kisses. It was also one that had been attempted by others. Claes had tried to seduce her from her concerns, and for a time he'd actually succeeded. She was wiser now. She would not give up her heart just to come second again. Not to Muir House, and not even for a man who made her believe that she could have passion in all parts of her life.

Jenna turned her face away from Dev's, but he wouldn't set her free. Instead he kissed her low on her throat, at the exact spot she'd earlier imagined kissing him. His tongue pressed against her skin, sending a thrill through her. Her ethical stance was losing ground to her body's instinctual response.

"Don't," she said.

"Don't what?" He cupped her breast, brushing his thumb against the nipple. Even with the barrier of clothing between them, it rose to his touch. "Don't want you as you want me?" he asked.

"Don't complicate things."

"They needn't be. We have this." His mouth again neared hers, and he whispered the one word she least expected to hear: "Please feel it, too."

As she drew in a surprised breath, he kissed her. She intended to push him away, but instead found herself flexing her fingers against his strong upper arms, like a cat kneading with pleasure.

Please. Usually it was a small politeness, casually spoken. Yet she sensed that in this instance, it was none of those things to Dev. It was a word of need, perhaps even capitulation.

Please . . . Pleasure . . . She let her tongue tangle with his.

She'd had enough displeasure in life. Maybe what he asked wasn't impossible. For the time that he remained in Ballymuir, she could keep her heart to herself, yet still enjoy his touch, revel in his taste, and perhaps even finally learn about passion.

Jenna drew back far enough to give him a quiet, "Yes."

His arms closed tighter around her. She rested her head against the crisp white cotton of his shirt and listened to the rapid rhythm of his heart.

After a moment he tilted up her chin until she met his gaze.

"I'm sorry I've told them about the house," he said. "If I could change matters, I would."

A jolt of alarm coursed through Jenna. His words tore at the gossamer-thin wall she'd built between pleasure and reality. "I don't want you to mention Harwood again."

He frowned. "But if there's something—"

She settled her fingers over his mouth. "Nothing more. I need your word."

He gently nipped at the pads of her fingertips, and then clasped her hand in his as she pulled it away. Dev looked at her for a beat of the heart, then two more. She couldn't imagine what he was seeking. Finally he kissed her palm. "You have my promise. And Jenna, you won't regret this."

Jenna drew him back to the sofa so they could wait for Maureen. No regrets, she thought as she relaxed against Dev. It was a wonderful concept, but impossible to achieve.

The shrill ring of a telephone jarred Jenna awake from a deep, warm sleep. She shifted, noting that she seemed to be atop Dev and that his arms were around her. It felt close to paradise. The phone rang again. Alarm shot through her when she recalled why she wasn't in her bed and for whom she waited.

"Sorry," she blurted as she untangled herself. Jenna scrambled off the couch, bounded to her desk, and grabbed the phone.

"Hello?"

"Jenna?"

The caller was whispering. Out of instinct, she pushed the phone closer to her ear. "Reenie?"

Jenna glanced over at Dev, who seemed to have come wide awake. He was sitting up and combing one hand through his sleep-mussed hair.

"Wait. Hang on," the voice on the other end of the line hissed.

"Maureen?" Jenna repeated.

Dev rose and came to stand beside her.

"I'm back," Maureen said in thin voice. "Thought I heard someone."

"Where are you?"

"I'm not sure."

"What?"

"I got a ride to O'Connor's and while I was there, I met these guys. They seemed nice, but now I can't get out."

Her sister's words had come in such a rush that Jenna struggled to sort one from the next.

"From O'Connor's?" She glanced at her watch. It was after three, well past legal closing time.

"No. We drove to another pub in Castlegregory and then back to their place. I kind of passed out. I woke up in this—this room. It's too high up to jump out the window, and I can't get out, so I'm using my cell phone to call you."

"What do you mean, you can't get out?"

"The door is locked from the outside. What the hell kind of country is this, with doors that can lock you into a bedroom? I mean, what if there's a fire, or an abduction—" Her breath hitched, just a fraction away from a sob.

Jenna spoke firmly, trying to calm her sister. "Reenie, think about what you saw when you were driving. Can you remember anything?"

"Of course I can," her sister snapped. "I'm not a total idiot."

That, as far as Jenna was concerned, would be a subject open to debate—once Maureen was safe.

Dev settled a hand on Jenna's shoulder. "Do you know where she is?"

"Maybe around Castlegregory." Not far by miles, but separated from Ballymuir by a stretch of mountains.

"Put her on the speaker phone."

Jenna did as directed.

"Maureen, this is Dev Gilvane. Can you describe for us what you saw?"

"When we drove from the pub, we turned right, up toward the mountains."

"How long did you travel?" Jenna asked.

"I don't know. It didn't seem that long, but I was kind of falling asleep."

"Like you 'kind of' passed out, huh?"

Dev frowned at her and shook his head in a firm "no."

"Sounds to me like she's near Camp," he said in a low voice to Jenna, referring to a village near Castlegregory. "Look out the window, Maureen. Are there lights from other houses about?"

"Yes, but not many." Now she was definitely crying. "I was going to start screaming, but then I thought, what if they come back? I mean, they locked me in, after all. Oh, God, I really messed up."

Feeling protective of her sister's dignity, Jenna switched the call off the speaker and back to the handset.

"I'm going to gather her home," Dev said. "The village is small enough that I'll not miss her."

"Hang on, Reenie." She muffled the mouthpiece with her palm. "She's my sister, I'll get her. I can call the Gardai, then head out," she said to Dev.

"Think about this, Jenna. Who has the faster car? Who has explored every drivable inch of land over the past week?"

His arguments were sound, practically unassailable, but relinquishing control made her stomach knot.

"Let me go to her for you," he said. "Please."

Again, a *please*. She could not refuse him.

"Jenna? Jenna?" she heard her sister calling. "Don't hang up on me!"

She uncovered the phone. "I'm here. Dev's coming for you, and I'm going to have to put you on hold while I call the police on my other line. Then I promise I'll stay and talk to you."

Maureen snuffled. "All right, but I think the battery on my phone is low."

"Okay. Then we'll save it. Give me your number." She did, and Jenna jotted it down on the pad and paper Dev scooped from her desk and handed to her. "Is there a light in the bedroom?"

"Yes."

"Keep flashing it on and off so Dev or the police can find you."

He nodded his approval.

"You'll be okay, Reenie," she promised. "Now hang up."

For once, Maureen obeyed.

"I'll need to get my suit coat from the library," Dev said. "And do you have a cell phone I could use?"

"Sorry. I think I'm the last person in Ireland without one."

He shook his head. "No, there's two of us, just now."

Before she could bludgeon herself with guilt, he leaned forward and quickly kissed her. "You call the Gardai, and I'll call you from Maureen's phone as soon as I can."

He left, and Jenna made her call, then settled in to worry some more. After a time she reached the point where she was checking her watch only every three minutes. The wind rattling the loose shutters outside her office window, the creaks and groans that were part of an old house's chatter, all of them seemed amplified to her ears.

Funny how being alone unsettled her when it had always been a comfort. Maybe that was because this time she waited for someone, when all the nights before she'd believed herself content in her solitude.

Life had grown so complicated. Nothing was occurring according to plan. In fact, she wasn't sure she could even recall the plan just now.

Minutes piled one on top of another until almost an hour had passed. Finally the phone rang, and Jenna grabbed it.

"Hello?" she said over the loud echo of her heart.

"I have her."

Dev. Sometime tonight the name had moved from being a curse to a more of a blessing. "Is she okay?"

"She's sleeping."

Jenna smiled. "She must be exhausted to pull that off, the speed you drive."

His laugh was warm and intimate. "Some Faheys have more trust than others."

"I'm trying to trust you, Dev."

He was silent a moment, as though testing her words for truth. "Thank you for that."

"Safe home," she said, giving him an old Irish farewell, though in this case she meant it as a welcome, too.

For however long, Dev Gilvane was now part of her life.

❋

Chapter Eleven

In spite of the fox's cunning, many a woman
wears its skin.

— IRISH PROVERB

Bone tired and resenting even another moment
awake, Dev drove the last of the road to Muir House.
He glanced over at Maureen, who was slumped
against the passenger door, dead out, the lucky little
fool. She'd had the shite scared out of her tonight, as
well she should.

In rescuing her, Dev had been faced with taking
the less direct route of the Connor Pass or threading
the perilous access road straight across the jagged
mountains to Camp. He had embraced danger. And
he'd arrived before the authorities, too.

With no sign of Maureen's semi-abductors, he'd
calmed her while considering the legal ramifications

of kicking in the door to a house not his. As it turned out, one of the late-arriving Gardai was more than happy to have a go. Dev didn't imagine they were presented the opportunity too often.

Dev rounded the last curve of the drive and smiled at the sight awaiting him. Jenna had left the house aglow, a warm welcome shining from its many windows.

"Maureen, we're home," he said.

The girl stirred, then sat upright. "Okay." The muzzy sound of her voice matched her appearance.

He parked the car and, as they were walking the path to the front door, handed Maureen her cell phone.

She managed an exhausted "thanks," one more added to the countless number she'd given him once out of the house in Camp.

They stood in the front entryway. "I'm going to crash," she said.

Interesting term, though he was too tired to comment. "First help me switch off the lights," he said.

She looked around, blinking owlishly. "Isn't there someone else who could do that?"

He didn't reply, just walked to the doorway to the right of the entry, reached in, and flipped the light switch. When he turned, Dev was pleased to see that she'd gone for the room to the far left. In less than a minute, they met at the foot of the sweeping stairway.

"Is there a room I could use?" Dev asked. "I'd rather not wake the people where I'm staying."

She nodded. "Follow me." Up the stairs they climbed.

"That's Jenna's room," she said as they passed a closed door. She pointed to the door opposite and the next one down. "This one's unfinished, and that one has a bed, but I'm not too sure there are sheets on it."

He shrugged. "Doesn't matter."

"Good night, then," she said and continued down the hallway. Soon he heard a door close.

Dev stood in front of his chosen door, hand resting on its oval brass knob. Nearby waited rest. But Jenna was also a matter of feet away. It would be so easy—and so gratifying—to take those steps. But he'd already given her much to think about, much to accept. If he weren't a selfish man, he'd leave her for the night.

But selfish he was just now, and hungry for comfort, too. He had excuse enough in telling Jenna that he was back. He retraced his steps down the hall and lingered outside her door. A few words, the crisp sound of her voice, they weren't much to ask.

Dev opened the door, stepped in, and closed it softly behind him. The drapes weren't quite closed, leaving a dim sort of light to guide his way. Jenna lay in bed, curled on one side, facing him.

He softly called her name.

She didn't stir.

"We're back. Maureen's off to sleep."

There, he'd done his duty, even if she hadn't awakened to hear the news. He could leave now. She sighed and murmured in her sleep, stretching one arm above her head to rest palm upward in a gesture of supplication.

Now, he told himself. Leave now. But selfish he remained. When he eased his weight onto the edge of her bed and sat, she didn't wake.

How had he ever, even for a moment, thought her plain? The tilt to her nose, the lushness of her mouth, even in dim light they were sights of beauty. He had started the night doing the right things for the wrong reasons, but ended up feeling an almost indefinable connection to Jenna.

What Dev did next was no more a matter of judgment than entering her room had been. This was about need. Slowly, quietly, he stripped down to his briefs, turned back the duvet and sheet, and stretched out on the bed next to her. Jenna's breathing was slow and steady, soothing him.

He was, he thought as he drifted to sleep, still the worst kind of opportunist. And very thankful for it, too.

Jenna dreamed. There was a man in her bed. A lover. His hands and mouth were sure, and she was open to him . . . the taste of his kisses, the hint of outdoors in his scent, and the feel of his body hard against hers. Her lover's hand slipped beneath the elastic waist of her boxer shorts and his fingers delved through the curls at the vee of her thighs. She sighed and spread her legs for him. One blunt fingertip ventured down. She was slick, hot with need.

At the first thrilling touch she shivered with excitement. No one had ever gotten it right; this man was magic. Hands seeking purchase on the bed, Jenna gasped and arched upward. He murmured something, but she couldn't quite catch the words. The tone she understood, though. It was low and rich and intoxicating.

"More," she begged as he teased, toyed . . . tempted.

Her skin grew damp and her heart pounded and her toes curled. For once she was flying in the moment, her mind shut down to everything but feeling. She had never been this hungry, this close to reaching that elusive release.

He pushed at the strap to her camisole, but it didn't give graciously. The sound of snapping threads intruded on Jenna's dream. She came fully, instantly awake. Whatever it was she'd been about to experience dissipated like so much stardust in sunlight.

"I want to taste you here," Dev said. Having given up on her camisole, he was tugging at her boxers. "And to come inside you and stay until—"

Jenna clamped one hand around his wrist. "Dev."

"Yes, love." He kissed her neck, then moved lower.

"*Dev.*" Jenna wriggled from beneath him and tried to think of what to say. She couldn't bear the disappointment. They would fail. *She* would fail.

"Give me a second," she said, edging toward the outside of the mattress.

He moved away. "I'm sorry," he said. "I thought you—"

"What time is it?" she asked, leaving the bed as she spoke. She looked at her alarm clock. Thank God, a valid excuse. "It's past *eleven?* Aidan will be looking for me, I'll have missed deliveries, and—"

"The Earth will have stopped turning?" Dev suggested. "Jenna, everything will wait. Come back to bed and let me love you."

He made it sound so simple, but it had never been that. She hurried to her wardrobe and pulled a clean jacket and pants from a hanger. "Dev, I have to work."

"Have I done something wrong?"

"No," she said, but then made the crucial error of looking at him. He was propped against the pillows, the covers riding low against his hips. Dev Gilvane was the most incredible man she'd ever had in her bed. He was virile, lean, and muscled, so perfectly golden-skinned and dark-haired. What any woman would dream of, and most would love to exhaustion. Except her.

She shook herself out of her trance. "Really, it's just that it's so late and—"

He blew out an impatient breath. "Work, then. But at three o'clock, you're mine until nightfall. I don't give a damn if you've got fish to scale, veal to pound, or bartenders to coddle. At three we take time for just the two of us. For pleasure."

She pulled herself together and tried to tease. "And the alternative?"

Despite the fact that her voice had been as high and reedy as a petrified virgin's, he played along. "The alternative? I bring you back into this bed here and now, peel that ridiculous smiling-face set of pajamas from you, and learn your body. I'll find out if the feel of my mouth against your breasts will make you sigh as you did minutes ago, and I—"

"Three o'clock," she blurted.

He shook his head. "And here I was thinking you were a smart woman. Have it your way, Jenna, for you'll be wanting it mine soon enough."

"Arrogance," she accused.

He smiled. "Truth."

"You can use my shower," she said, pointing to the door. "I'll go down the hall."

With Dev watching her, she riffled through her dresser, grabbed some non-smiley-face underwear, dashed into her bathroom, took her toothbrush, and then fled.

Less than fifteen minutes later, Jenna was showered, dressed, and in the kitchen. As though making up for yesterday's lapse, Aidan was firmly in command, leaving her nearly extraneous. He had handled the deliveries, assembled a sample of a proposed pasta entrée, and even seen to Evie, who had called in "tired."

According to Aidan, when asked tired of what, Evie's response had been "tired of working." No great loss. On the plus side, Saul had reappeared, and even Hector looked as though he'd skipped his nightly party.

In need of something to pull together her loose ends, Jenna wandered to the war room for a mug of coffee.

"Finally out of bed?" Vi asked from her seat at the table. "I was just ready to go wake you."

"I had a long night. What are you doing here?"

"I'm here to raid your larder and to check on Aidan for Deirdre, who's fretting about his wound. And I'm here to meddle, of course."

"Jenna, where can I—" Dev stopped just inside the doorway and scowled. "Hello, Vi."

"Hello, Dev. That's the same suit as last night, I'm thinking," she commented.

"An artist and fashion critic, too," he said, then

went to the coffeepot and rattled it about while pouring himself a mug.

"Late night, indeed," Vi said to Jenna. "To think of the fun I missed in not pulling back your covers."

Jenna gave her a glare meant to quell, but received laughter in return.

Dev pulled out a chair and sat. "You got our purse-swinger safely home, I take it?" he said to Vi.

"I did, though the way she wailed and carried on was frightful."

"No worse than me last night," said Maureen as she staggered into the room and toward the coffeepot. She poured a mug, then said to Jenna, "You left your toothbrush in my bathroom."

"Sorry."

"Sleep well?" Maureen asked Dev.

"Well enough," he replied.

Maureen joined the three of them. After setting her mug to her right, she rested her head on the table's hard surface.

"Irish whiskey is a tool of Satan," she proclaimed, then closed her eyes and feigned death.

Tapping one finger against her lower lip, Vi scrutinized the younger Fahey. Jenna had seen this look before, and knew that even if a freak tsunami were to swamp Ballymuir, it wouldn't be enough to tear Vi from whatever vision held her.

"You'd best get your sister about painting those bedrooms today," she eventually said to Jenna.

Maureen opened one eye long enough to ask, "Are you talking about *me*?"

"I am."

"I don't paint." She spat the last word as though it were plague-ridden.

"Ah, but I'm thinking you do. And to my everlasting surprise, very nicely, as well."

"Hah."

Jenna watched the exchange. "Do I get any input on colors?"

"Sorry, but definitely jonquil yellow for one," she said, following the order with a bold smile for Dev. Then she let her gaze settle on Maureen. "And blue for the next. Starlight blue, and well away from Miss Maureen's room."

Maureen peeled open both eyes and fixed Vi with a glare. "What the hell is starlight blue?"

"I'm glad you've asked. Drink up that horrible caffeine, then I'll run you to the hardware in the village. With a little coercion, Mr. Clancy will mix us just what you need."

Jenna's sister sat up and curled her lip with marvelous disdain.

"I know just what *you* need," she said to Vi.

"Excellent sex, and as frequently as possible," Vi replied agreeably, then whisked the coffee mug from in front of Maureen and set it next to the pot.

"Give me that back!"

"The day is running off without you. Time to go catch it." She snagged Maureen by the wrist and hauled her up. "You'll find the painting quite therapeutic, you know."

They were out of the room by the time Maureen spoke. Jenna was fairly sure that her sister said, "Witch."

Dev stood, then took a look into the kitchen.

"They're gone," he said. "And when I'm made king of the world, my first order of business will be to give Vi either a small nation to rule or a room in a comfortable asylum."

"Too late on both counts," Jenna said. "She has Ballymuir."

He smiled. "Right you are. She's dead on about the day running, though. I need to be making some plans."

"If you're too busy to come back at three . . ." she volunteered. After all, *Irish Gourmet* would be here in just days for their photo shoot, she had yet to place another call to her solicitor, and there was a new organic vegetable supplier in Kenmare she wanted to check out. And most of all, Dev's proposed pleasure made her feel cotton-mouthed and shaky.

He chuckled. "Pushing me out of your schedule already? You'll find that I don't leave well." He stood behind her and she tipped her face up to look at him. He brushed her lower lip with his thumb. "Ripe enough to eat," he said.

Some level of alarm must have shown in her eyes, for he brushed a quick kiss on her forehead, then added, "Oh, I'll wait. After all, a bit of wait only enhances the joy of the meal. See you at three."

And then he was gone. Jenna sighed as she considered the corollary to Dev's theory: With too much waiting, pleasure died.

At two-forty Jenna tracked down Maureen. Actually, not much in the way of tracking was required, since Maureen seemed to have found herself a radio and cranked it up loud. She didn't have music on, but what sounded to be a Radió na Gaeltachta talk show, which meant that the only words in English were those few for which no translation existed.

"Learning Irish?" Jenna asked when she entered the bedroom that Maureen had drafted for a yellow paint job.

Her sister looked up from where she knelt in front of the baseboard beneath the windows. "No, but it sounds pretty cool. I was just listening to something I don't have to think about. My brain hurts."

"Do you want some aspirin?"

"Just my brain hurts, not my head."

"I'm not sure I get the distinction."

"Much as I hate to admit it, Vi was right," Maureen said. "Once I got down the basics of what she and Mr. Clancy told me about painting, I've been able to do some thinking. Let's just say I've got a lot to figure out."

"Getting anywhere?"

"Well, I'll never drink whiskey again. Or go with strangers, or talk to men in general."

Jenna sat cross-legged on the floor not far from her sister. "The first two ideas sound pretty reasonable, but the last one's pushing it."

"Every time I talk to a guy, I end up toast." She dipped the very tip of her brush in the paint, sluiced off a few drops extra, then continued her work. "So when did you decide you wanted to be a chef?"

"The summer Mom hired the chef from Provence. Remember the food?"

"Not really."

Jenna had known that Maureen wouldn't. She'd been four at the time. Jenna had been twelve and learned the wonders of fresh herbs. Even earlier than that, she'd mastered the art of evasion, a skill her sister apparently also possessed.

"Let's get back to the guys and toast thing," she prodded.

"What's to get back to?" Maureen replied ever so casually.

There was no way to do this but leap in. "I saw the picture . . . you know, you, the fish . . ."

"Yeah, and Sam and the slut." She angled the brush just above the upper edge of the baseboard, drawing a perfect bead of jonquil yellow. "You, the fish and Sam and the slut," she recited. "It sounds like a demented cousin to a Dr. Seuss book."

Jenna laughed. "It does."

Maureen feathered the paint upward. "So while my life sucks, there's still humor to be found."

"Could be worse," Jenna said. "So Sam was the guy you fell in love with?"

"Sadly, yes. I met him at a party. I thought—" The paintbrush jogged, and a rivulet of yellow wandered down the white baseboard. She shook her head and stopped painting. "I thought that we had something real, but I was wrong," she said while using the corner of a rag to wipe away her mistake. "And the problem with being wrong with someone as well-known as Sam, it's like international news."

"I'm sorry," Jenna said.

Maureen flashed a hint of a smile. "I probably could have avoided the fish scene."

"What happened?"

"I was supposed to meet him at his hotel suite. I

went upstairs, and no Sam. I waited for a while, then gave up. On the way out I decided to check the bar, to see if he was just delayed. Instead I found him with Chloe. She's playing his sister in a movie he's been filming outside Paris."

"Maybe it was business."

"That's what I thought until I got close enough to see exactly where she had her hand. And I don't think they were discussing testicular cancer."

"Oh."

Maureen laughed. "God, you're blushing."

Jenna shrugged, but still wished she could be as open and relaxed about sex as Maureen and Vi.

"It's a little different hearing this stuff from you," she said to her sister. "The last time we talked, you loved horses and thought boys were disgusting."

"Now you've got me longing for the good old days, when I had a brain." Maureen picked up her paintbrush and readied to work again.

Jenna checked her watch. "Dev will be here in a few minutes to kidnap me, but don't forget to take a break and go down to the kitchen for the family meal at four."

"Only if I have the first coat on the walls," Maureen said. "Mr. Clancy says with the plaster, it will take at least two. Once I get the corners and edges covered, I'm going to roll the rest."

Jenna smiled at the spark of enthusiasm in her sister's voice. Perhaps she wasn't totally allergic to work. "You know, you really are pretty good at this painting thing. Ever consider making a career of it?"

"Shut up."

Now, there was the Maureen she was getting to know and love.

Dev had accomplished a number of Olympian tasks in his day, but luring Jenna off Muir House's property for even a few hours ranked among his proudest. Once she was seated in the Porsche, he'd taken the back route past Dingle. Now he wound his way up the road he'd traversed with Maureen last night. He could think of no place he'd be more likely to get Jenna alone. And here, away from all else, he might persuade her to let down her defenses. Here, he might learn why she had closed herself away from him this morning.

Jenna glanced at her watch. "I should have never agreed to stay with you until nightfall. The sun stays up too late this time of year. How about six o'clock?"

If the road weren't so bloody non-road-like, he'd have reached for her watch and flung it out the car window.

"Anyone who eats before eight doesn't deserve your company," he said instead.

They rounded a curve, clinging tight to the edge of a precipitous drop into nothing more than rock with its deceptively soft-looking blanket of green.

"You drove this in the dark?" she asked, sounding more angry than awed. "You must be crazy. It's even narrower than the Connor Pass."

So much for being lauded as a hero. "It's one sheep wide," he teased, "which is exactly what it needs to be."

"Sheep don't travel at fifty miles an hour."

"Neither would I, if I didn't have a deadline."

Jenna laughed. "Yes, you would."

Dev smiled. For not having known him long, she already knew him well indeed.

As he drove, Dev kept an eye out for a stopping point. Every so often there was a semicircular apron to the road, no doubt installed by souls exhausted by the choice of hitting head-on or backing down the mountainside. Dev saw one just ahead on his right. This particular pull-off was well situated, with no cliff to tumble from and no sheep claiming squatters' rights. He made it his.

"So we're stopping here?" Her expression was dubious at best.

He engaged the parking brake. "Our troubles can't follow us this high, now can they?"

The beginnings of a smile played at the corners of her mouth. "At least they'll have to work harder to do it."

She opened her door and climbed out, and Dev did the same. The air had been thick and still at Muir House, with a humidity that put him in mind of the tropical "calm before the storm" he'd experienced while doing site work in Costa Rica. Here, closer to the sky, a breeze managed to stir, and the air was much cooler.

"It's beautiful, isn't it?" she asked, gazing toward the Castlegregory side of the peninsula.

Dev agreed, though more to please her than out of honesty. And it did rank higher in his Wonders of the World than Jenna's favorite graveyard.

"That's Tralee Bay out there," she said, pointing. "You can see just a bit of the Magharees."

"The what?"

"Those islands—they're also called the seven hogs."

"Only in Ireland. I suppose there's a story to go with them."

"I'm sure there is, but I don't know it. I think it's my duty as a resident to make up a lie for you. And of course it has to involve someone of legend like Finn MacCumhaill."

Dev laughed. "Spin away. I'd never know the difference." He stood behind her and settled his hands on her shoulders. She leaned against him, and again he marveled at their fit. All those years wasted with tall women . . . He slid his arms down to loop around her waist, and she rested her arms on his.

"I'll be gone for a few days," he said. "Three at the most."

"Is it business?" she asked cautiously.

"Yes." Dev half-hoped that curiosity would get the best of her and she'd ask for more. He didn't like navigating his way through chat as though it were a minefield.

But Jenna only nodded. "Okay."

"I also want to apologize for what happened this morning," he said. She tensed, and he held her more firmly. "I have no excuse for being in your bed, except that it was where I wanted to be. I love the feel of you, Jenna . . . and your scent and voice, and even, God help me, the way you take my ego down to size. It's only natural that I want to make love to you, but I won't assume again that you're feeling the same way."

"Dev, I—"

He kissed the top of her head, resting there a moment to savor the soft feel of her hair. "You owe me no apologies and no promises, and I'll do my best not to rush you, though I'm giving no guarantees on that," he added with a rueful smile meant for himself. "Just know that when you're ready to come to me, it's your pleasure that matters most." His would follow, he knew.

"Thank you," she murmured, her voice almost lost on the soft breeze.

He kissed the side of her neck and smiled at her sigh. Then he let her go.

"I've brought some food," he said as he walked to the boot of his car. "Nothing very grand, but I didn't want you going the night without eating."

Dev began hauling out his treasures. First, three blankets and a pillow filched from the beds he was renting from Muriel. Overkill, perhaps, but hard ground didn't please his sensualist inclinations.

For their picnic spot, he chose the far side of the car, where they would be shielded from curious eyes in the unusual event that someone else should decide to take this crumbling road. He spread the sturdy blue woolen blankets, one atop the other, on the earth. He added the pillow, amused by the way Jenna was scowling at it. Then he reached into the boot again and emerged with a bag that he handed to her. She carried it to the blankets, where he joined her after closing the boot.

"So what do we have?" she asked, raising an inquiring brow at his brown paper sack.

"This and that. I have some of Muriel's brown bread, shaved ham, and butter," he said. "She was quite concerned that I might have starved while out of her sight." He reached into the bag again. "A wedge of brie and some raspberries and strawberries from Spillane's Market. It was odd . . . old Spillane said something about Ballymuir needing no new religion, and that I didn't look the part of clergy in any case. Do you have an idea what that might have been about?"

"None," Jenna claimed, though Dev was certain that the flags of pink on her cheeks had nothing to do with the cool breeze.

Dev pulled out the two plates, glasses, and cutlery he'd borrowed from Muriel, then reached for the last of the sack's contents.

"And I have a French rosé," he finished, pulling out a bottle. "Bright and pretty, just like you."

The skeptical look she gave him made him wonder about the people in her life who had failed to praise her. All had been fools; he would shower her with words while they were together.

He arranged their picnic, berries surrounding the cheese on one plate, and bread, ham, and fresh farmhouse butter on the other. Jenna took over opening the wine and poured two glasses. He took the one she offered and sipped it. The taste was light, with a whisper of sweetness, and it smelled faintly of roses. Dev imagined tasting it on her skin—between her breasts and in the slight hollow low on her belly.

He looked at her, sitting cross-legged in her silky white shirt and worn blue jeans, holding her glass cradled between her palms. She was gazing into the wine as though she were a Gypsy reading tea leaves.

"Can I get you some food?" he offered, since it seemed a polite alternative to pouncing on her.

She sipped her rosé. "Not just yet." Her gaze zigged about. She took in the sky, the ground, and the mountains beyond, but not once him.

"What's bothering you?" he prompted as he reached for a slice of Muriel's brown bread and topped it with a bit of butter.

"I need to say something, and I'm really no good at this at all."

Dev bit the corner off the bread. He steeled himself for an announcement that she couldn't forget, couldn't trust.

"I've never been comfortable talking about sex," she said.

At least with his mouth full he could say nothing daft.

She took another quick drink of wine, as though for courage. "I, ah, want you to know that you weren't doing anything wrong this morning. It's just I have this problem. I don't seem to be able to reach . . . to reach orgasm."

Dev swallowed, his food stopping in the middle of his throat, leaden and suffocating. He grabbed for his wine and downed a good half of the glass.

Oblivious to his difficulties, she kept talking. "You see, everything goes pretty much like I think it should, but then the guy is moving too fast or too slow—or something. And then instead of feeling anything, I'm thinking about the bad fish my supplier tried to slip me or how the cost of Italian wine is skyrocketing."

"And that happened this morning?" He was, in a word, gobsmacked.

It wasn't as though he didn't suspect that a girlfriend had manufactured enthusiasm a time or two, but in Jenna's bed? She'd do just as well to snip his parts right off as tell him that.

"No, but I began to worry that it was going to."

"So you executed a preemptive strike?"

"I guess," she said, still not meeting his eyes.

"Ah." He wasn't sure where to go with this. Except for some dirty talk in bed, none of his prior girlfriends had been this frank. He found he rather missed the illusion of males being perpetually godlike.

While he was staggering around in his thoughts, Jenna had been moving with more intent. Dev looked up to see her slip free the last button on her blouse. She lay back and spread the sides open, and she wore no bra. "I want to feel your mouth on me, like you said this morning."

"Is this—is this some sort of sacrifice?"

"No, this is for me."

Had she but looked at the increasingly uncomfortable fit of his trousers, she'd have known that it felt to Dev as if it were very much for him, too. He'd never seen skin so white or nipples such a glorious dusky rose.

His hands trembled as he took the pillow and tucked it behind Jenna's head.

"Well?" she demanded.

He smiled in spite of the fact that he'd never felt more set up for failure. "Too slow?" he asked. "Before I touch you, have you any other rules you'd like to share?"

She shook her head. "Um, no?"

"Good, then, because I do my best work without

them." After moving their picnic just past the top edge of the blankets, he stretched out on his side next to her and propped his head on his left hand. His right hand, he let near her, and watched her hazel eyes seem to darken as he did.

"Have you ever done this before, let the wind and the sun touch you? I can see the sun hasn't been blessed very often, for you're beautifully pale," he said quite conversationally. "The moon, perhaps?"

"No." Her answer was thin and breathy.

"We must, then, someday."

He let his fingertip hover above one pert nipple, puckered and begging his caress. She drew in a deep breath, her breast rising with it. Dev smiled. She would know anticipation by the time he was done. God knew he was well acquainted.

He brushed his finger against her lower lip. "Open for me." She did, and he put the very tip of his index finger against her tongue. "Suckle it," he said, "as you would have me taste you."

His voice shook like a schoolboy's. Then again, he felt a callow schoolboy, too. Jenna's eyes had slipped shut, crescents of lashes dark against pale skin. Her cheeks drew slightly inward as her tongue swirled around his fingertip. Dev's heart slammed faster, then faster yet. He drew his hand away and touched one nipple, wetting it.

She shivered.

"Now the breeze feels cooler, doesn't it?"

Eyes still closed, she nodded her head. "More," she whispered.

Ah, but he had heard that "more" this morning, and hard on its heels had come a "stop."

"You're sure?" he asked. "I might not be moving too fast?"

"Now."

Dev knelt, then reached for a strawberry and one of the wineglasses. He dipped the berry into the rosé and brought it to her mouth. Her eyes opened as he brushed the pointed tip of the fruit against the ripest part of her lower lip. He imagined the strawberry's small seeds felt rough against her tender skin.

"Taste," he urged as a droplet of wine escaped the berry. She opened her mouth just a bit and touched the tip of her tongue to the fruit.

"Sweet," she murmured.

He dipped the berry into the wine again. Her lips parted as she waited for more, but Dev let the liquid kiss first the tip of one crested nipple and then the next.

Jenna gasped, her hands clutching the blanket. Dev dragged in a ragged breath. The erotic sight of the strawberry tip-to-tip against her flesh would have brought him to his knees, were he not already there.

"I'm going to taste you now," he said as he dropped the strawberry into the waiting glass, then set them both aside. Dev moved over her, closing his mouth on her nipple. He tasted wine and some hint of sweetness that he knew was simply Jenna, and he shook with need.

She held on to his shoulders as though he might be thinking of stopping. Not bloody likely. He pulled away long enough to look down at her, one nipple glistening wetter from his kiss, then decided to create the same beauty on the other side.

Dev smiled at the pleased shock in her eyes. He nipped and laved and drew just hard enough to work a surprised gasp from her.

He kissed the valley between her breasts and asked, "Any bits of advice?"

She urged him upward, then kissed him hard, her tongue taking his mouth. When she was done, she said, "Don't stop."

He couldn't recall ever hearing finer words. He rolled to one side and struggled out of his shirt, desperate to feel her breasts against his skin. When the shirt was shed, he crawled back atop her and pressed his weight into her, mimicking the act he craved. Pleasure pounded harder through his veins when she wrapped her legs around him and rocked against his erection.

Dev hadn't planned on taking her here. This was to have been a slow seduction . . . just enough to leave her hungering for him. He dropped kisses in a line across Jenna's collarbone, trying to pay a bit less attention to the incredible feel of her hands skating across the skin of his back, then dipping lower to grasp his buttocks. He hadn't planned, but he was thankful that he'd been wise enough to tuck a few condoms into his billfold.

"I want you," she said while her smart hands slipped between them. She fussed with the closure to her denims, but then tugged at his arms. "Help me."

There had been no plea to her voice, just a demand that made him want to smile.

"Patience," he counseled, aware of the irony that he was near to losing it himself.

Concerned at the growing chill in the air, Dev

moved beside her. He reached across to grasp the far corner of the top blanket and tug it toward them.

"Get under this," he said. She quickly scooted beneath the blanket. Once he'd resettled the pillow, he joined her in their makeshift bed. Dev opened the copper button at the top of her jeans. Jenna's breath hissed in as he slowly brought the zipper downward.

Instead of pulling her clothing down, he insinuated his fingertips beneath the bit of fabric covering her curls.

"You're silken here, too," he said.

She urged her hips upward against his hand. "Hurry."

He knew once he'd touched the hot wetness that awaited him, he would have to be quickly inside her, so instead of complying, he took his hand away.

Dev moved from beneath the blanket and covered Jenna again. Then he crawled to her feet and pulled off her brown leather clogs and the white socks beneath them. Her toenails were painted a whimsical tangerine orange. She was full of secrets, Jenna Fahey. He pulled at the cuffs of her pants, and from beneath the blanket, she helped him make short work of them. Then she wriggled out of her panties and tossed them to him before he could blink.

Dev removed his shoes, then unable to fight the temptation of feeling her, he slid back under the blanket. He kissed her mouth and her breasts and traced the line of her ribs, down to her waist, and then traveled to her hips. He settled his palm over her mound and allowed his fingers to curve inward, between her legs. Still he didn't delve past the damp curls protecting her. Her breath came fast, and a sheen of sweat broke over his skin as he held himself back.

"Shall I touch you now, Jenna?" he asked, amazed that he managed to keep his voice level.

At her sighed "yes," he did. She was as he knew she'd be—hot, wet, and perfect. But he hadn't anticipated the primal need that was seizing him. He closed his eyes and struggled for control as he began a rhythm with his fingers, being sure to touch her where he knew it would please her most. She was ready for him, and he was beyond ready for her.

When he could bear the waiting no more, Dev kissed her hard, then said, "Do you want me inside you?"

Jenna could think nothing more important than reaching the other side of this excitement Dev was drawing from her.

To his question, she answered a simple, "Now."

He sat up, and the wind pushed through his black hair like a lover's fingers. *Her* fingers, she thought, marveling that she'd be naked beneath a blanket on a hillside and have no concern other than how much longer she'd have to wait for Dev to fill her.

He glanced skyward and frowned. "Weather's moving in."

"It doesn't matter."

His smile was intimate, and made her tingle with pleasure.

"I'll keep us warm enough," he said.

In deference to the cool air, he undressed the rest of the way beneath the blanket, then set his clothes aside. She touched him where she could as he reached for his billfold and withdrew a small packet.

After he'd sheathed himself, she lay back and urged him over her. He was more than willing to comply, but her body seemed less than able to accept him. She hissed a breath between her teeth as he pushed forward. He stilled, and she rocked against him, wanting the wait over, the sting to become something finer.

"I'm okay," she said, and it was only a minor lie.

"Good, then." He flexed the rest of the way home.

Their gazes met and locked. Dev began to move within her, slowly at first, then with more intent. As he did, something both magical and frightening happened. She was no longer Jenna, always unto herself. She was more. And less. Control was slipping away.

"Just feel," Dev commanded.

She did, and at first it was wonderful. But after a time it became too much. Her breath jittered from her. Her hair was damp with perspiration and clinging to her forehead. Something really, really good was about to happen, and it scared the hell out of her.

Focus.

No, relax.

Think.

Don't.

She heard the sound of a sheep bleating somewhere. The blanket began to feel scratchy beneath her, and she wondered what Aidan was doing in the kitchen back at Muir House.

Suddenly Dev withdrew, leaving her empty. He levered his weight above her on strong arms. "Not thinking about how many eggs in a teaspoon of Beluga, are you?"

"No." *Not exactly.*

Embarrassed that he'd caught her wandering, she wrapped her legs around him, tugged at his shoulders. He wouldn't give. Instead, he moved downward, taking the blanket with him, until he was between her thighs. Jenna trembled, but it wasn't with the chill wind bringing dark clouds.

He kissed her, his tongue hot and gently teasing against slick flesh she was sure could bear no more sensation. Except it could. Jenna rocked her hips against his mouth, unable to stop her cry of pleasure.

He drew back and looked up at her. "The price of butter lettuce, then?"

"No," she said, reluctantly smiling at the suggestion.

Another long caress, his tongue seeking—and finding—exactly the spot that made her world spin. Jenna tugged at his hair. "Dev, come back to me *now*."

He moved above her. "And here I was asking the same of you."

His breath was coming every bit as hard as hers, his chest rising and falling with the effort. He entered her easily this time, and then he kissed her. Jenna tasted him, tasted her, and was overwhelmed. Dev's rhythm was fast and sure. She could feel her muscles tighten as she neared that long-denied brink again.

"Come with me," he commanded, then reached one hand down beneath her bottom, changing the angle of her hips. "Don't be afraid."

It was the greatest leap of faith he could have demanded, but Jenna held tight and let the fear fly. Her act of courage was soon rewarded. A sensation so marvelous that she could feel nothing else took hold

of her. Out she spun, her cry marrying with his, drifting from the mountainside to a place she'd never
been, then slowly, wonderfully bringing her back
until she was Jenna, likely never unto herself again.

After they were recovered enough to do more
than cling together, Dev slid an arm beneath her
waist and moved so they lay face-to-face. She draped
her left leg over his lean thigh and sighed her contentment.

"Tonight, I'll be leaving for three days. I'm sorry I
have to go, but I've had this scheduled for a while,"
he said.

She felt open enough to ask, "Where?"

"Counties Roscommon and Kilkenny," he murmured, sifting a tangled lock of her hair between his
fingers. "And when I come back, I want a night with
you. Not a few stolen hours, but the full night and a
warm bed."

Jenna was about to say yes when cold, fat drops of
rain began to pelt them.

Muttering something dark about a damn country
never free from rain, Dev rolled her beneath him to
shield her from the sky. Jenna kissed away his dis-
gruntled expression, then laughed as the rain fell
harder.

There was something to be said for warm beds.

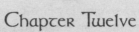

Chapter Twelve

There is no hearth like one's own.
—IRISH PROVERB

On the nightstand lay a mound of wadded-up tissue, Jenna's monument to impending death by common cold. Not once in the time she'd been at Muir House had she admitted to illness, let alone been brought down by something as trifling as this. It wasn't the lunacy three days ago with Dev on the mountainside, she told herself. It wasn't some curse visited on her by humorless gods who felt that she'd been flying too close to the sun. It was a simple, coincidental cold.

"You're truly sick," Vi marveled from her perch at the foot of the bed. "Thought you were too busy for that sort of nonsense."

"Don't gloat," Jenna said, pulling the covers up to

her chin and glowering at her so-called best friend. "Since you insist on witnessing my misery, at least make yourself useful." She waved one hand in the direction of the bedroom door. "Go down to the kitchen and check on Aidan. He's giving a test run on the menu for tomorrow's photo shoot."

Vi sprawled her tall frame across the end of the bed, head propped on one hand, red hair rippling like a living thing. "Ah, *Irish Gourmet*, is it? Aidan can take care of himself. I'd much rather enjoy you in this humble state. Adds a touch of humanity."

"Humanity?" Jenna croaked, scooting up on her elbows to lean back against the headboard. "I've got no time to be human. If you won't watch over Aidan, how about getting me some drugs? Something chock full of codeine so I won't care if I'm sick."

Vi made a disapproving little sound. "Don't be a ninny. It's just a cold." She sat upright and rummaged through the enormous velvet bag that went everywhere with her. "I'll brew you up a little tea. Some horehound, peppermint, and sea kelp and you'll be right as rain."

"Not on your life, Kilbride. I want a real bottle of medicine."

Vi chuckled. "What do you think they use to make those miracle drugs?"

"Not pond scum, I'll bet," Jenna said, her stomach churning at the thought of swallowing one of Vi's "family cures."

"Then you'd best not read the list of ingredients on this too closely," Vi said, tossing a comfortingly commercial box in Jenna's direction. "I bought the 'chesty cough' mixture, you'll see. It won't do a thing for your cold, but I'm thinking that those chemicals could conspire to grow you a real chest."

Jenna pulled her loose-fitting flannel nightgown away from her collarbone and through the gap surveyed the relatively flat terrain below.

"Not even one of your concoctions could do that," she said, still looking down.

"Ah . . . Jenna," said a male voice.

Jenna quickly released the nightgown's neckline. She looked up to see Dev in the doorway, a tray in his hands. Her first impulse was to send him away. When he'd called to talk this morning—his sixth call in half as many days—she'd told him that she was sick and best left to suffer alone. She looked awful, with matted hair, sallow skin, and a red nose. And he, as always, looked wonderful. His black polo shirt fit to perfection, and his khakis didn't have a wrinkle anywhere.

"Aren't you going to ask him in?" Vi prompted as she scooted from the edge of the bed, lithe as any feline.

"I come bearing gifts," he wheedled. "Cooked it myself, too."

This, she could not resist, even if it meant relinquishing yet more of her dignity. Not that she had a great deal left after he'd caught her mid-geographical-survey.

"Okay, but I make no promises that I'm not contagious."

He grinned. "I'll risk it." Dev settled the bedtray on her lap, then said, "It's scrambled eggs and toast. Yesterday on the phone, you told me that was your favorite comfort food."

His calls had been a welcome distraction from her ills. They'd talked for hours about everything except what he might be doing in his travels. Jenna needed to leave that door closed.

"Try the eggs," he urged.

Eggs? There *was* a sodden brownish-yellow mass that could conceivably be eggs. The charred black squares might once have been toast. . . .

Vi stood on the opposite side of the bed, peering down at the plate. "He cooked it himself, Jen. Be gracious and have a bite."

Where was the royal food taster when one was needed? Jenna lifted the fork, snagged a tiny bit of the egg mixture, and brought it to her mouth. After she'd finished chewing she said, "Interesting texture."

Vi smothered a laugh.

Dev shifted from one foot to another like a schoolboy called on the carpet by his principal. "Aidan told me that I had the heat too high, so I turned it down, but everything was sticking in one godawful mess. And then I forgot all about the toast."

"As they say, it's the thought that counts," Vi offered while Jenna chiseled a corner off the blackened bread. Thankful that her taste buds were deadened by illness, she chewed a bite and washed it down with a sip of orange juice.

"Fresh squeezed," Dev said.

"Perfect," Jenna answered once the last of the seeds had settled in her stomach. "Couldn't have made it better myself."

"You're a poor liar," he said, softening the words with a smile.

"You've caught me on an off day." And tonight was to have been *their* night. Since that was a matter best discussed in Vi's absence, Jenna dug for a relatively neutral topic.

"Was Roscommon pretty? I've never been there," she said.

"It's lacking the appeal of Ballymuir," Dev replied.

The tension marking his face translated itself to Jenna. Her heart began to beat uncomfortably fast. Frowning, Dev picked up the tray and looked about the room for some other likely spot to put it down. Vi took it from him and set it just outside the door.

"You're home for while now?" Jenna asked.

"Other than a meeting in Killarney this afternoon, I'll be here."

From the window where she gazed out at the sea, Vi murmured, "Quite the traveler. One would think that the circle has nearly closed." She turned. "Jenna, has Maureen finished with the yellow room?"

Jenna smoothed the comforter over her lap. "I think so. Why?"

"Eventualities," she said. "One can never tell . . ."

"No, one can't," Jenna said. "But as I tell you every time you pull your clairvoyant act, a little detail might help, if at all possible."

She smiled. "Chesty cold medication I can give you, detail, I can't."

Dev watched Vi with an unsettling intensity. Her unwavering green eyes met his dark ones. Suddenly Jenna felt more spectator than participant. She didn't much like it.

"We can't outrun those eventualities, can we?" Vi said to Dev.

He shrugged and turned toward the door. "Perhaps not, but we can damn well try."

After he left the room, Vi shook herself and turned back to Jenna. "I'm going down to brew you some tea. Don't worry, you'll taste no nasty surprises, either," she briskly added on her way out, leaving Jenna to ponder precisely what "eventualities" might await her.

Dev walked Muir House's rocky shore, picking his way between clumps of seaweed. It was treacherous footing, but no worse than finding himself cornered by the eerily perceptive Vi Kilbride.

"Eventualities," he said. He wondered whether the word painted the same dark hues in Vi's mind as it did in his. He doubted it.

Dev bent down and picked up a chunk of rock worn smooth by water and time. It was chill, slick with algae, but had a nice, solid heft to it. He flung it as far into the tide as he could, a dissatisfying act. The rock was gone from sight, but eventually it would return, pushed willing or not back to shore.

Eventualities.

He'd crossed an ocean, built a life, become a man to envy. But now he was back in Ireland, and those specters of old failures haunted him. He bent to find another rock, another missile to fling against the inevitable.

"What are you looking for?"

Dev turned to see Vi standing on the verge where sea grass met rock. From his vantage point on the lower shore, she seemed to tower impossibly tall. With her wild hair snaking about in the strong wind, she lacked only the spear and shield of a warrior.

"Are you speaking on a metaphorical plane?"

She laughed, the sound as bold as her appearance. "No, I was speaking of you down here sorting among the rocks. It's raining, or did you not notice?"

He shrugged. "A soft day, not much more than a mist."

She easily navigated the round boulders to stand by him. "If I didn't know the type of man you are, I'd say you're sounding quite at home."

"It's an easy place to be comfortable." Only after he'd spoken the words did their truth strike him. Much as he wanted to continue to dislike Ballymuir, he couldn't. It had given him too much—perhaps more than he'd bargained for.

"But the sea is greedy," Vi said, picking a white feather from where it spun in the foam and tucking it into her skirt's pocket, "and the land not willing to part with its secrets. If you watch and listen with care, though, a balance can be struck. But you'd not be understanding that, would you?"

He understood more than he cared to. "Do you ever talk your way straight at anything?"

"I'd say that would be best answered by those doing the listening. You're hearing what you're able to." She bent down and picked up a stone. "Ah now, this is a special one, worth the wet and your dark mood." She held it out in the flat of her hand to show it to him. "A hole worn through the middle, and yet whole." She slipped it, too, into her pocket. "It will be on one of my silks before the day's end."

He envied her and the sure knowledge with which she conducted her life. Until recently, he, too, had been that way.

"Do you care for her?" she asked.

The quicksilver shift in conversation took Dev aback until he realized that was where she'd been headed all along. "I want to see Jenna grow, to make her see the possibilities outside her rules."

"I didn't ask what you wished for her. I asked you a very simple question, do you care for her? Will you treat her heart with care?"

Jenna had not offered him her heart. In their hours on the phone, she steered their conversations away from anything that touched her too closely. He should have considered this the perfect situation: passion without obligation. But already it had begun to rankle.

"She's very beautiful," he offered up as a non-answer to Vi.

"Any fool can see that. I'm asking if you'll be sure not to harm her when you run."

He flinched at the last word.

"The truth can be an uncomfortable thing," Vi said. "Until you come to own it." She pushed her hair back behind her shoulders and shook out the folds of her long purple skirt. "It's back to the studio for me. Jenna's sleeping, but if you can, pop in before you leave. Check the yellow room, too." She paused for a moment, gazing at the water.

"Eventualities," he said.

Vi nodded, then climbed the ridge to gaze down on him. "Stay for a while. I'd think you must be tired."

Just past teatime Katherine Connolly Gilvane pulled into the car park adjacent to Muir House and switched off her Mercedes. The house was looking brilliant, years younger than the last time she had stopped by. She gave a moue of a smile at her reflection in the car's rearview mirror. If only the same could be said for her. Still, she was doing well enough for a woman of a certain age. Dev had seen that she was well-coddled, if not often visited.

Katherine slipped from the car and tucked her keys into her pocketbook. Whatever niggling bits of guilt she felt for coming to Ballymuir unannounced drifted away on the sea wind. How could one ever feel truly repentant for coming home?

The gardens leading to the house put her in mind of Provence. She wondered if this Jenna Fahey that her friends who'd dined here had told her about had spent much time there. Low, scruffy lavender bordered the pathway. Katherine imagined it would smell quite lovely here, once summer's warmth had done its job.

She climbed the front steps and peeked in the side window, much as she had done on her last visit. This time, though, there was no need to rub away dirt in order to mourn sad neglect. Muir House thrived.

Katherine pushed the buzzer. After a few moments a young woman came bounding down the stairs and to the door. She pulled it open, and Katherine did what she could to mask her surprise. Even with a smear of blue paint down one side of her face, and a shirt and denims wearing both that blue and a lovely shade of yellow, the girl was arrestingly beautiful. And very young.

"You must be Jenna Fahey."

The girl laughed. "Not this lifetime. I'm Jenna's sister, Maureen. Jenna's upstairs, sleeping off a cold."

"I'm Katherine Gilvane," she said, relief warming her voice. "A friend heard that you're beginning to take overnight guests. I had left a message this morning regarding a room."

The girl's smile grew. She would break a man's heart one day, this one.

"Gilvane," young Maureen repeated as she ushered Katherine inside. "Are you by any chance Dev Gilvane's mother?"

"I am."

And she'd been greatly relieved that Devlin's arrogant little sports car wasn't in the car park. She'd already made a call to a girlfriend in the village and knew that Dev had great interest in both Muir House and its mistress. Katherine would bide her time, though. In dealing with her son, a position of strength was always preferred, but seldom gained.

"This is too bizarre," the girl said, and Katherine was sure it wasn't directed at her. "I finished what must be your room yesterday."

"*Before* I called?"

She smiled. "Yes, and I'm pretty proud of what I've done. Would you like me to show it to you?"

Katherine nodded.

Maureen Fahey took the stairs two at a time, talking over her shoulder. "I named your room the Áine Suite. I found a book in the house library and it said that Áine was—"

"The last true Irishwoman to live in this house," Katherine finished.

That gave the slip of a girl pause. "How did you know that?"

"I grew up in Ballymuir."

"Oh."

Maureen started down the west hallway, then paused at a massive oaken door. "I think you're going to like this."

Katherine stepped inside and smiled. The walls were a glorious yellow, muted just enough not to jar one's senses, and the bed was hung with rich ivory velvet.

"Yellow. My very favorite," she said.

"I know."

"Really, now?"

"This is Ballymuir," the girl said with a shrug that was purely American.

"That it is," said Katherine, smiling at the thought.

"So, should I have someone send up your bags?"

"I believe you should."

Maureen Fahey left, and Katherine walked to the bank of windows and pulled wide the drapes. This was indeed Ballymuir, and she planned to never leave again.

That evening Dev sat in his car outside O'Keefe's B&B, trying to work up a veneer of politeness. The real thing had deserted him hours before. Never had he spent so many hours accomplishing so little.

Days ago, after meeting Muir House's eccentric owner in London, a backup to the site had suddenly seemed prudent. After making love to Jenna, though, the need had become both urgent and personal. His conscience seemed to have made a tardy yet dramatic entrance. If he was to share her bed, he needed to make a good-faith effort to save her home.

Outside the Roscommon town of Boyle, he'd looked at the former vacation house of an American movie star. He'd hoped it would be the sort of place that Trevor, his boss, would go wild for. Unfortunately, it lacked the drama of Jenna's home.

After that, Kilkenny had been dismal and Killarney this afternoon, little better. The land agent there had either misunderstood his requirements or thought him a fool. Either way, he had returned empty-handed and with a head still ringing with Vi Kilbride's talk of caring and eventualities.

Dev knew that he couldn't sit in his car forever. As he made his way toward his rooms, he paused at the statue of Molly Malone.

"I'll give you this, Molly. You're the quiet type—no comments sharp enough to bleed a man to death. We need to sit you down for a chat with Ms. Kilbride."

Molly's smile was vacuous, not proof against a woman like Vi.

"Or then again, perhaps we'll keep you away from her," he said with a sorry shake of his head. "She'd have you in her coven in no time, cockles, mussels, and all."

Dev was three steps short of the door when Muriel flung it open. "You've had some packages arrive," she said. "I've left them in the breakfast room for you. And a tea tray, too, since you look near to starving."

"Thank you," he said, taking in her altered appearance. She seemed to have cast off the frilly apron in exchange for some fun. "You're looking fit for a night in Dublin, Mrs. O'Keefe."

She smoothed her hands over her dress, matronly in cut but bold red in color. "Well, thank you for that, and there's a reason, too. I'd make you a full dinner, boiled veg and all, but himself's about to take me dancing in Tralee. You'll be by yourself, if you don't mind very much."

"I'll be fine." Alone was all he was suited for, just now. He followed Muriel into the breakfast room and shot the courier's boxes a scowl.

"Grand, then," she said. She was about to push through the door into the kitchen, but turned back and gave him a smile that was impossible not to return. "Oh, and should you be interested—and I think you might, the way you're frowning—there's a bottle of Paddy's in the cupboard next to the stove. For medicinal purposes, of course."

"Of course," he echoed with a mock gravity to match hers.

She nodded firmly, then left. Moments later Dev heard the diesel engine of the O'Keefes' sedan make its coffee-grinder start, then chug away from the house. He was, as he'd wished, alone. Instead of going upstairs and sitting in a darkened room, as suited his black mood, he bypassed the tea, rooted out the Paddy's, and poured himself two fingers.

Back in the breakfast room, Dev pulled out a chair and sat in front of his waiting parcels. He knew that among them were a land survey of Muir House and also those of the adjacent property where he'd secured a purchase option. He hadn't the stomach to deal with them, wanting only the burn of Paddy's.

He'd had just a sip when his replacement cell phone—courtesy of Lorcan O'Connor in the village—burbled its song. Dev slipped it off his belt, set it on the table, and willed himself to ignore it. He couldn't, though.

Resigned to his fate as a slave to technology, he answered. "Hello?"

"Dev?"

He smiled when he heard Margaret's voice. "Are you still in the office? You should get that husband of yours to take you dancing."

His assistant seemed to be shocked into silence. Dev didn't consider that he'd said anything untoward. He'd be dancing with Jenna, if he could. Under the stars on Muir House's terrace, perhaps, or better yet, at the foot of her bed.

"Arthur dance?" Margaret finally said. "Quite unlikely. I'm at home, though. Did the package I sent you arrive?"

He took a look at the table and developed a yen for his whiskey. "I've a number of them. Haven't quite opened them yet."

"Find the one from me and open it. You've a problem, Dev."

No mollycoddling from his Margaret today, either. He sifted through the stack and came up with one bearing sender information from Harwood International.

"Got it," he said. "I'm going to put you down a minute while I open it."

Inside the flat cardboard package was one sheet of paper. Dev looked at it and felt his gut knot. It was an organizational chart of the Resorts Division—*his* division. The bottom rows of the pyramid were the same as always, stacked heavily with toilers. The middle rows showed some alarming gaps, and the top two were enough to have him driving to Shannon and waiting for the next flight out.

He picked up the phone. "Where did you find this?"

"In the rubbish bin by the copy machine."

He knew better than to ask what she'd been doing nosing about in copy discards. Margaret's many skills had held him in good stead.

"No talk in the office?" he asked.

"Trevor's secretary was home ill today."

And Trevor was nowhere on the chart. Dev remained in his block and Sid Barrett was crushing him from above.

"Is Barrett still there?"

"He's back to New York this evening, thank God," Margaret replied. "But do remember, this could be nothing, Dev."

He set down the paper. "I know."

Perhaps it was no more than Barrett committing the paper equivalent of masturbation. There were no markings on the page that indicated this was part of a longer or more detailed document, and none that gave its origin. It could well be nothing. Or perhaps he was about to be royally screwed.

Dev allowed himself a sip of Paddy's, then said, "Let me know if Trevor's secretary is better tomorrow."

"I will."

"And thank you, Margaret. I don't know what I'd do without you." This time the words were deadly earnest.

"Tomorrow will be better," she assured.

After they said their goodbyes, Dev turned off his cell phone before closing it. He wanted no more business intrusions, and knew that Jenna was likely working when she should be resting. He would not be hearing from her, and knew better than to call.

Dev sat in Muriel O'Keefe's fussy breakfast room and wished that he was no longer alone. He longed for the scent of Jenna's fire, and more than that, he longed for her taste and touch.

Did he love her?

He had known her only a matter of weeks, surely too brief a time to be making a reasoned decision. Ah, but the question was a valid one, resonant with a truth having nothing to do with days, hours, or minutes.

Did he love her?

With Muriel's saints and virgins looking down on him, he couldn't swear that he did not.

Chapter Thirteen

Bit by bit the castles are built.
—Irish Proverb

Just past six in the morning Jenna stood in front of the bathroom mirror. Her skin had picked up a healthy pink tone, and her eyes once again looked more hazel than bloodshot. All told, not bad for a woman who'd considered herself one tissue away from death the day before. Vi's tea seemed to have worked, though Jenna had no intention of puffing her friend's ego by telling her so.

The crew from *Irish Gourmet* was due at eleven. The shoot was to be of appetizers in the style of Muir House, and the article to focus on Jenna's philosophy of fostering local farmers and suppliers to produce the very best for the restaurant. Other than assuring herself that the food's presentation was perfect, her most pressing goal for the day was to slink out of camera's range. If given a choice between having her picture taken and eating worms, she'd go with the worms—especially if given sufficient garlic in which to sauté them.

Because she knew that she was unlikely to be offered the option, Jenna took the extraordinary step of applying not only mascara, but also eye pencil, blusher, and lipstick. She glanced again at her face in the mirror, a passing regard that grew to be something more, something startling. She looked like someone with a marvelous secret, a woman desired by a man whom she desired in return. She was not glamorous, but she was Jenna. And today at least, she was glad for it.

Resolving to be merciful and not to shake Maureen awake until at least nine, Jenna cleaned her bedroom, then made her way downstairs for a quick breakfast. She greeted and fed Harold, safe in his lobster world for one, then foraged for her own food.

As she pulled open the door to the walk-in fridge, she paused, hearing a noise not part of the house's usual repertoire. The sound, like two pieces of china tapping against each other, was gone so quickly that Jenna decided she'd imagined it. She stepped in, pulled a box of strawberries and a container of homemade vanilla yogurt, then emerged.

Jenna yelped. In front of her stood a stranger. The strawberries hit the floor and the yogurt was nearly a victim, too.

"I'm sorry if I've startled you," said the woman, bending to pick up a berry that had rolled to rest at the tip of one ivory leather pump. "I'm Katherine

Gilvane. Your sister said she'd mention to you that I had arrived."

Jenna closed the fridge, struggling to simultaneously calm jumping nerves and recall whether Reenie had been in her room last night. It was a possibility; Jenna had slept the sleep of the exhausted as her cold left. She did have some hazy memory of Maureen saying something about the yellow room and one-hundred-twenty euros a night. The sum, at least, had to have been based in viral delusion.

"Well, welcome to Muir House, Mrs. . . ." She trailed off, realizing she'd lost her guest's name along with the berries. "I'm sorry, what did you say your name was?"

"Gilvane, Katherine Gilvane. I understand you know my son, Devlin."

Feeling as though her world had been tossed in the air and was still tumbling wildly, Jenna very carefully set the yogurt on the counter. Then she looked at the woman in front of her. Beneath the lapels of her ivory suit jacket lay a scarf—jonquil yellow, of course. Mrs. Gilvane had eyes as dark as her son's, and an elegant black bob threaded with silver. The similarities were unmistakable. And for someone who claimed that she was no psychic, Vi Kilbride was piling up some unsettling statistics.

Mrs. Gilvane extended her hand. Out of an instinctive sort of politeness, Jenna managed to shake it.

"Yes, I know Dev," she replied. Whatever cordial tidbit she should have added after that affirmation escaped her. "How long will you be staying with us, Mrs. Gilvane?"

"Call me Kath—" She shook her head. "No, call me Kate. I'm hoping to have left Katherine in Dublin, where she can dust my furniture and sit placidly through Altar Guild meetings."

Bending to pick up the box of strawberries, Jenna smiled at the whimsical thought. She'd seen flashes of the same humor in Dev.

"And as for how long I'm staying, I'm really not quite sure," Mrs. Gilvane said. "I have friends I'm needing to visit, and I've had a thought of perhaps finding a place of my own in Ballymuir."

Like mother, like son, again.

"Your berries are tumbling," Kate said in an amused voice. "Now hand me the box and go sit. I've clearly given you a fright."

Jenna obeyed, walking the few steps to the oak table in the war room. She sat, and mindless of the makeup she'd so carefully applied, leaned her elbows on the table and her face in her hands. She could hear Kate Gilvane in the next room, humming to herself as she turned on the taps to the sink, no doubt washing the fallen strawberries.

There was no arguing that she could use a paying guest. Several, even. In any bidding war, the Fahey deep pockets were negligible when compared to the wealth of a company like Harwood. And there was a certain irony in earning money from the mother of one of Harwood's executives. Except Jenna had thoughts of getting the executive in question quite naked, and having his mother under the same roof might be an impediment. But really, debate was pointless. Kate Gilvane was here, and from the sounds of it, as comfortable in Jenna's kitchen as she.

Kate appeared in the doorway with a bowl of freshly washed berries in her hands. "Bring in the yogurt," she directed Jenna, "and we'll have ourselves a fine breakfast and a chat."

Jenna rose. "Coffee or tea?" she asked before she lost total control of the meal.

"Tea sounds grand."

Jenna escaped and started a kettle. "Would you like some eggs or an omlette? I can do better than just berries," she called as she assembled a tea tray.

"Another morning, perhaps," Katherine answered. "I'm not often awake this early. I was too excited to sleep."

Jenna returned to the table with yogurt, a paring knife, spoons, and two parfait glasses.

"You're very pretty," her guest commented.

Instead of making one of her standard self-denigrating comments, Jenna said simply, "Thank you." She sliced berries into the base of each glass, spooned in some yogurt, then layered in more of the same.

"You might want some sugar," she warned Kate. "I make my own vanilla yogurt, and it's not as sweet as store-bought."

"I'm sure it will be perfect. That is, after all, your reputation. I've read reviews of your cooking."

"The water should be ready," Jenna said. She slipped from her chair, tarried in the kitchen as long as she thought she could, then finally returned. If Kate had found the delay surprising, she didn't show it. They ate in silence.

"And how did you come to be at Muir House?"

Kate eventually asked as she poured out more tea for Jenna and herself.

Because Kate was both Dev's mother and an unknown quantity, Jenna gave the generic "for strangers" answer. "I was visiting the area. When I passed the gates on the main road, I had to see more."

"Simple enough," Kate said, but the arch of her brows implied she wasn't quite buying in. "And now you're the house's mistress. You've done well by it."

"Whatever I've given Muir House, it's given me back double."

"Then I'd be saying your arrival here is fate."

"Or insanity on my part."

Kate chuckled. "There is that."

Jenna sipped a bit more of her tea, thinking she might well develop a taste for the drink, which she'd selected this morning out of sheer politeness to her guest. It had seemed the Irish thing to do. "Did Maureen give you any keys last night?"

"Two," Kate said.

"Well, I'll assume one is for the front door. On nights that the restaurant is open, it's unlocked until the last guest leaves, sometimes as late as midnight. After that, you'll need the key."

Kate laughed. "I won't be closing the pubs. At least, I don't think I will. Is Rory O'Connor behind the family bar?"

Jenna nodded. "Rory and his daughter, most nights."

"Then I'll be needing that key, after all," Kate replied in a pleased voice. "Rory will keep me talking until the sun rises."

Knowing Rory, Jenna didn't doubt it. "I'm assuming the other key you were given is to your bedroom," she said. "You should know that it's the same skeleton key that opens every other bedroom door. I'll call a locksmith and see if I can persuade him here, but until then, I hope you won't mind too much."

Kate settled her teacup in its saucer. "I'm sure I'll be fine, and it's no surprise. The security of this house came from the strength of its owners, not locks."

"You know Muir House?"

"I've loved her all my life," Kate said simply. She rose. "I don't mean to seem lacking in chat, but it's time for me to be gone if I'm to see all I want to today."

"Dev should be stopping by this afternoon," Jenna offered, thinking Kate would want to know.

"Oh, I'll find him when I'm ready," she replied, then smiled. "I expect he'll be quite surprised, though not nearly as much as I was to learn that he was nosing about in Ballymuir." She looked ready to leave, but paused and said, "Tea and porridge with a bit of fruit should be fine for the morning, and I promise I'll not bother you until seven-thirty at the earliest."

"Would you like a dinner reservation for this evening?"

"Thank you, but it's O'Connor's for me. A toasted cheese sandwich and some of Rory's horrible jokes, I'm thinking."

"I'll see you in the morning, then," she said to Kate. "Have a wonderful day."

Kate Gilvane's answering smile was every bit as full of the devil as her son's. "Of course I will. I'm in Ballymuir."

Yes, Kate Gilvane was in Ballymuir, and an hour and a half later, Jenna was still in the kitchen wrestling with both a moral dilemma and a consommé. The dilemma was proving every bit as complex as the raft she had assembled to flavor and clarify the smoked quail consommé for her *Irish Gourmet* visitors. As Jenna carefully submerged a small ladle to vent the center of the egg white, ground meat, herb, and onion concoction that floated on the surface of the deep pot, she sought an equally tidy solution to the arrival of Dev's mother.

It wasn't as though Kate had ordered Jenna not to mention her arrival, but her words of finding Dev later had carried an implicit message to stay silent. Much as Jenna's conscience balked, muttering that she owed Dev a word of warning, the rest of her mind was intent on getting him into her bed to find out whether they could recapture the breathtaking wildness they'd shared on the hillside . . . and doing it before he caught sight of his mother.

She suspected that Dev, quick man that he was, would overlook the ethical issue in favor of the end result.

"You look like you swallowed the Mona Lisa." Maureen lounged in the doorway.

"Jesus, Reenie, how long have you been there?"

"Long enough to see you grow that smile, and I have to say, it's hot."

Jenna set aside the ladle and checked out her sister. Reenie seemed to have dug back into the worn-out hippie wardrobe that had been retired since her luggage had arrived. "Well thanks, though I have to say that you look, um . . ."

"Ready to paint. I want to get the blue room finished, which means putting a second coat on the ceiling, plus a decorative effect above the wainscoting."

She sounded as though she'd been watching too many decorators' shows on the BBC. "What sort of decorative effect?"

"Ragging. It seemed to suit me," she replied.

Jenna smiled. It might be time to give her sister credit for having a little self-knowledge.

"Anyway," Maureen said, "I'm in a hurry. I've got a feeling that your friend the witch is about to go two-for-two."

Jenna kept her voice mild as she said, "Which reminds me, you might have mentioned last night that our guest is Dev's mother."

"I was saving the news until you weren't delirious. All the better to get a reaction out of you."

Jenna winced. "Kate beat you to it."

"Nice lady, isn't she? Maybe even mother-in-law material." Maureen batted her eyelashes.

"Funny."

"I wasn't joking—too much."

Just to occupy her hands, Jenna again picked up the ladle and fussed with the raft's inner edge. The scent of the stock Aidan had made yesterday wafted up to her, smoky and delicious.

Reenie moved next to her and peeked into the pot. "I don't want to tell you what that stuff floating on top looks like."

Jenna smiled. "The raft's there to add flavor and help clarify. It looks a little foul, but trust me, once it's done its job and been discarded, this will taste like heaven."

She received a dubious "uh-huh" in response.

"I've got kind of an off-the-wall question for you," Jenna said after a moment.

"My favorite kind."

She drew in a deep breath and blurted one of the worries that had been nibbling at her composure. "Do you think it's possible for a woman to deal with sex as a no-strings act?"

Reenie laughed. "You're blushing! I figured that when a female reached a certain age, she'd at least get to outgrow some of that stuff."

"I'm not even thirty!"

Her sister was unrepentant. "Yeah, but you've got a few years on me."

"Look, I'm serious."

Reenie frowned. "This doesn't have to do with Dev Gilvane, does it?"

Jenna nodded.

Her sister hesitated a moment, toying with the black bandanna she'd tied to cover the top of her head. "Okay, sex with no strings . . . Lots of women do it well. Professionals, for example. But you? You're a Fahey, which means I figure that you're a lot like me. Everything you do smacks you right in the soul. You could no more have sex without strings than you could boil that senile lobster living in your kitchen."

Jenna gave up on harassing her consommé. "That wasn't the answer I was looking for."

"So, either you're working up the nerve to jump Dev's bones, or you've already done it."

She ignored the color still climbing her cheeks. "The deed's been done."

"And now you have regrets?"

"Not regrets, exactly. It's more like I'm trying to figure out how to disconnect my heart so I can do it again."

"Disconnect?"

"We've got some . . . issues. If I talk about it, I'm just going to get more uptight, and—"

"Maybe you should take a clue from that old shoe commercial. You know, just do it."

"The problem is, I don't 'just do' *anything*. If I had been you in that restaurant, Sam Olivera would have been safe from the fish. I would have been deciding how to best throw them while he slipped away."

Maureen chuckled. "Maybe if the gods took the two of us and mixed us into one person, we'd come out a fairly normal female."

"Well, it's too late for that."

"And I'm going to be too late for Vi the all-knowing if I don't get painting." Maureen headed back toward the kitchen doorway, then lingered. "For what it's worth, I like Dev—a lot. When he rescued me the other night, he was nice. And after he had me home, it was over. He hasn't mentioned my dumb move once. Stupid as it sounds, I think he's really a noble kind of guy."

These were the words Jenna needed to ease her tension. "I hope you're right," she murmured.

"It's not like I'm trying to push you back into bed, but I could think of worse ideas."

"Like throwing fish?" Jenna suggested.

"No, like *not* sleeping with him again." And with that easy piece of encouragement, Reenie was gone.

The *Irish Gourmet* crew didn't arrive at eleven, as arranged. Though Jenna's nerves were pulling tighter and the burn in her stomach began making itself known, she wasn't fully alarmed. Part of the charm of Muir House was getting lost on the country roads that led to it. And when the magazine people finally arrived, they would see undeniable magic.

In the dining room the round table beneath the Waterford chandelier was topped with an intricate handmade lace runner, aged to a golden hue. It was Vi's contribution to the day. The lace was, she'd said when she'd flitted in and out at around nine-thirty, a piece much loved by her nan. Even though her grandmother was no longer on Earth, Vi said that Nan was most proud to know that her work would be in a magazine.

In another family touch, antique silver serving pieces shone under the chandelier's lights.

"Thanks, Mom," Jenna murmured as she realigned the oyster forks. Last summer the silver had arrived instead of her mother—the one time Sheila Fahey had come close to violating her policy of benign neglect by scheduling a visit. Sheila's change of plans had been the table's gain.

In a kiss of color, a lush and rambling arrangement of fuchsia, yellow flag, and roses—all local flowers—sat beneath the chandelier. When presented with the florist's delivery, Jenna had assumed that the magazine had arranged for it. Then she'd pulled back the paper protecting the blossoms and discovered a note from Brendan Mulqueen—one word written in angular blue script: *Comhghairdeas*, the Irish for "congratulations."

Jenna was touched. She knew that Brendan, like many of her regular patrons, had mixed emotions about her burgeoning success. He was pleased for her, but would much rather keep Muir House, and all of Ballymuir, a well-guarded secret.

Kitchen matters were less serene than those in the dining room. When the oysters arrived from Caherciveen—across the bay—Jenna had requested that Saul, her help in the kitchen this morning, rinse and scrub them until they were picture perfect. She might have overmanaged the process; now, if she entered his range of vision, he developed a twitch. Seeing the wisdom in not enraging a man with access to knives, she had left him alone with the prawns and scallops.

Careful not to make eye contact with Saul, Jenna skirted to the back of the kitchen. The pheasant consommé had been carefully ladled from the hole in the center of the raft and put into another pot. The liquid was a gorgeous deep amber in color. All else was at the ready, too. Tiny goat-cheese cakes were breaded and biding their time in the walk-in before browning. The baby greens and raspberry coulis to finish the cakes' presentation were set and could go no further before the crew arrived.

Noon passed and the clock crept toward one. Jenna actually remembered to refresh her makeup. After that, a call to *Irish Gourmet*'s offices yielded only the fact that Tracie Butler, who would be writing the article, was indeed somewhere in Kerry. The slow burn in Jenna's stomach intensified.

In need of comfort, she called Dev's cell phone, but found a mail message instead of the man. Much as she enjoyed the low and musical timber of his voice, she needed more. Much more. Since they'd missed their evening together, he'd said nothing specific about when he might next be by.

Jenna was lingering near the front entry when finally the bell rang. She knew it wasn't Dev; he was far too bold to ask permission to enter. She opened the door to Tracie Butler, who looked to be about her age, but with far greater experience in reeling out excuses. By the time Tracie had finished, Jenna still wasn't sure whether a flat tire, a cousin who lived nearby, or a farmer crossing his sheep to a high field had caused the delay. And honestly, she didn't care. She wanted the shoot over and Dev there.

With Tracie was a wiry and balding photographer, whom she introduced as Reggie. After less than ten minutes in his presence, Jenna was developing a twitch to rival Saul's. Reggie trailed after her in the kitchen, the autodrive on his camera whining as he fired away. He was too close for comfort yet just far enough off that she couldn't claim he was a hazard.

When she put a dollop of sour cream atop a thin slice of potato, Reggie snapped. She touched a pan, Reggie snapped. She inhaled, Reggie snapped.

Come now, Dev was Jenna's constant unspoken plea.

"Soon you won't be noticing Reggie at all," Tracie promised.

She'd have better luck disregarding a six-hundred-pound canary perched on her shoulder.

Aidan, who had arrived and begun to set up his station for the evening's menu, watched the insanity with a smirk that demanded retribution.

Jenna's smile was sweet when she asked, "Reggie, have you met my second-in-command, Aidan Lynch?"

While Aidan muttered something in Irish that Jenna was thankful she couldn't understand, the photographer turned to him and nearly gasped. "You . . . you've stark and glorious features."

Clearly not enamored with his admirer, Aidan scowled.

"We need you in a shot. Off-center with the contrast of your white jacket against—"

The photographer hesitated as Aidan smiled, dipping his fingertips into the dish of blood oranges he was neatly sectioning.

"And?" Aidan prompted as he ran one hand across the front of his jacket, leaving deep crimson stains.

Reggie looked as though he'd been deflated. "I don't suppose you'd be having a fresh jacket?"

"I don't suppose I would." Matter closed, Aidan returned to his oranges.

As she finished off dishes, Tracie peppered her with questions, Reggie got in her face, and Maureen joined the group. Glad for the photographer to have a target other than herself, Jenna made the introductions. As she'd hoped, Reggie was again awed.

"You outshine the Rose of Tralee," he said to Maureen.

"Which is?" Maureen muttered to Jenna as they carried finished appetizers to the dining room.

"Beauty queen," she whispered back. "Big contest every year."

"Lame, but I'm a sucker for praise."

"The two most beautiful sisters in Ballymuir," Reggie proclaimed as they set out the dishes. "This must be captured." Then he frowned at Maureen's paint-splattered appearance. "I'll be needing you to . . ." He finished the statement with a dictatorial wave of his hand in the direction of her raggedy clothing.

Maureen smiled. "Give me five minutes and I'm yours."

While Reenie changed, Tracie coaxed Jenna through a recitation of her credentials, from the Cordon Bleu training to the renowned four-star Provençal chef with whom she'd done her first *nestage*, or apprenticeship, to the opening of Muir House. Facts Jenna knew as well as her own name were coming out stilted, nervous. If Muir House was about local charm, it was suffering a drought.

Maureen returned to the dining room. She'd swapped her painting attire for a form-fitting black cocktail dress with an asymmetric neckline.

"No fish in any of the pictures," she directed Reggie.

Jenna laughed, and the photographer gave it a befuddled, "Sorry?"

"Inside joke," Maureen said. "Where do you want me?"

"Here, by the table, but you'll have to be sitting," he replied. "We don't want you towering over our star, now do we?"

He turned and pointed at Jenna. "Bring your glorious self this way and we'll be done in no time."

Jenna sent up one last mental plea of *Now, dammit, Dev.*

And because he was not only smart, but a man of consummate timing, Dev Gilvane ambled into the dining room.

Chapter Fourteen

If it's good, it's high time.
— Irish Proverb

Jenna's heart soared, and that was well before Dev came to stand in front of her. He was dressed for business, dark, lean, and lethally handsome.

"You're feeling better," he said, the words more assertion than question. Smiling, he tipped up her chin and leaned down until his mouth met hers. The kiss was too brief for Jenna, but not so short that Reggie didn't catch it with his camera.

Dev glanced over at him. "You won't be using that one," he directed.

Knowing the voice of authority, the photographer quickly agreed and focused his attention on Maureen, who had decided to open a bottle of champagne.

Dev drew Jenna away to a corner. "I've missed you," he said, toying with the collar to her jacket. "When they're gone, I'm taking you up to your bedroom and I'm finding what you have on beneath this."

"Nothing at all," she promised.

A jolt of pleased shock crossed his features, thrilling her. Finally she relaxed. Finally the interview flowed. And finally, an hour later, Tracie and Reggie were gone.

"Now," Dev said, snagging what was left of the champagne from its chiller.

This was the moment she'd been hungering for, yet now that it was here, Jenna felt so thoroughly unprepared. Her sister's "just do it" advice warred with worry that she'd be unable to strike the emotional balance needed to survive such intimacy.

"I'll meet you in my room in just a minute," she replied, then left to tell Aidan that she'd be unavailable for a few hours.

Maureen, who had ferried the food back to the kitchen, was nibbling at the greens surrounding the goat-cheese cakes. She stopped long enough to give a singsong chant of "Jenna's got a *boy*friend."

Aidan let loose some of his rare laughter. "That being the case, if you have any sense about you, make it the night. We'll thrive fine enough without you."

As she climbed the sweeping staircase to the room where Dev waited, Jenna wondered just how well she was going to thrive upstairs.

A martyr had entered the room. Dev bit back a sigh. He should have known better to leave Jenna alone with her thoughts for even a bloody second.

"Champagne?" he offered, pouring the drink into a slender crystal flute before she could answer.

She took the glass from him, held it in a white-knuckled grip, then drank. Her expression was as blank as if she were sipping water instead of bubbling, vintage French wine.

"Jenna, what's the matter?"

"What if I mess up? What if I can't . . ."

She hadn't hesitated in voicing her concern, and for that he was grateful. He took the glass from her and set it on the dresser. "After the other day I'd say we have no problem. But if we do, then we try again. And again. And again until we both find pleasure."

He took her hand and led her to the windows. Light flooded in, and her hair shone with its incredible chestnut hues.

"Jenna, there's no wrong or right way, here. There's just us."

"Okay," she said, clearly hesitant. "I know I'm a lot better. Still, maybe if you're worried about cold germs?"

"I'm immune," he teased.

But his heart was falling victim to the worry on her face. He'd never met a woman more compelled to be perfect in all she did.

"This is supposed to be a messy, joyous thing. No one's died. There's no one downstairs keening in the parlor," he said, bringing out to play all the Irish he usually tried to subdue in his speech.

At least he had eked the beginnings of a smile from her.

"So what would make you happy?" he asked, giving her the one thing that he knew pleased her: control.

She smoothed her hands down his suit's lapels. "I want the businessman gone."

"Done," he said, taking off his jacket, then pulling loose his tie.

Because she was Jenna, his perfectly tidy Jenna, she took them, opened her wardrobe, pulled down a hanger, and put the businessman away. She returned and walked a circle around him.

"Still not enough," she said when she was before him again. Her frown was tempered by the light dancing in her hazel eyes, making them greener than he recalled ever seeing before.

She began undoing his belt, and what had been a waking arousal grew impossibly hard. Content to have merely unlatched the belt's buckle, she moved on to the buttons of his shirt. Dev allowed the breath he'd been holding to ease from his body. He held out each wrist as she unbuttoned his cuffs and willed his heart to beat more slowly as she tugged the shirt from beneath his trousers, finishing the last few buttons. When she slipped it from him, she was satisfied to set it atop her dresser instead of giving it a hanger.

She circled him again, this time stopping to run her hands down his back. His muscles jumped beneath her touch.

"You must work out," she said from behind him.

"Back home . . . in London," he managed to say. In giving her control, it appeared that he was losing his.

"Beautiful," she said, then he felt the damp heat of her mouth on his skin—just below his left shoulder blade. "I didn't get to look at you nearly enough the other day." She wrapped her arms around him from

behind, working her fingertips beneath the waist-
band of his trousers. He drew in a sharp breath.

"It seems warm in here," she murmured, dipping
her fingers even lower.

Dev closed his eyes and prayed she'd stop this
game and wrap her hand about the part of him needing it most.

"Hot, even," she said in a nearly conversational
tone. "I think I'd like a breeze."

Jenna slid her hands free. He couldn't recall the
last time he'd felt such crashing disappointment. She
walked the few steps to the windows and opened
one a bit. As she moved to the other, she looked over
her shoulder and said to him, "Your shoes and socks
will have to go."

Dev sat on the edge of the bed and complied. Taking orders was new to him; he wasn't entirely sure he
liked it. Except this was Jenna, and her happiness
here, today, and on this bed soon, God willing, was
paramount.

Shoes and socks discarded, he waited for her next
directive. He also wondered if she knew that she'd
set her fate. She had only to command, but until she
did . . .

"Why don't you come back over here?" she said.

Dev smiled. "Of course." When he again stood before her, he said, "And now?"

She tapped a finger against her chin, affecting in-
decision. Dev knew better.

"I *think* I want the rest of your clothes gone, too,"
she announced.

"You're sure?"

She hesitated, then nodded. "Yes."

His hands went for his belt, but she stayed him. "I want to do it."

She was killing him by slow pleasure, and what a fine way it was to go.

Jenna had gotten Dev Gilvane naked. Wonderfully, gloriously naked and hers to touch as she would.

He wasn't in the least bashful about standing there nude for her pleasure, and he shouldn't be. Bathed in the golden sunlight, he was beautiful. No other word suited. She circled him again, letting her palm follow the curve of his tight buttocks, then up his back. Around to the front again, where the view was . . . well, largely impressive and maybe a little daunting. She was a small woman and he was in no way small.

She brushed her fingers against the dark hair on his pectorals, then followed the thin line of it down toward his navel. Oh, he wanted her. She was tempted to touch that thick shaft, to enjoy the feel of him hot in her hand, but she wasn't ready to speed to failure. She'd rather dance around the end moment and savor the present.

"Would you like some champagne now?" she asked as though she hadn't just been looking at the most intimate part of him. As though her hand still didn't hover there as she spoke.

His dark eyebrows rose. "You're trying to drive me mad, aren't you?"

Dev walked to the dresser, lifted her champagne glass, and downed the swallow or so she'd left in it.

"Would you like some more?" Jenna offered, gesturing to the bottle on the nightstand. She had to admit that she liked entertaining a naked man while still she remained fully clothed. It was a fitting reverse of all those paintings of naked Renaissance women dining al fresco.

Dev firmly set the glass back on the dresser. "What I'd like is for you to lose those clothes so I could see you, Jenna, but this about *your* pleasure. Would you like me to see you?"

The voice of temptation, she thought, luring her to a forbidden place.

"Yes," she said.

She toed out of her clogs, then bent down and awkwardly removed her socks. She stood and began to shed her clothing. He walked one circle around her, as she'd done to him. Jenna felt her skin grow even hotter under his regard. Silent, he watched every button go, every snap. The only sounds in the room were that of the songbirds outside and of her heart pounding, which she was sure Dev could hear.

She moved close to him, very close so maybe he wouldn't notice that she wasn't as beautiful as he.

"Who'd have known?" he said.

A vein throbbed at the side of his throat, and Jenna was mesmerized by the sight. "Known what?"

"That you truly look like polished ivory all over. I'd convinced myself that I'd dreamed it about you." He shook his head as though bemused. "So very perfect."

"Perfect? Obviously you're not talking about the size of my breasts."

He stepped back and looked at her, which made Jenna immediately regret the comment she'd let fly. Still, she didn't try to cover herself. God knew she'd offered him this part of the view before.

"But I am talking about your breasts, too. They're perfect," he said, then smiled. "And with your height, you'd want to be carrying around great melons?"

"A couple of grapefruit would have been nice."

He laughed, and the awkward moment passed.

"I'd like you to kiss me," she said.

"Where?"

"Here." She touched her index and middle fingers to her lips. "And here," she added in a stroke of boldness, cupping her breasts. "I really liked that the other day."

One side of his mouth quirked, as though he might be holding back a smile. "Right, then."

He kissed her, taking time to send his tongue to venture. A whisper of the tangy taste of champagne he'd drunk lingered, but more than that he tasted hot and potent, addictively so. Then he bent and kissed her breasts with a slow and languorous intent. Not once, though, did he touch her, except with his mouth.

Dev stepped back. "Like that?"

If she couldn't see the obvious effect she was having on his body, she might have felt stung by the casual, almost teasing, tone of his voice.

"That was very nice, but do you think you could touch me?"

"I'm sure I could. Anyplace in particular?"

"Where—where you kissed," she said. "And kiss me again, too."

He complied, taking his time with each taste, each caress. As much as she wanted to touch him in return, she didn't. The anticipation was translating into a sort of excitement she'd never felt before. She was weak with it, but somehow strong, as well.

"I want you to touch me here, too." Her voice had come out no more than a tight whisper, but Dev had gotten the message. His eyes grew darker, hungrier as he watched her brush her fingers over the curly hair at the vee of her thighs. She was so sensitized that even her own brief touch had jolted her.

He copied her caress exactly, a brief tease and no more. Still, Jenna's knees started to give, and she had to hold on to him.

"More," she said.

"More, how?" he asked, his smile hot, knowing, the devil's own. "Show me."

She was burning a fiery red and didn't care. Jenna slid her fingertips to touch herself.

"Like this," she said.

She tipped back her head and closed her eyes. It was too much, using all of her senses. She needed to focus on this . . . *now*. The low moan she heard could have been his or hers, she wasn't sure. All she knew was that he was replacing her touch with his, and that she was sure she was going to spin out of control.

Dev scooped her up in his arms. "No more," he said. "I've waited all I can."

She landed on her bed with a decided lack of gentleness. "Condom," she said once she'd settled out.

"Yes." He was looking about the room. "In my billfold."

His trousers lay in a heap on the floor, where she'd left them. She didn't think now was the time to hang them up.

"Try the nightstand," she said while scuttling the best she could under the covers. It was so much easier to dispel her fears when they were touching.

He pulled open the drawer and retrieved the box she'd bought in Tralee days earlier—just before her cold had set in.

"Well planned," he said.

She smiled but doubted it was much to look at. She still felt edgy. *"Mise en place*—everything in its place."

He opened the box, pulled out a packet, and smiled as if to say "and we know where this is going." Once he was sheathed, Dev folded back the covers.

"No hiding," he said. "And no secrets between us." He stretched out on the bed next to her, then rolled to his side.

She reached over and touched his face. The beginnings of his beard were rough under her fingertips. This sign of humanity, of being less than his usual polished self, sent a wave of tenderness through her.

"I want you now," she said. That much of herself she could safely give.

He kissed her. His touch found places it had been before and ventured to newer territory, too. Dev whispered phrases of praise and of awe. They weren't all that different from the few bits she'd heard from other lovers, except for one thing. They didn't ring empty and rote; he meant them.

After he'd settled between her thighs and eased his way inside her, he leaned his forehead against hers for an instant.

"There are no words for how right this feels," he murmured.

But there were words, all of which had to do with emotions Jenna struggled to hold in check. She wanted to simply *feel*.

He began to flex and withdraw in a careful rhythm, one so tender that she felt the start of tears in her eyes. He covered her mouth with his and used his tongue to caress her with slow thoroughness.

"I could do this forever," he said, keeping the same easy pace.

A lock of dark hair had fallen over his forehead. Jenna's hand trembled as she reached up to brush it back. Their gazes met and held, but it was too much for her.

"No, don't look away," he said. "Let me watch you."

"I can't."

"Then watch me. I'll close my eyes."

What he suggested was nearly voyeurism. The thought was exciting and oddly freeing.

"Okay," she whispered.

A half-smile curved his mouth as he let his eyes slip shut. He moved with more intent, and she wrapped her legs just above his hips.

"God in heaven," he moaned as their contact grew increasingly intimate. Still, he didn't open his eyes.

She braced one hand on the headboard as he drove harder into her, moving them both up the rumpled sheets. Color suffused his cheeks, and his breath came in sharp gasps. Harder yet, faster and more. Sweat covered them, and as their bodies rose and fell the sound of their joining grew louder, more primal. His teeth clenched as though he fought back words.

Jenna closed her eyes, struggling to hold in a cry that welled from deep inside her.

"Let go," Dev said, his voice tight, almost unrecognizable. "You did it before, and you can do it again."

Jenna's eyes flew open. He was watching her when he'd promised not to. She stared into brown eyes with flecks so dark that they were nearly black and she trembled.

She had lied to herself about their earlier lovemaking. Her response had come from her heart, as it was now. Still frightened, she was about to look away when Dev drew a sharp breath. Shock, surprise, ultimate pleasure, all were written on his face as he came. He groaned, but still held himself above her so she could watch.

Lost, she felt herself arch into him. She cried his name, then gave herself up to Dev Gilvane: body, heart, and soul.

Twilight had turned to darkness, and Dev was exhausted. They lay in Jenna's bed, the covers tangled at their feet and spilling onto the floor. He had never felt this replete . . . this complete. He should have known that Jenna would take to learning his body with the same intense enthusiasm she brought to her cooking.

How does it feel when I touch you here? and *Could we try it like this?* and *Do you like this, Dev, or maybe a little harder, do you think?*

Jesus, but he'd loved it all. Loved her joy, loved watching her inhibitions fade when she realized that pleasure was hers to own. He'd been right, those days before; he was well and truly captured by her.

He looked down at her, so small, so soft, and for once so at peace.

A phrase came to him, one his mother had called him when he was small. Or perhaps he'd heard it in a dream.

"Mo chroí," he murmured.

Jenna stirred, her body warm and damp against his. "What?"

"Mo chroí . . . my heart." He drew her even closer. "You have become my heart."

"Oh, Dev." She kissed the skin over that vulnerable heart of his, then settled to rest against once again. After a few minutes he felt wetness against his chest and sat up, bringing her with him.

"Are you crying?" he asked.

She nodded, then wiped beneath each eye with one knuckle. "But I'm not sad. I promise."

"What, then?"

"You were right, what you said the first time we made love tonight."

He chuckled. "Technically, that was this afternoon."

"True," she said, her voice sounding less shaky—a vast relief since he wasn't much good at dealing with weeping women.

"I was afraid to let go."

"Ah, I see."

She took his hand and settled hers against it, palm to palm, matching their fingers. "I guess you're the first person I trusted enough to lose my control near."

"And a fine sight it was. Given time, you might even prove to be a wee bit of a screamer."

She reached down and pinched the skin of his inner thigh. Though it was nothing more than a nip, he gave her the *ouch!* she seemed to be seeking.

"The control thing . . . it was just another hang-up from my stellar Fahey upbringing."

"Well, now you've got me curious."

She scooted up on the bed, then leaned over him and reached to the floor below to retrieve a fallen pillow. Once she'd settled it behind her head, she spoke. "My family is like most others, but even more so. What you see of us in public doesn't have much to do with the rest of our lives."

She took his hand again, and he wove his fingers between hers, giving her, he hoped, a link to his comfort.

"My father has problems."

Whose doesn't? he thought. His had been a bitter man, always feeling slighted. Dev knew he'd been blessed not to often live with him.

"Was it matters like the changeling comment?" he asked Jenna.

"More than that, really. My mother always calls him 'moody,' but there are a lot of clinical terms that fit better."

He lifted her hand to his mouth and kissed it—scant comfort, he feared.

"When I was little I never knew whether I was going to be his 'best little angel' or if he'd shout for the nanny to come haul me off. Sometimes he'd wake me at three in the morning to look at the stars or to play. Other times, he'd stay in his rooms for days.

"By the time I was a teenager, I couldn't stand it. When he was on a downswing, he'd bully me, pit me

against Maureen, embarrass me in front of the household staff. Never in front of outsiders, though. There,
we were the perfect family. Perfectly happy, perfectly
prominent, perfectly rich." She paused, then said, "I
left when I was seventeen, the day after my high
school graduation. No screaming, no scenes, I just
packed and moved to Paris while he and my mother
were traveling in Asia."

"Bleak," Dev said.

"But hardly tragic," she replied. "That's why I feel
so stupid about the way all the chaos made me turn
out."

"Which is?"

"Afraid. Afraid to let go. Afraid that if I do, I'll
find that I'm just like him."

God, he was so ill-equipped to deal with this sort
of thing. He'd been raised by teachers and house-
masters in the fine tradition of "stiff upper lip" and
"carry on." What could he do but gather her to him
and give her the truth?

"My heart," he said, "you are as straight and
steady as the day is long. You are *not* your father."

She laughed, and it was a thin sound. "Oh, I
know."

But did she believe? Dev wasn't so certain. And he
wasn't about to find out, either, for it seemed that
Jenna had moved on. She wriggled from his grasp
and knelt above him.

"Dev, do you think we could try making love
standing up?"

He was momentarily taken aback. "Had you
asked the first or second time, maybe even in the
shower before we napped, I'd have been pleased to

be of service," he said. "But now? You've left me boneless."

"Not totally," she said, running her fingertips over the part of him that was to be the death of the rest of his body. "And if we can't try it standing up, at least I get to be on top this time."

He sighed, the sound meant for her pleasure. "Bossy woman. If you insist."

"I do."

And she did with great abandon, until Dev was sure he'd been wrung dry.

"Are you thirsty?" he asked, once he found a wee reserve of strength—just enough to speak.

Jenna lay facedown, one arm dangling off the side of the bed. She nodded. "Hungry, too."

"Then one of us is going to have to venture out."

She turned her face toward him. "I elect you."

As he'd expected.

Keeping in mind that Miss Maureen might still be about, Dev crawled from the bed, stepped into his trousers, and zipped them. He also pulled on his shirt, but skipped the buttons.

The house was quiet, but not dark. It appeared that tonight, Maureen hadn't found someone to remind her to switch off the lights. Dev padded down to the kitchen, for the first time thinking how odd it must be to live in one's place of work. Then again, perhaps no odder than the way he carried his work with him everywhere, always processing in his mind.

The kitchen lights were also on. A woman stood, back to him, at the range burners. He blinked and was half tempted to rub his eyes like a child waking from a nightmare.

It had to be exhaustion coupled with bizarre, sub-liminal guilt over the last hours' total sexual aban-don, for he couldn't believe who he was seeing.

"*Mum?*"

She turned. "Devlin, whatever are you doing here?"

"*Me?* What the—what are *you* doing here?" he stammered as he fumbled with the buttons on his shirt.

Teakettle in hand, she came around to his side of the counter.

"It's grand you're dressing, but you're still bare-foot, which I'm sure violates health rules," she pointed out, delicate brows arched. "You'll note I have on slippers with my wrapper."

"You're having a fine time with this, aren't you?"

She smiled. "My best in quite a while."

"Grand," he muttered.

She gestured at the kettle. "Come join me."

He followed her to the small room just off the main kitchen, where she poured water into a waiting pot.

"Sit," she ordered, pointing at one of the chairs around the old wooden table.

Dev sat. This was his night for being bossed about.

"Don't run while I put back the kettle."

As if he could. She had returned before he'd even fully managed to accept that this was no bad dream.

"You're looking tired, Dev."

Sheer repetition had worked when he was a lad, so he asked again. "What are you doing here, Mum?"

She laughed. "I wasn't able to sleep, so I'm having *an cupán tae*, of course."

Jesus, had she swallowed an Irish lesson book?

He tried again. "I don't mean this very minute, but in general?"

She fussed with the cuff to her wrapper, a bright red silky affair that was lovely on her, but not at all fitting for a woman her age, Dev thought.

"I'm staying here while I look for a place of my own."

"A place of your own . . . in Ballymuir?" he blurted before logic could kick in and tell him she surely wasn't looking for one elsewhere.

"Yes, and is it so strange? I grew up here, after all."

"It's mad, Mum. You've a lovely home in Dun Laoghaire, with a view of the sea—"

"I knew you wouldn't understand," she said, her tone rich with that "poor, benighted mother who hasn't the love of her only child" tune.

"We'll discuss this later. Jenna's waiting."

"She'll wait a few minutes more. Shall I pour you a cup? It will still be a bit weak, but you're looking in need."

He was more in mind of a single malt from the Reserve shelf in the bar, but he nodded anyway.

"I need a change of pace, Dev."

"A change of pace? You're active with too many charities for me to track, your gardens are practically a tour spot, and you've more friends than—"

"And I'm lonely. I have club friends and charity-work friends, but if the clubs and charities were to disappear tomorrow, I'd see none of them again. And I can't say I'd be missing them overmuch, either."

"So you're going to pack it all up and move to a

place with more sheep than people?" he asked before having a sip of tea.

"It's hardly that." She poured out a cup for herself, then set the pot back on the tray. "I'll keep the house until I'm sure. But I was born here, and I believe I'd like to die here, too."

Dev's cup hit its saucer with a sharp clatter. "Is there something wrong, something you've been hiding?"

She shook her head and gave him a coy smile. "No, I'm fine, just thinking about the inevitable. Not that I'd have much difficulty in hiding something, what little I see you."

It was clear the parent from whom he'd inherited his killer instincts in business.

"So long as I shouldn't be planning a wake," he replied with equal cheerfulness.

"Should God be willing, and my son less aggravating, no, not quite yet."

"Fine, then. So you're in Ballymuir for a visit."

"An indefinite visit," she clarified.

"That being the case, perhaps you'd like me to find you a house of your own to let?" Out of sheer habit, he reached for his cell phone, then recalled his state of under-dress.

His mother laughed. "When morning comes, don't you think of badgering poor Margaret. I'm staying here."

Which could knock hell out of his sex life.

As his mother lectured him on something or another, Dev began to turn over possibilities. There had to be a stone tower he could stick Mum in, or perhaps arrange for the trip to the United States she'd been wanting. Anywhere but—

"Dev, are you listening to anything I've been saying?"

He gladly shook off thoughts of sex and mothers. "Sorry. Just pondering a business point."

"Which is the reason you're nearing forty and not yet married. You're all about business and nothing else."

Yes, she was having far too much fun, indeed. "I'm thirty-five, Mum."

"Close enough," she said. "So will you be marrying that Jenna girl upstairs or are you just after ruining her fine name?"

It was, Dev thought, a pity he was too old to cry, for at that moment he wanted nothing more than weep like a wee, wretched babe.

He was back with Mum again, God help him.

Chapter Fifteen

Never cross a woman who has been crossed in love.
—IRISH PROVERB

By early Thursday afternoon, a gray and sullen rain had settled over Muir House, driving in sheets off the bay. Sky, water, and building all held the same drab color. Even the vivid green of the hills was muted by a blanket of fog.

It would be an evening for comfort food in the restaurant, assuming much of anyone braved the elements. Kate Gilvane hadn't seemed slowed, though. She'd disappeared this morning before Jenna could even make her breakfast, leaving a note asking for an eight-thirty dinner reservation.

Just now Jenna, Aidan, and Saul were preparing ingredients for Jenna's delicate lamb tenderloin rendition of shepherd's pie. Throughout the kitchen tempers simmered—except Jenna's. She remained cheerful, almost to the point that she annoyed herself. Oh, she was sorry that Dev had left in a foul mood, and she supposed she could have handled him with more finesse last night when he'd come back to the room after finding his mother.

In retrospect, "The walls are thick, she'll never hear us," probably was a narrow response. But Dev had his share of blame to shoulder, too. If he hadn't just spent hours showing her the incredible responses his body could finesse from hers, she might have thought in terms other than sex.

Too late, though. He had put back on his black, tailored businessman's armor and left just after sunrise, saying that he had to go to Wexford and would call her as soon as he could. When he did, she'd coddle him and commiserate over the unfairness of mothers showing up unannounced. And if that didn't do the trick, she'd wait until he was back in her bedroom, then make him moan so loudly that he'd be thankful for those stone walls after all.

As she worked, Jenna hummed the tune of a folk song that Vi sometimes sang on *sessiun* night down at O'Connor's Pub and laughed at Aidan's good-natured darts about his employer's relentless happiness. Then a rain cloud came storming in the doorway. Maureen stood with her arms wrapped about her midsection and her blond hair tumbling wildly over her shoulders. She looked to be only a fraction of a second away from tears.

"You have to make him go away," she demanded.

"Who?" Jenna asked, feeling as though she'd been dropped into a foreign land with no map.

"Sam."

"Sam?" The name was familiar, but after last night, her brain was as fogged-in as the weather.

"Yes, Sam," Maureen repeated in a sibilant hiss. She waved one hand as though directing traffic through an intersection. "You know . . . me and Sam and the fish and the tramp."

Realization dawned. Jenna set aside her knife. "He's *here*?"

"At the front door and he says he won't leave."

"So you spoke to him?"

"Sort of." The sour cast to her sister's features made Jenna fairly certain that communication had been of the one-fingered variety.

"Just get rid of him," Maureen said.

Jenna walked to the sink. Buying time, she washed, then dried her hands.

"What if—" she began, but was cut off by the ringing of the kitchen phone.

"Don't answer it!" Maureen cried.

Giving a put-upon shake of his head, Aidan walked to the phone and picked up.

"What if I just come talk to him with you?" Jenna said, finishing her suggestion.

Maureen's eyes grew wide. "Are you crazy? I'm not going back there. This is your house. You throw him out."

"Mr. Olivera's personal assistant for Miss Maureen Fahey," Aidan announced in a voice dry enough to parch the River Shannon.

"Take the call, Maureen," Jenna said.

"No."

"Miss Fahey's gone round the bend, quite mad,

serious meds needed, if you get what I'm saying," Aidan said into the phone, then hung up.

Maureen glared at him. "I'm not crazy."

"Come to the door with me," Jenna wheedled. "Aren't you curious about what he wants?"

"No."

She changed tacks. "Fine, then just cower here in the kitchen."

Her sister squeezed herself into the small space between Harold's tank and the start of the counter. "Works for me."

Jenna gave up and left to face the actor alone. When she reached the front hall, she peeked out the glass to the side of the door. She wanted to get a quick first look at the guy who had her bold sister hiding next to a lobster.

Sam Olivera appeared somewhat older and harder in person than he had in the photographs she'd seen. Just now, he was wetter, too. Arrogance and anger were stamped on his handsome face as he paced the covered portico, ignoring the rain blowing horizontally. Sam appeared to be a man accustomed to getting his way.

Past Sam, down at the foot of the drive, sat a limousine with tinted windows, its windshield wipers battling the deluge. A smaller car waited behind the limo. She supposed she was lucky to be facing just one wet, angry actor.

"Hi, Sam. I'm Jenna Fahey," she said, opening the door. "Maureen has mentioned you."

"I'll bet she has," he said as he stepped inside. When he slicked his hand through his wet hair, Jenna hid a smile. She could almost hear Vi's appraisal. It would run something like "He's got a fair bit of Hollywood about him."

Just before closing the door, Jenna glanced outside. Two people had left the limo. One was an older woman, intently speaking into a cell phone. The other was a muscle-bound guy holding an umbrella over the female.

"Who are your friends?" Jenna asked.

Sam answered without looking back. "My assistant and my bodyguard. I'm assuming the babysitter from the production company hasn't gotten out of his car."

The assistant she had expected. The other two came as surprises. Jenna selected the one that most concerned her. "You have a bodyguard?"

"No threats, just groupie problems," he said with a shrug.

Hollywood all the way.

"Why don't you come into my office, where we can talk?" she suggested. Her best chance of getting this done politely was to do it away from an audience.

"Are you sure? I'm kind of wet."

Jenna smiled. "Trust me, there's no part of this house that can't stand up to rain."

He smiled in return, and her initial impression of hardness faded.

As she led him down the hallway, Sam asked, "Is Maureen hiding?"

"More or less."

"Figures. Your sister can be a real pain in the ass."

They stepped into the office, and Jenna closed the door behind them. "My sister seems to have been under a good deal of stress," she said, with gentle emphasis on the phrase "my sister." She didn't want him thinking that she might side with Hollywood over sisterhood.

Sam had the good sense to look contrite. "I'm sorry. And I hate sticking you in the middle of this. If you could just find Maureen . . ."

"I'd like to accommodate you, but I can't. She's not ready to talk."

Sam paced the room, glancing at the upholstered sofa and apparently deciding not to sit. "Look, I know Maureen. She doesn't cool down well. The longer I leave her alone, the more angry she'll get. It took me a few days to track her down, and I would have been here right after that, but it's a little complicated when I need to break from my schedule."

"Sam, you seem like a nice enough person, but Maureen's upset and I have to—"

He spoke, looking at the rug. "I love her."

Jenna's senses sharpened. "What?"

His gaze met hers, and she saw a mix of pain and humor. "I said that I love her. Really. Not that I want to. Or even that I feel real happy about it. But here's the bottom line—you need to tell Maureen that I'm not leaving until we have this fixed."

He was an actor, skilled and sufficiently famous to be tabloid fodder. If he chose, he could put out lines with the best of them, but Jenna sensed truth.

"Love. That changes things, doesn't it?" she said.

"If by change, you mean totally screw up my life, then yeah, love changes things."

She thought of Dev and the course her life had taken over the past weeks. Her heart lurched, and she struggled to maintain a calm demeanor.

Dev, love, and chaos.

She was in deep, deep trouble.

Immersed in his own troubles, Sam pushed back his sleeve and glanced at his watch. "I get the feeling I'm not going to make it back to the airport tonight. Or knowing your sister, maybe not even in the next week," he added with a quick smile. "Do you rent rooms?"

"In an involuntary sort of way, yes." The same way she had ended up with a room painted starlight blue.

"Maybe if I—" he began.

"Sam, I don't think this is a good idea. You need to give Maureen some space."

"She loves me. I know she does. She just needs me around to remember, so even if you don't rent me a room, believe me, I'm going to be here."

He had hurt Maureen. By bringing him into Muir House, Jenna might be risking the delicate beginnings of the relationship that she and Maureen had started. But if Sam truly loved Reenie, here was an opportunity for a Fahey sister to come first in a man's heart. She could think of no better gift to give the sister she'd overlooked for so long.

"I saw the pictures from Paris," Jenna said, testing.

An unwilling smile tugged at his mouth. "The fish, huh?"

She nodded.

"I deserved them."

"Really?"

"Okay, maybe not actually the fish. It's not like I asked Chloe to—" He stopped, seemed to consider his words, then spoke again. "It was just a case of bad timing with Maureen coming to the table when she did. But you know, I've done so many shitty things in my life that I've decided the fish were kind of a cosmic smack. And Maureen, that she had the guts to do what she did . . . Well, I guess I don't have to worry about her being intimidated by my fame."

He'd passed the first trial—barely.

"What's your favorite color?" she asked.

He looked at her as though she'd just sprouted an extra head. "Blue, I guess. Why?"

And the second. "No reason."

"So, about a room . . ."

"And your entourage?" she asked, tacitly giving consent. "Where do you plan to stow them?"

"Here?"

"Impossible." She was willing to deal with Sam— and to make Maureen do the same—but the Fahey sisters needed to keep control of the house. "The bodyguard can stay, and only because I'm not in the mood to scrape groupies off the house. I'll give you the names of some bed-and-breakfasts in the area. The others can find rooms there."

"I need my assistant."

Faced with this Dev-in-training, she wanted to smile. In a few more years he'd be using the assistant to hunt down cases of organic butter lettuce. "Then I'm afraid you'll all have to go."

"Don't do this."

"Look, if you're tough enough to deal with Maureen, I think you'll survive without a personal assistant hovering over you. In fact, you might even like it."

His expression bordered on incredulous, but he managed a grudging, "Okay."

"Fine," she said, and went to her desk to dig for extra keys. "That will be two hundred and fifty euros a night per person for the rooms and breakfasts."

"Two-fifty each? Do I look stupid? That's black-mail."

Reenie wasn't the only one who could drive a bar-gain.

"That's my rate for guys who mess with my sister's heart. Want to add the annoyance surcharge, too?"

"Thanks, but no."

"Good, then we'll stick with two-fifty per person. The restaurant's open for dinner Tuesday through Saturday. You'll need to let me know at breakfast whether you want a dinner reservation for that night."

She held out the keys to him. Just as he was about to take them, she closed them back within her grasp. "And Sam, remember that while you're under my roof, you follow my rules. I'm in charge here. One step out of line, the smallest bruise to my sister's heart, and you'll have reason to know just how skilled I am with a chef's knife."

Sam's laugh was a little bitter about the edges. "You Fahey girls don't mess around, do you?"

Smiling, Jenna tossed him the keys. "Damn straight we don't."

"About Maureen . . ."

"Why don't we just keep the rest of it between you and Maureen?" Now that she'd made the critical error of linking Dev and love in her mind, she had

enough to handle in the way of emotional entanglements.

"Fair enough," he said.

The greater question was whether Maureen would
see Jenna's meddling as "fair."

Stewing in sorrow, Maureen watched from a second-
floor hallway window as Sam walked down Muir
House's drive and out of her miserable, tragic life.

There. It was done. He was gone and she never
had to see him again. This scary sound, kind of a
muffled howl, worked its way up from her throat.
She turned away, unable to watch him leave, then
turned back because she was so pathetically weak
that she needed one last look.

Except he wasn't leaving. He was at the window
of the car behind the limo, and it looked as if he was
handing the occupant something. As he returned to
the limo, not even bothering to bend or shield himself from the rain, her howl turned into a sob.

She'd never gotten to see him naked or even to
touch him like Chloe-the-bitch. And even forgetting
that stuff, which was like forgetting she had ovaries,
she would never, ever again get to talk with him for
hours. Or slow dance in his suite, just the two of them.
Or go for a late-night walk, just the two of them—plus
Steve, Sam's bodyguard, who was really an okay guy,
even if he didn't talk much. If life was like Shake-
speare, she'd be jumping from the window about now.

The limo driver got out and opened Sam's door.
Tears ran down Maureen's face. She'd screwed up
and she had to pay the price.

"Goodbye," she whispered.

Sam was saying something to the driver, who then closed the door while Sam stayed in the rain.

Shit. She couldn't be seeing this right.

Maureen moved close enough to the window that her nose nearly touched the glass. Whether it was because he caught the motion or because he was one intuitive son of a bitch, Sam looked up. She froze as the cars pulled out of the driveway, leaving Sam Olivera behind.

Shielding his face from the rain with one hand, he used the other to wave at her. His smile was the classic "I've got you now, babe" grin she'd seen in every one of his movies.

Heart slamming, Maureen backed from the window, turned, and dragged in enough air to scream, *"Goddamn it, Jenna Fahey, what have you done?"*

More than rain surrounded Muir House tonight, Kate Gilvane thought as she made her way downstairs. Emotion was thick in the air, swirling down the old house's hallways, seizing even her, when she'd reached a point in life that she had nothing left to speed her blood this way.

Perhaps it was walking into the midst of a Fahey battle royal this afternoon, with the sisters having a high-volume go at each other right in the front hallway. Lacking in propriety, to be sure, but ever so entertaining.

Or perhaps it was that handsome young Sam who'd been walking about the house in search of Maureen, who refused to be found. The actor put her in mind of Dev—before he'd started hiding the best of himself beneath that businesslike attitude.

Whatever had summoned the spirits, it was high drama for all tonight. Kate smoothed her hands over the pale lilac linen dress she'd chosen to wear—her spit in the eye of Nature, who'd deprived her of a day fit for much hiking. She knew she looked fine in this dress, the color bringing out the silver threads in her hair and complimenting the slight cast of gold her skin naturally carried.

"I'm Kate Gilvane," she said to the hostess.

The girl smiled. "And I'm Niamh Leary. You used to watch over my da after school, while my grandmother was still to work."

"Hugh Leary," Kate mused.

"He told me last night that he was mad in love with you when he was ten," Niamh said while pulling a menu.

Kate had been fourteen and found him a wonderful nuisance, the way he'd mooned after her. "Do give him my best."

"I will. Would you be liking a seat in the library before you dine?"

"Where's the most to watch? I've a mind for a show tonight."

"Well, right now that would be the dining room," she replied.

"Then the dining room it is."

Soon settled at her table, Kate looked about. Young lovers—honeymooners, no doubt—sat nearby. Not far away was Sam, alone, though seated at a table for two. At the setting opposite him lay a rosebud. Romantic boy, though she expected that a more assertive approach would be required to lure Maureen from her room tonight.

Disappointed that there was not more to watch, Kate took a glance at the wine list, then smiled. It was grand news that Jenna carried her favorite Bordeaux by the glass. Kate summoned her waiter and ordered one. It appeared nearly like magic, and she settled in to read the menu. Only a few moments later, a soft American voice slipped into her thoughts.

"Do you mind if I join you for a few minutes?"

Kate smiled at Jenna Fahey, thinking that the girl grew prettier each time she looked at her. Even now, when dressed in the not especially alluring uniform of a chef, she sparkled.

"Please do," Kate said.

Jenna pulled out a chair. "I don't often get the chance to do this, but it's a slow night, which usually happens when it rains sideways." She hesitated, then asked, "Have you heard from Dev yet today?"

Kate knew that Jenna joining her had nothing to do with being a charming hostess, and all to do with delving for information. Somehow it made her like the girl all the more.

"My son's been silent, though I'm not surprised. I'm sure he sees my being here as meddling." She paused to consider the concept and then laughed. "I've not been much for nosing in his business, but I have to say the sport could grow on me."

The chef was doing her best to tame a smile. "So," she said, "did you have a good day?"

"I did, despite the wet. I picked up some more practical clothes in the village, then had a visit with the ogham stone."

"Tennac's ogham?"

Kate smiled at the delight in her hostess's voice. "Yes, it was once a favorite spot of mine."

"Mine, too. It's kind of a hopeful place, if you know what I mean."

Kate nodded because she did, indeed.

"Dev mentioned that he attended school in England. . . ."

Ah, the expedition had begun.

"He did. His father inherited a good bit of money from an aunt. I persuaded him that a child as bright as Devlin needed more advantages than we could offer." She sipped her wine, swallowing some of the pain she would not voice. "Dev was just turned eleven when we sent him away. He's done well for himself, degrees from Oxford and even one from Harvard, grand house, women . . ."

She paused just long enough to watch for Jenna's reaction and was pleased to see a flash of jealousy in the girl's eyes. "Yet sometimes I wonder if he wouldn't have grown up happier at home."

Niamh appeared with a bottle of still water and a tumbler of ice for her employer. Jenna thanked her, and Kate could tell that it was a sincere thanks, not the lip service one's superior frequently gives.

"You must have missed him very much," Jenna said after Niamh had left.

"He was my heart," she answered simply.

The chef looked down at the tablecloth, and Kate watched as color painted the girl's cheeks. It seemed that her son might have found *his* heart. The thought brought joy, but not without a nip of jealousy that Kate knew was wrong, but so natural.

Because both women were trained to be hostesses

and gloss over the dark, they picked up the chat with ease. Kate asked of Jenna's plans for Muir House and learned that she'd like to run hobbyists' cooking classes during the off-season. Nothing as advanced as the professional courses offered at Ballymaloe Cookery School over in Cork, but just for fun.

Pretty girl and a head for business, too. Muir House had always thrived best in the hands of a woman. It seemed that its time to rise had finally come again.

She was about to ask another question but stumbled over her tongue at the sound of deep laughter coming her way. The fine hairs on Kate's arms rose. *You're dreaming,* she told herself. *Over thirty-five years gone and you're still dreaming.* She took a nervous swallow of wine, then picked up the frayed ends of the conversation.

"Well thought out, using both your kitchen and your rooms," she said.

"That's the challenge of having chosen an out-of-the way location."

"Filling the slow months?"

Jenna chuckled. "Actually, staying in business at all. I've been lucky, though."

Kate glanced over Jenna's shoulder. The spirits had come to call, for a ghost stood in the doorway.

"Dear God," she whispered, again reaching for her wineglass. Her knuckles brushed its side, and it spilled across the table. "I'm so sorry!" she cried, her voice sounding loud, humiliatingly loud. She began to blot at the spill with her napkin.

Niamh, who had been in the company of the ghost, appeared and efficiently took care of the spill.

Kate stared at her hands, fingers knotted together and shaking. Finally, though, she surrendered to the inevitable.

"That man over there." She gestured at a table for two in an alcove lined by books. "Do you know him?"

Jenna glanced over and smiled. "That's Brendan Mulqueen. He's a regular."

Kate permitted herself to look directly at him. Their eyes met, his seeming blank of recognition. She should have been relieved, but anger overrode all else.

How could he forget?

She looked no more different than he. Half a lifetime gone, and still she could pick him from a crowd, know him by voice alone. Did she merit no less?

Nearly dizzy with rage, she stood. "I'm feeling a bit tired, I think. If you don't mind . . ."

Jenna rose, also. "Of course not. Would you like me to have Niamh bring a tray to your room? Some soup and bread, at least?"

Kate glanced over at Brendan. "No, you needn't put anyone out. Some sleep is what I'm wanting."

She was to the front stairway when the voice she'd never thought to hear again sounded from behind her. "You're as beautiful as the day I last saw you, Kate Connelly."

Bastard.

She swung around and gave him a cool, careful appraisal. "Well, Brendan, at least this time you have your trousers on and no girl hanging off you."

He tipped back his head and laughed, the robust, life-by-the-short-hairs sound she recalled.

"So are you still chiseling names on gravestones?" she asked, knowing far better.

"For friends and enemies, I do."

And am I either? she wanted to ask, but didn't, for then she'd have to decide what this man was to her. And though it was impossible, she'd much prefer that he remain a ghost.

"Come, Kate, don't run again. Join me for dinner."

She could refuse, but then she would merge back into that state of aloneness that had been eating her soul to nothing. Better angry and alive than polite and dead.

"I suppose I might, but if I'm to eat with you, spare me your lies, Brendan Mulqueen."

"Your luck is strong," he said. "I'm too damned old to lie anymore."

She rolled her eyes at this patent falsehood. And when Brendan laughed, Kate could do nothing but join in. Still, when he reached his hand for hers, she would not take it. She had stood well enough on her own.

"Let's eat," she said, "and you can tell me how you've passed a life."

He looked at her in surprise. "It's hardly over."

Was it not? Hers seemed to be frozen in ice most days.

As they walked back into the dining room, she saw that Jenna was still waiting, a concerned expression on her face.

Kate stopped. "Sorry for the bit of a scene."

Jenna smiled. "By Fahey standards, that was hardly a conversation, let alone a scene."

Kate laughed, recalling the afternoon. "Right you are. I'll be joining Brendan for dinner."

"Wonderful," she said, surprise well masked behind polite interest. "I'll have Niamh bring your wine over."

"Perhaps a full bottle of what Kate's drinking," Brendan said. "I suspect I'll be needing it."

The young chef's smile shone bright. "I see."

Kate and Brendan weren't long seated when he said, "So you're home to Ballymuir. I often wondered if you'd last in Dublin."

"Thirty-six years? I've lasted well enough," she replied before another thought occurred. "You knew I was in Dublin?"

He set his hands on the table and looked down at them. Kate looked, too. She could remember those hands when they were less scarred by work and age, when they'd touch her with a sureness that made her cry out. So many years gone . . .

"I've known many things," he said, "and seen your son now, too."

"And you, what are you doing here, Brendan? I'd heard you live in America." She'd also tracked his success through friends in the art world and lain awake at nights wondering what if she hadn't fled?

"I've kept a small summer house nearby."

She pointed out the obvious. "But it's not yet summer."

He laughed. "It was when I got here three years ago. I keep forgetting to leave."

The waiter arrived with their wine. Brendan ordered absently, requesting "the usual," whatever that might be. After he had, he looked across at her, seeming almost surprised. "I'm sorry, I should have waited. I mostly dine alone. What would you like to try, Kate? Jenna's a miracle in the kitchen. You'll not go wrong."

She ordered the lamb dish. If they substituted sawdust, tonight she'd not know.

"You never married," she said after the waiter had left.

He laughed. "Well, don't be thinking it was on your account."

Kate could feel her blush rising. "I didn't mean it that way."

He leaned back in his chair and took a sip of his wine. "I meant to marry, just never got around to it."

"Isn't that an Irishman? Gone past fifty and found no time to marry. What about that girl?"

"Nancy, you're meaning?"

"Yes, Nancy." Whom she'd last seen Brendan wearing.

He shook his head. "I've no idea. You well and truly caught me with her, though."

"Why?"

He didn't pretend to misunderstand. "You scared the holy shit out of me, Kate. I couldn't be the man you demanded I be."

"A simple 'we don't suit' would have sufficed."

He laughed. "Aye, it would have." He looked away for a moment, then back to her. "I didn't mean for you to see us, you know. She was an ego stroke, nothing more."

"You're not improving your situation, telling me this. I'd have found it more palatable were she your one grand love and you lived in bliss forever. But for a wee stroke of the ego or otherwise?"

He chuckled at her blunt assessment. "You'd married Gilvane by the time I knew myself for a fool and came looking for you." He paused. "Were you happy?"

"Sometimes" was all she said.

James Gilvane hadn't been an easy man to live with, and she'd become pregnant with Dev within weeks of marriage. James had known she'd married him on the rebound from someone, but he'd never asked about it, and she'd never volunteered the information. But her marriage had given her Dev, and though he had been acting the perfect snob these past several years, he was her son, and for him—and nothing else—she'd be thankful to James.

"He's gone now?" Brendan asked.

"Yes."

"I'm sorry."

This is it, Katie me girl.

She leaned forward, took her old lover's hand, and said, "Yes, but as you've so well reminded me, my life's not over, Brendan Mulqueen."

In fact, there was a grand possibility that it had just begun.

Dark nights, dark truths.

Dev sat alone in a hotel in Wexford, which a resort owner desperate to sell had told him was like the Miami of Ireland. Of course, he'd also been desperate enough to make the journey. Wexford and Miami, then? True enough, if a man didn't let trivialities like location, weather, and attitude cloud his vision.

At the end of the day it had taken a phone call from Sid Barrett, of all people, to make Dev recall what was important. Sid had insinuated that Dev was losing his edge, and as one friend to another, maybe he should think of a vacation. Or even a change in career. Bullshit, all.

But that word that Sid had used so deceitfully—*friend*—had given Dev pause. Did he even have friends? Like his mum, he had friends at work and friends at his club, yet had one of them even called him while he'd been in Ireland? Or had he thought to call them?

The answer was a very ugly no.

Dev pulled aside the curtain and looked out his window into the darkness. He longed to be in Ballymuir. Turning away, he checked his watch. It was nearly midnight, minutes ticking down in another meaningless day.

Tomorrow he would visit an estate being offered out Hook Head. He prayed to God that it would be the break he was seeking, but even if not, at least it was fractionally closer to Jenna and Muir House. He despised the thought of taking Muir House from Jenna, but there it remained, close and ugly, pounding in his head.

Over on the nightstand his phone warbled. He considered leaving it, dreading more prods from Sid. But at the last moment he answered, and the voice that greeted him pushed the darkness away.

"My heart," he said. "How I've missed you."

And how he wished to never cause her pain.

Chapter Sixteen

Three things that can't be seen: edge, wind, and love.
—IRISH TRIAD

All at Muir House was not as Dev had left it four days earlier. He'd scarcely cleared the front gate when he received his first hint that life had proceeded apace without him. He slowed his car to a crawl and watched as one imposingly large, dark, and muscled man in mirrored sunglasses escorted two camera-bearing girls from the house grounds. And here he'd thought that the genius of returning to his heart on a Sunday when the restaurant was closed was not having to share her with strangers.

Hint number two came to his ears soon after he'd left his car. A "Peg O' My Heart," "Wild Irish Rose" medley rendered American and blisteringly off-key invaded his hearing.

Dev laughed at the sound, inspiring in its volume if nothing else. "Has she hired entertainment now?"

Then he noticed that someone had taken one of the wooden benches from the back terrace and planted it on the lawn. And that particular someone was the soul now butchering maudlin folk melodies.

Dev left the pathway to check out this newest oddity. The male who was sprawled on the bench, bottle of beer in hand, looked as though he'd not slept in days. He also looked familiar, the way a face might after encountering it at a few parties or whatnot. He stopped singing, and Dev was certain that dogs for miles around were sobbing with relief.

"Grand day, isn't it?" Dev offered, counting the empty bottles littered on the ground about the bench.

"Better with a beer," he received in reply. The man pushed an ill-tended mix of brown and blond hair away from his face, scrutinized Dev, then smiled. "You're Dev Gilvane, aren't you? I met your mom last night." He took a swig of beer. "Cool lady . . . very cool. You look just like her."

So Mum had been chatting up the local drunken tourist? Unbelievable. "Don't be taking this the wrong way, but I hope it's not my mother you're singing to."

"Hell, no. But she's pretty damn hot for a lady her age. This is for the love of my life, Maureen. I'm Sam, by the way."

Dev finally made the connection of name and face, unshaven and haggard as it was. "Olivera, right? I've seen a few of your films while on the London-to-New York hop."

"Yeah, that's me. Up-and-coming superstar, not that anyone in this house seems to care."

He smiled at Sam's dejection. Life grew difficult when one was no longer king. "It's nothing personal. If God Himself walked in the door, the Fahey sisters would have Him dancing to their tune. So, how goes the serenade for Miss Maureen? Is it working?"

Sam waved his bottle in the direction of a second-floor window, and a drape was yanked shut in response. "No, but since I've already run through all of my soliloquies and groveled until the skin on my belly's gone, I thought, what the hell."

Which likely echoed Maureen's thoughts at this moment. Sam would be starring in no musicals.

The actor squinted up at him. "You're looking for Jenna, right?"

"I am."

"She left about an hour ago . . . said she needed some peace."

No great surprise there. Since her car had been parked where it always was, Dev asked, "Which way?"

Sam draped one arm over the back of the bench and pointed to the hills with his bottle. "Up."

Thankful that he'd stopped at Cois na Mara for a change of clothes and to prove his continuing, well-fed existence to Muriel O'Keefe, Dev set off. At least today there was no rain, and his footwear was practical—perfect for tracking Jenna, who'd apparently bought herself a bit of Bedlam in his absence.

One foot in front of the other, up Dev climbed. Perhaps it wasn't so much what he was seeing, as *how*, but he noticed things he hadn't before. In the crooks of rocks grew flowers so small that he marveled at their will to survive. Jenna would have the names for them, but at least now he knew they were there.

Far ahead he saw her. She sat by a stone similar to the one she'd so fancied in that bleak churchyard. An ogham, as he recalled—and one that he'd missed on his last climb. He shook his head. Overlooking flowers was one thing, but a whole bloody monument?

Equally amazing was that Jenna hadn't noticed his approach. Face tipped down, she seemed to be writing in a journal of some sort. Dev drew closer and noted a scattering of objects on the red blanket she'd spread to sit upon. Photographs held down by stones, a swatch of fabric, a yellow glass vase, leafy stuff of some sort . . . He wouldn't hazard a guess.

"*Mo chroí,*" he said.

She looked up, eyes wide. The smile that took her face was answered by the feeling of utter contentment settling in his bones. He would never be able to pin down the precise moment he'd become a romantic, but it had happened all the same.

"Come join me," she said as she rearranged her collection of items to make room for him.

"What have you here?" he asked as he sat.

"I'm working on the summer menu. Just give me a second," she said, turning back to her notebook.

He plucked the scrap of fabric from beneath its stone anchor. The silk was streaked with azure blue and a green that matched this hillside. "From your friend, Vi?"

Jenna nodded. She scribbled frantically, like a student at exams with ten seconds left to define the undecipherable essence of James Joyce.

"Tough to chew, isn't it?" he teased, drifting the fabric against her lips.

She brushed it away, then replied, "It's inspiration, not food."

After a few moments she gave a satisfied smile, flipped her notes closed, and tucked them into a day-pack that lay at the blanket's edge.

"Inspiration," he said. "And here I thought a chef would open a file packed with recipes, and that would be the end of it."

She moved closer, and he drew her within the circle of his arms. "Not me," she said. "I surround myself with things that look like how I want my menu to taste. Then I close my eyes and think of foods . . . of textures and flavors and colors. After a while I start writing ideas." She tipped her head back to look at him. "I must sound crazy to you."

"No," he said. "I think I'm seeing it. Colors . . . Textures . . . This is the Zen approach to menu planning, then?"

She laughed. "I'd never thought about it that way, but I suppose it is. And after the Zen interval comes the tough stuff like working out ingredients, perfecting portions, and—"

Dev shifted Jenna so that his mouth could easily meet hers. He kissed her once, twice, hungry nips meant to whet her appetite for more. "Could I persuade you to set the menu aside for, say . . . the texture of your sheets against your bare skin?"

He reached his hand up under the loose-fitting blue shirt she wore and let it follow its desired path to cup her small breast. She sighed, and he knew it was with pleasure, for he felt it in his veins, too.

"And flavors?" she asked, her voice wavering ever so slightly. "Do I get flavors, too?"

He rubbed his thumb over her nipple and smiled as it crested to his touch. "I get the sweet of this wee bit, and the salt of your skin low on your throat after I've loved you."

She settled her hand over his erection, which rode hard against his khakis. "But I was asking what I get." She added just enough firm pressure that Dev closed his eyes and fought back a very pleased moan. "What do you have to tempt me with, Dev?"

"Anything you want," he managed to say.

She leaned closer and licked the side of his neck, a cat at cream. "What about color?"

With great regret, he slipped his hand from beneath her shirt, then moved hers away from him before he found himself begging for skin against skin. Here. Now. "Color? I'll give you midnight, for that's when I'll let you rest."

She sighed. "Nine o'clock."

"What?"

"You'll have to settle for the color of nine o'clock, because after that we'll be at a bonfire by the shore."

"We will?"

She nodded. "Vi decided that Maureen needs one."

He understood, even if he lacked in appreciation. "And it's to be at Muir House, of course. This is generous of Vi, indeed. Four days gone and I return to bodyguards, groupies—"

"Damn, that was fast," Jenna muttered.

Dev plowed on. "And drunken serenading actors. It's not as though we haven't spoken, you know. Is there any other news you forgot to share with me by phone?"

Jenna gave him an apologetic half-smile. "Well, I think your mother has a boyfriend."

Since Mum wasn't in sight, Dev glared at the mountains beyond. "Jesus. Forget I asked."

Jenna knelt and began reaching for the bits of Zen inspiration still on the blanket.

"They're wonderful together, Dev. It's so romantic."

He scowled at his lover's smile. "And fast, don't you think? She's not been here a week."

"Not much faster than us," she said while pulling to her feet. "Off the blanket. If we only have until nine . . ."

Dev stood, unable to let loose the idea of his mum and some man.

"And besides," Jenna was saying, "they've known each other forever. They were lovers back when she was seventeen."

"You've—you've talked to my *mum* about lovers and such?" Somewhere beneath his shock he realized that he sounded like a musty Victorian prig ready for museum display, but Christ in heaven, this was his mum!

Jenna's laughter was well earned. "Yes, we've talked—though if it makes you feel any better, it's not like we got down to the details."

He should have packed Mum off when the thought occurred. "Who is this man?"

"Brendan Mulqueen. Silver hair . . . Tall . . . You've seen him around the restaurant." Jenna pulled the blanket from the ground and tucked it into her pack.

Yes, and Dev had even sensed that he might have liked the man, given the chance to talk. Which just went to prove how wrong his instincts had turned.

"Grand," he said.

Jenna was about to swing her daypack into place when Dev recovered at least enough of his manners to retrieve it from her.

A small line appeared between her brows. "Shouldn't I have told you about your mother? I figured after the way I messed up her arrival, I'd get this news out right away."

"No," he said, trying to sound sincere. "You did the right thing, telling me." He just damn well wished that he were deaf.

Dev shouldered the daypack. Jenna flitted close and kissed him.

"Let's go home," she said. "Maureen's walled herself in, Sam has to have lost his voice by now, and Kate's off somewhere with Brendan. Best of all, in the bedroom it's just the two us."

Just the two us. Dev could think of no truer definition for *Paradise.*

Long after Dev had loved Jenna into utter relaxation, questions of a Zen nature drifted through her mind. . . .

What was the color of love? And the feel of it?

On this incredible afternoon, she knew this much: Love was sunlight drifting in the window as Dev and she held each other and talked. She could never know enough of him. Cocooned in their world, they had started a lovers' game.

"Jenna at nine?" Dev asked.

She smiled. "Horse-crazy and fat."

"*Fat?* That's no way to speak of my heart."

"Okay, chunky. *Really* chunky." She laughed as he pinched her bottom. "Dev at eleven?"

"Very alone."

His voice was so somber. Jenna's muscles instinctively tightened as she realized she'd picked the age at which he'd been sent from home. She wanted to know more, but refused to ask and risk the sunlight they shared.

They lay quiet in each other's arms, and she willed contentment to return. It might have been a trick of the light—or a trick of the heart—but as the room fell into a shadow, he spoke.

"It was no great joy, being the 'stupid Irish git,' " he said. "And I wasn't even rich Irish, with a family they'd heard of. My clothes were wrong, my accent an abomination, and I was lower than a pariah."

"I'm sorry," she offered.

"As was I."

Knowing Dev, the man, made Dev, the boy, seem nearly unimaginable. His confidence and flair were so much a part of him that it seemed he must have been born that way. "Why didn't you ask to come home? I'm sure your mother would have let you."

He shifted, moving her so that she was spooned against him. "At first, it didn't even occur to me that I *could* ask. It felt like prison, and I was there to serve my term. No questions. No complaints. Keep your bloody gob shut no matter what the others do to you."

She closed her eyes, trying to think of something other than the cruelty of children, which she knew had insidious ways of surpassing that of adults

"And then I learned," he said. "I learned to be faster, smarter . . . the best. But most of all I learned to act as though I gave less than a shit about what they said or did. And when I was done, simple bastards that they were, most of them liked me. Even those who didn't knew I was not to be ignored. By the time we moved on to university, I doubt they remembered when I'd been the 'stupid Irish git.' But I've never forgotten." He paused, then said, "You've heard the old adage . . . that which doesn't kill us makes us stronger."

"Or totally screws us up," she added, thinking more of herself than Dev.

"Leave a man his comforts, would you?" he said, a note of humor in his voice. "So now you know Dev, eleven to seventeen—definitely not the golden years." His hand, which had been resting on her stomach, moved lower. Excitement began to hum at his intimate touch.

"And Jenna right now?" he asked.

"Wanting you," she said, giving half the truth. The other half—*loving you*—was a powerful secret, too strong to send crashing into their world. And so she would hold it close, in her control.

They loved again, and for all the sweet sounds of their pleasure—the sighs, the words, the breath hitching as release neared—for Jenna, the most memorable sound of all would be that of the words she could not give.

Dev had never been so close to total peace. For the first time he could recall, the need to have more, faster, better wasn't riding him. This moment, this woman . . . they were enough. Except he knew that he could hold on to neither. Time slipped away on its own. And Jenna, he would surely lose her if he could not turn Harwood's interest from Muir House. Of course, without appeasing the corporate gods, he'd lose all he'd fought for these past years. Neither could that happen. It was a thin line he traveled, and as Vi Kilbride had before noted, he was growing weary.

This moment, this woman. How to have more of both? He looked at Jenna, stretched out on her stomach, dozing. Her hair lay in wild curls that would appall her with their lack of order. And he could not resist. As was his habit, he wrapped a curl around his index finger, a link, however tenuous, holding them together.

She stirred and murmured, "It's too light to be nine."

"No, we have time," he assured with a confidence he didn't feel. He'd done much thinking while east in Wexford, and had even cobbled together a plan of sorts. To his mind, it was solid. He'd lose nothing and he'd give Jenna the status she deserved.

God willing, she would see it that way, too. He stopped toying with her hair and asked, "Have you ever thought of taking an executive position?"

She didn't move, but opened her eyes and smiled. "You mean where I'm on top? We just did that."

He laughed. "I've never met a woman who thinks so often of sex. It's a grand trait, but I meant as a chef."

"Oh, that. No more often than I've thought of becoming a nun."

"That bad, eh?"

She rolled onto her back, then yawned and stretched, flexing even her fingers. "I'm a chef because I love to cook. Me, my kitchen, my restaurant . . . that's all I need." She hesitated, then added, "I know I'm going to regret asking, but why are you bringing this up?"

Dev kept his voice casual. "Harwood is in need of someone to oversee the restaurants in their resorts. Obviously, your name came to mind."

She shuddered. "A corporate job?"

"It would be very high-profile. And think of having Zen menu sessions around the world. The two of us on a beach in Bali . . . A chalet in Zermatt . . ."

"Dev—"

"The pay is substantial," he added casually.

"Maybe, but the only thing I need money for is Muir House. Taking the job would defeat the purpose of earning the pay."

"Think about it, would you, Jenna?" *Damn.* Immediately he knew that too much concern had slipped through. He could not reel it back any more than he could regain his lost feelings of peace.

She sat up. "Harwood is considering other sites, isn't it?"

Here, he did not have to lie. "Yes."

"Anything better than Muir House?"

"In ways, yes." Also not quite a lie, but no site had been overwhelmingly better.

"Then I don't want to talk about this anymore, okay?" she asked, anxiety simmering in her voice. "You're doing all you can, and I'm doing the same. Let's just forget it."

Which would save him this moment but lose him this woman. There was no forgetting that life in London also proceeded apace without him. Plans were being drawn, numbers studied. Even if he managed to get a sniff of interest from Harwood on either the Roscommon house or the one he'd actually rather liked, out Hook Head, they would not set Muir House aside while they looked at the others.

He eased Jenna into his arms, giving comfort when he had none for himself. "I'm sorry, *mo chroí*. I didn't mean to upset you."

"I'm not upset." And that, he knew, was her lie to comfort him.

"Well then," he said, "let's rest so we're ready to face the fire."

She slipped back into sleep, his Jenna. But that was one voyage Dev could not make. He lay awake, thinking of eventualities, of what he could have and what he could not. At eight, he gave up. He woke Jenna with kisses and promises of eternal gratitude if she'd fix him just the smallest bite to eat. They showered, dressed, and then went downstairs . . . to madness.

Dev was aware that Vi was about drama—not that she manufactured it, more that it was the definition of the woman. Still, he had hoped that tonight wouldn't be as large as the gathering of two weeks earlier, but it was looking to be just that.

Jenna and he peeked out a back window and tried to count people on the terrace, never mind the stray girls that Sam's bodyguard was extracting from the shrubs.

"Sixteen . . . eighteen . . . twenty," Jenna tallied.

She smiled with an excitement that made him feel damned selfish. "Looks like I'm cooking for more than you. I'll find you as soon as I can." After giving him a quick kiss, she hurried to the kitchen.

Dev headed in the direction of the bar. The door to the library was occupied by a tall, thin man swinging it open and shut.

"Squeaks," he said.

"That it does," Dev agreed.

"I'm Clancy, from the hardware in town," he said, then gave Dev a stern look. "Someone needs to see to this."

Dev agreed that was so, then was permitted to enter. Once in the room he found Rory O'Connor of the pub family behind the bar.

"Haven't seen you in over a fortnight," O'Connor said. "Have you been too busy to stop down, or did you just figure you'd learned all you needed to know?"

Dev gave a nod to the man's perceptiveness. Of course when first arriving in town he'd gone straight to the pub to learn about Ballymuir. What better way? "I'll visit again, and just for a drink. You have my word."

"Good, then. Now what can I get you? Brendan Mulqueen's buying the house a drink."

"That being the case, a bottle of the Château Margaux," he said, naming one of the most expensive wines he recalled seeing on the restaurant's list.

O'Connor laughed. "You'd best stick with what I can find back here. There's a fine recent-vintage Australian Shiraz. A full bottle should be sting enough for Mulqueen."

"Sold," Dev replied.

"Not much for your mam taking up with him?" O'Connor asked as he retrieved the bottle and a corkscrew.

Dev walked to the side of the bar and reached for a wineglass. "Haven't decided yet," he lied.

He didn't trust Mulqueen. In fact, he doubted he'd trust any man near his mum. She'd been too sheltered; she had no idea what men today were about.

Rory opened the wine, then said, "Hate to see what you order to drink when you do decide." While he was pouring a glass, he glanced over Dev's shoulder. "Ah, now, there's himself."

Dev turned. Mulqueen and his mum had come into the room. He did the polite thing and thanked the man for the drink, getting an assessing nod in return. Dev's gaze went to his mum. It was then he noticed that she and Mulqueen were holding hands. But something startled him more.

"What's that you're wearing?" he asked his mum.

"Brendan and I have been hill climbing, so I borrowed a pair of young Maureen's denims. They fit perfectly."

If she hadn't sounded so bloody thrilled he'd have told her that denims like that were for teenage pop stars, not mothers pushing the far end of middle age. Instead, he took his glass and his bottle and said, "See you outside."

Dev "helloed" his way through the crowd, slowly escaping the sour mood that chased after him. A group was gathered around one of the three large, circular tables that had been among the new arrivals while he'd been in County Wexford. He joined the party and watched as bets were made and money changed hands.

Arm-wrestling looked to be the challenge of the night. Danny Kilbride, Pat Kilbride, Sam Olivera—now sober and looking like a man determined to have a laugh—and Sam's bodyguard, who Dev learned was named Steve, matched up. Vi, who was acting as referee, flirted outrageously with Steve. With a toss of her long red hair, she promised him a fire to light if he'd teach her brothers a wee bit of humility.

Soon Jenna, Maureen, and others came out of the house, bearing food. Dev helped them set it up on another of the tables. By the time all was done, the Kilbride twins had learned there still existed unstoppable forces in their world. Vi was leading Steve down to the shore to start a fire that the bodyguard was sure to find disappointingly literal.

Dev and Jenna walked hand-in-hand to the stone ring behind his mum and Mulqueen. When the man paused to kiss his mum, Dev determined that he was calling Margaret at sunup. By noon he would know Brendan Mulqueen down to the brand of toothpaste he preferred. And if the smallest fact disturbed him, Mum would be winging her way to Los Angeles by supper.

Jenna tugged at him gently. "Dev, you're crushing my fingers."

He gave her a rueful smile, followed by an apologetic kiss. "Sorry." In stopping, he made Maureen nearly trip over them.

"Watch it, guys. I'm sticking close to you tonight," she said.

Dev glanced downhill at Sam, who stood at the stone circle by himself. He felt sorry for the poor bastard, and would have felt sorrier yet if he didn't know how close to disaster his own life remained.

"Talk to him, Maureen," Jenna said just before they reached the fire. "He's going to leave and you're going to spend the rest of your life regretting this."

"I fear young Maureen's determined to make her own mistakes," Dev's mum chimed in. "Just see that you take less than a lifetime to fix them."

Maureen remained mutinously silent and didn't move from her sister's side.

Once the fire was lit and a song was sung, groups broke off for chat.

"Shall we go back up to the terrace?" Dev asked Jenna, who stood in the circle of his arms.

"In a minute."

He glanced down at her, then smiled at the way the flames held her mesmerized.

"Beautiful," she murmured.

"Yes," he answered, meaning her.

From the opposite side of the fire a voice announced, "*Now*, Maureen."

In a parody of concern, Maureen looked around. "Did you hear something?"

Sam circled to their side. "I mean it, Maureen. I'm about fifteen minutes short of hung-over, and when I get there, it's going to be real ugly. The way I see it, you can deal with me now or you can deal with me then."

"I'd pick now," Jenna suggested.

Maureen must have hesitated a fraction of a second too long, for the actor hauled her over his shoulder with an ease that had Maureen cursing.

"Looks like now to me," Dev said as the couple disappeared into the darkness down the strand.

Dev and Jenna made their way up to the terrace. When she headed toward the table where his mum and Mulqueen sat, Dev balked.

Jenna impatiently tugged on his hand. "Maybe I can't put you over my shoulder, but I'm not without leverage, if you get my naked-upstairs-soon drift."

"Right, then," he said. At least the table held a bottle of wine to compensate for the pain of the company.

"Do you mind if we join you?" Jenna asked.

Mulqueen gestured at the two fresh wineglasses. "We were hoping you would."

Dev grudgingly took a seat. Jenna pulled a pack of matches from her back pocket, lit the four small white candles in glass votives at the center of the table, then sat.

"Do you remember the story of Muir House, Dev?" his mum asked.

"Story? I'd never heard of the place until recently." Nor did he especially want to talk about it now.

In the dim light he could see Mum give a shake of her head. "But that's not so. I even took you down the drive and to the house one summer. You were seven, I think. It was one of our few vacations, do you not recall it?"

Looking back, he recalled sitting in the back of a car, feeling carsick and listening to his parents argue over whether they'd missed a signpost, if breakfast had been overcooked, and did she have any idea how much all this was costing. He recalled wishing he could disappear, or make them do so. Of what they saw, he recalled nothing.

Rather than give his mum all that unhappiness, he said, "No."

"Well then, I'll refresh your memory, for this is a tale that Jenna should be hearing," she replied.

Next to him Jenna edged forward in her seat. Dev resigned himself to listening politely, for his mum had always liked her stories—even those he chose not to remember.

"In another time," she said in the smooth voice of a practiced storyteller, "so long ago that the land was still rich with people and free of English, a house stood here. Now, it had no fine name and not nearly so many rooms as what we're seeing today, but it was nonetheless a place to be envied—especially by the men. You see, the house passed mother to daughter when none other did. Women tended the house, made her flourish, held her safe from men's wars."

"And the men?" Dev felt compelled to ask, though he already deemed the story a great lot of nonsense. "Did they serve a purpose?"

His mother laughed. "Oh, they served purpose enough on a cold night, but you're making me lose my tale. You see, the English arrived for the first time, and one of the Desmond clan came out from Tralee. He believed he'd captured the house. Instead, the house's daughter captured his heart. They married, and because he loved her, he agreed that the land should be handed down as before."

Dev began to rise. "That was a grand story, Mum, but if you'll excuse us . . ."

"We're only halfway home, Devlin," she chastised. Brendan and Jenna laughed. Dev sat, and his mother picked up again.

"Because this is Ireland and others want what is hers, in time there came another wave of invaders from across the water," she said. "They saw these formerly English as purely Irish. And this time the daughter of the house didn't fare so well."

"Áine," Jenna said. "I've seen her name in books, but thought it was just a legend."

His mum took a sip of her wine, then said, "It's truth. It's also said that she was a beautiful girl. Dark of hair and eyes, and filled with spirit. An Englishman wanted her, and she, him. But she had her pride, our Áine. Before she would be his, she made him promise that the land must pass as it always had. He spoke the words, but did not live them. Instead, he seduced this place from beneath her. Once he'd tired of her, he killed her family and cast her out. After that day the land passed through males, and the family that held it knew horrible luck. The chain had been broken."

Beside Dev, Jenna shifted uneasily in her chair. "That's so sad."

That's rubbish, he thought, but still his heart skipped a beat, as though some unseen woe had come his way.

"Aye," said his mother. "It was tragic, indeed. And a sorrow I've always felt when I visit here. You see, I'm descended of Áine, who died giving birth to the Englishman's child."

His mother raised her glass. "And that is why I toast our Jenna Fahey, the owner of Muir House. You have brought life to a place I've always held dear."

"Thank you, but you should know, Kate, that I don't own it. And unfortunately," she added, sending a wry glance Dev's way, "I'm not the only interested party."

His mum set down her glass. "Well, I'd heard in the village that Dev had been looking, which seemed a fine thing until I met you. And now with the two of you, well . . ." She trailed off. "If you don't own Muir House, who does?"

Dev grasped the danger of this question and hastened to evade it.

"An elderly Englishwoman by the name of Weston-Jones," he said before Jenna could speak. "Which unfortunately, Mum, knocks the legs from beneath your tale. The house was held by a woman and still didn't thrive. Until Jenna, that is," he added, knowing that all he could do now was mitigate.

"And has this Englishwoman been here?" his mother demanded. "Has the house whispered to her as it has to Jenna? If it had, she'd be here still."

"How did you know what I've heard?" Jenna's voice sounded thin, frighteningly so.

His mum waved off her question. "Because I've heard it, too. I'd wager even Dev has sensed something, except he's decided to be too thick to understand." She stood and glared at him. "Contrary to your approach to life, ownership is more than a piece of paper, Devlin. It's caring and loving, and sometimes it's even dying for a place such as this. Don't talk to me of ownership and Englishwomen."

She marched away.

Brendan sighed, then stood. "She's always had a temper, my Kate. I'll see to her. You two enjoy the rest of the night."

After he had left, Dev looked at Jenna. "Interesting tale."

She sat, silent. The light was too dim for Dev to discern doubt or any other emotion in her eyes, but he felt something chilly coming his way.

"I'm not Áine's Englishman," he said.

"Of course you're not," she replied so quickly that he knew some ease. "Still, you carry both his blood and Áine's." She toyed with her glass for a moment, twisting the stem so that the candlelight danced blood red through the wine. "Let's go upstairs, Dev. I think I've had enough for one day."

Dev couldn't have agreed more. And as he followed Jenna into the house, then upstairs, a ghost hovered behind him.

Chapter Seventeen

Youth cannot believe.
—Irish Proverb

On a romantic moonlit night, how long could two very angry people sit on the boulders edging the shore and say nothing at all? Long enough that Maureen's butt was beginning to ache.

Not that she was about to move. Sam had been pretty clear with his "stay" command. And if she had to be honest with herself—which she really hated doing—she didn't want to leave.

She could hear Sam, one cold, hard rock away, fumbling with his cigarette pack. Then a match flared, which was a definite provocation. She'd have to break the silence for the sake of the jerk's health.

"Don't light that. You know I hate it when you smoke."

"That's rich. Besides, there's a lot of things you do that I hate."

She noted that despite his protest, he'd left the cigarette unlit.

"Name one," she demanded.

He put the cigarette back in the pack, and the pack away. "Running off because you're too scared to face me."

Maureen scooted off her boulder. "I did *not* run," she said, then picked her way across the uneven blanket of smaller stones until she stood at the water.

Low laughter sounded from behind her. "Right, like you're not running now."

Okay, so he had her on that count.

"Look, I'm going to say this once—and just once—even though I think you already know it. . . . I didn't sleep with Chloe. She was making a move, and I was getting around to rejecting her."

Maureen felt tears welling. She hated them. Hated Sam. "You sure as hell were taking your time about it."

He came up from behind her. "No, I wasn't, and you also know that Chloe's not the real reason you left."

She hugged her arms about her midsection. "Do I? Want to remind me what that reason might be?"

"I've been trying to since I got here."

"Well, here's your big shot."

She heard him release a long, slow breath. Was it relief or resignation? She didn't know and told herself that she didn't care.

"You're scared, Maureen. The fact that you can't say two words without being sarcastic proves it.

You've never felt this way about anyone and you
don't like it." His voice was nearly hypnotic. Her
eyes slipped closed as she listened. "You wake up
alone in the morning and you feel incomplete. Your
plans, your dreams, everything seems wrong now—
like it just doesn't fit. In fact, you're sure that if you'd
never met me, you'd be one hell of a lot happier."

She couldn't stand being so transparent, every
thought and emotion out there for people to read.
Maureen fixed her gaze on the water, dark and mysterious. "Nice try, but you're wrong."

"No, I'm not. And do you want to know how I've
figured all of this out?" He paused, and Maureen
stilled, trying to catch his next words. "It's because
I'm scared, too."

Now she'd heard everything. She turned on him.
"Don't treat me like a child. I might be a little younger
than you, but I'm not stupid, okay? Like anything
about me could scare the great Sam Olivera."

He said nothing but took her hand and placed it
over his heart, which slammed a rhythm faster than
even hers. "I'm scared of losing you and I'm scared
of having you. Jesus, Maureen, I should have been
back to Paris days ago, but I'm still here because I'm
afraid to leave. So don't tell me—" His voice broke,
but she was already a sniveling, sorry mess. "Don't
tell me that I'm trying to play you."

If she tried to talk, she was going to screw this up, so
she flung herself at him instead. She kissed him. It
wasn't a very together kiss, since she could hardly
breathe for her tears, but she was pretty sure that he
was getting the message. And when she was done kissing him, she said something she'd never said before.

"Come to my room with me . . . please."

He pulled her hips tight against his, and based on the action between them she knew that he wasn't exactly opposed to her suggestion. He kissed her throat, her cheek, and then her mouth again. "No."

Maureen stepped back. "Did you just say *no?*"

He stood with his hands propped on his hips, head tipped toward the stars. "Yeah," he said, with something in his voice that Maureen could only describe as wonderment. "I think I did."

This was not working out at all the way she wanted it to. "Why?"

"Because I love you?"

Okay, at least that was really good, even if a little confusing. *"And?"*

"And some things are too important to mess up, you know?" He took her hands. "I'm not going to lie to you and say that before you, I've never told a girl that I love her . . . but this time is different. I want this to be perfect. There's no way I'm spending the night making love to you when I know that I'm leaving in the morning."

"You're leaving? But—"

"No, wait. It's my turn to talk. Yes, I'm leaving and I'm sure as hell not taking you back to Paris, with Chloe and the groupies and a pissed-off producer all waiting to make my life suck. We need a better start."

"It's cool the way you're getting all assertive, but nothing's stopping me from showing up there," she pointed out.

"Except you know that it's not right. This is serious stuff, Maureen . . . the biggest I've ever dealt with. I want us to begin as we mean to continue."

And she wanted him now because she knew he couldn't really mean any of this. She'd dumped fish on him, ignored him, and acted like a bigger diva than even Chloe. The way Maureen saw it, this was her last chance at stealing a memory to live on forever. "Come on, Sam, what difference will it make if we go upstairs and—"

He used a kiss to cut off what was going to be the most detailed description she could summon.

"What I'm asking for is some faith, okay?" he said. "You didn't show it by running, and I think we both need to see it now. You love me, right?"

"It's looking that way," she admitted.

"Then you have to trust me." At her choked sound of disbelief, he pulled her close. "I swear to God, I'll be back for you . . . two weeks, three at the most. And then I'm taking a few months off. It will be just the two of us, Maureen. We'll figure out how to build our future."

She briefly closed her eyes. How could she ever believe him? And without giving up on love, how could she not?

"Anything you want. Anywhere you want. Name it," Sam said.

His voice was shaking, Maureen realized with a start. Hell, *he* was shaking! Vulnerability was something she'd never associated with Sam. But what she saw under the wash of the moonlight made her love for him absolute and irrevocable. With one hand she smoothed the tightness of anxiety from his features.

He folded his hand over hers and, eyes closed, kissed her palm.

"All I want is you," she said.

Maureen felt the tension leave him and joy return. Laughing, he hugged her hard. "Just me? You're far too easy, love of my life."

Kisses and promises later, they walked hand-in-hand to Muir House.

They were nearly there when Maureen gave it one last shot. "So you're really sure about this no-sex-tonight thing?"

"Positive," Sam said without slowing.

"Major bummer." The love of her life wasn't proving easy at all.

By mutual, unspoken agreement, Jenna and Dev did not make love. Jenna wasn't certain whether she should be happy or sad for the fact. She did know, however, that it had been the right choice. Physical release was too easy a way around his mother's story, when they needed to get through it.

Jenna shifted beneath the bed's covers, trying to find a comfortable spot. She had left the window open, and along with the slight scent of wood smoke, one of Vi's songs drifted in. It wasn't a happy tune, and it seemed to Jenna that the house mourned with it. Fire, music, and mood, this night could be taking place now, or just as easily, three hundred years ago.

Jenna rolled onto her side and watched Dev sleep. He was a decidedly modern man, with his perfectly trimmed hair and features unscarred by battle or grueling physical labor. No, he could not be Áine's

Englishman any more than she could be Áine. She
was, however, vulnerable.

A strange knot of fright or maybe foreboding
seemed to have settled at the base of her throat, making it difficult to breathe. And for the first time in
days, her stomach hurt. She tried again to resettle,
and must have disturbed Dev, because his eyes
opened.

He smiled a bit, then reached out to rub one of her
curls between his fingers. She loved the tilt to his
eyes and the small laugh lines that angled out from
their corners. Jenna scooted closer, trying to focus on
this moment and put the rest behind her.

"Can you not sleep?" he asked.

"I guess I'm feeling a little restless."

"And myself, too," he agreed. "But I've been trying to pretend otherwise. I don't think it will work,
though, until I say what I need to."

And now she felt a lot restless. She laughed, but
the sound was forced. "You make it sound so omi-
nous."

"It's not . . . or at least I don't think so. God, I'm
making a mess of this," he muttered, then sat up,
propping a pillow behind himself. "All I'm trying to
say is that I love you."

Jenna closed her eyes. "You don't have to do this."

"Do what?"

"Say things you don't mean. It's just this night
and that story of your mother's. You're saying it because you have to . . . you think it might make me
feel better." She curled onto her other side, facing
away from him.

"So you think I'd tell you that I love you to separate myself from Mum's tale of the Englishman?" He moved closer, pulling her against the warmth of his body. "I thought you knew me better than that. I'm too selfish to feel that I *must* do anything. I love you and I don't give a damn about my mother's ungodly meddling, Áine, her Englishman, or anything else outside this room."

She wanted so very much to believe him.

"Jenna, would you please at least look at me?"

She turned to face him again.

"Do I look like a man who'd lie to you? I've said I love you and I mean it. I don't think you have the vaguest idea of how rare you are, or how special. You've made a world for yourself and filled it with beauty. You've made me see all I've been missing, all I could be. How could I not love you?"

He looked strong and sure, all the things she wasn't at this moment. What he asked was even a greater leap of faith than the one she'd taken to find pleasure.

Dev shook his head, the motion almost impercep- tible. "All right, then. I won't give you the words if you're not ready. But at least think of this, Mum's Englishman—who, by the way, I'm not believing was real—he'd have told the girl that he loved her, too."

Jenna's pulse jolted. She'd been imagining a se- duction, a smooth, sexual, sinuous act of plying the land from beneath her. She hadn't considered that the Englishman would have claimed love, too.

"You're right," she said, feeling oddly cheered.

He nearly smiled. "And in being right, I've done myself no favors. Forget the story. Listen for the truth in my words, and ask yourself what's in your heart. Because I felt it this afternoon, and I know it's real."

He was her heart. With the dark mood of the night stripped away, it was that simple. Admitting that she returned his love still might be nothing more that whistling her way through the unknown, but whistle she would.

"I love you, too, Dev."

"Thank God." His kiss was hungry and confident. "See, I'll just take it and not argue that you don't mean it. Now, shall I try telling you one more time, and let's see if you can get it right?"

"That would be nice," she replied, as though he'd asked her to take a stroll.

"Just *nice?* How about brilliant or wonderful or the best thing that's ever happened to you?" he teased.

Smiling, she nodded. "Okay, those, too."

He took her hand and kissed it. "Jenna, I love you."

"Of course you do. Who wouldn't?"

His eyebrows arched. "Getting bold already?"

Her smile grew truer now, easier. "Trying, at least."

He rolled her beneath him and caged her there. Kneeling above her, he looked down and laughed. "God in heaven, you're wearing those yellow smiling-face pajamas again. I didn't even notice when you climbed into bed."

"I suppose we could get rid of them," she suggested.

He ran his fingers down a camisole strap. "A ritual burning under a full moon might do the trick."

"There's always this." She shimmied her way out of the top.

"You American girls always were clever," he said, gazing at what she'd bared.

Smiley-bottoms disappeared as easily as the smiley-top. Very soon Dev's black silk boxers were gone, too. As she lay beneath him, their limbs twined and hearts pounding, Jenna knew she'd never tire of the feel of him deep inside her, of the shattering joy they shared.

He'd painted her outlook on the world with incredible hues. Possibilities were infinite, bright, and astounding.

"I love you," he whispered as their bodies rocked together.

Higher she climbed, cresting on a wash of emotion so vast that she prayed it would never end.

"I love you," he groaned as she urged him onto his back, took him once more into her body, and rode him hard.

She cried out as a climax seized her, leaving her sprawled atop Dev's strong chest. There she lay, weak but not wanting, for she had love.

Maureen woke early on Monday. She picked through her wardrobe, seeking a farewell outfit that would make Sam so totally sorry he'd been noble and slept alone last night.

Giving a critical eye to her choices, she settled on her favorite flame-red Versace dress. Maureen wriggled into it and scrutinized her reflection in the wardrobe's mirrored door.

She frowned. She'd always loved this dress; it was

undeniably the hottest thing she owned. But today something was wrong. She turned sideways to see if maybe she'd gained weight from Jenna's cooking, and that was why it didn't seem to fit. No, it still skimmed her perfectly. It just wasn't working its usual magic.

Maybe the vintage Dior, then? She stripped down and tried again, but no.

Armani? No.

Clothing landed in heaps.

Stella? After all, McCartney had never done her wrong. Another critical look in the mirror. Maureen's palms grew clammy. Could it be that she was experiencing her first-ever fashion crisis?

Fine, then, she'd go all-out with Alexander McQueen. When she'd finished lacing, the verdict was kinky, but seriously no.

Chanel? Understated, yet still wrong.

Maureen's panic grew. Jesus, how could a girl own so many clothes and still have nothing to wear? She looked at the bedside clock. It was already seven.

What if while she was up here playing princess, Sam had left without saying goodbye?

Panic doubled.

From the wardrobe's lower drawer—which remained fairly unmolested—Maureen grabbed a white silk V-neck sweater with three-quarter length sleeves. She pulled it on, and it settled sleek and simple against her skin. Her heart slowed. She reached into the wardrobe and brought out one of the few items still hanging—a plain black skirt. She slipped into it and exhaled a slow breath.

Yes, she thought, taking in her reflection. This was

who she'd been looking for all along, who she wanted to be.

A knock sounded at the door.

"Come in," Maureen called.

Jenna stepped inside. Her eyes widened as she took in the mess. "What are you doing?"

Maureen smiled at her sister. "Changing."

Just before five Monday evening, Dev found his mum in the garden, taming a knotted bramble of raspberries by the far wall. It seemed she had taken full liberty of Maureen's wardrobe, for now she wore a ragged pair of denims and a red T-shirt that appeared to have seen even more use.

"Brendan Mulqueen has fathered four children," he said as he approached.

His mother started at his voice, but quickly recovered her composure. She turned to fully face him and then closed her clippers. "So we're just dancing by 'Hello, Mum, sorry I was an ass last night'?"

"I could have chosen my words more carefully," he lied. Actually, he'd been doing his damndest just to stay ahead of the storm.

"Fine, then," she said with a stern nod. "And yes, Brendan has fathered four children. With three different women, too, from what he tells me."

"And married none of them."

"My, but you've put poor Margaret through her paces today, haven't you? Did it occur to you that I'm old enough to tend to my own affairs?" She gave an annoyingly content smile before adding, "Literally."

"I'm concerned, Mum."

"Concerned . . ." She sounded out the syllables as though testing them for the word's true meaning.

"Yes, concerned."

She laughed, then turned back to nipping dead stalks out of the raspberries. "He'll not be getting me pregnant, if that's what's bothering you. Sad news that it is, I'm afraid you're destined to be an only child."

Dev knew he should take the light breeze of her humor to shore, but it was his duty as her son to have done with this conversation. "I'm worried that you're not prepared to handle a man like Brendan. You've not had much experience with his sort."

"And you would know the experience I've had in the past fifteen years? You, who can't be bothered to step outside your suite on the few occasions you've come home? I could have had an affair with every man in Dublin and Dun Laoghaire, too, and you'd not know it. Don't be presuming to know anything about the woman I am."

"He has a reputation."

"You're a fine one to be pointing this out. Until Jenna, the best way I had of knowing where you were or who you were seeing was to pick up a newspaper—and I don't mean the business section."

It was impossible to argue against years of salacious press. "Then I'm the right one to be pointing this out."

Sighing, she sheathed the clippers in their leather sleeve. She pulled off a pair of worn gardening gloves and tucked them into a back pocket as she walked to him.

"Dev, I've carried Brendan Mulqueen in my heart

every day since I was seventeen years old. I know he's far from perfect, and I know that more hurt might be waiting for me."

"Then stop now. Please."

She shook her head. "But I love him."

Love. God, but it was mucking with all and sundry. "You're quite sure?"

"Yes."

His proper mother, taking up with a man who had children scattered from Bali to Boston. "What will people think?"

She laughed, the sound musical on the cool breeze. "Think? I should be caring what they think?"

"Mum . . ."

"Fine, then. They'll think that your father's been gone over fifteen years. They'll think that neither Brendan nor I are hurting anyone in finally grabbing our happiness. And they'll think that my son's standing in line to be the Pope."

Dev rubbed absently at his forehead, then tried again. "I'm just saying this because I love you."

His mum nodded. "And now it's been said. But I can't just sit about and wait for my life to end."

She opened her arms to him, and he hugged her, his real mum, not the fine figure he always imagined sipping tea in Dun Laoghaire.

"You know, one thing keeps bothering me, Devlin," she murmured while patting his back as if he were still ten years old.

"And that would be?"

"You've bought a new residence in Knightsbridge, yes?" she asked while releasing him.

"I have."

She freed her gardening gloves and began pulling them on. "And my friends in Dublin tell me that it must have cost a million or more."

"Your friends are needing some new hobbies."

She laughed. "True enough. But this got me to wondering, Dev, why would you be looking at Muir House?"

Since she'd always known when he was lying, he gave her the truth. "I was looking on behalf of Harwood."

"And Jenna knows this?"

"Yes."

Frowning, she adjusted the thumb of her left glove for a better fit. "You've stopped Harwood, then?"

He sighed. "That's like stopping the tide from coming in. I'm just doing what I can to save us from the flood. It's a mess, Mum, I found this place and told them about it. I didn't expect to fall in love."

"One seldom does. But now that you have, you must make the right choice."

As though he had the freedom that the word *choice* connoted.

"I've one question for you," he said.

"Yes?"

"That story last night . . . Áine and her Englishman, were they real?"

"On your father's grave, it was the truth." With that, she turned and pretended that he was no longer there.

As Dev left the garden, he had but one thought. If only she'd loved his father a wee bit more, he just might have believed her.

Chapter Eighteen

Eastward lies my journey, and westward lies my love.
— IRISH PROVERB

May gave way to June, but not without a fight. As the days passed, Jenna relaxed into a new rhythm. It wasn't so much that she let things slide at Muir House; she could hardly afford to, with rumors of approaching *Guide Eireann* critics growing louder every day. Instead, she learned that if she moved with less frantic intent, more seemed to get done.

Dev and she were together nearly every free minute. Of course, with his travels around Ireland and back to the London office, those minutes were fewer than she wished.

This lazy Monday morning, Maureen and she sat in the blue salon. Between the breaks in clouds, sunlight streamed into the room. Jenna worked on supply and grocery lists while her sister scribbled in a journal, something she seemed to be doing every minute that she wasn't on the phone with Sam.

Jenna picked up her pencil and added "2 cases baby aubergine" to her notes. "Do you want to go set aside your journal long enough to go into town with me?"

"Nope. Besides, Sam's supposed to call."

"If you're looking for company, I'll come along," said a much-loved but unexpected male voice.

Jenna looked toward the doorway. "Dev! You told me that you'd be in Wexford."

"Change of plans," he said as he approached. He leaned down and kissed her to the sound of Maureen's, "Would you mind? Some of us don't need to see that."

"So we're going to the village for what?" Dev asked.

"To visit with an organic supplier."

He arched a brow. "Looking for an unlimited supply of butter lettuce?"

She laughed. "With you around, it couldn't hurt."

After meeting with her supplier, Jenna joined Dev at O'Connor's Pub. It was a quiet place after lunchtime, with Rory behind the bar and the television chatting for companionship. Dev and she chose a small, round table near the front, where some light actually managed to creep in through well-shuttered windows.

They savored Rory's famous artery-clogging, Cream-of-Whatever's-Fresh soup and ate brown bread thick with butter. Dev drank a pint while Jenna stuck to bottled water.

"Come to London with me," Dev said just as Jenna was taking a sip.

She swallowed her surprise at the request and said, "Okay, when? December for Christmas, maybe?"

"How about tomorrow?"

"You're joking, right?"

He shook his head. "No, I have to go tomorrow, for four days at the most. If you came with me, you could see where I live, and maybe meet some of my friends."

"Dev, it's one thing to take a few hours away or even a night, but four days?"

"Three, then," he bargained. "I'll tighten my schedule and have you back Thursday night. It will be fun. I've visited your haunts," he said, waving a hand around, "but you've yet to see mine."

His words couldn't have been more of a shock. She had come to think of Ballymuir—and Muir House especially—as Dev's world, too. He spent more nights in her bed than in the rooms he kept at Muriel O'Keefe's.

"I just can't," she managed to say. "The Guide Eireann critics are going to visit the restaurant soon and—"

"Would you know them if you saw them?"

"No."

"Is your staff not well trained?"

"With the exception of Hector on a hung-over night, yes."

"Then your presence would change their meals in what way?"

"I just need to be there to cover it." She knew she

was sounding mulish. "This winter, I swear anyplace you want to drag me, I'll go."

He was silent, seemingly occupied by shredding the coaster that had been beneath his glass.

"What's wrong?" she asked.

"Nothing at all." He smiled, but seemed distracted. "Don't worry yourself. We'll do it in the winter, then."

She wanted to relax, but it was no easy trick. In their relationship the ground she would not tread was that occupied by Harwood. When Dev traveled, she would welcome him home, never asking about the tense lines that bracketed his mouth or the sudden fierceness with which he made love to her. It seemed she'd developed quite a talent for whistling her way through the unknown.

Tuesday lunchtime, Dev met with his boss, Trevor, in a smoke-filled "Ye Olde English" bar of a chain hotel on the edge of London. After becoming accustomed to Rory's sparkling clean establishment, this place was more a pox than a pub. In any case, Dev had to wonder at the bizarrely clandestine nature of the meeting.

"Not quite our usual surroundings, I know," Trevor said with an apologetic smile as Dev came in.

"At least it was convenient to my flight," he conceded, then sat.

Trevor was looking a wee bit more smug than usual. "I needed to catch you before you arrived at headquarters," he said. "There's changes coming, and as one of my best men, I wanted you to know. I'd have called you, but it seems that I can say nothing over the phone without word leaking." He shook his head. "And life in the office is little better."

Dev managed a neutral nod while thinking of his own Margaret riffling through the trash bin.

"So tell me of these changes," he prompted.

"On July first I'll be moving to manage the commercial real-estate division," Trevor said, his chest puffing, as was his due. After this promotion he had only the executive board left to attain. As a man yet in his forties, Trevor could aspire to the heights. And naturally Dev aspired to fill the slot he'd left.

"Congratulations," Dev offered.

"Thank you. This means, of course, that there will be a transition within the resorts group." Trevor drew on his cigarette, clearly waiting for Dev to ask about his fate.

Dev bit back on his impatience. To appear anxious was to appear weak. He smiled at a passing waitress, and when she stopped, he asked for a coffee and thanked her. Then he raised an expectant brow at Trevor, but said nothing.

"We'll be placing you to manage the Tokyo office," his employer announced. "It will be two years, three at the most."

"Tokyo," Dev repeated, unbelieving. He knew that his shock was showing and knew equally that Trevor was enjoying this infrequent slip.

"Consider it part of a rise to the top. I passed a stint in Tokyo, myself," Trevor said. "Some of the best years of my first marriage, in fact. Camille wouldn't come along."

Dev pulled out the smile he knew was expected.

"This is a perfect time for you, Dev. You've no con-
nections or commitments that can't be severed."

He did, for he'd be losing his heart.

"If it's your flat that concerns you, relax," Trevor
assured. "Your payments will be covered while
you're abroad."

His flat. Christ, that was the bloody least of his
problems.

"It won't be so dreadful. Now they've even an
Irish pub, I'm told."

Ah, give the paddy his pub and all would be well.

Dev knew that Trevor likely didn't deserve such
bitterness. On the whole it was a lucky thing that he
still had the composure to hold his tongue.

"And when you come back, you'll move to be second in command to me."

Dev asked a question for which he already knew
the answer. "Who's heading up resorts?"

"Barrett."

Aye, Sid bloody thief Barrett. "I see."

"It's not my choice."

Which changed nothing. "And if I turn down
Tokyo?"

"You'll be Barrett's direct report. Surely that's
enough to make the Ginza sound appealing?"
Trevor's attempt at a hearty laugh fell on an unrecep-
tive audience.

The waitress arrived with Dev's coffee. After she'd
left, he glanced at the lipstick remnants on the cup
and absently pushed it aside. The thought of Tokyo,
a world away from Jenna, was an abomination, but
he had bigger problems yet.

"What's to become of the Ireland project?"

"We're moving ahead. I'm stepping back to a consulting role, and Barrett will have the final site approval. You've done some fine work, Dev. Two of the sites in particular were charming—in a rural sort of way."

"And the site that's been selected?" Dev asked in as casual a voice as he could summon.

After one last pull on his cigarette, Trevor stubbed it out. "Do try to act as if you don't know when I tell you in our meeting this afternoon, but it's the County Kerry location. Ballymuir, is it?"

There, the worst had happened. Dev had supposed that when this moment finally arrived, he'd know a sense of relief, or at least resignation. He'd been wrong.

"Yes, Ballymuir," he replied.

"Barrett and a site group will be visiting on Friday. If it passes personal inspection, we'll push ahead with negotiations."

And it would pass, for it was the ideal site.

"I've an extra set of plans in my car if you'd like to see them before we meet at the office," Trevor offered.

This was rather like seeing the drawings of the scaffold from which he'd swing.

"Yes. Yes, I would," he heard himself replying. If he was to be hanged, he might as well go knowing.

Early Wednesday morning Dev did the unthinkable. Instead of heading to the office for the full raft of scheduled meetings, he arranged for a driver and went to the airport. After leaving his half-finished and very empty Knightsbridge flat, he didn't pull his cell phone and call Margaret. This was one matter in which even she could be of no help.

In Gatwick's Departures Hall, while waiting for the short flight that would take him back to Ireland, he considered his fate. Beside him sat a drab brown cardboard tube carrying plans that were enough to damn him with every last soul in Ballymuir. True, the development would be a boon to the economy, but the personal cost was immeasurable.

On the flight to Shannon Airport, Dev closed his eyes and imagined himself taking another path, one to Tokyo. He pretended that he had never met Jenna, had never loved her. He remained glib, confident . . . and starved to the bottom of his soul. Vi Kilbride, near witch that she was, had told him not to hurt Jenna when he ran. He would not run; he had grown past the impulse. But he would hurt her all the same.

Once landed, Dev retrieved his car and tossed his bag and the plans on the seat next to him. It was not much past noon when he pulled down Muir House's drive. The assortment of vehicles parked in a lot usually nearly empty this time of day rattled him. He had envisioned the way his talk with Jenna was to go, and no audience was to be included. Still, there was no way but forward and past this disaster.

Dev entered the house and followed the sounds of talk and delighted laughter to the dining room. He wasn't quite sure how to define what he'd walked in on, except that it was the last thing he wanted to see.

A large group sat at the round table beneath the chandelier. His mum, Brendan Mulqueen, Vi, and Maureen he recognized for certain. With them were another couple he recalled from the night of the

Beltane fire as Vi's elder brother, Michael, and his wife, Kylie.

Jenna stood at the table, a flute filled with what looked to be water held aloft. "Everyone knows that Vi's the one with the talent for speeches, while I stick to my kitchen. But this toast is from me, and even if it's a little rough, know that it's from my heart. To Michael and Kylie, who will be wonderful parents," she said. "Thank you for bringing your joy to Muir House."

When everyone had honored the couple, he—destined to be the outsider in all parts of his life—stepped the rest of the way into the room.

"If it isn't our semi-resident," Vi called, spotting him first. "Welcome home, Dev."

Home. He managed what he was sure was a fair travesty of a smile. "Thank you, Vi."

As Jenna came to him, he exchanged quick greetings with the others at the table. When she was near, he closed her in his arms, needing to feel her love this one last time.

"Come to the kitchen with me, where I can welcome you home without an audience," she said after rising on tiptoe and giving him a brief kiss.

"We'll be right back," Jenna called to the others, then took Dev's hand and led him off.

The delicious scents of spices and grilling meats and a sweet something wafting from the convection oven were too much for a system already gorged on guilt. Dev lingered just inside the doorway, only a few steps from the lobster's tank. He knew Jenna expected another kiss, but he couldn't . . . simply couldn't.

"I'm glad you're home early," Jenna said while fussing with a family-style platter of salad sprinkled with paper-thin slices of red pepper and what looked to be tiny violets. "I've missed you, and I'm sorry I wasn't nicer when you left, too."

He worked up that same awful smile he'd shown in the dining room. "What have you going on?"

She smiled. "Other than an impromptu celebration since Kylie's just back from the doctor and confirmed pregnant, it's a victims' dinner."

"A what?" He was too distracted to care much, except the name of the dinner gained his attention.

"A victims' dinner," she repeated.

Fitting, indeed. Pity they didn't yet know to what they were falling victim. Jenna needed to know, and now, before he lost the numbness that insulated him.

She didn't seem to notice that he was hardly there at all. "Okay, I know it's only lunchtime, but the theory holds," she said. "You see, I invite over a bunch of friends and experiment on them with my new recipes." She waved a hand at the dishes lined up and ready to be taken out. "These are from my Zen session, by Tennac's ogham."

His bleakness must have left him looking a totally thick *eejit*, for she slowly repeated, "Tennac's ogham, you know, the stone on the hillside."

"Yes," he said. "Of course."

"There's room for you at the table," she offered.

"Not—not just now. How long do you think this will last?"

"Not too much longer or Aidan will have me skewered and turning on a spit. He needs the kitchen ready for dinner."

Dev nodded. He must tell her now. Each minute he delayed would only deepen the hurt.

"Jenna," he began, his voice rough, almost choked.

She looked up, hazel eyes wide as if she'd just seen the shadow of a ghost. "Yes?"

"I—" Jesus, in his life he'd coolly let staff go, cordially ruined the hopes of those competing against him, and competently rejected women with a note and a gift, all without feeling a twinge of remorse. But this, it would kill him. "I love you," he finished.

Awareness passed between them, the unsaid shouting louder than the said. And then she seemed to push past the moment.

"As you should, since I love you," she said. She scooped up a plate. "By the way, I think I left some notes in your car on Monday, when we came back from the village. Have you seen them?"

The forced cheerfulness in her voice sliced through him. Dev moved a step nearer the door. "Yes. I put them in the glove compartment."

"Good," she said, balancing a platter on the inside of her forearm, then filling her free hand. "I'd hate to have to redo the work." She came around the counter. "Are you sure you don't want to eat?"

"I'll just wait in the library," he said.

"Okay," she said. "I'll get rid of these guys as fast as I can."

Dev watched as she pushed through the door, leaving him alone. He took his time walking to the library, stopping to look at portraits and mementos on the walls, imprinting in his memory the scent of this place, the spring of the carpet beneath his feet—even the squeak of the library's door. Then he stood and gazed into the empty fireplace, cleaned free of the ashes from fires he'd watched.

"Dev?" called a woman's voice from behind him.

His shoulders slumped. "Why aren't you eating, Mum?"

"And why aren't you?"

"Not hungry," he said, then sat in his favorite chair.

She came to stand in front of him. "Whatever's the matter? You looked like death when you came into the dining room."

Keeping his gaze somewhere about her feet, he shook his head. "Nothing's the matter."

"Devlin, look at me."

God, that command, how many times he'd heard it as a child. Any half-truth, any wiggling away from an unpalatable situation, and he'd be told to meet her eyes. And she'd know, damn her, she'd know in whatever mysterious ways a mother did.

"It's my turn to be concerned," she said.

Keeping his eyes averted, he shook his head. "I'm just needing some air. Go back and eat, Mum." With that, he left.

Dev took the service hallway to the kitchen. Jenna was tasting a sauce as he passed by. She tossed the spoon into the utility sink by the back door just as he grasped the handle and swung it open.

"I thought you were waiting in the library. Where are you going?" she asked, but he didn't slow.

"Taking a stroll," he replied, forcing a false note of joviality into his voice for Jenna's sake.

Dev walked the tamed pathway to the front of the

house, then left for the rougher land beyond. Up the hill, grass and weeds wet from an earlier rain, on he walked. Only when he'd lost some of his anger did he slow. Instinct had brought him to a place he'd been before. To the ogham stone.

It was timeworn, far from grand, but held a strange power, sitting on the crest of the hill. Just as he'd seen Jenna do, Dev bent down and brushed his fingers across the odd, angled lines cut into the ogham's side—an alphabet pagan and evocative.

She'd said this was Tennac's stone, and so it must read. Still, Dev felt its deeper meaning: *I am. Long after I am dust washed down to the sea, remember: I am.*

Tennac had his stone lording it over a land empty of Tennac for years uncountable. With the terrified arrogance of the living, Dev scoffed at the thought.

But then a voice, low and sibilant, curled around him with the grip of the wind.

And what does Dev Gilvane have?

He wouldn't permit himself to turn heel and run. He wouldn't be cowed by a goddamn rock, or thoughts of the spirits that lingered. It was nothing more than the voice of his own distress.

He rubbed at his forehead, then frowned at the tremor in his fingers.

Fear? Dev Gilvane had no fear.

He had a flat in Knightsbridge that cost more than the whole bloody town of Ballymuir. He had the wealth to travel.

He had . . .

He had . . .

Jesus, after today, what would he have?

Without regard for the wet or the bite of the earth, Dev sat next to the stone of Tennac.

Everyone was fed and generally content, except for Kate, who was looking pale. Jenna would have asked what was wrong, but Kate was busy whispering to Brendan.

Jenna drew Maureen aside. "Would you mind playing hostess? I need to find Dev."

Maureen gave no hesitation, no flip answer, only a plain, "Well, get going."

And so Jenna did.

There were two places at Muir House that seemed to call to a soul: the hillside and the sea. Figuring the odds were even, Jenna opted for the uphill climb.

She saw Dev long before she reached him, and in all that time she wondered if he'd spotted her at all. He sat perfectly still next to the ogham, feet flat on the ground and his wrists propped on bent knees. If the wind hadn't been moving his hair, she'd have thought him a statue.

"Dev," she called as she neared him.

He looked up, but his gaze seemed almost blank of recognition.

Jenna did her best to sound cheerful, to lighten a moment she didn't understand. "Did you enjoy your stroll?"

He gave a slight nod and then rose.

Did he have any idea he'd be wet from sitting on the ground? It didn't seem so. She pointed to the fog pushing down the mountainside and toward the shore. "The weather's turning. We should go back to the house."

Dev nodded, but seemed in no hurry to beat the fog, which was slithering downhill, swallowing whole all in its path.

"Let's move," she urged. "I'll build a fire in the library. This is an afternoon to stay warm."

He followed, but was as silent as the blanket of white behind them. They were nearly to the drive when she recalled that she needed her notes.

She stopped. "Is your car open?"

"Yes," he said.

"Then I'm going to grab my notes. I'll meet you at the house."

He said nothing, but she was becoming used to this silent Dev. Jenna angled off toward the car, checking once to see if he continued toward the house. He did, so she took care of her task.

Jenna opened the passenger door of the little Porsche. In order to open the glove compartment, she had to push aside Dev's fancy travel bag and a cardboard courier's tube that lay atop it. She reached in and retrieved her notes. After she'd closed the compartment, she resettled Dev's things. It was then that she noticed someone had written *Muir House* in marker on the tube.

She wasn't above snooping, especially when the subject was her home. Jenna brought the tube out of the car and turned it over in her hands. At the far end was a label showing the name and address of a London architectural firm. Centered on it was the phrase, "Revised 4 June."

The fourth of June. Less than two weeks ago.

Jenna tucked her notes into her jeans' pocket. Hands shaking, she dislodged the contents from the tube and unrolled it across the hood of Dev's car. The drawings were pages thick, but the first was enough to tear the breath from her.

"Oh, God."

On a schematic, her house was nothing more than a small block off which grew more shapes—huge, monstrous land-eating buildings, labeled "Conference Centre" and "Sports Complex." The walled garden was consumed by a day spa, the hillside with rental cottages, and Mr. Horrigan's farm was a golf course.

Jenna peeled back a sheet and found the front elevation of Muir House. Nothing, not even the placement of the entry was the same. They would eat it alive. Rain began to fall, one cold, heavy drop after another pelting the drawing. She wished for the ink to run, the ugliness to be washed away, but it stared back at her, firing her fury.

"I planned to tell you as soon as I arrived," Dev said from behind her.

Jenna wondered how long he'd been standing there. She kept her head down, staring at the travesty in front of her. "These were last revised on the fourth of June, Dev. Did we make love that day?"

"I would think we did."

"And didn't you feel a little guilty?"

"No. I love you."

His words were empty, she knew that, but her tears joined the rain anyway. "They never stopped looking at Muir House, did they?"

"No."

"And you knew this."

"Yes."

"How could you?"

"Damn it, there was nothing I could do about it. Don't you think I've nearly killed myself, combing every mile of road, following every lead, no matter how poor, trying to find some other way for this to end?"

She wanted to turn and fling herself at him, bite and howl and sob until the fury left her, but she wouldn't. "You should have told me."

She wasn't alone in her anger. His hand settled on her arm, and he spun her around.

"That's shit and we both know it. You didn't want me to tell you. Every time I'd come home, I wanted to share with you, to tell you how goddamn awful my trip had been and how frightened I was that I'd not fixed this mess. But you, all you wanted to do was talk about your days or Maureen or almost anything except this. You knew, Jenna. You've always known."

With a brutal, stabbing motion he pointed at the plans. "So here it is . . . what they're doing. Even with your money and mine, it won't be enough. And I know how Harwood works. I wrote the rules of the damn game. If they want this place enough, they'll make it impossible for others to have it."

"No!"

"You made me bear this alone even though we both knew it was happening. And I was willing to do it, to take those dark nights myself, because I love you."

He was a liar. She didn't want to hear this. She

turned, thinking to flee, but he caught her and held her tight against him. "It's here—this bloody horrible mess—and now we have to bear it together or bear it alone."

He didn't understand; she *couldn't* bear it. Jenna pushed away, then shoved her wet hair from her face. "I need you to leave. And Dev, don't come back."

Dev watched as Jenna gained the front steps of the house she loved so well, then disappeared inside. He picked up the plans, folded the sodden mass in half and stowed it on the passenger seat of his car. If he were a brave man, he'd go inside and confront her. But just now he was worn and weary, and heartbroken nearly to death. Jenna had her sister and Vi to comfort her. He had no one.

Dev climbed into his car and left as Jenna had asked. He had no particular destination in mind when he drove to town and parked. That he was in front of O'Connor's seemed fitting. He went inside, sat down, and ordered himself a whisky, neat.

Rory O'Connor had the good grace not to ask why Dev would be wanting this at not even two in the afternoon, or to argue overmuch when he swallowed the first and immediately demanded a second.

Rory wiped down the bar in front of Dev. "And what made you decide to be my best customer?" he asked.

"Turned my lover against me."

O'Connor extended his palm. "Hand over your keys, then," he said with a pitying shake of his head.

"Wouldn't want to hurt that fancy machinery of yours."

Dev complied. Rory pocketed the keys, then settled a whiskey bottle in front of him. Maybe a quarter left, he measured, but it should be enough.

"There's a room at the top of the stairs," the bartender said. "Stop drinking while you can still climb."

Chapter Nineteen

Women don't drink wine, but it disappears
while they're present.

— IRISH PROVERB

By the time Dev stepped outside O'Connor's Pub on Thursday morning, jungle drums must have found their way from the rainforest to Ballymuir. Either that, or while he'd slept the sleep of the totally sotted, someone had tattooed "Evil, Grasping Bastard" across his forehead. Though he'd spoken to no one but O'Connor, it seemed that everyone in town knew what had happened.

Mrs. McCafferty, market basket full to brimming, passed him by. His subdued "good morning" was answered by a sound he could only interpret as a hiss.

His hello to Mr. Clancy, the owner of the hardware, went totally unmet, unless one counted the fact that the man spat into the gutter.

Dev had been a pariah before. And in the manner he'd learned as a boy, he stood taller, set his expression to one of amused superiority, then got the hell out of the village.

Back at Cois na Mara, he bypassed his habitual hello to the Molly statue, went upstairs, and showered for as long as he thought he could without Muriel pounding on the door and calling to see if he might have drowned. Head tipped back, hot water pounding the poisons from beneath his skin, he damn well wished that he could.

Half an hour later he was downstairs again. He pushed through the breakfast room door and found Mum waiting for him.

"Spent the night at O'Connor's, did you?" she asked.

"Jungle drums once again," he muttered.

"Don't be daft, your car was out front. I was worried last night when I called here and no one had heard from you, so Brendan took me looking."

"And here I am, still among the living." *Barely*.

She walked to the cupboard and pulled a box of the cereal that Muriel kept for her guests. Though the door to the kitchen remained closed, she said in a conversational tone, "Some milk, if you could, Muriel."

In the time it took Dev to blink, the door opened a crack and a pitcher was pushed through. His mum took it and went about putting together a bowl of cereal.

She set it in front of him and said, "Eat."

He suspiciously glanced over at the Fruits of Nature box before taking a spoon to the food. These shriveled bits looked too dubious for his protesting stomach.

"We have some questions," his mother stated.

"We?" he asked, happy to delay his first bite.

"Jenna, Vi, Maureen, and myself."

"Ah, the coven."

"Mind your mouth, Devlin."

He filled it with cereal instead.

"Jenna's seen the plans, of course, but she was in no state to be asking for details yesterday. This morning's a different thing. It's time to know just what she's facing."

"Yet you're here and not Jenna."

"Her heart's broken, Dev."

He set down his spoon and gave up on the pretense of eating. "It's not only hers."

"I know, which is why I came," his mother said. Now she wore the look of the saints, and he wished for the stern face instead.

"Tell Jenna that representatives of Harwood will be visiting Ballymuir tomorrow. If matters are as I presented, then we move ahead and step up negotiations with Muir House's owner."

"We?"

"We . . . they . . . Dammit, Mum, don't be picking apart my words."

"Ah, but they're important ones, those words of loyalty and choice." She reached forward and patted his hand. "I'd say we've just hit on your first order of business today. After eating your cereal, that is."

Then Mum stood and walked from the room, leaving Dev alone with his cereal, his portraits of saints, and his litany of sins.

Morning at Muir House was an ugly thing. Jenna had spent an hour on the phone with her solicitor. He'd deluged her with lawyer-ese about what "market value" meant and how the courts might view differing appraisals. She'd also received an apology. Mr. Keene agreed that nearly two years ago, they shouldn't have relented in their demands that Miss Weston-Jones fix a sales price for the property.

Mr. Keene had also suggested that Jenna could fight the sale, should one occur. Harwood's proposed use of Muir House was unforeseeable. Jenna should not be forced to pay the same value.

She'd asked one question—could she win?—and received twenty minutes of hedging, hemming, and hawing. The bottom line appeared to be that she'd be bankrupted by legal fees before she'd ever know.

So now, when it wasn't yet noon, she, Vi, Maureen, and Kate sat around the table in the war room, drinking mimosas and eating the dark chocolate truffles presented in the restaurant with after-dinner coffee. Between the alcohol and the chocolate, she hoped to become sufficiently anesthetized that her heartache would ease. It seemed to be slow going.

"God in heaven, get your face off the table," Vi said to her. "It's not as though this is your last day on Earth."

"But it feels that way," she replied, sitting up before her bossy friend resorted to stronger tactics.

Her last day on Earth . . .

Years ago, in her first restaurant job, the staff

would sit and drink for hours after the place had closed, waxing philosophical. A recurring topic was how one would fill that final day, if given the choice. Most of the answers had centered on mind-boggling amounts of sex with various celebrities. Since at that point, sex had been a bleak thing for her, she'd always been the very odd girl out, proclaiming that she'd spend her last day cooking.

Maureen came around the table with more champagne, topping everybody's glass. As Jenna watched, an idea began to bubble—an absurd and pointless one, if she were to think past today. She wouldn't, though, because in all ways that counted, this *was* her last day on Earth.

Tomorrow, pompous executives would snoop and sniff around Ballymuir, then leave feeling smug. Tomorrow, this chapter in her life would begin to end.

"I want a celebration . . . tonight," she said, then waited for her extended family's reactions.

To her right, Kate said nothing, but subtly moved Jenna's glass of anesthesia from her reach.

"Sounds good to me," proclaimed Maureen, ever the party girl.

Vi frowned. "What will we be calling it? It can't be Midsummer's, for that's still a week off."

Her friend was no doubt contemplating the varieties of wood appropriate for her fire. "It's my last-night-on-Earth party, so feel free to burn anything you can get your hands on."

The thought seemed to cheer Vi, since she voiced no more objections. Jenna felt cheered, too. She was moving forward, standing bold in the face of the inevitable, just as one should on her last day.

"Maureen, get the reservations book and call any of tonight's guests who we have numbers for," she said. "They're welcome to join us at no charge, but whatever I feel like cooking is what they'll eat."

"How about the reservations I can't reach?"

"I guess they get to be surprised."

"Perfect," Maureen said before grabbing both her glass and the remaining champagne, then taking off.

"You're sure you want to do this?" asked Kate. "It seems a bit mad."

"I can't sit here and mourn all night."

And both she and Dev's mother knew that she had more to mourn than Muir House. Jenna still loved Dev—and probably always would—but the joy was so twined with hurt that she didn't think she'd ever be able to separate them again.

"A party it is, then," Kate said with forced joviality. "What shall I do to help?"

Jenna struggled to maintain a gloss of composure. "Could you and Vi spread the word in town? I want everyone invited."

"I'm to assume that invitation doesn't extend to my son?"

She shook her head. "I can't see him."

Kate's smile held no happiness. "Don't be waiting thirty-six years, Jenna. My son loves you, and you'd best not forget that you're hurting him, too."

Vi rose. "Since I'm not one to be standing in the way of a celebration, it's off to O'Connor's, then. I need to see some people about music. Care for a lift, Kate?"

"That would be grand."

Vi stopped long enough to fold Jenna into a hug scented of exotic eastern spices and Irish peat smoke.

"You'll survive this," she said. "I know you will because I see a room sparkling with gold."

Jenna held her best friend close. If only Vi's vision could have been of a place within the walls of Muir House.

Home truths. It was a phrase Dev seldom if ever used. But just now, as he sat in his car outside Muir House's gates, the words came to him.

He hadn't slowed enough in years to ask himself what his home truths might be. He had been satisfied amusing himself with pretty women and accruing wealth. And he'd always believed he was master of his destiny.

His first truth had been handed him by Trevor in that miserable smoke-filled bar two days ago. He, Devlin Gilvane, was as much a slave to corporate whims as the next man. Expensive suits and a glib tongue did not make him invincible. In fact, they had an odd way of landing him on the wrong side of the world, far from where he wished to be.

His second truth had been with him for far longer. Through those black iron gates across the road was everything of value in his life. And because last night he'd wallowed in self-pity, he was a beggar on the other side of the wall. But he was a better man today, even if a wee bit hungover.

Dev's final home truth had arrived this morning. It had been slow in forming, no doubt pickled in last night's whiskey and misery. But now that it was here, it was grand and mad and enough to give him hope that he'd cross those gates again.

Dev pushed an autodial number on his cell phone and waited until his call went through.

"Margaret, my love, I need some information."

Surely a man who could do a job to perfection could undo it just as well.

As far as last nights on Earth went, Jenna found this one nearly perfect.

In the kitchen this afternoon, she had soared. The flavors, the scents, the mix of subtle and bold, all had combined in a wild whirl. She supposed this was fate's way of compensating for her other losses.

Now evening had fallen and Aidan had barred her from any further madness. She was to drink and chat and if she so much as thought of crossing the kitchen's threshold, he'd put the Kilbride twins on her as guards.

As Jenna wove between the revelers crowding the terrace and spilling onto the grounds beyond, she stopped to talk to both familiar faces and new.

"It's a fine hooley you're having. Everyone's having a grand time, so relax, darlin'," Breege Flaherty said as she pressed a glass of wine into Jenna's hand. "Whatever else happens, you've done well, bringing life back to this house."

Breege flitted off and joined her friend Edna in the circle of musicians setting up next to the outdoor bar Vi had rigged. Jenna walked on, wondering if a single citizen remained in the village. Even Roger, Vi's dog, had taken up residence beneath a table and was snuffling every dropped morsel of food. But Jenna knew who was missing from this party, for she was empty without him.

Dev had been right yesterday. She hadn't asked him about Harwood because she didn't want to know. And when she'd learned, she'd acted as though he'd failed her. In truth, she'd failed him. The physical act of loving, the speaking of endearments, these she had done. But to truly love Dev, she should have shared the bad the same way she'd hungered for the good. And knowing the truth did nothing to ease the pain.

Maureen couldn't recall the last time she'd been so alone in a crowd. Luckily, Niamh had just taken over for her in delivering food to the masses. Maureen intended to make herself scarce.

Because a beach was best seen with wine in hand, she first stopped at the terrace bar and had Rory O'Connor pour her a plastic cupful. Rory, who on probably his only night out until the tourists left, chose to linger by the bar. You could take an O'Connor from the pub, but you couldn't take the pub from an O'Connor.

Sipping her wine, Maureen nodded greetings to Emer, Danny, and the other Muir House staffers as she wandered down to her favorite rock by the shore. She leaned the cup against the base of the boulder and stretched out on her back across its rough surface.

She'd never known that sorrow could be such a physical thing. Maureen ached for her sister and for herself. Even though they spoke nearly every day, she missed Sam so much that she could howl with wanting.

"Take me now," she said to the moon, staring up at its shadows and secrets.

"That was my plan."

Maureen scrambled upright. "Sam?"

Now that she'd wished a lover home, she'd have to rethink her skepticism about magic.

He picked his way down the rocky shore toward her. "Sorry I'm late."

"Like almost two weeks late," she said, trying to work up something close to a dramatic snit. Funny thing, though. She didn't seem to have it in her.

He stood before her. "This is where we begin. This is where we do it right."

She managed to squeak out an "okay."

He took her hands in his and said, "I love you, Maureen. We've probably met each other years before we should. God knows I have a lot of growing up to do and so do you. But every night, for the rest of my life, I need to come home to you."

"Okay, now that you've got that out of your system, would you please, *please* take me up to my room?"

Laughing, Sam put her over his shoulder and began the climb to the house. "Every night, Maureen. Every night."

Dev knew better than to enter Muir House through the front door. But now night had fully fallen, and he was sure he could just sneak around the side and find Jenna without raising too much of an alarm.

He rounded the corner of the building and nearly ran into a couple. In the dim light he saw Michael Kilbride kissing his wife Kylie as though she were the most desirable woman on Earth. And perhaps she was—to Kilbride. Dev's tastes ran more to short Americans.

"Sorry, there," he murmured and worked his way around the lovers, who didn't seem to notice him.

He had almost made the back terrace when a tall figure stepped in front of him.

"Not so quickly," Vi Kilbride said. In each hand was a wineglass and at her feet was her stumpy little dog.

Dev looked about. Christ, how many more Kilbrides had he yet to find?

"So what's it to be, Vi? Are you going to set your dog on me and have me run to the other side of the gates?"

She laughed. "Perhaps you should fear Roger. He's a keen judge of personality, and an ankle can bleed as well as an arm."

"I mean trouble for no one."

"Yet you've managed to cause much," she said before drinking down the remainder of the dark contents in her left-hand glass.

"True."

"So why should I let you by, Dev Gilvane? Jenna's nearly having a pleasant time. Two or three more wines and I expect we'll have her the rest of the way there."

"You should let me by because I love her, and there's a lot that needs fixing."

"So you're saying it can be done?"

He smiled. "With luck, persuasion, and a few words in the right ears."

"Well, I like you well enough, and even Roger

does, too. Still, there are plenty who'd relieve you of your teeth and a few other bits, were Kate not your mam." She held out the empty glasses. "Fill these with red and bring them to my friend and me by the fire. If you live through the crowd, you're meant to be here."

As Dev made his way to the bar, he kept an eye for Jenna but saw her nowhere. He was seen, though. Nobody said a word to him, and really only his mum and Mulqueen looked pleased.

"Two reds, Rory," he said to his host of the prior evening.

"And no whiskey for you?" O'Connor asked, grinning. "I'd think you might be wanting a shot of courage."

Dev managed not to shudder. "Nothing, thanks. Have you seen Jenna about?"

"Not since the music started."

He took the wine and started back through the crowd. As he left the terrace, he did his best not to look back over his shoulder, where he was sure he'd see gossip springing like fleas from one group of Ballymuirians to the next.

Vi's fire was a living thing, rising and swelling with the music that drifted from the terrace. Dev was no pagan, but tonight he could feel something in the air, almost an echo of what he'd heard by the ogham stone.

Tonight, though, he accepted. Tonight he understood.

At the beach edge of the fire he saw Vi. He'd assumed that the other glass he carried would be for a man, drawn to her as so many were. Instead, she stood with Jenna.

He paused, but Vi urged him on, "Don't be losing your heart now, Gilvane."

How she could have chosen those words, so perfect and so terrifying, Dev could only put down to magic, too. She held out her hands, and he gave her the wine.

She passed a glass to Jenna, murmuring something about a golden room that Dev couldn't quite catch.

To the others standing about the fire she said, "To the terrace, if you don't mind. My flames have some work to do."

And all too soon it was just he and Jenna. She wouldn't meet his eyes. She held her glass cupped between her palms and gazed into it as she had on the hillside, the first time they'd made love.

"If you want me to leave . . ." he offered.

"No."

That was grand, since he'd been lying. He'd no sooner leave here than he'd move to Tokyo. Jenna was his home and his truth.

"Well," he began, suspecting that he was about to choke on his formerly glib tongue, "I've made a mess of things these past few days, but I want you to know that I'm here to fix them. I love you, and while that might not sound enough just now, it's where we start."

She looked up. With the fire's dance of light and shadow flickering against her face, she was a new mystery to him.

"You told me it couldn't be fixed."

He shook his head. "I was missing the magic, the illusion."

"What do you mean?"

"What I do for a living is all about illusion." Words began to spill from him and he knew he must sound moon-mad. "People come to a resort to escape what's real. It's a place where the good is exaggerated and the bad unwelcome. For a week or a fortnight, they're wealthy and pampered. Their children are never sullen and their lovers are never bored. That's what I was missing, *mo chroí*. Illusions can cut both ways."

Jenna very nearly smiled, and Dev felt his spirits buoy.

"I can make no promises, but I've been doing some thinking. No later than noon tomorrow, three men from Harwood will be here. They've seen photos of the house and the village, they have my assurance that the environment is right, but things change, if you know what I'm saying?"

"I'm—I'm not sure."

"The pictures are just that, a moment in time that's gone. And after that moment, well, who's to say what can happen in a place such as this?"

"So you want to scam them?"

"A harsh word, though accurate. A junkyard and a few other bits might sour Harwood's taste for Ballymuir. Do you think we might be pulling together a few of your friends? I've made a list or two."

"You'll lose your job, Dev."

"Better that than my heart." He reached for her glass and tossed the rest of the wine into the flames. "Will you do this with me? Shall we make it right together or at least go down fighting?"

"Yes," she said, but it didn't have quite the joyous ring he'd hoped for. And when he drew Jenna into his arms, she held herself just distant enough that Dev knew he wasn't home yet.

Chapter Twenty

*Never call a Kerryman a fool until you're
sure he's not a rogue.*
— IRISH PROVERB

Friday dawned wet and dismal, as though the sun had never shone over Ballymuir and never would. Considering the day's inhospitable purpose, Jenna could have wished for nothing better.

Well before sunrise, Dev had begun to coordinate his plan. When he'd gathered everyone last night and begged their help, Breege Flaherty had summed up Ballymuir's feelings by calling him "a frightful sharp man." Of course, he'd soon won them over. Ballymuir's citizens enjoyed nothing more than a good meddle. And if repelling a British incursion came with the game, all the better.

Dev had organized his troops brilliantly. There

was little point in altering Muir House itself, since Harwood's plans were to obliterate it. Matters outside her home's walls were the main focus.

Jenna knew that by now her neighbor Mr. Horrigan would have taken truckfuls of sheep for a visit to the village—a day to see the sights, as it were. He'd been quite anxious to help, explaining that he'd agreed to the purchase option only because it was contingent on Harwood also buying Muir House. He'd taken a hefty bit of deposit money, feeling certain that he'd never actually have to sell, since he knew how much she loved her home. Now that he had all the facts, he and his flock were in open rebellion.

Those who usually parked their cars on the village's tight streets had agreed to relocate for the day to give the beasts their run. Ballymuir wasn't to be so much a ghost town as a pungent sheep town.

Soon the landowners across the road from Muir House would be putting the finishing touches on the auto repair yard they'd yesterday decided to open. Every last rusted relic usually lingering behind its owner's shed or decomposing in a field should be nicely tucked in opposite her house's beautiful entry, ugly but not in violation of land use laws, either.

As for the other dynamics of Dev's plan, they weren't as static as crumpled and flattened cars, or quite as fluid—so to speak—as frightened sheep could be.

Lorcan O'Connor had been enlisted to aid with communications using his legion of cell phones and walkie-talkies, all assigned to roadside sentries. As the Harwood contingent approached, livestock would be brought from high fields to low, a slow process known to hold traffic for long stretches. And when the executives finally reached Ballymuir, yet another set of challenges awaited. Those, Jenna planned to see for herself.

She hurriedly dressed, then stopped to pound on her sister's door. "Get up, you two. The show's about to begin!"

Dev was well pleased with the sheep. He was also well pleased that the rain had crept into the mountains long enough for his other diversions to proceed. In making his plans, he had relied on two essential components for a resort site: acceptable access and surroundings conducive to relaxation. God willing, Harwood would find neither.

He had equally addressed matters of human nature. Trevor, whom Margaret had told him to expect, was about to move to the corporate pinnacle. What happened in Ballymuir was no longer his burden. He would make polite noises, but his brain would be elsewhere. And Dev knew Sid Barrett for a lazy man, one interested in the surface aspects of business. Ballymuir would be the Costa Rican deal all over again, with Sid trying to grasp the nuances well after the fact.

From Dev's vantage point in the window of Spillane's Market—hidden behind a tall display of laundry soap—he watched a black sedan inch its way downhill. In it were four men, including Sid, who according to the last farmer creating a bovine roadblock, was "spittin' mad."

Dev didn't doubt it. Sid and patience seldom

crossed paths. This was not the group's first trip through town, but their third. The signposted road to Muir House was regrettably under construction and the detour, sadly circular, an act Dev knew he couldn't maintain much longer. Even Vi Kilbride's marvelous flirtation skills could keep the local Gardai's heads turned from a spurious roadblock for only so long.

Dev smiled as Barrett marched from the car and tried to clear wet and stupid sheep from a parking space. Black suit, white sheep . . . there was a certain grand simplicity to the scene, though it appeared Sid was finding nothing grand about the sheep's leavings. Dev wasn't sure who was more frightened, Barrett or the sheep. The sheep held the edge in the eerily expressionless department, though. Finally, after Trevor and a man Dev recognized from the New York office also climbed from the car and lent a hand, the humans managed to claim a bit of the curb.

Now some grand fun would begin.

"Come watch," Dev urged Jenna, who tiptoed from behind the tinned vegetables to join him.

In addition to the sheep, Dev had arranged for a ladies' tea on the sidewalk—in full wedding guest regalia, of course. Edna McCafferty's lace-draped hat was at least three feet across. Concealed in its frippery was a walkie-talkie, the mate to which rested in Dev's hand.

But even if Ballymuir's visitors might have been inclined to examine Edna's hat, there was too much else to take their attention. Tiny Breege Flaherty was nearly missing beneath her screaming yellow chapeau. The rest of the village's senior set was arrayed in peacock brightness, making their stretch of side-walk as difficult to navigate as the street.

Barrett approached the women. "Hello, can you help me?" Each word was delivered slow and ear-splittingly loud, as though his audience might be ad-dled, non-English-speaking, or both.

Edna looked him up and down. "I don't recall inviting you to the ceremony, young man."

"Look," he said, waving one hand as he had at the sheep, "all I'm trying to do is—"

Mr. Clancy stepped from a doorway. The hard-ware store owner spat a fraction of an inch from Bar-rett's glossy shoes then said, "You nearly hit my favorite sheep, parking up there."

Barrett pulled his gaze from the glob of spittle at his left toe. He looked itching to brawl, but appar-ently still possessed enough composure to hold back. "We're trying to find Muir House."

"Follow the signs," Clancy replied with all the graciousness for which he was renowned.

"We've followed the signs three goddamn times and we always end up back here."

"So you're lookin' for another way, then?"

An unhealthy purple tinge climbed the New Yorker's face. "Of course we're looking for another way. Do you think we like driving through this god-damn river of sheep?"

"You needn't be rude," Breege Flaherty called to Barrett before passing tea cakes to her companions.

Barrett took an aggressive step toward her, but Edna rose. She was an impressive figure of a woman, enough to slow any man not interested in finding his teeth relocated.

"Fine, then," Clancy said. "At the end of town, you'll see a roadside well. Turn right. The road might not look like much, but it will be gettin' you there."

"Great," Barrett snapped.

"And mind the sheep," Clancy added as the man stalked back to his car.

In the market Jenna kissed Dev. "The old Dingle Road? It's nothing more than weeds and ruts. I wouldn't send my worst enemy up that."

He smiled. "But we just did."

Jenna jogged downhill toward the harbor and the arts village, where she'd left her car outside Vi's studio. Breathless with a mix of excitement, fear, and general under-exercise, she turned right and nearly ran into two women coming the opposite way.

"Sorry," she called, but didn't slow.

"Wait!"

Knowing she had time before the Harwood people found their way back down the long-abandoned path they'd been sent to travel, Jenna turned back. "Yes?"

A blond-haired woman who Jenna thought was her age or maybe a bit older asked, "You're Jenna Fahey, from Muir House?"

"I am."

"I won't be taking much of your time. I just wanted to say that we visited Muir House last night. It was, without exception, the most, ehm . . . *unusual* meal I've had."

Jenna smiled. "Sorry, I threw away the rule book last night."

"Then you might consider leaving it in the bin,"

the woman said as her companion nodded in agreement. "I've never done this before, but as it will be some time before I'm back this way again and we're tossing out rules . . ." She extended her hand, and Jenna automatically shook it. "I'm Eibhlinn Darcy from *Guide Eireann*."

Jenna worked up a squeak she hoped would pass for a polite response.

"I'm advising that we raise you to three stars, just so you know. You'd be one of twenty in the guide, so I'm expecting that you'll be visited by others on staff before it's final."

"Thank you! Wow . . . I . . . Hell." Clearly and maybe forever wordless, Jenna hugged Eibhlinn Darcy and then followed up with a kiss to each cheek.

She had her stars, but would she keep her home?

It was nearly three by the time Barrett and his friends arrived at Muir House. Their sedan, which seemed to be dragging a good portion of its rear bumper, shuddered to a stop in the drive. As Barrett, Trevor, and the other New Yorker made their way to the entry, Dev straightened the cuffs to his shirt and gave a check in the mirror as to the rest of himself. It wouldn't do to look less than his best—like, say, his soon-to-be-former co-workers.

Dev opened the front door. "Welcome to Muir House, gentlemen."

If they were surprised to see him, they were too weary to react. Barrett had unmentionable stains on his suit, and Trevor was digging at an empty cigarette pack as though a phantom smoke might still lurk within.

"You said this site was less than three hours from the Shannon Airport. It's bloody closer to five, and that's not counting the death march we just survived," his boss said in way of a greeting.

Ah, the airport driver Margaret had secured had done well. "Five hours, really?" Dev said. "I hadn't noticed."

"And that's if the ferry is running on time," Barrett added.

So they'd had a full tour of County Clare, including a ride across the mouth of the lovely River Shannon. How wonderful. "Well, you're here now and that's what counts, yes?"

"No," Barrett replied flatly. "This place is the back ass of nowhere and populated by a pack of goddamn loons. Sheep everywhere and dressed-up old bats having tea on the sidewalk."

"Too much local color?" Dev asked.

"Rather grotty junkyard out front, too," Trevor added.

Dev managed an apologetic wince. "That's new, I'm afraid. The McCauleys are weary of farming. Now, would you like a look around?"

"No," Barrett spat.

"No?" Dev echoed.

"No. What I want is to get on a plane and never see you or another sheep for the rest of my goddamn life. I know when I've been screwed with."

The moment was here, but somehow Dev felt far away. Perhaps on some level he'd seen this day coming for years now—though admittedly not quite in this form.

Dev produced his finest corporate smile. "That's grand, Barrett. Now, I can do nothing about the sheep, but I can promise you'll see me no more." He pulled an envelope from his breast pocket. "Trevor, this is for you. It's been a wild time working for you, but I'm done."

Trevor's brows arched with disbelief. "You know what you're giving up?"

"Yes, but I know better what I'm gaining."

Trevor looked to the two Americans, then back at Dev. "Is there someplace private we can speak?"

Dev ushered Trevor toward the blue salon. He hid a smile as Jenna, Maureen, and Sam quickly ducked into the library doorway just as he and Trevor rounded the corner.

Dev closed the salon door behind himself and the man who had been his mentor. Before speaking, Trevor took a loop of the room, stopping to look at the photographs of Jenna with friends and family.

"She's quite lovely," he said in the offhand way that was his trademark.

"Quite," Dev replied with equal understatement.

"And would I be amiss in guessing that you're throwing away a career over her?"

Trevor had always been remarkably perceptive. "Since I love her, I prefer to view it as righting my course."

"Righting your course?" Incredulity had crept into Trevor's even tones. "Did you not understand me when we spoke in London? Two years, Dev, then it would all be yours. Two years after how many?"

"Almost eleven," Dev replied.

"Insanity."

Dev expelled a slow breath. "Trevor, I'm not asking you to understand this, or to give me your opinion, or even to wish me well. I thank you for the years and all I've learned, but it's time for me to do something else."

"Here?"

"Yes."

"And how many hours is it from Shannon Airport to Muir House by the *direct* route?"

Dev permitted only a hint of a smile to escape. "Two, when I drive. Two and a wee bit more for anyone else."

Trevor nodded. "As I suspected." He picked up a photograph of Jenna and smiled. "God knows I'm no romantic, but it appears that you just might be."

"That I might." Dev hesitated just long enough to send a quick and silent prayer skyward before asking the greatest favor of his life. "Will you steer Sid elsewhere for me?"

Trevor set the photograph back on the mantel. "To the degree it's needed, yes. I've never seen a man outside politics hate Ireland as fiercely as Sid Barrett."

"Then Ireland is well blessed."

Laughing, Trevor extended his hand. "I do wish you well, Dev."

Together they walked back to the front hall, where Sid was picking bits of whatever off his suit.

"Gentlemen," Dev said, "there's another car waiting for you in the car park by the gates. Shall I see you out?"

"You can see yourself to hell," Sid spat.

Trevor, Sid, and the silent minion left. With that, all Dev had worked for was gone.

And he was . . . vastly relieved.

Jenna came round the corner and flung herself in his arms.

"Will you marry me, *mo chroí?*" he asked, after spinning her in a dizzy circle.

"*Yes!*" she cried, and never would Dev doubt for the depth of her joy. Home, heart, and truth, all were now his.

Chapter Twenty-One

Health and long life to you;
the love of your heart to you;
land without rent to you;
and may you die in Ireland.

—IRISH TOAST

With the coming of autumn, tourists drifted through Ballymuir, content to stroll instead of dash. Jenna and Dev slowed, too, though neither of them were exactly souls of leisure. Once he'd sold his house in Knightsbridge, Dev had invested in a number of business partnerships—including one that made Jenna owner of Muir House both in her heart and in the eyes of the law.

No surprise to anyone, Dev would never be a passive investor. He was underfoot in the restaurant enough that Padraig the bartender had grown territorial about Dev's poaching on his domain.

Sam and Maureen had settled in Malibu. Maureen had started college there, at Pepperdine University. Jenna was shocked but pleased with her sister's growing maturity. Kate and Brendan had decided to "live in sin," a phrase Kate employed to mercilessly tease Dev. Jenna didn't doubt that Dev's mother and Brendan would marry one day—once Kate was sure that staid Katherine had been permanently abandoned in Dublin.

As for Jenna, she remained in firm control of her kitchen, as befit a *Guide Eireann* three-star chef. Sometime after the last-night-on-Earth party, the publication had sent another critic to determine whether on an evening without moon, magic, and madness, Jenna's food still held. It did.

Tonight, though, Jenna hadn't even ventured near her realm. Tonight she was a bride. Around her, Muir House's dining room glittered, transformed into a fairyland. Vi's wedding gift had been bringing her vision of a gold room to life.

Restaurant linens had been replaced with rich silk. Instead of flowers, at each table sat a wild arrangement of greens adorned with hand-made golden ornaments in a Celtic motif. From the center of the greens rose tall and slender gold tapers, their tiny flames dancing.

Friends and family laughed, danced, and sang. Gifts ran from the sublime of Vi's room to the wonderfully silly Molly Malone statue that had previously resided in front of Muriel O'Keefe's bed-and-breakfast. When they'd come back from church earlier in the day,

Jenna had been knocked nearly wordless at the sight of Molly on Muir House's lawn.

"Your man seemed to have a liking for it," Muriel had explained. "More than once I saw him chatting her up as though she were his bosom friend."

Judging by the size of Molly's bosom, Jenna decided that it must be an enormous friendship.

"Herself won it in a parish raffle," Mr. O'Keefe had added, fiddling with his unaccustomed tie. "Can't say I'm sorry to see it gone."

And even more wildly miraculous than Jenna's surroundings was the man who sat next to her. Dev was so open in his love, so without pretense or subterfuge that she couldn't look at him without becoming filled with joy.

Dev reached over and took her left hand, turning her gold wedding band in a slow circle. His smile was intimate and smacked of an ownership that might have offended if she didn't feel exactly the same way about him.

"Has the day been everything you were wishing for?" he asked.

"Even better," she replied before kissing him.

Just then Vi rose. "And now here we are at my favorite time of the evening, when I get to talk."

"And I'm timing you," called her brother Michael. "Don't be talking till the wedded couple's first anniversary."

The crowd laughed, and even Vi managed a grin at her brother's obligatory prod.

"Tonight I have a rare tale," she said. "It's one of Irish lovers who managed to get it right without bloodshed or war." She hesitated, then gave Jenna and Dev a rueful shake of her head. "Well, almost without war.

"One green spring day a dark man came to Ballymuir. It wasn't just that he was dark in looks . . . he also carried a certain emptiness in his soul. Now, if you'd have said that to him at the time, he'd have laughed. Still, it was to Ballymuir—and Muir House—that he was led to heal."

Jenna looked to Dev, who was exchanging with Kate one of those "don't say 'I told you so'" expressions that pass so well between mother and son. Jenna took her dark man's hand and held it tight.

Smiling, Vi waited a canny beat to focus her listeners' expectations. "I'm sure that those of you without too much champagne fizzing about in your brains know where I'm traveling. And more than one of you is saying to yourself, 'That Vi Kilbride's ready to be boxed and shipped to the asylum, for everyone knows that Jenna is no more Irish than the Statue of Liberty.' And this is where you're wrong.

"God has given me three fine brothers with size enough among them to make one or two more. But what He seemed to overlook is that a woman needs sisters. Michael was kind enough to give me one by marriage in Kylie. I, however, claimed another for myself." She smiled at Maureen and added, "And my thanks to you, Miss Maureen, for sharing."

In smooth strides Vi walked to Jenna and Dev. "Jenna, you are in every way my sister, and as such, clearly Irish, too." She held her glass aloft. "Muir House has known the sorrow of Áine and her Englishman—and don't you be doubting the tale's truth, Dev Gilvane. But now these walls will know the joy of Dev and Jenna and their children's children. I wish you both a love that will always shine true and bright."

After everyone had drunk their toast, Vi said, "Now, if you don't mind, I'll be going off to have myself a wee bit of a cry. All this happiness is hard on a single woman." Her content smile, however, belied her words. "And as for the rest of you, there's a fire to be lit."

With that, Jenna took her husband's hand and led him to the shore, where together they would light a blaze to burn their whole lives through.

**Visit the Simon & Schuster
romance Web site:**

www.SimonSaysLove.com

**and sign up for our
romance e-mail updates!**

Keep up on the latest
new romance releases,
author appearances, news, chats,
special offers, and more!
We'll deliver the information
right to your inbox—if it's new,
you'll know about it.

POCKET BOOKS

2800.02

Visit
❖ Pocket Books ❖
online at

www.SimonSays.com

Keep up on the latest new releases from your favorite authors, as well as author appearances, news, chats, special offers and more.

SIMON & SCHUSTER
A VIACOM COMPANY
www.SimonSays.com

Pocket
Books